HOCKEY PENGUIN 3PEAT

By Luke Anderson

With Contributions by Megan Martino

To Caeden,

I hope Hockey Penguin 3peat
makes you laugh 3 times as
much! Happy Reading!

Copyright © 2014

All Rights Reserved

To My Readers,

You'll notice in this book that there is a team in this book by the name of the Reno Five Ohhh!. The exclamation point is part of the spelling of the team's name, and therefore not considered as punctuation. It may be immediately be followed by periods, commas, question marks, etc. I know it looks funny and isn't exactly proper, but it is how I chose to do it in this particular series. Just thought I'd clear that up before I get a million hits on hockeypenguin.net or the Hockey Penguin Facebook page telling me how many errors were left in the book.

Also, I have to give thanks and credit to Emma Rose of C.T. Sewell Elementary and Vanessa from Charlotte Hill Elementary for their creation of Penny Penguin. They each submitted the winning character, creating the same animal with the same name and the same story line for my Nevada Reading Week 2013 Hockey Penguin 3Peat create-a-character contest.

Happy reading! ☺

– Luke Anderson

Chapter 1: Big Changes In The IAHL

It took just one season for the Las Vegas Gamblers to go from worst to first. Now, after two seasons, they've won back to back Anderson Cups.

The team's recent success has many wondering if the Gamblers could possibly be the first team in IAHL history to win four straight Cups. Their winning ways garner not only the attention of the hockey world but the attention of the entire world. All thirteen players and their monkey coach, Safari Chip, explode from hockey superstars to worldwide celebrities.

Gamblers t-shirt, hat, and jersey sales go through the roof, and team apparel is only the beginning of the Gamblers merchandise that is mass produced. Lunchboxes, posters, cell phone covers, wallets, watches, iPods, DVDs, playing cards, poker chips, greeting cards, toys, stuffed animals, dinnerware, pencils, notebooks, collector's cards, and thousands of other items are rapidly manufactured for a demanding public. Some products have the Gamblers logo and others have pictures of the players. Several Gamblers get tagged with trademark slogans that appear on much of their merchandise. After Safari Chip's speech at the end of last year's Cup Finals, *Big Game, Big Stick, Big Chick* becomes one of the most popular catchphrases. *I'm a Lovey, Not a Fighter* gets tacked to Lovey, the team's fighting grizzly cub. Merchandise with the dogs is often adorned with a question. *Who Let the Dogs Out?* Harlan, the Gamblers turtle goalie, is labeled *The Mean, Green, Goal Stopping Machine*, and most of the merchandise for the captain, Rodman T. Penguin, simply bears his nickname, Hott Rod.

The Gamblers are famous everywhere they go, but nowhere more so than in Las Vegas. They can't walk down the street in their hometown without being mobbed by adoring fans, and their popularity only grows on account of all of their offseason appearances on TV and radio. Rodman is constantly called on to do commercials, celebrity appearances, celebrity auctions, charity events, and he's invited to be a guest on multiple radio shows. He even competes in a game show in which he squares off against other celebrities to survive different tasks and win money for his favorite charity. After twelve weeks, Rodman emerges victorious, wining over three hundred thousand dollars for a charity that deals in finding a cure for childhood cancer. His happy-go-lucky personality and his keen mind make him a natural star.

Rodman's not the only Gambler who gets to be on TV and radio however. Big Chick, a former all-pro kicker at the collegiate level, is hired in the offseason to talk college football on ASPN, the nation's leading animal sporting network. Lovey, Undertaker, Kane, and Apple Jack each do guest spots at different times on the radio to talk about upcoming MMA fights. Beary becomes famous for his flashy and extravagant fashion sense and is asked to co-host a weekly fashion segment on one of the radio stations, and Safari Chip gets his own weekly radio program called *Cashing In With The Gamblers* to talk about the goings on of his team week to week.

The Gamblers enjoy every minute of their postseason celebration and their new found celebrity. They even try to one up their Cup celebration from the year before. They have parade from downtown to the Strip again, but this year the parade ends at the Fontana Hotel where they throw a pool party inside the lagoon out front that houses the hotels magnificent water show.

When the parade stops, the Gamblers crawl through a trap door in the bottom of their float into a tunnel under the streets that leads into the inner workings of the pool. The crowd clamors for their hockey team to come back until suddenly, the Gamblers pregame music begins to play over the speakers in front of the Fontana. The crowd turns to the lake in front of the hotel to see if the show is starting. What they see instead is each Gambler shot high into the air out of an underwater chute. They glide through the air like a stream of water in the show and then splash into the pool. While some of the Gamblers swim to a platform in the middle of the pool where the Cup has been put on display, other Gamblers continue to fly through the air and fall into the pool.

When all the Gamblers and their coach are on the platform, they dance to the rest of their pregame music while water shoots in the air all around them. At the conclusion of their song, all the water cannons shoot a massive burst of water high into the air at the same time. The burst sounds like heavy thunder, and it entirely clouds the Gamblers from sight.

The crowd goes bonkers until the mist clears and Rodman and the rest of the guys can be seen once more.

Rodman holds a microphone while wearing his trademark smile. He holds it to his beak and yells, "It's time to party once again Las Vegas!" He spins and points to all the animals lined up around the lagoon. "So, on my count, I want all you crazy animals to join us here in the pool."

Everyone around the pool grips, stands on, or prepares in some way to jump over the railing into the pool.

"One! Two! Three!"

On three, the fans dive into the pool like penguins jumping off a cliff during fishing season. Fans swim with the Gamblers, take pictures with their the Cup and their favorite players, watch Harlan sit underwater and hold his breath for over an hour, and someone puts up a net for a massive water volleyball game. The party rages on for hours.

Come the next morning, after all the Gamblers have long since left, the employees of the Fontana Hotel still have to fish a few straggling fans from the pond.

The pool party is just one example of the many Gamblers celebrations. Later, at the New Orleans Hotel, where the Gamblers play their games and live during the season, a pair of statues is unveiled. One statue depicts Rodman being joyously tackled by his all black, except for his white goatee, Lhasa Apso teammate, Morty "Undertaker" Curtains with his other teammates, Keith Kane, a shabbily trimmed black and white Shih Tzu whose whiskers grow out like a handle bar mustache, Lovey Bara, Liten Mus, a mouse, and Harlan T. Turtle, racing to them to join the celebration and Safari Chip jumping up and down on the Gamblers bench. The other statue portrays Big Chick standing stunned on the ice as his teammates, Sammie Lou, a koala, Apple Jack, an all white Lhasa Apso, Bruce Goose, and Maverick Limpright, a horse, mob him in celebration. In the background of this statue Beary Nelson Riley, the team's panda backup goalie, throws his arms up in celebration, and L-Rod, a peewee hockey penguin turned pro, has his head lowered as he cries tears of joy on the bench. Each statue commemorates the moments directly following the gaming winning goal from the Gamblers two Cup Finals. Each Gambler poses by the statue of himself to reenact the winning moments for publicity photos. L-Rod isn't exactly thrilled to bow his head and cry, but he wasn't on the team for their first win, and after everything he went through last season just to make the team, winning the Cup was too much for him, and he burst into happy tears.

The proud hotel puts the statues right out front of the building, near the street for all passersby to see. The hotel also unveils giant posters of the Gamblers that line the walls both outside leading up to and inside of the arena. Each of the Gamblers is given a paintbrush and a can of paint to autograph their wall print.

Later, the Gamblers and the New Orleans Hotel partner for a Win-A-Date-With-A-Gambler fundraiser to help their favorite charities. Everyone is sure Rodman will bring in the most money, and he brings in a winning bid of $2,150, but they're all surprised when a couple of hens engage in a bidding war over Big Chick that results in a winning date at the cost of $3,025. The rest of the guys each bring in at least $1,000 for a total amount of $20,975. The only Gambler who doesn't participate is L-Rod. He's too young to go on a date. Instead, the Gamblers have him participate in a pizza party with the school that sells the most chocolate bars for charity.

The mayor of Las Vegas declares July 3rd as Gamblers Day. He also gives the team the key to the city. ASPN does numerous interviews with the team and airs countless specials about their rise from the depths of the league. Rodman does hosting duties on the late night sketch comedy show Monday Night Live. Each Gambler gets a chance to throw out the first pitch at a Las Vegas Cowboys baseball game. They tour local schools doing guest speaking. They visit sick children at local hospitals. Lovey's favorite part of the off season is when the other Gamblers, along with the Cup, tour some of the overseas military bases. And the coup de grace is the invite they get from the president of the United States to come to the White House.

　　With all they have going on, the Gamblers have very little free time during the offseason. They love it though. It's why they play so hard all season long. They know there are seven other teams sitting at home, waiting for the next season to start, wishing they could be partying Gamblers style.

*

　　While the other seven teams wait for the season to start, their general managers make it a point to figure out what the Gamblers have been doing so right. They fear if they don't figure the Gamblers out quick, they might not be able to compete with them in the upcoming seasons.

　　During a round of golf, the general manager of the Stockton Lightning, a hound dog named Bill Turner, and the general manager of the Bakersfield Trains, a buffalo named Sam Kennedy, discuss a trade and the Gamblers success.

　　"You know when all their success started?" Turner steps out of their shared golf cart.

　　"When?" Kennedy asks, following behind Turner.

　　"When they signed Rodman. He turned that team of losers around." Turner grabs a club from his bag.

　　"Yeah," Kennedy agrees.

　　"And I'll tell you another thing. The Gold Rush signed Jason Vyand that same year." Turner sets his ball on the tee. "And which teams have been in the past two Cup Finals?"

Kennedy thinks about the answer to the question for a moment. "The Gamblers and the Gold Rush."

Turner interrupts his own swing to turn and face Kennedy again. "That's right. And do you know why?"

"No."

"Think about it. What have they got that we don't?"

Kennedy can't come up with an answer.

"Penguins!" Turner shouts. "They signed penguins, and the next thing you know they're unstoppable."

Turner turns back to his golf ball and gives it a whack. He and Kennedy watch the ball sail down the field. Once it lands, Turner turns back to Kennedy.

"We don't have penguins."

Kennedy waves Turner off. "Awww come off it. Rodman being a penguin isn't the reason the Gamblers turned their fortunes around. He's the best player to ever play the game. He's the type of star player who elevates the play of everyone around him. That's why they started winning. Guys like him don't come along but once a generation. And the Gold Rush were good even before they had Jason."

"The Gold Rush *were* good, but after two straight Cup wins five and six years ago, they fell short of reaching the Finals the next two seasons. So, they go and get Jason, and he gets them right back to the top."

"Yeah, because Maulbreath, Haas, Iggy, Rapture, Smooth, Auggie, Ranger, Metz, Packer, and Peanuts didn't have anything to do with their success," Kennedy says sarcastically. "They more or less have six captains for crying out loud."

"You can think what you want, but penguins are born on the ice. They grow up on ice. They know how to maneuver around on ice. It's only natural they'd be the best players."

"I think Rodman and Jason... and L-Rod for that matter, all come from the tropical beaches of Capetown, South Africa," Kennedy argues.

Turner looks at Kennedy agitated. "Fine. Be stubborn, but I'm getting out of here."

"Where are you going?"

"I'm headed to Capetown. They have to have some more star-powered penguins down there." Turner abandons his ball and starts walking off the course.

Kennedy looks at his own ball on the tee, digesting the conversation he just had with Turner. Suddenly, he jumps into the golf cart and flies past the hound dog.

"Hey! Where are you going?" Turner shouts.

"Capetown!" Kennedy calls as he speeds off the green.

Turner chases after Kennedy. "Hey! That was my idea! Wait! I'm coming with you!"

*

Turner and Kennedy's scouting trip to South Africa leads to Turner signing Rodman's ex-teammates, Pencil Spoedige, a forward, and Chad "Dolvy" Doelverdediger, a goalie, and Kennedy signing another of Rodman's old teammates, another forward named Pablo Pikkewyn.

When they come home and announce their signings, ASPN does a piece about the hockey playing abilities of the South African Penguins of the Capetown Chill. It becomes a huge topic in the world of hockey, and it sets off a rash of penguin signings. The prevailing thought becomes, *if you don't have a penguin, you don't have a prayer*.

The other IAHL teams frantically race to Capetown to see what's left to pick from. The Chill are completely raided. The Californians sign Rugby Storm. The Potatoes sign Ty Mosienko. The Fishermen sign Andy Dapper and P.V. Dermeer. Even the Utah Thumpers, the last team to make it to Capetown, sign Johnny Starkweather, a player with only one year under his belt as a Chill. Each signing is less talented than the one before it, but each of the IAHL teams is just happy to have a penguin.

The Chill's coach, The Coach, is dumbfounded when he learns he's lost all of his players. There's no way he'll be able to replace his entire team in time to start the season. With a heavy heart, he informs the heads of the South African Hockey League that the Capetown Chill will be going black until further notice.

*

The offseason isn't all fun and games and penguin signings though. It's a very busy time for the IAHL. With its growing popularity, the league decides to merge the modest eight team league with the Animal Kingdom Hockey League, doubling its size to sixteen teams. Prior to this season, the AKHL had been the minor league affiliate of the IAHL. Among the teams joining the professional ranks is the Fairbanks Pilots, headed by coach Lou Brown, the gorilla coach who helped get L-Rod get into playing shape last season when he was sent to the minor leagues for a few weeks. Also joining the IAHL are the Seattle Rampage, Fort Collins F-14s, Dallas Cacti, Reno Five Ohhh!, Fresno Fire, Albuquerque Quakes, and Portland Pirates.

The expansion of the league allows the IAHL brass to develop an expanded playoff schedule. Instead of two teams making it to the championship series, now the top four teams will make the playoffs. In round one, the team with the best record faces the team with the fourth best record, and the second and third best teams will match up. Round two becomes the Finals where the winners from round one will compete for the Cup.

Even with all the new teams and a longer and tougher playoff schedule, the Gamblers are still the heavy favorite to win it all.

True to his word, Safari Chip plans to expand his roster. After seeing how well his team performed with the additions of Big Chick, Beary, Apple Jack, and L-Rod, he swore he'd fill his roster completely with the maximum seventeen players. This means he has two forward and two defensemen positions to fill, but just when he thinks he has a plan all prepared, he hears a knock at his office door.

"Chip?" Beary pokes his Navy captain's hat clad head into Safari Chip's office.

"Come on in Beary. What can I do for you?" Safari Chip motions for Beary to take a seat.

Beary walks in wearing yellow bell bottom jeans with a red shirt that reads HUGS across the chest under an opened blue bathrobe, and a custom made Gamblers scarf around his neck. He sits down in the only chair in the office other than Safari Chip's. "I want to talk to you about the upcoming season."

"What about it?"

"I had a great time last season in my backup role, but I think I'd like a more everyday role this season."

Safari Chip's heart sinks. *Here we go again*, he thinks.

Beary sees the look on Safari Chip's face and quickly adds, "Don't worry Chip. I'm not looking to replace Harlan. I would never do that to my buddy."

"What do you mean then?"

"Do you know what the biggest thrill for me was last season?"

"Winning the Cup?" Safari Chip guesses.

"Aside from that."

Safari Chip shrugs.

"Game one of the season."

Safari Chip is confused.

"I got to suit up and play the wing.

Safari Chip is still confused.

"I scored the game winning goal," Beary elaborates.

"Oh," Safari Chip says still thinking things over. Then, suddenly, it dawns on him. "Ohhh! You want to play the wing?"

"Yeah."

"But you're the best backup goalie in the game. If Harlan goes down, and we don't have you, we'll be up the creek."

Beary doesn't understand Safari Chip's expression. "Could you swing that in ragtime?"

Now, it's Safari Chip who doesn't understand Beary's expression. "Pardon me."

"Swing that in ragtime for me. That thing you just said."

"Swing that... ragtime? I don't understand what that means."

Beary sighs. "It means could you repeat what you said."

"I asked what you said."

"Before that."

Safari Chip can't remember what he said before, or how the conversation wound up here. "Let's start over. We can't afford to lose you if Harlan gets hurt."

Beary frowns. "So it's a no go?"

Safari Chip hates to disappoint his players, but he has to think of what's best for the team. "It's a no for now, but let me think it over. Maybe something can be worked out."

"Alright." Beary sounds less than enthused as he shakes Safari Chips hand to seal the deal.

As Beary leaves the office, Rodman walks in.

"Hi Chip." Rodman waves.

"Hi Rodman. What's up?"

"I'm hoping you would consider doing me a favor."

"Anything," Safari Chip says.

"You remember my old coach right?"

"The Coach."

"Yeah. Well, he lost his whole team this season."

Safari Chip shakes his head. "I saw that. That was the darnedest thing. What's he going to do?"

"He had to forfeit the entire season, but he plans on rebuilding the team during next offseason. So, the favor I was hoping you'd grant me is, do you think you might need an assistant coach this season since Liten will be back on the ice?"

The question catches Safari Chip off guard. His initial reaction is to turn the idea down. That's what he would have done last year, but this year he ponders the notion for a while. When Liten wasn't driving him batty, finishing all of his sentences, it was nice having someone to work and game plan with. "Let me get this straight. You want me, Safari Chip, a two time Cup winning coach, to share my team with a minor league coach?"

Rodman frowns. "Well I thought maybe…"

"Ok." Safari Chip smiles.

"Ok?" Rodman was sure by Safari Chip's tone he was going to say no.

"Yeah. I'd be a fool to say no. We can only benefit by having the guy who taught Rodman T. Penguin how to play hockey. He can probably even teach me a thing or two about coaching."

Rodman jumps from his seat and pumps his flipper. "Hot dog!"

Together, Rodman and Safari Chip call The Coach and extend to him an offer to come help coach the Las Vegas Gamblers. The Coach is overwhelmed at their offer and accepts in a heartbeat.

The visits to Safari Chip's office don't end there. One by one the Gamblers file in with concerns and requests for the upcoming season. One of the pop-ins is Lovey, the team's official promotional jersey night jersey designer. He has ideas for eight different jerseys. The four designs he and Safari Chip agree on are tie dyed jerseys for 70's night, pink jerseys for ladies' night, mint chocolate chip ice cream jerseys for 21 Flavors Ice Cream Parlor's night, and roulette style jerseys for casino night, a night in which all the money collected by the hotel's casino gets donated to several of the Gamblers favorite charities.

After all the Gamblers have their chance to pop in, Safari Chip is finally able to spend some time going over stats and reports on players that will be available at the upcoming IAHL Free Agent Meetings. As the days go by, he spends hours upon hours prepping. The Coach arrives a few days before the meetings, and he's able to help Safari Chip narrow down his search. They have four spots to fill and twelve targets to choose from.

Chapter 2: The Gamblers Bolster Their Lineup

Safari Chip and The Coach bring Rodman, Lovey, and Big Chick along to the Free Agent Meetings. It's never a bad idea for a team to bring its best players to help recruit other players, especially when those three players have combined to win both of the Rookie of the Year awards, both Cup Finals MVP, and both league MVP awards the last two seasons. In his rookie season, Rodman became the only player in history to win the triple crown of awards, earning the Rookie of the Year award as well as the league and Cup Finals MVPs. Last season, he took home another league MVP, but it was Big Chick who earned the Rookie of the Year award and the Cup Finals MVP. Always a groomsman and never a groom, Lovey doesn't have any awards under his belt yet, but he always plays at a high level, coming in third in the Rookie of the Year vote in his first season, top five in last season's league MVP voting, and runner up for Safari Chip's vote in last season's Cup Finals MVP.

The Gamblers set up a booth with a couple of tables inside a humungous convention center. All around them, the room swirls with teams setting up their camps, players talking to one another, agents preparing their players, and reporters running around trying to find out who signed where so they can be the first to break a big story.

The Gamblers finish setting up about the same time as the team next to them. Safari Chip doesn't recognize anyone from the team, so he walks over to introduce himself. He reaches out his hand to a yellow duck in a suit wearing a pirate hat. "Hi. I'm Safari Chip, head coach of the Gamblers."

"Hey! Wow. It's nice to meet you. I'm Buck Wild, head coach of the Seattle Rampage."

The coaches shake.

"You say you coach the Rampage?"

"Yep." Buck Wild turns and point to his team's logo, a burst of hockey pucks shattering the letters S and R, on the banner above his tables.

"I thought for sure you would have been the coach of the Pirates."

"Why?" Buck Wild asks.

"Well I just…" Safari Chip doesn't know exactly what to say. "I mean I guess with…"

Buck Wild stares at Safari Chip.

"What's with the pirate hat?" Safari Chip finally asks.

"I don't know. What's with the safari hat?" Buck Wild turns and walks away from the Gamblers coach insulted.

Safari Chip turns to The Coach. "Make a note to send that guy and his team some Double Double Bonus Banana Split Sundaes and an apology for my comments about his hat the first time we play them."

"Check." The Coach makes a note in his notebook.

"Hey Coach," Rodman calls.

Safari Chip and The Coach both turn around. "Yes?"

"Oops. I meant The Coach."

"Oh," says Safari Chip.

"Some of the guys from the Chill are here. They want to say hi," Rodman says.

The Coach goes with Rodman to see his former players. He's greeted by Spoedige, Pikkewyn, and Dolvy. "Hey fellas."

"We just wanted to let you know we're sorry about what happened to the Chill," Spoedige says.

"Yeah. We would have never left if we knew it was going to destroy the whole team," Dolvy agrees.

"It's not your fault guys. I'm glad you're all getting an opportunity to play in the big leagues, and it's even given me a chance to come here and coach," The Coach assures them.

"We know what the Chill means to you though, and it means a lot to all of us too," Pikkewyn says.

"There's a lot of history behind that team. We don't want it to end," Spoedige adds.

"Fellas. Fellas. Fellas." The Coach pats the air with his flippers to calm them down. "It's ok. The Chill aren't through. They're just on hold until next season."

The other penguins are mighty glad to hear that. They visit with Rodman and The Coach for a while longer before they split to join back up with their new teams.

*

At the Alaska Gold Rush table, Coil Wraparound, the team's snake head coach and Copper Cashbrenner, a their number one pig scout, await their first meeting of the day.

Coil turns to Copper. "You had better hope we can still sign him after that crap you guys pulled in the Finals."

Copper doesn't respond.

Coil motions for Jack Haas to come over and have a seat. Haas, a light grey furred hare, has been his goalie for the past seven seasons. He's won Coil and his team two Cups and has taken the Gold Rush to four Cup Finals, but because of a misunderstanding during last season's Finals that strained the relationship between Haas and Coil, the coach of the Gold Rush isn't sure he's going to be able to re-sign his all-star goalie.

"Hi Jack," Coil says.

"Hello Coil."

"Jack, I see no reason to beat around the bush with you. I need you. This team needs you, and we're willing to pay any amount to keep you." Coil, lays his cards on the table.

"I appreciate that," Haas says.

"So, what's your price?" the snake hisses.

"I don't have one."

"What do you mean?"

"I don't think I want to play for the Gold Rush anymore," Haas says.

"What? Why not? If this is about what I said during the Finals I…"

"It's not that," Haas is quick to interrupt.

"If it's not that, and it's not money, what is it?"

Haas looks Coil straight in the eye. "I don't want to play with Jason and some of the other guys. There are lots of players on the current Gold Rush roster who don't play the right way, and they make it not fun. But Jason is the worst. I think if he weren't here, I could tolerate the rest of the guys, but his influence is just too bad. And as long as he's here, I don't think this team is going to win it all, and I really want to win again."

Coil is speechless.

"I'm not asking you to pick me or him. He's a really good player…"

"So are you," Coil interrupts.

"Thanks. You've been a great coach, and I've enjoyed playing for you. But I think it's time for me to move on."

Coil stares across at his soon to be ex-goalie, trying to figure out a way to keep him. He turns an incensed eye to Copper. The pig, after all, was in on the plan that sent Haas over the edge. Coil knows Haas is right about Jason being a bad influence, and he's had his own thoughts about the Gold Rush not being able to win while Jason is a part of the team. Now it appears Jason's presence in Alaska and his influence over the team is going to cost Coil one of the league's top goalies.

"Is there nothing I can do to change your mind?" Coil asks.

Haas shakes his head.

Coil sighs. "Well, good luck to you Haas. You're a class act."

Haas stands up, taps the table, points to Coil, and leaves.

*

Back at the Gamblers table, Safari Chip looks over to the Rampage table. He sees Buck Wild talking to Ed Norton, an established right wing aardvark that had a breakout season last year. He's projected by all the analysts to be one of the top twenty guys in the league this season.

Buck looks in Safari Chip's direction as he talks to Norton.

Safari Chip shoots Buck a thumbs up.

Buck doesn't return the gesture.

Things at the Gamblers table aren't going so well. They've interviewed half of their targets, but they haven't come close to signing any of them. Some of their targets come only with their apologies, having already signed with other teams. Others receive better offers in terms of money or their role on the team or both from other teams.

"This sure isn't going well, is it Coach?" Rodman asks.

"No it isn't," Safari Chip and The Coach answer in unison.

The two coaches look at each other.

"Oh," says Safari Chip. "You were talking to him."

"No, this time I was talking to you," Rodman says.

"Rodman. This is our third season together. How many times do I have to tell you…"

"I know. It's Chip, not Coach," Rodman interrupts.

"That's twice now that we've gotten confused. Say Coach, what's your real name?" Safari Chip asks.

The Coach shakes his head emphatically.

"No?" Safari Chip asks.

"He'd never tell any of us, and I've known him since I was a peewee," Rodman explains.

"Come on Coach. You can tell me. I promise I won't tell anyone or make jokes. Besides, we have to know which one of us the guys are talking to or we'll be confused like this all season," Safari Chip pleads.

The Coach looks at the three Gamblers looking on in anticipation of his real name. He grabs Safari Chip and pulls him aside. "Ok. I'll tell you, but you have to keep it secret."

Safari Chip crosses his heart with a finger.

"It's Sue," The Coach says.

"Sue?" Safari Chip asks astonished and a bit too loud.

"Shhhh, shhhh, shhhh," The Coach shushes Safari Chip. "I know. It's a stupid name. I don't know what my parents were thinking."

"A boy penguin named Sue," Safari Chip says again. "Well that won't do. We'll have to find something new. But what shall we call you?"

"Are you kidding me?" The Coach asks.

"What?" Safari Chip questions.

The Coach moves past Safari Chip's rhyme and thinks about a new name for a bit. "Flip."

"Flip," Safari Chip repeats. "That could work. Chip and Flip. I like it."

The two coaches return to their table. Their next interviewee, a rookie defenseman named Bruce Moose, is waiting for them and talking to the other Gamblers. He stands up as the coaches approach. He extends his hoof to each of them.

"Nice to meet you Mr. Moose. I'm Safari Chip, and this," Safari Chip points to The Coach, "is my assistant, Flip."

"Flip?" Rodman looks suspicious.

"Flip? I can do a back flip," Lovey says.

"I like when you do back flips," Big Chick says.

Before Safari Chip can stop him, Lovey runs into the aisle to get some speed. He hops, plants, and jumps into the air, spinning backwards with the greatest of ease and lands a perfect back flip. He usually pulls off this trick while on the ice wearing skates. It's easier in shoes.

"Awesome!" Big Chick grins.

Safari Chip and Flip like Moose from the get go. He's big, strong, and smart, everything they want in a defenseman. They only have one other defenseman left to interview, and they haven't been impressed with the ones they've interviewed to this point, so after a brief private discussion to make sure they're both on the same page, Safari Chip and Flip tell Moose they're seriously interested in signing him.

"This is great," Moose says. "Let me get my agent so he can work out the details of a contract with you guys."

"Sounds good." Safari Chip stands up and shakes Moose's hoof again.

Moose takes off.

"Who's our last defenseman?" Safari Chip asks Flip.

Flip searches through a stack of papers. "Oh. Here he is. It's Snickers Doodle Anderson."

"Snickers Doodle Anderson?" Safari Chip can't believe his ears.

"Yep. The third."

"As in son of Snickers Anderson Jr. and grandson of Snickers Anderson, for whom the Cup was named?" Safari Chip asks.

"That's the guy," Flip informs him.

Safari Chip scratches his head. "I didn't even know he was still playing? He's got to be a hundred and fifty years old."

"It says here he's two hundred and sixty-six."

"Two hundred and sixty-six!?"

Flip examines the notes on Snickers a little closer. "Oh wait. That's in dog years. He's thirty-eight."

"That's still pretty old for a hockey player. What sort of numbers has he been putting up lately?"

Flip pulls out Snickers' stats. "His numbers have been progressively declining over the past three seasons, but he's still better than average. What he's lost in speed over the years he's made up for in knowledge of the game."

"I see he's missed a lot of games lately. Is he injury riddled?" Safari Chip peeks at the papers in Flip's flippers.

"I wouldn't say he's injury riddled, but he's definitely got some wear and tear."

"Bring him over," Safari Chip says reluctantly.

Flip walks away from the table to get Snickers. He comes back with another Shih Tzu, who, unlike Undertaker, Kane, and Apple Jack, is clean cut.

The first thing Safari Chip notices is that the black parts of Snickers fur have lightened to brown and part of his white fur has grayed. He stands up and greets Snickers with a handshake. "Hello Snickers."

"Glad to meet you Mr. Chip," Snickers says.

"You're sort of IAHL royalty, aren't you?" Safari Chip notes.

Snickers waves off Safari Chip's claims. "I don't know about that."

"Grandson of the first ever coach to lead his team to a championship, and the son of a three time Anderson Cup champion, I'd say you come from a royal pedigree."

Snickers seems uncomfortable with the comparison. "Despite all of my father and grandfather's accomplishments, I sit here a seventeen year vet who hasn't even played in a Cup Finals. And let's face it. I'm not getting any younger. I've bounced around four teams in the last five years, and with the expansion of the league, I fear if I don't play with the Gamblers this season, I may never get to play in a Cup Finals."

"Why do you say that?" Safari Chip asks.

"That I won't play for a Cup if I'm not a Gambler?"

"Yeah."

"With your current roster, the Gamblers have a legitimate chance to be the first team in the history of the league to win four straight Cups. I know playing with you guys isn't a guaranteed ticket to the Finals, but I feel I'd have a better shot with you guys than I would with any of the other fifteen teams."

"What sort of penalty minutes have you been putting up lately?" Flip asks.

"I've cut them in half from what they were ten years ago."

"Playing smarter?" Safari Chip asks.

"Kind of. Mostly I've just mellowed. I'm playing more and fighting less."

Flip leans over to Safari Chip for a private word. He whispers, "I don't know about you, but I think he'd be a great asset."

"You do?" Safari Chip whispers back.

Flip nods.

"I'm not sold. What am I missing?" Safari Chip asks.

"Think about it. He said he thinks the Gamblers have a chance to win four Cups in a row, so that means he's got faith in the team. And, since he's never won a Cup, he's going to bring a desire to win, especially since his playing days are numbered. And, maybe best of all, he's someone the other dogs can look up to. Maybe when they see he's not fighting all the time, they'll mellow a bit too, and the Gamblers won't have three of the top five fighters this year," Flip says.

"We had four of the top five fighters," Safari Chip corrects. "Don't forget, Lovey was at the top of that list."

"Oh yeah," Flip sighs.

"But you make some good points Flip."

The two coaches turn back to Snickers.

"Would you be opposed to a one year contract?" Safari Chip asks.

"I was hoping to do three years. I want to play at least until I'm forty, I'd like to not have to worry about where I'm going to be playing at the end of each year, and I'd really like to end my career with a class team like the Gamblers. But, to have a legitimate chance to win a Cup, I'll take whatever you guys are willing to offer," Snickers says.

Safari Chip ponders the idea of having Snickers around for three years. He was really hoping to sign the older dog to a one year deal and possibly re-sign or not re-sign him at the end of the year based on his performance.

"Well, go get your agent. I'm sure we can work out a deal," Safari Chip tells him.

Snickers goes and gets his agent. He and Moose arrive back at the table with their agents at the same time. Safari Chip rounds out his defensemen, signing Moose to a three year deal and Snickers to a two year deal with a team option for a third year. Though he initially wanted to sign Snickers to a one year deal, he decides if he gives Snickers at least two years the veteran dog might play better without the worry of whether or not he might be playing all next season, and if he exceeds Safari

Chip's expectations, the team option gives him the opportunity to get his wish to retire as a Gambler.

After signing his new defensemen, Safari Chip and Flip meet with Bing Hope, a right wing chimp, formerly of the Idaho Potatoes. He gives a great interview, and both coaches want to sign him, but Bing's reluctant. In recent seasons, Bing seems to have been an on ice punching bag for the Gamblers. They find Bing and hit him with explosive power all the time. Two seasons ago, Undertaker illegally hit him and gave him a concussion, and last year he ran into the brick wall that is Big Chick several times, landing hard on his tail each time. No matter what, he always seems to have the puck at the wrong time when he's on the ice against the Gamblers. An ASPN countdown of the top ten hockey hits from last season had Bing as the victim in three of the highlights, and each time the opponent lighting him up is one of the Gamblers.

Safari Chip has Bing meet the three Gamblers he's brought with to show him that they're not really bad guys. Bing relaxes slightly, but he's still not sure if he wants to sign with them until Flip makes the comment that if he plays with the Gamblers, he won't have to worry about getting pounded by them. At that, Bing signs a Gamblers contract with a quickness. His agent insists on a panic alarm clause though. The special clause allows Bing to terminate the contract at any time if he feels unsafe. It's a silly request, but Safari Chip grants it because he's sure it will never be an issue.

The interviews roll on until Safari Chip realizes they've interviewed all the players they came to interview, and they're still one player short. "We still need another forward."

"You want to go over the guys we interviewed again?" Flip asks.

"We're going to have to."

They start going over their notes about the three forwards they interviewed that haven't already signed elsewhere. Each comes with his own pros and cons, and none of them stand out to either coach. Flip suggests that they leave without signing anyone. Perhaps they can go scouting elsewhere in the world the way Safari Chip did when found Rodman.

Safari Chip doesn't get a chance to respond to Flip's suggestion, because Haas comes to their table and interrupts. "Hey Mr. Chip."

"Hi Jack." Safari Chip stands up and shakes the hare's paw. He points to Flip. "This is Flip. He's going to be my assistant coach this season."

"Hello." Haas waves.

Flip stands up and extends his flipper. "Hi."

"He's the guy who coached Rodman in South Africa," Safari Chip explains.

"Nice."

"So what brings you by the Gamblers table?" Safari Chip asks.

"I wanted to congratulate you guys on your second straight Cup. I also wanted to apologize for what happened during those games in Alaska…"

"Rumor has it that your involvement in that little scandal was nonexistent," Safari Chip quickly waves off Haas' need for an apology.

"Well, I still knew what my teammates did, and I didn't stop them. So, in my own eyes, I'm just as guilty."

"For what it's worth, my guys and I don't hold any ill will towards you. What do you say we let bygones be bygones?"

"Sounds good."

There's a small gap in the conversation.

"Well hey, thanks for your time. I have to find my agent. He's around here somewhere shopping my services," Haas says.

"You're not playing for the Gold Rush this season?" Safari Chip is floored.

"Nope."

"They didn't cut you did they?"

"No. It was my call. I want to play with guys I can trust and guys who make playing the game fun. It was great playing for Coil and most of those guys, but I'd rather be the third goalie on your team behind Harlan and Beary than play one more season with guys like Jason and Maulbreath."

"You would?" Flip asks.

"Yep."

"You mean it? For real?"

"You bet."

Flip pulls Safari Chip aside. "You know, if we signed Haas, it would allow Beary to play the wing like he wants, and we would have both goalies from the last two Cup Finals."

Safari Chip smiles wildly. The slot machine jackpot noise that plays over the arena speakers when one of the Gamblers scores a goal plays in his head.

Both coaches turn back to Haas.

"Listen Jack. If you're serious, go grab your agent and bring him this way. Let's see if we can't work out a deal to get you into Gamblers black, red, and gold," Safari Chip says.

"Serious?" Haas is surprised.

"Serious."

Haas sprints away to find his agent.

"Looks like we have a full roster," Flip says.

"Indeed," Safari Chip agrees.

Both coaches are unexpectedly approached by a familiar looking turtle wearing a ten gallon cowboy hat, a plaid red and black shirt tucked into his tight cowboy pants that are held up by a belt buckle just slightly smaller than a wrestling championship belt, cowboy boots, and a patch over his eye. Even more curious is the fact that the turtle has a long handlebar mustache even though turtles can't grow mustaches.

"Hello sir. My name is John Wayne," the turtle says with a heavy 1800's style cowboy accent and extends his flipper to Safari Chip.

"Hi." Safari Chip stands up, shakes the turtle's flipper, and tries to get a better look at his face under the cowboy hat he has pulled over much of his eyes.

John Wayne looks away. He doesn't want Safari Chip to get a good look at him. "I represent a hockey player by the name of Trigger McCoy that you can't afford to pass upon if you're seriously interested in threepeating."

"I'm sorry Mr. Wayne, but we just filled our entire roster," Safari Chip apologizes.

"Awww come on now. You can surely take a look at my boy. He's the real deal. They don't call him Trigger for nothing."

"Why do they call him Trigger?" Flip asks from his seat.

"Because, when he sees an opening in the net, he pulls the trigger on the shot. And let me tell you, he's a deadeye. He'll score you a lot of goals," John Wayne states.

Flip gets a better look at the turtle from his seated vantage point. He can see who the turtle is and it's not John Wayne.

Safari Chip rifles through some papers. He can't find anything on a Trigger McCoy. "I've never heard of him."

"Let me bring him over to talk to you. He's a red panda you see. You'll love him." John Wayne motions for Trigger.

Over walks a regular panda bear with his white fur dyed red, not a red panda. Safari Chip continues rummaging through his papers as Trigger approaches. Flip shakes his head at the shabby disguises of Harlan and Beary.

"I still can't find anything on him. What position does he play?" Safari Chip asks, still looking at the papers.

"Well, he prefers the wing, but he can play any of the forward positions," John Wayne says.

Safari Chip looks up from his papers to greet Trigger. One look at the supposed red panda, and he can tell what's going on. He extends his hand to Beary. "Nice to meet you Beary."

"Nice to meet you too Chip," Beary says with no disguise in his distinctive voice. He realizes he gave himself up and tries to correct it. "I mean, my name is Tigger."

Harlan nudges Beary with his elbow and whispers out of the side of his mouth, "It's Trigger."

"I mean Trigger," Beary says.

Safari Chip reaches over his table, takes off Harlan's cowboy hat, and rips off his mustache.

Harlan and Beary both gasp.

"Harlan," Safari Chip declares.

"Hey!" Beary exclaims nervously, trying to keep up the charade. "You're no my agent, Bruce Wayne."

"It was John Wayne," Harlan says, giving up the rouse.

Safari Chip turns to his backup goalie panda. "Beary."

"Awww nuts. How'd you know it was us?" Beary asks.

"Because I have eyes," Safari Chip says.

The other Gamblers, who have crowded around to see what is going on, have a laugh at the expense of the silly goalies.

Rodman takes Harlan's cowboy hat from Safari Chip and tries it on. "Nice cowboy hat Harlan."

"Thanks." Harlan smiles.

"I just want to play the wing this season so bad Chip," Beary begs.

At that moment, Haas and his agent return.

"Well kid, if we can sign this guy, you've got your wish," Safari Chip explains.

"Really?" Beary asks.

"Really," Safari Chip assures him.

"Then you better sign him, whatever it takes," Beary says so seriously it makes everyone around burst into laughter.

Less than fifteen minutes later, the Gamblers have a new backup goalie signed to a one year deal. The length of Haas' contract is as short as it is because after the Gamblers most recent Cup win, Safari Chip signed Harlan to a six year extension, and Haas knows he's in his prime. He wants to play with a team like the Gamblers, who have a chance to win and restore his faith in what teammates should be, but he also wants to start. It would be a waste for him to spend more than one season as a backup. Some would even say one season as a backup is a waste, but for Haas, it's something he needs to do.

Safari Chip and the Gamblers couldn't be more thrilled with the way the Free Agent Meetings go. They leave feeling like they have the strongest team they've ever had.

Chapter 3: L-Rod Is Orphanage Bound

On the ice, before practice starts, the new guys introduce themselves to their teammates.

"Hey," Moose extends a hoof to one of the Gamblers. "Nice to meet you. I'm Bruce Moose."

"Bruce Moose!?" Goose exclaims his wing extended for a shake. "I'm Bruce Goose."

"I know. And from what I hear, we're going to be on the same line," says Moose.

"It looks like it's going to be Maverick, Goose, and Moose from now on," Maverick laughs.

At the opening of training camp, Safari Chip finds he has a full roster, an assistant coach, and none of the problems he had to deal with last season at this time. The dogs aren't bugging for Apple Jack to get a tryout because he's already on the team, Harlan and Beary are getting along, Lovey isn't busting his chops about new jerseys, Sammie isn't sleepy, Liten's arm isn't broken, Maverick and Goose are getting playing time, Big Chick is no longer working in a grocery store, and Rodman hasn't surprised him with any more orphaned penguins.

But, just when it seems like nothing can go wrong, when the hockey world is so right, when the team's joy is at its zenith, the arena doors open and in walks a woman coyote with two hotel security guards. Everyone stops at the sight of her and the guards. She walks directly to Safari Chip and pulls him aside. She hands him some papers, explains something to him, and points at several different lines in the papers.

"Who's she?" L-Rod asks Rodman.

"I don't know."

"What do you suppose she wants?"

Rodman turns to his little buddy. "If I don't know who she is, why do you think I would know what she wants?"

The Gamblers watch as Safari Chip suddenly starts yelling and flailing his arms around enraged. The woman tries to calm him down, but he only gets angrier, jumping and stomping around on the ice. When the coyote can't calm him down the security guards make their way towards the irate monkey.

The Gamblers make a move to protect their coach, but Safari Chip promptly brings his tirade to an end and motions for the guards to stand down. Both guards and Gamblers back down.

Safari Chip breathes in deep and sighs heavily. He turns to his player and yells, "L-Rod, Rodman, come here."

L-Rod's smile fades.

Rodman frowns too. Whatever news Safari Chip has for them, Rodman knows it's bad, and whatever the news is, it must have something to do with L-Rod, otherwise Safari Chip would never involve him.

"What's up Chip?" L-Rod asks as they approach.

"L-Rod, this is Ms. LeJuene from social services," Safari Chip says.

"Social services!?" Rodman exclaims.

"What's social services?" L-Rod asks.

"It's a government program that protects the rights of children," Safari Chip explains.

"Hi," L-Rod greets her warmly. "Are you here to set up a social services night?"

"I'm here to bring you in," Ms. LeJuene says bluntly.

"Bring me in where?" L-Rod asks.

"To the orphanage," Safari Chip explains.

L-Rod gasps and skates away from the adults. He goes and hides behind Big Chick and the dogs.

"Why are you taking him to the orphanage?" Rodman demands.

"Let me ask you Mr. Penguin, whose care is he under?"

"Mine."

"And where is he staying?"

"With me, in my hotel room."

"In your hotel room?" Ms. LeJuene says skeptically.

"It's a suite. It's more like a condo," Rodman explains.

"Are you married?"

"No!" Rodman cries.

"Mmm Hmmm."

"What?" Rodman asks.

"How is it that Canter came to be under your care?" Ms. LeJuene asks.

"It's L-Rod, and he snuck onto our plane last year before it left South Africa. He rode stowaway in my luggage all the way into my hotel… my suite. One thing lead to another and before we could send him back to South Africa, he became a Gambler."

Ms. LeJuene looks confused.

"What's the matter?" Rodman asks.

"I just have so many questions. How old is he? Is he being educated? Is he even a legal resident of the United States?"

Rodman shrugs.

Ms. LeJuene is aghast.

"He's fifteen," Flip interjects.

"What about his education and residency?"

"We can get him a tutor and a green card," Rodman says.

"Is it true you once lost him?"

Rodman hesitates to answer.

"Where are his parents!?" Ms. LeJuene asks.

"He's an orphan," Flip answers.

"Look Mr. Penguin. You can't just have a fledgling. You have to have papers. He has to have papers. You have to show that you're a fit parent, capable of caring for a child. You can come to my office tomorrow to discuss the adoption process. But rest assured Canter is leaving with me tonight."

"His name is L-Rod," Rodman says angrily.

"Whatever." Ms. LeJuene motions and calls for L-Rod.

L-Rod remains where he is.

"Wait," Rodman says.

Ms. LeJuene looks to him.

"Can't we work something out?"

"Like what?"

"Like, can't we keep him through the paperwork process?"

"I'm afraid that's impossible. If something was to happen to him, and we allowed him to stay with you, knowing the process had not been completed, we could get into a lot of trouble."

"But, I'm Rodman T. Penguin. Surely there's something I can do to persuade you."

"What do you mean?" Ms. LeJuene asks.

Rodman rubs his flipper together, making the international symbol for money.

"Are you trying to bribe me? You know, this could reflect very poorly on any attempts at adoption," Ms. LeJuene admonishes Rodman.

"No! No! No! No bribe." Rodman uses his flippers to frantically wave off the suggestion.

"Look, I don't have time to waste. I have to get going." Ms. LeJuene turns back to L-Rod. "Come on Canter. We have to go."

"You can go. I'm ok," L-Rod shouts.

"Very funny young man. Now, let's go."

"Seriously," L-Rod yells, "I'm ok. You can go."

Ms. LeJuene turns to the security guards. "Would you go get him please?"

L-Rod skates fast away when he sees the guards coming to get him.

"Wait. Don't do that. You're scaring him," Rodman shouts.

The security guards continue towards L-Rod. He's fast, and they have to try to run along the ice to get him. They slip and fall while he glides away from them with the ease of a figure skater. The guards continually fall as they chase L-Rod around the ice with the Gamblers cheering him on. Sometimes the guards get close to L-Rod, but when they do, L-Rod skates by his teammates, and they trip, push, or hip check the guards, knocking them down and giving L-Rod more time to escape.

It almost becomes a game. L-Rod knows he can outrun the guards all night if it comes to that. He glides around and past them, but suddenly, he finds himself being held from behind. He turns his head to see Ms. LeJuene with a paw full of his jersey.

The Gamblers rush to L-Rod's aide, but the security guards step between them and Ms. LeJuene with their night sticks pulled.

The sixteen other Gamblers hold up their hockey sticks in response.

The guards back down.

Safari Chip puts a stop to all the lunacy. "Ok guys stop!" He turns to L-Rod. "You have to go buddy, but don't worry. Rodman, Flip, and I will be down there to spring you at 6:00 a.m."

"You can be there at 6:00 if you want, but we open at 9:00," Ms. LeJuene says. She takes L-Rod to his room and allows him to gather his stuff. All he takes is a small bag of clothes. He doesn't plan on being in the orphanage for long.

Chapter 4: Jailbreak

Safari Chip can't get his guys to focus on hockey drills after L-Rod is taken away. The Gamblers are more interested in arguing him about letting L-Rod be taken. They talk over him about what they'd do if they got their paws, hooves, wings, or flippers on Ms. LeJuene. Unable to get his guys to settle down, Safari Chip cancels the first practice of the preseason. He orders his players to go to bed and not worry about L-Rod. He assures them by tomorrow night L-Rod will be back with the team.

The Gamblers leave the locker room under the pretense of obeying Safari Chip's orders, but they all go to Rodman and L-Rod's room to come up with a plan.

"We can't let the little dude stay in that prison all night," Kane says.

"What can we do about it though?" Undertaker asks.

"We could do to social services what we did to that one team who hurt our captain," Apple Jack suggests.

"The last time we tried that we all ended up in jail for a night," Lovey says.

"Yeah. We can't just pee on everyone that makes us mad. We need a real plan," Rodman says.

At that moment, Rodman gets a text.

"It's from L-Rod," Rodman informs his teammates.

"What does he say?" Liten asks.

"He says we have to get him out of there," Rodman answers, and responds to L-Rod: *We'll have to wait until tomorrow to come get you. What else can we do?*

The room is silent as the Gamblers wait for L-Rod's response.

Silence.

Silence.

More Silence.

BEEP!

The Gamblers huddle around Rodman to read L-Rod's response.

Come down to the social services building and wait for my signal.

*

The Gamblers, minus Bing, who is too nervous to join them, pull up outside the social services building in the team limo with Big Chick at the wheel. He parks the limo in front of the building, and the Gamblers wait inside for L-Rod's signal.

"Where is he?" Goose asks.

"I don't know. I can't see anything," Maverick says, looking out the window.

"Look there." Beary points to a flashing light from a window on the fourth floor. "Is that him?"

"That's him," Rodman says. "Get ready Big Chick."

Through the darkness, the Gamblers can barely make out L-Rod throwing several bed sheets tied together out his window. Their little buddy shimmies down the makeshift ladder to the ground. He scopes the grounds until he's sure the coast is clear. Satisfied that it is, he makes a break for the fence that surrounds the building and its yard. His breathing is under control, and his heartbeat is normal as he walks calmly towards the fence. A quieter, calmer escape is probably best. Plus, with his teammates there to help him, what could go wrong?

Suddenly, sirens wail and L-Rod is drenched in bright lights. His movements have triggered an alarm. With no time to waste, he makes a mad dash for the fence. He waddles as fast as he can without looking back. A window in the social services building behind him lights up and then another and another.

Rodman and the dogs get out of the limo. The rest of the Gamblers all poke their heads out of the windows, and quietly clamor for L-Rod to hurry.

L-Rod picks up the pace. He ducks out of the way of one of the security lights and keeps a steadfast pass for the fence. Behind him, the double doors of the building open and four orderlies step outside. One of them shouts for a spot light.

L-Rod hits the fence.

"Hurry L-Rod. Climb!" Rodman panics.

L-Rod looks up and points to the razor wire atop the fence. "I don't think I can get past that."

Without hesitation, Snickers scales the fence, braves the razor wire, and jumps onto the other side. "Jump on my back."

L-Rod does as he's told, and Snickers jumps back onto the fence. Behind them, the spot light continues to crisscrosses the field in search of who set off the alarm.

Undertaker and Kane scale the fence too. They grab the razor wire from a safe position and pull it down so Snickers won't have to cut up his paws again. Snickers jumps over the fence and safely deposits L-Rod on the other side.

"Thanks Rodman," L-Rod says.

"Don't thank me. Snickers is the one who just scaled that razor wire to get you," Rodman says.

"Thanks Snickers," L-Rod says.

"We might want to save all the thanks yous for later and get going?" Liten calls from inside the limo.

"Yeah. Come on. Let's go!" Apple Jack shouts and pushes the penguins and the other dogs into the limo.

"Go Big Chick! Put the pedal to the metal big fella!" Sammie yells when the limo doors slam shut and everyone is accounted for.

Big Chick does as he's told. He slams the pedal all the way to the floor. The tires spin around and around on the ground for a few seconds before they get traction. The squealing tires send the smoke of burning rubber into the air. The spotlights hits the limo just as the tires grab ahold of the road. The back of the limo is lit up for a split second before it peels off into the night.

Inside the luxury car, all the Gamblers scream as Big Chick drives like a madman away from the social services building. Big Chick zigs and zags, weaves in and out of traffic, and runs more than one yellow light. He takes a tight corner that shifts everyone to the right side of the limo. The weight of the sixteen players combined with the sharp turn causes the limo to tip onto two wheels. Gamblers fall on top of other Gamblers. The excited screams of the players get louder. This jailbreak and escape has several Gamblers having the time of their lives.

"Someone needs to move their weight to the other side of the limo to knock us back down," Rodman says, trapped under the weight of Lovey, Harlan, and several other players.

"Big Chick, you're the biggest. Move over to the other side," Undertaker shouts.

"Ok," Big Chick agrees.

"No!" Liten screams.

It's too late. Big Chick lets go of the wheel and crawls over Haas on the passenger's side of the front seat.

Haas screams as the limo goes completely out of control and into oncoming traffic with no one at the helm.

Big Chick tries a few times to pound the limo down from the passenger's seat, but the other side of the limo is still too heavy with Gamblers. "It's not working."

Liten claws his way to the front seat and assumes driving duties.

"Let's help Big Chick," Snickers rallies the defensemen.

The other dogs, Maverick, and Moose fight their way to a standing position.

"On the count of three," Snickers says.

At his three count, the six defensemen and Goose all jump into the seats on the passenger side, knocking the limo back onto four wheels. They hit the ground with a bang, but other than dazed and a little petrified, everyone's ok.

"Snickers, you're bleeding," Moose notices.

"Eh, just a few knicks. Nothing to worry about," Snickers says, examining his paws.

"Is anyone following us?" Liten asks.

Rodman looks out the back window. "I don't think so."

As if on cue, red and blue police lights flash through the limo windows.

"Oh nuts!" Harlan says.

"It's the fuzz!" Lovey smiles.

"Rodman, what should I do?" Liten asks.

"Pull over," Beary says. "We can probably talk our way out of this."

"Outrun them," Apple Jack laughs.

"No. Pull over," Beary repeats.

"Outrun them," Undertaker and Kane both urge.

Rodman looks back and forth between the two parties' suggestions.

"Rodman?" Liten asks again.

Lovey mouths the words *outrun them* to Rodman, and most of the other guys nod their heads in agreement.

Just as it dawns on Rodman that the last time he tried to talk his way out of something it ended with L-Rod being taken away, Beary caves and says, "Oh what the heck. Outrun them."

"Floor it Liten," Rodman says.

"Ok, but we have one problem," Liten says.

"What?"

"I cannot reach the pedals!" Liten screams.

"Oh for Heaven's sakes. Scoot out of the way." Maverick crawls up front, moves Liten out of the driver's seat, sandwiching him between Haas and Big Chick in the overcrowded front seat, and takes over driving duties. He maneuvers the limo off of the main road and onto the highway.

In the back seat, the Gamblers give Maverick updates on the distance, speed, and actions of the three cop cars chasing them. Maverick moves the limo from the lane on the right side of the highway to the far left lane. The three squad cars follow him.

Goose pops his head into the front seat and gets in his buddy's ear. "Hurry up Mav. They're coming up on us fast."

"Don't worry. I have an idea."

"What are you going to do?"

Maverick pulls ahead of a semi-truck in the center lane and gets in front of it. "I'm going to get back into the slow lane."

"You're gonna do what!?" Goose exclaims.

"I'm going to use this semi as a blocker between us and the cops. Then, I'll hit the breaks, and they'll fly right by."

Maverick gets into the slow lane just as the cops pull up alongside the semi-truck in the fast lane. He slams on the break and the cops fly by as the limo grinds to a halt near an exit. Maverick hits the gas again but pulls the limo off the highway.

"We've got to get back to the hotel," Rodman says once they're back on the surface streets. "Take some back roads Mav so we can stay mostly out of sight."

"You got it," Maverick says. "How's L-Rod?"

Rodman looks all around the limo for his buddy. The little guy's been unusually quiet for the duration of the ride. He spots L-Rod way in the back, sitting with a look of shock plastered to his face. "L-Rod, are you ok?"

L-Rod doesn't answer, doesn't move.

"L-Rod?"

"L-Rod?" Sammie shakes the little penguin.

L-Rod doesn't answer.

*

The Gamblers enter the New Orleans Hotel from the back. They sneak L-Rod in and get him to the elevator undetected. The bell dings and the doors open. They all file in with Ed, the old goat elevator operator.

"Whoa! Whoa! Whoa sirs! Are all yall getting into my elevator at one time?" Ed asks.

"Sorry Ed. It's an emergency," Harlan says.

"Well now I do declare. An emergency? What kind?"

"We're ducking the law," Lovey chuckles.

"Was that yall that I heard about on the news?" Ed asks.

"What did you hear?" Rodman asks back.

"They said a limo pulling away from social services tonight led police on a wild goose chase before escaping."

"Lead police on a what?" Goose asks.

"Oops. I do apologize Mr. Goose."

"It was more like a wild Gamblers chase," Undertaker laughs.

Everyone in the elevator laughs.

"That was us," Big Chick admits.

Ed's face grows grave. "Did yall bust out young Mister L-Rod?"

The Gamblers part the elevator to show L-Rod, still in his unmoving state, to Ed.

"I do declare!"

The elevator dings as they reach the top floor.

"Top floor! Penthouse!" Ed says as he always does when they reach the top.

The doors open, and the Gamblers hurry out with Big Chick carrying L-Rod like a bag of luggage.

"You could do us a big favor Ed," Rodman says.

"I'm the only one working this late, and I didn't see none of you Gamblers leave your rooms. Definitely didn't take any of you for no elevator ride," Ed says.

"Thanks Ed. We owe you one. A big one." Rodman races to join the rest of the guys.

"You just win a third Cup this season," Ed shouts.

Rodman has Big Chick bring L-Rod to his room. Big Chick sets L-Rod down on Rodman's couch. "What do you think is wrong with him?"

"He might be in shock," Rodman says.

"What should we do?"

"Maybe a cold shower will snap him out of it."

Big Chick shrugs and does as Rodman suggests. He picks L-Rod up and brings him to the shower. They set L-Rod down in the tub and turn the water on. L-Rod doesn't respond immediately, but he eventually starts shivering and shaking. He jumps from the tub and fights to catch his breath. He stares a hole through Rodman and Big Chick as he huffs and puffs.

"Relax. At least you're safe and sound at home," Rodman says.

Big Chick heads for his own room with L-Rod safe at home again, and Rodman and L-Rod look for a hiding place for L-Rod in case Ms. LeJuene comes looking for him.

*

Big Chick slips his key card into the door and enters his hotel room. A light is on inside. He doesn't remember leaving it on. In fact, he's almost positive he turned it off. He hates wasting electricity.

"That's weird."

Big Chick walks further into the room. As he gets further into his suite, he sees a mess of white and yellow feathers that grows bigger and bigger the more the room gets visible.

"Holy cow. What happened here?" he asks aloud.

A loud thump startles Big Chick. He runs to his living room closet and grabs a hockey stick. He holds it over his shoulder like a baseball bat. From the hallway, he hears voices squawking in his room. He hides to the side of the hallway entrance and waits for the intruders to come out.

He doesn't wait long before three tiny chickens come running out of his hallway into his living room, chasing and hitting each other with pillows that spew feathers all over.

Big Chick jumps back terrified. Then he gets a good look at them and whispers to himself, "Oh no!"

The three tiny chickens are too busy with their pillow fight to notice him.

"Hey!" Big Chick shouts.

The three chickens drop their pillows and turn to him nervously.

"What are you guys doing here?" Big Chick asks.

"Grandma got sick," the first chicken says.

"So our mom and your mom had to go and take care of her," the second chicken says.

"And they sent us here to stay with you," the third chicken says.

Big Chick slaps himself in the forehead with his wing. He knows he's in trouble. His cousins, Chicken, Noodle, and Soup, weren't nicknamed El Pollos Locos for nothing.

Chapter 5: Hiding L-Rod

Bang! Bang! Bang!

Safari Chip shoots out of bed at the loud ruckus coming from his front door.

BANG! BANG! BANG!

Safar Chip scrambles to get out of bed and answer his door. He stops only to grab his safari hat on the nightstand.

The three loud bangs come a third time.

The monkey is awake enough at this point to be angry at the noise disrupting his sleep. He walks in his safari hat and his banana patterned pajama pants with matching night shirt to the front door. "I'm coming. I'm coming. I don't know which one of you is banging on my door, but whoever it is, you better have a darn good reason or you're going to be in a lot of..." Safari Chip opens his door to find Ms. LeJuene and four police officers. "Trouble."

"Where is he Mr. Chip?" Ms. LeJuene demands.

"Where's who?"

"Canter." Ms. LeJuene stares at Safari Chip agitated.

"Who?"

Ms. LeJuene sighs. "L-Rod."

"Oh. Isn't he with you?" Safari Chip asks.

"No Mr. Chip. He is not."

"Why not?"

Ms. LeJuene's only response is a blank stare.

"What?" Safari Chip insists.

Ms. LeJuene tries to get a read on Safari Chip, tries to figure out if he's truly clueless. "Do you really not know?"

"Know what?"

"Last night, L-Rod escaped from his room and ran to a limo parked outside our building, waiting to take him away."

"Someone took L-Rod!?" Safari Chip is aghast.

"It was your team!"

"My team? How do you know that?"

"Who else would be picking him up in a limo?" Ms. LeJuene asks.

"Well, just let me grab my safari hat, and we'll head to each of their rooms until we find him." Safari Chip turns to look for his hat.

"It's on your head."

"What is?"

"Your hat."

Safari Chip reaches for his head. Sure enough, his safari hat is already there. "Oh." Safari Chip leads Ms. LeJuene and the police officers to Liten's room next door to his.

Ms. LeJuene leaves one officer to question Liten. She then directs one office to Maverick's room and another to Goose's room. She turns to Safari Chip. "Where is Rodman T. Penguin's room? I want to start there."

"It's all the way down at the other end of the hallway." Safari Chip leads her to Rodman's room.

Once there, the officer bangs on Rodman's door the same as he banged on Safari Chip's.

Rodman, already awake and eating breakfast with L-Rod, walks to the door and peeks out the peephole. He sees the policeman and turns to L-Rod. "It's Ms. LeJuene, and she brought the fuzz."

L-Rod panics.

The office bangs on the door again.

"What do we do?" L-Rod asks.

"Go hide," Rodman says.

L-Rod runs to the laundry room and hides in the dryer. Rodman answers the door.

"We're here to get Canter, Mr. Penguin." Ms. LeJuene pushes her way into Rodman's room without an invite. "You can make things a lot easier on everyone, especially yourself, if you just tell us where he is."

"Isn't he with you?" Rodman plays dumb.

"You know he isn't. And you know where he is." Ms. LeJuene directs the officer to check for him in L-Rod's room.

"I promise you, he's not here," Rodman says. "You're welcome to turn the place upside down, but what I want to know is, if he's not with you, and he's not with me, then where is he?"

Ms. LeJuene looks around the living room, under the couch, in the fireplace, and behind the television stand. "You know he's here." Ms. LeJuene turns and heads for the kitchen.

Safari Chip looks to Rodman and shoots him a look that asks *what's up?*

Rodman points to the laundry room.

"In the laundry room?" Safari Chip mouths.

Rodman nods.

Ms. LeJuene notices two breakfast plates on the kitchen table. "Do you always eat two breakfasts?" She questions.

"Yes," Rodman answers.

Ms. LeJuene eyeballs him unbelievingly.

"I'm a big strong hockey player with an appetite to match."

She looks around the kitchen a bit. "Do you object to me checking your room?"

"I do, but go ahead anyway," Rodman answers.

Ms. LeJuene walks out of the kitchen, down the hallway, past the laundry room, and stops. She backs up, looks at the washer and dryer, and opens the washing machine lid.

Rodman and Safari Chip start sweating.

She keeps moving towards Rodman's room.

"You get him out of here while I keep her distracted," Rodman whispers to Safari Chip.

"No!" Safari Chip protests. "You're in a lot of trouble. I don't want to get mixed up in this."

"Yes," Rodman argues back. "You're our coach. You're supposed to protect your players, and if I go down for this, you're going to be down two penguins instead of one."

Safari Chip hesitates.

"Besides, if we get him out of here, no one is going to get in trouble."

Safari Chip sighs. "Fine. Get in there and distract her."

Rodman enters his room, leaving Safari Chip alone in the hallway.

Safari Chip looks around. When the coast is clear, he pops open the dryer door and sees L-Rod inside. The little penguin looks up with terror in his eyes. Safari Chip holds a finger to his lips and shushes L-Rod.

The sound of the officer's boots clonking on the tile gets Safari Chip's attention. The officer exits L-Rod's room. Safari Chip slams the dryer door shut, creating all sorts of noise.

The officer eye balls him suspiciously.

Ms. LeJuene comes out of Rodman's room and calls for the officer. "I need your help. He won't let me in the closet."

The officer moves past Safari Chip and enters Rodman's room, leaving Safari Chip alone with L-Rod. This time, the monkey wastes no time in extracting L-Rod from the dryer. He rushes him out the front door. There, they're met by Rodman's neighbor, Sammie.

"Chip, what's going on? I keep hearing all sorts of banging and I see tons of cops in the hallway," Sammie asks.

"Since you guys decided to jailbreak L-Rod last night, and you were seen, Ms. LeJuene brought the police to find him."

"Uh oh."

"Yeah, uh oh."

"What should we do?" Sammie asks.

"We've got to hide him. I have to go back in there. So you take him, and hide him in your room." Safari Chip hands L-Rod over and runs back inside the penguins' suite.

Sammie and L-Rod make their way down the hall to Sammie's room, but they hear a door open down the hallway a bit, and they see an office step out. The two Gamblers run to the closest room on the other side of the corridor and feverishly bang on the door.

Kane answers. "Hey guys. What's up?"

Sammie and L-Rod push their way in without answering.

"Hey!" Kane barks.

Sammie and L-Rod run into the living room shared by the four dogs. They're met by the other three dogs eating Muchos on their couch and watching the stock market channel.

"Hey Sammie, L-Rod," Undertaker says.

"No time for talk," Sammie says.

"What's going on?" Snickers asks.

"The police are here looking for L-Rod," Sammie explains.

"No way!" Apple Jack sprints to the door, peeks out, and sees Harlan, Haas, and Flip being questioned by the police.

With each interview, the officers are moving closer and closer to the dogs' room.

Apple Jack slams the door and runs back to the living room. "What are we going to do?"

"We've got to hide him," Sammie says.

The six Gamblers look around the dogs' room for a place to hide L-Rod, but no place seems good enough. Before they can find a place, there's a banging on their door.

Apple Jack runs back to the front door. He peeks out the peephole. "It's Rodman, Chip, Ms. LeJuene, and a cop!"

"Stall them," Snickers orders.

"How?"

"I don't know. Think of something."

Apple Jack turns to the door. "Ummm. Hold on!" he shouts. "Just a second. Ummm. Undertaker messed on the floor."

"Hey!" Undertaker complains.

Apple Jack shrugs at his buddy.

"What?" Ms. LeJuene asks.

"Sounds like he got nervous," Safari Chip says.

Rodman shrugs at her. "It happens."

Apple Jack turns back to the living room and gets the high sign from Kane. He opens the door. "What's going on?"

"Is L-Rod in here?" Safari Chip asks.

"Why would he be in here?" Apple Jack questions.

"They lost him at the orphanage," Rodman antagonizes Ms. LeJuene.

"You know you guys took him. How much longer must we play this game." Ms. LeJuene seethes.

"Well, you're welcome to come in and check for yourself." Apple Jack moves aside.

Ms. LeJuene leads the officer into the room. She sees Undertaker and Kane enjoying their Muchos. "What are all of you doing in here?"

"This is our room," Kane says.

"Yeah, and I didn't mess the floor," Undertaker says. "Apple Jack spilled some water."

"I thought you said there were four dogs Mr. Chip," Ms. LeJuene questions.

"There are," Safari Chip answers.

"Where's the fourth?"

"He went to get more Muchos," Kane says.

Ms. LeJuene seems skeptical.

"I told you hockey players have big appetites," Rodman tells her. "And theirs are monster sized."

"Just start in their rooms," she orders the officer. "I'm going to stay out here, near the front door, so no one leaves."

*

On the outside ledge of the dogs' giant city view window, Sammie and Snickers cling to the wall and work together to get L-Rod to the next room.

"This was a stupid idea," Sammie says.

"We'll be fine. Just don't look down," Snickers says.

Immediately, Sammie and L-Rod look down.

"I just said don't do that."

They reach the window of the next room and look inside, but they don't see anyone. They bang on the window for someone to come and let them in.

Finally, Bing walks by the window and sees his new teammates out on the ledge. The sight is too much for him. He faints and falls to the ground.

"Oh nuts," L-Rod says.

They bang on the window for a while longer, but the chimp remains down.

"Let's move on to the next window," Snickers says.

The three Gamblers cautiously move down the ledge to Beary's window. Snickers peeks inside and sees Beary talking with one of the officers. "Man. We can't catch a break."

"What's wrong?" Sammie asks.

"There's a cop in there."

"We'll just have to wait it out."

"I guess." Snickers looks down. "Oh nuts!"

"What?" L-Rod asks with worry in his voice.

"I think I'm going to lose my Muchos."

"You said not to look down."

"I know." Snickers holds a paw to his mouth. He fights the nausea buiding up in his tummy as long as he can. He tries to keep from hurling, but the puke comes up anyway. The sick dog tries to not spray it all over by holding his paw over his mouth, but puke seeps through between his fingers as the pressure in his mouth builds. He can't hold it back any longer and blows chunks over the side of the hotel. As he vomits, his body involuntarily lunges forward, causing him to slip from the ledge.

Sammie and L-Rod reach out quickly, grab Snickers by the shirt, and pull him back up.

"Thanks guys," Snickers pants.

"That was cool," L-Rod says.

"Are you crazy? That was the scariest thing I've ever seen." Sammie's heart races.

"Yeah, but his throw up landed on top of that van." L-Rod points.

All three Gamblers look down at the vehicle and share a laugh. They'd laugh even harder if they knew it was the social services' van

"That is kind of cool," Snickers laughs.

"Is the officer gone?" Sammie asks.

"Let me check," Snickers turns back to the window. He's met by the face of Beary, staring at him from inside the room. Snickers screams and falls backwards off the ledge again.

With his catlike reflexes that made him the best backup goalie on Earth, Beary opens the window, grabs Snickers, and pulls him inside. "What are you doing out there?"

"We're hiding L-Rod," Snickers says.

Beary looks out the window and sees the other two Gamblers. "Get in here you nut jobs."

L-Rod and Sammie climb into Beary's room.

"Are the police gone?" L-Rod asks.

"They're gone for now, but they're still milling about the hallway, talking to the other guys," Beary answers.

"We've got to get L-rod out of the hotel," Sammie says.

Snickers spots Beary's breakfast on a cart. It gives him an idea. He picks up Beary's phone and dials a number.

"Room service," the attendant answers.

"Hi. This is Snickers of the Gamblers. I'm upstairs in Beary Nelson Riley's room. I'd like to order four Muchos."

"Sure thing sir. We'll have them up to you in no time."

Snickers hangs up.

"Muchos? That's your bright idea?" Sammie asks.

"You'll see," Snickers says.

*

In the dogs' room, Rodman continues to antagonize Ms. LeJuene. "I have a question for you Ms. Social Security Lady."

"It's LeJuene, and I'm from social services, not social security."

"Even though you lost him, and now he's missing, am I still able to come down and start the adoption process?"

"I suppose you could, but you can rest assured when we find Canter, if he's here, I'll see to it you never see him again."

Inside, Rodman gulps, but outside, he keeps up his tough guy façade.

*

Snickers waits by the door for the room service cart to arrive. He watches out the peephole and opens the door before the attendant has a chance to knock. "Come in. Come in." Snickers literally pulls the guy and his cart into the room.

"Whoa!" the attendant yells. "What's going on?"

"Give me your uniform," Snickers demands.

"For what?"

"I can only tell you that I need your uniform."

The attendant can tell the Gamblers are in a bind. His face turns smug. "What's in it for me?"

"How about season tickets?" Snickers offers.

"I already have those."

"A team autographed jersey?" Sammie offers.

"I have two of those."

"What do you want then?" Snickers asks.

"A thousand dollar tip and a PTO?" the attendant beams.

"A PTO!?" Sammie.

"Yeah. See, I played junior college hockey, and I want a shot to play in the big leagues."

Beary steps up to the guy. He gets right in his face, and bumps him with his chest. "How about a thank you and we don't tell your boss you insulted the Gamblers?"

The attendant sees he's pressed his luck. "That sounds good." He steps out of his uniform and hands it over to Snickers.

"It's too small. One of you guys are going to have to do it," Snickers says to Sammie and Beary.

"Do what?" Beary asks.

*

Beary and Snickers peek out of Beary's front door. Ms. LeJuene and the police are in the hallway with Rodman, Safari Chip, and now Flip too.

"Ok man, go." Snickers turns to Sammie.

"This better work," Sammie says in the room service attendant's outfit. He pushes the cart out of the room towards the gathering at the end of the hallway. L-Rod peeks out from under the curtain on the bottom of the cart. Sammie plays the role of room service attendant very well. He stops by each of the Gamblers rooms and picks up their used breakfast trays.

The Gamblers in the hallway see Sammie but don't recognize him until he's right next to them. When they do recognize him, they give him baffled looks, but Sammie passes them by as though nothing out of the ordinary is going on.

"I don't understand. I know he's here somewhere," Ms. LeJuene says.

"We searched each of their rooms high and low," one of the officers says.

Sammie picks up the tray outside Rodman's room and makes his way to the garbage chute at the end of the hallway.

"We didn't get to check Sammie's room," she states.

Sammie stops at the mention of his name.

"I can let you in," Safari Chip offers and leads Ms. LeJuene and the officers down the hall.

Sammie opens the garbage chute and starts pouring the leftover food from the room service trays down the chute. He nudges L-Rod under the curtain giving him the sign to jump out. "Hurry," Sammie whispers.

L-Rod jumps out from behind the curtain and into the trash chute as fast as he can.

The police don't find L-Rod in Sammie's room. Ms. LeJuene starts to question whether or not the Gamblers have him. If they don't, she doesn't know how she's going to find him. She mills about the hallway for a while longer with the officers, discussing their next move. The Gamblers could be hiding L-Rod in any one of the rooms in the entire hotel.

Safari Chip and Flip hold a meeting of their own in the hallway with Rodman, Sammie, Snickers, Beary, and a few of the other Gamblers who have made their way into the hall.

"What's going on? Where's L-Rod? And why are you dressed up like a room service attendant?" Safari Chip demands.

"I needed a disguise to get L-Rod past the police," Sammie says.

"To get him past the police?" Safari Chip is confused. Then, he sees the trash chute. "Oh no. You didn't."

Sammie nods.

"Well someone better go get him," Safari Chip demands.

"I'll get him," Snickers says.

"Take the other dogs with you. But wait until she's gone." Safari Chip turns to Rodman. "Well that answers two of my questions. What's going on here Rodman?"

"We busted L-Rod out of the orphanage."

"I can see that, but why?"

"We couldn't bear the thought of him in that place while we're all playing hockey. He begged us," Rodman explains.

"Yes. Do not blame just Rodman. We all wanted to do this," Liten agrees.

"You guys should have waited to see what they had to say at the social services office. You had better hope we don't get caught, or we're all in a lot of trouble," Safari Chip warns.

*

The dogs enter the basement of the hotel where the garbage chute empties.

"Hey L-Rod. It's Undertaker. You can come out now."

L-Rod pokes his head out of a trash pile. "She gone?"

"Yeah. We tricked the heck out of her," Kane laughs.

L-Rod jumps out of the dumpster and joins the dogs.

Apple Jack covers his nose with his paw so he won't have to smell L-Rod's funk. "Nasty!"

"What?" L-Rod asks.

"You need a bath," Apple Jack jokes, and the dogs have a laugh at L-Rod's expense.

Chapter 6: Fire In The Hole

For the next month, Ms. LeJuene attends several Gamblers practices to make sure L-Rod is not with the team. This forces the team to hold two practices each day, an early one for the entire team, and a midnight practice where players rotate turns training with L-Rod.

They all worry when the adoption paperwork for L-Rod hasn't come through the night before the season's first game.

"What are we going to do about tomorrow?" L-Rod asks Rodman inside their suite.

"You'll just have to miss a few games," Rodman says.

"Nuts!" L-Rod frowns.

A knock on the door interrupts their conversation.

"That's probably Chip." Rodman walks to the door and answers it without checking out the peephole first.

"Hello Rodman," Ms. LeJuene greets him.

"Hi," Rodman gulps.

"May I come in?"

"No!"

Ms. LeJuene looks at him puzzled.

"I mean sure." Rodman turns to the living room and elevates his voice. "Come on in Ms. LeJuene."

L-Rod scurries into the hallway.

"What can I do for you?" Rodman asks.

"I came here to apologize that I accused you of kidnapping L-Rod. I mean, if we had spent as much time trying to find him as we did trying to catch you with him, maybe we would've found him by now, but we kept our focus on you, and obviously you don't have him. Now he's lost. I never should have taken him from you in the first place." Ms. LeJuene sobs.

Rodman pats her on the shoulder to comfort her. "It's ok. He'll turn up."

"I hope so, and if he does, he's all yours."

L-Rod's head perks up in the hallway.

"His papers came through?" Rodman asks.

"Yeah. I put a rush on them so that if he turns up, he can come back to a place he knows, a place where he's safe," Ms. LeJuene bellows and hands Rodman the adoption papers.

L-Rod, feeling invincible, walks out from the hallway. He stops in front of the crying coyote and clears his throat.

Ms. LeJuene looks up. Her crying stops, and she almost chokes on her tears. "What…? You…? I mean." She stands up. "You had him the whole time!"

L-Rod shrugs arrogantly.

Ms. LeJuene grabs L-Rod. "Come with me young man."

Rodman grabs L-Rod by his other flipper. "Whoa! Wait. I have legal guardianship of him now. You can't just take my son from me."

Ms. LeJuene drops L-Rod's flipper. Rodman is right. "You may have legal guardianship of him, but that can be revoked." She stomps her way to their front door, stops before opening it, and turns back to the laughing penguins. "And don't think for one second that I won't be all over you to make sure he's being taken care of properly. I mean it. If so much as one feather on his head gets wrinkled, I'll involve the authorities and have him taken away from you for good." Ms. LeJuene slams their door behind her on her way out.

Both penguins blow her a kiss and blow off her threats.

"Want to play IAHL Hockey on PS3?" Rodman asks.

"Heck yes I do." L-Rod high fives his buddy.

"I call the Gamblers," Rodman says.

L-Rod makes a fist and grinds his beak. "Nuts."

*

In the hallway, Ms. LeJuene runs into Big Chick and El Pollos Locos.

Big Chick has been hiding them from Safari Chip and the rest of the guys. He's caught by the coyote trying to sneak them back into his room from a late night meal.

"You too?" she asks rather loudly.

Big Chick panics. "Me too what?"

"Where did those chicks come from?" she demands.

Safari Chip pops his head out of his room to see what's with all the commotion.

Big Chick turns and sees his coach. He panics even more. His hope was that his grandma would be feeling better and he could send them home before anyone knew they were there.

"Where did those chicks come from?" Safari Chip asks.

"That's what I want to know," Ms. LeJuene says.

"These are my cousins, El Pollos Locos," Big Chick comes clean.

"El Pollos Locos?" Ms. LeJuene asks.

"That's what we call them. That's Chicken. That's Noodle. And that's Soup?" Big Chick points out each tiny chick.

"You're kidding" Safari Chip says.

"No," says Big Chick.

"What are they doing here?"

"They're staying with me while our grandma is sick."

"Oh brother." Safari Chip removes his safari hat and wipes his brow.

Ms. LeJuene huffs and puffs and storms past them on her way to the elevator room. She turns back to Big Chick before rounding the corner. "I'll be keeping my eye on you too."

"Me!?" Big Chick points to himself.

"And you too," Ms. LeJuene warns Safari Chip.

"Me!? What did I do?"

"You're the coach of this screwy team,"

*

The next day, before the season's first game, Safari Chip is on edge with all that has gone on in the preseason. He and Flip arrive early and lock the office door to get some peace and quiet.

The dogs are the first players to arrive in the locker room after the coaches. They instantly get busy filling green and brown water balloons that look like grenades. They're in such a rush filling the balloons that they splash water all over one another. Undertaker is so excited that he rushes a tie job on his balloon, and one of his long nails pops it, drenching him and splashing the others. He runs around the room scared. It makes the other dogs laugh so hard, they drop their balloons, and water sprays all over. The four dogs laugh and joke until the last balloon is tied, and they're all placed into two buckets.

Sammie shows up next.

"Sammie!" Kane yells.

The dogs rush to him.

"Sammie!" Undertaker repeats.

"What?" Sammie finds himself surrounded.

"Last night, Snickers told us about this trick he used to play on an old teammate of his in the minors," Kane starts.

"And one thing led to another, and we came up with our own trick." Apple Jack's tail wags.

"What's the trick?" Sammie asks.

"Our trick isn't exactly the same," Undertaker says.

"But ours is even cooler," Kane says.

"What is it?" Sammie asks again, his curiosity peaked.

"Before each game, we're going to hand out water balloons as players comes into the locker room," Snickers starts.

"But we're only handing out sixteen balloons," Undertaker interrupts.

"And there's seventeen players on the team," Kane cuts him off.

"So the last guy in, we all jump out and yell 'FIRE IN THE HOLE!' Then we unload our water balloons on him," Apple Jack finishes.

Sammie chuckles. "Every game?"

The dogs snicker and nod.

"Sounds fun. I'm in." Sammie takes a balloon from the bucket and goes to his locker.

One by one, the Gamblers file into the room. Liten, Harlan, Beary, Rodman, L-Rod, Lovey, Big Chick, and Moose arrive respectively. All of them love the idea of fire in the hole.

Haas enters the room next and draws all sorts of attention his way. He's dyed one of his long floppy ears black and the other red to match the Gamblers team colors.

"That's so cool. I want to dye my ears too," Lovey says as he examines Haas' ears.

"It's easy to do, and it washes out after a few days. I can show you how," Haas offers.

"Awesome!" Lovey says.

Apple Jack hands Haas a water balloon and informs him of their plan. The Gamblers hold onto their water balloons anxiously awaiting the next arrivals.

"I hope Bing doesn't come in next," Undertaker says.

"Why?" Apple Jack asks.

"Because that will leave just Maverick and Goose, and they'll probably come in together." Undertaker says.

"If they come in together, we can just nail them both," Snickers suggests.

"Hear that everyone?" Apple Jack yells. "If Bing comes in next, and then Maverick and Goose come in together, we're going to hit them both with our water balloons."

The door cracks open just then and draws rapid head jerks from each and every Gambler. Those with fingers have them crossed that Maverick and Goose will walk in together.

They get their wish. The horse and goose walk in next, are promptly informed about the prank, and given their water balloons. Now, the Gamblers heartbeats really race. The next time the door cracks, the new guy, Bing Hope, is going to walk in and be greeted by sixteen water balloons. The Gamblers giggle, breathe heavy, and hide. They can barely stand the wait.

After several long minutes that feel like hours, finally, the locker room door swings open, and Bing walks into what he thinks is an empty locker room. No one is in sight, and the place is dead silent. He looks to the clock on the wall unable to believe he's the first one to arrive. For a second, he thinks he might be so late that everyone is already on the ice.

The chimp's confused thoughts are interrupted by Apple Jack, who jumps out of his locker, screaming at the top of his lungs. "FIRE IN THE HOLE!"

Bing is startled beyond belief. He's so frozen with fear at the scream that he doesn't even react to Apple Jack rearing back and firing a fast ball at him. The balloon whizzes through the air, hits Bing square in the forehead, and explodes. The cold water causes a violent shiver up and down Bing's whole body and a momentary loss of his breath. As more Gamblers jump out of lockers, from behind tables, chairs, and corners, and peg him with one water balloon after another, Bing struggles to get his lungs working again.

Incredibly, all sixteen balloons hit Bing dead on. No one's aim is off even slightly.

The Gamblers can't contain their laughter. They hunch over, hold their bellies, roll on the floor, lean against lockers for support, and pound the walls from laughing so hard.

Bing, on the other hand, doesn't laugh. He shakes, petrified. Between assaulting him with water balloons, players walking the window ledges outside of the hotel, and orphanage breakouts, he wonders what sort of psychotic teammates he's inherited. He doesn't wait to find out. Without a word, he turns and runs from the room, and he doesn't stop until he's at the airport with a ticket back to Idaho.

The Gamblers look around the room at each other. They're worried, baffled, and uneasy.

"What just happened?" Lovey asks.

"Where did he go?" Rodman asks.

"He just took off." Kane points to the door.

"Right out the door." Undertaker scratches his head.

Harlan walks to the locker room doors and peeks into the hallway. "He's gone. I mean long gone. And I don't think he's coming back."

"Uh oh," says Beary.

"Who's going to tell Chip?" Big Chick asks.

Panic sets in. No one wants to tell Safari Chip.

"You should tell him," Undertaker says to Kane.

"Me? You tell him." Kane pushes Undertaker.

Undertaker pushes Kane back. "I'm not telling him."

"Well, I'm not telling him either," Kane says. "You tell him Apple Jack."

"Why me? It was Snickers' idea," Apple Jack says.

"It wasn't my idea. I just told you guys a story. You came up with the plan," Snickers says.

"Well, you're one of the alternate captains," Apple Jack argues.

"Yeah. You're supposed to be setting a good example for us," Kane says.

"So go and give us an example of what it looks like to take one for the team," Undertaker says.

Snickers growls at his apprentices. Then, he has a thought. "Hey. I'm just an alternate. Rodman's the captain."

All eyes turn to Rodman.

Rodman gulps loudly. "Me?"

All at once, there's a collective nod from the entire team.

Before Rodman has a chance to protest, the rest of the guys scurry to their lockers. The Gamblers captain goes to his own locker and tries to think of just the right way to put it to Safari Chip, but there is no good way.

After things settle down a bit, Beary walks around the locker room giving all of his teammates decorative scarves just like the ones he wears. He went to great lengths during the offseason to find scarves that fit the personalities of each of his buddies. Most of the Gamblers graciously accept their gifts even though they aren't keen on wearing them every day like Beary does. Lovey, however, receives two and puts both of them on immediately. He puts the one with green and brown Army camouflage around his head like a bandana, and he ties the other one, a plain yellow one that was supposed to represent bananas and go to Bing, around his right arm.

At Rodman's locker, he preps his gear and gets dressed for the game. All the while, he hopes Bing will return so he doesn't have to tell Safari Chip what they did. After he laces up his skates, he takes a marker and writes the word THREEPEAT on them. Safari Chip had the word painted above the locker room exit, so everyone sees it before they hit the ice each night.

Safari Chip's door bursts open. "Game time!"

Rodman watches the dogs and several other players, hightail it out of the room. One by one, all the Gamblers escape the locker room until Rodman is alone with Safari Chip.

Safari Chip pushes Rodman towards the door. "Come on Rodman. Let's go. I thought I'd see a little more pep in your step for opening night. Is everything ok?"

"Actually Chip," Rodman starts and then stops.

Safari Chip grows overly concerned. He grabs Rodman's shoulders and shakes his captain. "What's the matter Rodman?"

"Ummm." Rodman hesitates again.

"Come on man. Spit it out." Safari Chip continues shaking him.

"Bing is gone."

Safari Chip releases Rodman. "What do you mean Bing is gone?"

"He's gone. He left."

"Where'd he go?"

"I don't know. He just ran out of the locker room."

"That's odd." Safari Chip scratches his head. "What the heck are we going to do?"

"I guess we can all take turns rotating turns on the third line. We've had lighter rosters than this. We'll make it work."

Safari Chip breathes a sigh of relief. "You're so smart. Have I told you that before?"

"Once or twice."

Safari Chip puts his arm around Rodman and leads him out of the locker room. Underneath his feet, the carpet is wet and squishy. He stops and looks down. Water forms around his feet when they press down on the carpet. "Remind me to call a plumber. There must be a leak under the floor. It's all wet."

Rodman knows he's off the hook for now, but sooner or later, Safari Chip's going to find out what happened. Then, they're all going to be in trouble.

*

The Gamblers open the season against the yellow and green clad Dallas Cacti. Despite the hopes of most fans that the original eight teams would start the season against another of the original teams, the IAHL decided to start each of them against a new team to help introduce them throughout the league.

After the opening night ceremonies, Safari Chip calls his regular starting lineup of Rodman, Liten, Lovey, Undertaker, Kane, and Harlan to the bench. He huddles his entire team around him. "Ok guys listen up. I know there's been a lot of talk around the league about these new teams being minor league, but I'm telling you now to get that notion out of your heads. Treat this game like it was a game against the Gold Rush."

The Gamblers holler indistinguishably in unison.

"Now, everyone get in here and let's get a one, two, three, Gamblers." Safari Chip throws his hand out.

The rest of the Gamblers pile on their hands, flippers, wings, paws, and hooves.

"One, two, three GAMBLERS!"

Safari Chip sends his starting six onto the ice.

Rodman lines up across from Ross Ambrose, a hedgehog. Rodman does as Safari Chip instructed and plays his hardest. He focuses on the puck, puts his head down, waits for the drop, fights for it, and wins the season's first faceoff.

Lovey snags the puck and races for the blue line. He's defended by a lizard named Chris Justice. He flicks the puck past Justice, swerves around and past the lizard, and wins the race for the puck behind the net. Justice and one of the Cacti defenseman, a bulldog named Shaun Cary, fly in from either side to jostle the puck away, but Lovey bangs it around the boards out to

Undertaker. The Gamblers dog races out in front of the net and fires a shot.

The Cacti's goalie, another hedgehog and Ross' brother, Dean, makes the save with his body. He's unable to stop the puck from bouncing back towards Rodman and the oncoming play. Rodman fires the rebound right back at him. Dean makes another save, but once again, he's unable to control the loose puck. This time, just as Cary and a peacock named Brad Fryar, fight to clear it, Liten skates in, steals it, and fires at the open side of the net. It goes in, and the goal lights go off. The slot machine jackpot noise plays for the first time this season.

The Gamblers go up 1-0 in the first twenty seconds of the game, and they never look back. Safari Chip's early warning to play the Cacti tough guides them to a 5-1 victory over Dallas. After Liten's goal, Rodman scores two, Lovey tallies one, and Goose gets the other. Assists go up and down the roster, and the defense allows only ten shots on goal all night, meaning Harlan starts the season with a win and a ninety percent save percentage.

After the game, the entire team celebrates at the food court with some Muchos. Kane, Apple Jack, and Snickers, three of the team's four Mucho fiends, are the first three to show up. Conspicuously absent is Undertaker. One by one the other Gamblers continue to arrive.

"Where the heck is Undertaker?" Kane asks.

"I don't know, but I'm not waiting for him much longer," Apple Jack says.

Kane looks and sees several of his teammates already chowing down. He turns and sees more teammates coming, but not Undertaker. "Here comes Maverick, Goose, and Moose. Where is this dog?"

Apple Jack shakes his head. "Come on Snickers. Let's get some Muchos."

Snickers gives the food court one last glance, and then, with wagging tail, he and Apple Jack get in line.

Kane continues to wait for his buddy, but Undertaker never shows up.

Chapter 7: Bing Reemerges

Game two arrives, and one by one, the Gamblers file into their locker room. As they enter, Apple Jack hands each of them a water balloon.

"I don't know if this is such a good idea after what happened last time," Rodman says as he reluctantly accepts his.

"But we all agreed it was ok," Apple Jack argues. "No one else is going to have a meltdown like Bing did."

Rodman ponders Apple Jack's claim for a moment.

"Come on Rod. Don't be a party-pooper because of one kooky experience," Apple Jack pleads.

"Yeah," L-Rod agrees. "It was fun."

Rodman thinks it over a while and smiles. "It was pretty fun."

"Alright!" Apple Jack pumps a fist.

Rodman and L-Rod take their water balloons and head to their adjacent lockers.

Undertaker strolls in next.

"Well, well, well. Where were you?" Kane demands.

"Where was I when?" Undertaker asks back.

"Last night. When we were all eating Muchos and celebrating our opening night victory."

"That was last night?"

Kane looks at his buddy in disbelief and slaps him upside the head. "Yeah bonehead. You missed quite a party."

"Don't worry. We're going to have plenty more," Undertaker assures him.

*

Lovey can't run down the tunnel to the Gamblers locker room fast enough. He has big news. He jumps as he approaches the door, kicks it open, and runs in screaming. "You guys!"

That's all he's able to get out before Apple Jack jumps out of his locker, screaming, "Fire in the hole!"

The rest of the Gamblers jump out of their hiding spots and rear back to peg Lovey. Their grizzly cub has run right into the line of fire. The Gamblers barrage Lovey with a water balloon attack. He has no choice but to stand there and take the water balloon blitz like a man. He closes his eyes and takes one hit after another without moving. He counts them in his head. Thirteen. Fourteen. Fifteen whizzes past his ears and splatters on the wall behind him. Sixteen nails him right in the snout.

Lovey shakes the wetness out of his fur and goes right back to screaming. "It's an Olympic year!"

"An Olympic year?" Beary asks.

"Yeah! We're going to be playing for two weeks in the Olympics!" Lovey pulls an IAHL/Olympics committee official flyer from his pocket that has all the details.

The Gamblers crowd around their wet, drippy, teddy bear. The excitement of playing for a gold medal spreads like wild fire around the room.

Lovey grabs Rodman by the shoulders and shakes him. "Dude, we've won two Cups together, and now we're going to be gold medal buddies too. This is so cool!"

Rodman frees himself from Lovey's grasp and steadies himself from Lovey's overzealous shaking. "I hate to burst your bubble dude, but we won't be teammates on the Olympic team."

"What? Why not?"

"I'm from South Africa. I'll be on team South Africa."

Lovey suddenly realizes he might not be playing with several of his Gamblers teammates. He spins to them. "Hey. Which of you guys here are Americans?"

Only seven of the remaining fourteen Gamblers raise their hands.

Lovey is flabbergasted. "Sammie, where were you born?"

"Australia."

"What about you Liten?"

"You know I am German."

"Beary?"

"China."

"Harlan?"

"The Galapagos Islands."

"Maverick? Moose? L-Rod?" Lovey finishes.

"We're Canadian," Moose points to himself and Maverick.

"And I'll be on the South African team with Rodman," L-Rod says.

"Oh nuts!" Lovey, who was so excited about the Olympics a minute ago, slouches down depressed at the idea that he won't be playing with a lot of his friends. "Well, that's going to suck, all of us on different teams."

"It's just for two weeks Lovey, and it'll be fun to see how well we play against each other," Rodman says.

Lovey perks up. "That actually will be fun."

"You better go get changed out of those wet clothes."

Lovey looks down at his damp clothes. "Yeah I should."

*

Safari Chip comes out of his office. "Game time!"

The Gamblers jump up and run out of the locker room. They hit the ice prepared to take on a familiar foe in the Idaho Potatoes, but they're not prepared to see who's wearing a Potatoes jersey and standing on the ice across from them.

"Is that Bing?" Liten points out the chimp skating around the ice with the other team.

Before any of the other starters can answer, Max Derlargo, the Potatoes wolf captain grinds to a halt in front of the Gamblers. "Yeah, that's Bing. And you guys better not target him like you have in the past."

"What do you mean target him?" Kane asks.

"Yeah, what do you mean target?" Undertaker repeats.

"Two years ago you concussed him!" Derlargo points to Undertaker and then turns to Lovey. "How many fights did you pick with him last year?"

"My fighting days are done. I'm a…"

"Lovey not a fighter," Derlargo interrupts. "I know. I know. I've heard your dumb catchphrase. But Kane hits him every chance he gets. Apple Jack has put hits on him that had him seeing stars. Even Big Chick has knocked him on his tail."

"I promise we don't target him. He's just always in the wrong place at the wrong time," Rodman promises.

"And I hit everyone every chance I get," Kane adds.

"Oh? You don't target him? So, was your locker room, last night, the wrong place at the wrong time?" Derlargo snaps.

The Gamblers are too ashamed to answer. They know they did Bing wrong.

"You guys better stay away from him if you know what's good for you," Derlargo warns and skates away.

"RODMAN!" Safari Chip screams from the bench.

Rodman turns and sees Safari Chip irately motioning for him to come to the bench. Standing next to Safari Chip, Flip shakes his head.

Rodman is positive this has something to do with Bing. "Yeah Chip?"

"What is fire in the hole?" Safari Chip crosses his arms.

"It was just a prank."

Safari Chip points to Bing. "Well take a look across the ice. That's what your prank cost us."

Rodman frowns. "Sorry Coach."

Safari Chip shakes his head and sends Rodman skating for center ice to take the game's first faceoff.

Both teams fight and claw to get an edge in the game. In the first period, they trade goals. The Gamblers score on a wrister from Sammie, and the Potatoes tie the game on one from Derlargo. Bing puts the Potatoes up 2-1 with his first goal of the season, and soon thereafter, Big Chick ties the game back up.

The Gamblers steer clear of Bing, and Derlargo sees to it he's safe. Any time someone even comes close to Bing, Derlargo is there to check them down. Bing becomes so wide open that he scores two more goals in the second period.

While the third line is on the ice with Rodman filling the spot that should have been occupied by Bing, Snickers sits on the bench with the other dogs.

"Man, that guy is killing us," Snickers says.

"Which guy?" Apple Jack asks.

"Bing." Snickers points to the chimp. "Someone's got to put a hit on that guy."

"You heard what Max said," Undertaker warns.

"We have to stay away from him," Kane says.

Snickers furrow his brow and growls. "We'll see about that."

Rodman comes to the bench with his flipper raised for Big Chick to take his spot. The rest of the third line follows close behind Rodman. Snickers jumps over the wall before Maverick is all the way back to the bench.

There's such a jumble of players changing lines that Undertaker and Kane lose sight of Snickers. Even Apple Jack, who jumps on with Snickers, can't find the older dog on the ice.

The Potatoes secure the puck that had been dumped by the Gamblers and head back towards Harlan. As they cross the blue line, the Gamblers try to set up on defense. Apple Jack still can't find Snickers and tries to defend the front of the net alone.

Dusty Poole, a turkey on the Potatoes, makes a move past Sammie and shoots the puck to Bing. Bing, in turn, makes a move towards the net. He has a clear shot, rears, back, and prepares to fire. Out of nowhere, he's met by a vicious but legal blast from Snickers, who reemerges from thin air like a magic trick. The hit sends Bing flying through the air. He lands on his tail and slides into the boards with a loud thud.

No one saw Snickers coming. Not Bing, not Derlargo, not the players on the ice, and not the players on the bench.

"Oooh!" Kane throws a paw over his mouth.

"Snap!" Undertaker shouts.

"Did you see that?"

"He came out of nowhere and leveled him."

"Like a shark."

"Like a dog shark!"

Derlargo's eyes go wide. He's slow in reacting, but he makes his way towards Snickers as play moves the other way. He grabs Snickers from behind, spins him around, and throws a punch at the old dog. Snickers takes the first punch and then a few more. Finally, he gets a block and throws a haymaker of his own. He catches Derlargo in the snout, stunning the wolf momentarily. Snickers isn't looking for a fight, so instead of punching Derlargo more, he throws the wolf to the ice and allows the referees to separate them.

After his penalty expires, Snickers joins the other dogs on the bench. "Now that's how you put a hit on someone."

"Dude. That was cold," Kane says.

"Awww, that was nothing. Just a little love tap to let him know we're watching him," Snickers waves off Kane's remarks.

"A love tap?" Apple Jack laughs.

"That was the most brutal hit ever," Undertaker says.

The four dogs laugh.

Snickers knows they're still losing though, so he gets the younger pups to focus. He knows Safari Chip made special concessions not only to allow him on the team but also to make a fourth captain's spot for him. He knows he owes a lot to Safari Chip and the Gamblers, so on his next shift, he leads the second line on a shift that ends with him assisting Beary on a goal.

The third period sees Derlargo trying his best to get back at Snickers for the hit he put on Bing. This causes him to play sloppy and careless. He gets one penalty for cross checking that leads to a power play goal from Rodman that ties the game, and later, he commits a boarding penalty that leads to another power play goal from Apple Jack that gives the Gamblers a lead they hang on to. They win the game 5-4.

Snickers apologizes to Bing after the game, during the handshakes, but Bing wants none of it.

In the locker room, Safari Chip gives his players a stern talking to for what they did to Bing, and he reminds them to stay focused on their goal of a threepeat.

Chapter 8: The Gamblers vs. The Five Ohhh!

The Gamblers have four days between their game with the Potatoes and their next game. Safari Chip leaves Flip in charge of practicing the team while he sets out to find a replacement for Bing. It takes him all four days, but he finally finds a suitable replacement. After much deliberation, Safari Chip signs a pigeon named Michael Williams. He's six year vet of the IAHL, who hasn't played for the last two seasons due to what his agent and the IAHL classify simply as personal reasons.

The fact of the matter is Mike was forced out of the league to do some psychiatric evaluations and "take a break" from hockey for a while. But, he had decent numbers with the Lightning at the time of his departure from the league, and during a light skating session for Safari Chip, he shows that he still has what it takes to play the game.

After getting Mike cleared to play again by the IAHL board, Safari Chip, Mike, and his agent all agree that the pigeon should get into playing shape with some minor league warm up games before joining the Gamblers. Safari Chip works hard to keep the signing a secret. He doesn't want to distract his team from doing their jobs, and he wants Mike to be able to get into playing shape at a comfortable pace.

*

With the Gamblers next four games all on the road, Big Chick has to decide what to do with El Pollos Locos. He tries to hire a babysitter, but they convince him that they're old enough to take care of themselves. He makes them promise to behave and to not stray far from the hotel until he gets back. He gives them his cell number, Safari Chip's cell number, Flip's cell number, and the number to all the arenas and hotels where the Gamblers will be staying and playing.

All four road games are all against new teams. The first game is a 7-0 blowout of the Albuquerque Quakes, a game in which Sammie and Lovey each get hat tricks, and Haas gets his first start, first win, and first shutout as a Gambler. The Gamblers second road game sees them lead 2-0 all the way up until the final seconds when the Fort Collins F-14s score with their goalie pulled and the Gamblers already on the penalty kill. The Gamblers manage to hold on anyway for a 2-1 win. They run their record to a perfect 5-0-0-0 with their third straight road win, this time a 6-2 pounding of the Portland Pirates.

The Gamblers are scoring goals in record numbers and winning with ease. By the time they head for Reno for their first Game against the Five Ohhh!, they're feeling unstoppable and very confident in their abilities. In their minds, they cannot be stopped. They may not even be able to be contained.

Their airplane flies in over Reno. The players look down upon what seems to them like a miniature, rundown, redneck version of Las Vegas. None of them are very impressed. Nothing changes in their minds after they land and walk through the halls of a tiny airport to baggage claim. The entire airport seems cramped and dirty, and the animals inside give them the heebie jeebies. They get crossed eyed stares from everyone there. It gives the Gamblers a feeling of anxiousness. They all just want to hurry up and get their bags so they can get out of the place.

Their escape from the unfriendly airport is delayed at the baggage carousel. They get tied up when L-Rod's bags never come out. Rodman has to help him fill out some paperwork to have his bags delivered to their hotel upon being found.

With the paperwork done, they go to meet a bus driver pre-hired by Safari Chip. They find the guy, greet him, and are greeted back by little more than a grunt. The bus driver leads them to a rundown bus that doesn't nearly resemble the bus Safari Chip looked at online. The short ride to the hotel, which is built into the Five Ohhh! arena, is uncomfortable and slow.

Finally, the bus arrives at the arena, appropriately named The Biggest Little Arena In The World. The Gamblers make their way inside, and head straight for their locker room so they can unload their gear before they check into their hotel rooms.

Safari Chip tries to navigate his team through the foreign corridor to the visitor's locker room, but he has a hard time of it in the unfamiliar arena. The walls are lined with cracks and holes, the paint job looks thirty or forty years old, lights in the ceiling are sporadically broken, ancient and seemingly broken equipment is scattered throughout the halls, and the entire place smells like a junior high school gymnasium.

Sammie takes off his sunglasses. "The Biggest Little Arena In The World looks like the biggest dump in the world."

"Yeah," Beary agrees.

"I guess you guys have been in the pros for so long that you forget what it's like to play for a minor league team, in a minor league city, and in a minor league arena. They don't have much money for upkeep and repairs," Moose says.

"But this is a major league team," Goose is quick to correct.

"They were minor league just a few months ago though," Maverick reminds him.

"Have you seen their uniforms?" Beary asks Harlan.

"They're tacky," Harlan says.

"Why are they tacky?" Haas asks.

"They're made to look like blue police uniforms with a long tie painted down the front," Beary says.

"And their captain and alternates have their letters inside of little badges that are painted on their jersey." Harlan laughs.

"You guys know what else is minor league about this team?" Apple Jack asks the entire group.

"What?" L-Rod asks.

"Their players," Lovey jokes.

Most of the Gamblers have a hearty laugh at the expense of the Five Ohhh!, but the couple of guys up front, Rodman, Safari Chip, Flip, Big Chick, and Liten, curb their laughter. They're the first ones to see the players of the Five Ohhh! standing in front of them, and it's clear by the looks on their faces and their tough stance that they've heard all, or at least most, of the comments the Gamblers have been making.

The Gamblers stop in their tracks. A long awkward stare down ensues.

The silence is broken by the ox captain of the Five Ohhh!. He snorts and steps forward. "You guys lost?"

"We're looking for the visitor's locker room," Safari Chip says.

"You must be the Gamblers."

Safari Chip nods.

"They don't look so tough to me," says a rat.

"They're not," says the koala from the Reno team.

Lovey steps up for the Gamblers. "Lots of teams have made that mistake."

A black bear for the Five Ohhh! steps out from the crowd of Reno players and approaches Lovey. He circles the white teddy bear, looking Lovey up and down.

Lovey clenches his fists.

The black bear flicks Lovey's bandana. "Who are you supposed to be? Miss Cleo?"

Lovey growls.

"What's with the ridiculous bandana?" the black bear asks.

"I happen to like it," Lovey defends Beary's gift.

"Well I hate it. In fact, I dislike it." The black bear pulls out his phone and snaps a picture of Lovey fuming in his bandana.

"What are you doing?" Lovey growls.

"I'm posting it on Facespace so I can dislike it."

"Yeah?"

"Yeah."

"And just who are you?"

"I'm Dislike."

"Dislike?"

"Yeah. Dislike."

"What kind of a dumb name is that? Did your parents dislike you from birth?" Lovey jokes.

Some of the Gamblers laugh.

"Actually, it's a pretty cool nickname," the ox draws everyone's attention back his way. "You see, he's the guy who invented the dislike button on Facespace."

"I've heard of him," Undertaker whispers.

"He doesn't like anything on Facespace," Kane says.

"Allow me to introduce the entire team. I'm Jake "The Ox" Trailor, that's Dislike, we call the four dogs over there Hoss, Stunner, Crush, and Crunch." Ox points to a Boxer, a Rottweiler, and two Pit Bulls. "The rat is Joey Ratone. The panda is Greg Claymore. The koala over there is Sammie Two…" Ox stops and points to Sammie Lou. "I believe you two may know each other already."

The Gamblers look to Sammie Lou, who frowns uncomfortably.

"We call the albino penguin here Mad Man, and the little penguin is Samanya Fiscal…"

"Samanya?" L-Rod can't believe it.

"Hello Canter." Samanya grins menacingly.

"It's L-Rod."

"It's Mud." Samanya makes a fist with his flipper and pounds it into his other flipper.

"The horse, Canadian goose, and moose are Ice Man, Slider, and Big Deuce," Ox continues. "Our goalies are Marlon C. Turtle, no relation to Harlan T. Turtle, and Rabbit X."

The Gamblers stare across at the Five Ohhh!. It's like looking into a mirror, an angry mirror. There's a Five Ohhh! animal counterpart for each Gambler.

Big Chick smiles when he doesn't see anyone to oppose him. "Well, you guys don't have a big chicken."

"Oh how rude of me. How could I have forgotten? You're right. We don't have a chicken, but allow me introduce The Colonel." Ox snaps his hoof.

From the back of the crowd of Five Ohhh! players glides a red fox with a toothy grin. He stands up straight and tall and waves at Big Chick. "Hello!"

Big Chick's eyes go wide with fear. He clutches his heart and falls to the ground. The Gamblers scurry to wake up their fainted chicken.

Laughter erupts from the Five Ohhh! side.

The Gamblers get Big Chick back to his feet and calm him down.

"Well, we're the Gamblers. No introductions necessary. We didn't mean to offend you guys, and we apologize sincerely for any hurtful comments we made," Rodman says.

Ox nods contemplatively. "Oh. Ok. Well in that case, apology..." he stretches out his hoof for a handshake with Rodman.

Rodman reaches out his flipper.

"NOT ACCEPTED!" Ox shouts and pulls his hoof away from Rodman before they can shake. "And as part of not accepting your apology, we're going to show you just how minor league we're not by kicking your tails tonight." Ox turns abruptly away from Rodman and motions for his team to follow him. "Come on guys."

Alone with his team, Safari Chip admonishes them. "Good going fellas. That wasn't nice."

"They weren't nice," Lovey argues.

"We started it," Safari Chip shoots back. He turns to Flip. "Make a note to send them an apology after the game and to have some Double Double Bonus Banana Split Sundaes waiting for them in their locker room after their first game in Las Vegas."

Flip makes the note.

*

The Gamblers put their gear away, check into their hotel rooms, and start getting focused on tonight's game. They stop making jokes and cracking whip, and by the time they take the ice, they're ready to play. Early in the first period, they go up 1-0 with a goal from Beary.

Shortly thereafter, Lovey scores despite the defensive efforts of Dislike to put the Gamblers up 2-0. "Why don't you dislike that on Facespace?" Lovey taunts the black bear.

Each of the goals sends Marlon C. Turtle spinning around the ice on his shell like the Harlan T. Turtle of old. The Gamblers seem to be rolling right through another inferior new team, and Safari Chip notices his team starting to showboat. They try trick shots, make fancy passes, and belittle the Five Ohhh! like a hockey version of the Harlem Globetrotters beating up on the Washington Generals. They head into the first intermission cocky, proud, and brash.

The second period rolls around, and the Gamblers hit the ice the same way they left it, but they soon find things spinning out of control. While trying to fend off an attack in front of Harlan, Rodman swipes and misses at a puck controlled by Ox. This gives Ox an opening to send a pass to Ratone. The rat speeds towards the net after breaking free from Liten and fires the puck past Harlan, getting the Five Ohhh! on the board.

Later in the period, Crunch fakes a blast from near the blue line. Everyone moves to defend the fake shot, allowing Crunch to change directions and fire at the empty side of the net. The shot gets through and ties the game.

A few minutes after tying the game, Sammie Two skates with the puck towards the offensive zone. He knows Sammie Lou is rushing up on him from behind, so he stops and allows Sammie Lou to bump into him. During the commotion of the collision, Sammie Two hooks his arm around Sammie Lou's arm. Then, he tries to skate away, faking as though he's being held. He even sells it by stumbling backwards and falling to the ice. He throws his arms up at the referees looking for a penalty.

Everything happens so fast that it appears to the referees as though Sammie Lou was actually holding Sammie Two. Sammie Lou receives a penalty, and the Five Ohhh! go on the power play. The result of which is a goal scored by Sammie Two and a 3-2 Five Ohhh! lead. Sammie Two doesn't stop there. On his next shift, he picks a fight with Sammie Lou and really pummels his koala counterpart. The crowd cheers raucously when Sammie Lou hits the ice.

Meanwhile, the Gamblers can't get anything going, not offensively, not defensively. Marlon turns into a brick wall, the Gamblers first line is shut down, The Colonel chases Big Chick around the ice, rendering him and his precision shooting useless, and L-Rod is targeted by Samanya.

Towards the end of the period, Beary draws a tripping penalty that could easily have been called a flopping penalty on Greg Claymore, but instead, the Gamblers go on the penalty kill once again. The Five Ohhh! pass the puck around and around and around. They get a few shots off, but either Harlan or one of the Gamblers defenders are always there to block the puck.

Then, Dislike does something none of the players has ever seen. He drops his stick, turns to Harlan, stares him in the face, and starts making funny faces at him and waving his paws around all crazy. Harlan tries not to let the distraction get to him, but whenever he moves to get a clearer view, Dislike moves with him and gets right back in his face.

Harlan tries to push Dislike away from him, but they next thing he knows, the goal light is going off as Raton bounces a shot off Dislike's skate, and ricochets it into the net.

While the Five Ohhh! high five and celebrate with snide chuckling, Safari Chip waves Harlan over to the bench. Harlon skates off the ice to antagonizing cheers of the Five Ohhh! fans.

Haas takes over in net with the hopes of being able to stop the bleeding, but on the first shot he faces, he gives up a goal. About an hour later the Five Ohhh! win the game by a score of 6-2.

Both teams do their customary end of the game handshakes, but they are far from friendly. Instead of *good game*, some of the Five Ohhh! tell the Gamblers *bad game*. Sammie Two flinches at Sammie Lou as they pass, and Dislike high fives no one, giving them a thumbs down instead.

As Ox shakes Rodman's flipper he asks, "Who's minor league?"

Chapter 9: The Gamblers vs. The Gold Rush

Before heading back to Las Vegas, Safari Chip chews the hides of his players for their behavior in Reno, but the Gamblers don't need him to tell them so. They know they acted like jerks, like punks, like... like the Gold Rush. It makes them sad, but it shapes them up as well. They write a letter of apology to the Five Ohhh!, that all of them sign.

Back home, two limos pick the Gamblers up at the airport. The team has grown so much that seventeen players, two coaches, and all their equipment just don't fit into one limo.

For most of the Gamblers, arriving home is a relief. For Big Chick, it's a nightmare. He finds room service trays, candy bar wrappers, toys, and clothes, including some of his jerseys, strewn all around his living room. His refrigerator door has been left open, there's a weird stain on his carpet, a pillow and blanket fort built in his living room, the cushions on his couch are missing, and one of his lamps is broken, though it appears someone has tried to glue it back together.

"What the heck happened here?" Big Chick asks aloud. Then, it dawns on him. "Chicken. Noodle. And Soup."

He doesn't know what he's going to do about his little cousins. He picks up a room service tray. On it is a receipt. The total at the bottom of the bill is over two hundred and fifty dollars, and in the corner is a running unpaid total El Pollos Locos have run up since the Gamblers hit the road. Big Chick's eyes go wide at that total, almost four thousand dollars. His cousins certainly don't have four thousand dollars.

The front door opens, and Big Chick spins around at the sound. Chicken, Noodle, and Soup walk in, each carrying a wing full of arcade game prizes and tickets. They stop in their tracks with looks of horror when they see Big Chick.

"Big game." Chicken waves.

"Big stick," Noodle says.

"Big Chick?" Soup asks when Big Chick doesn't respond to the other chickens.

"Big trouble," Big Chick informs them.

*

The Gamblers have two days after they arrive back home to rest and prepare for their next game, which happens to be their first game of the season against the Alaska Gold Rush.

On the second day, the Gamblers take a trip as a team for one last swim before the hotel closes its pool for winter. Big Chick brings El Pollos Locos along. They ran up another five hundred dollars in arcade play while he was gone, and in his estimation it will be harder for them to get into trouble while they're with him.

Kane looks around the crowd of Gamblers for Undertaker. Usually, the two of them are side by side making plans for tricks they're going to pull and who they're going to throw into the pool. Kane has Apple Jack to his left and Snickers to his right though, and Undertaker isn't with them at all.

"Do you guys see Undertaker?" Kane asks the other dogs.

"He said he had some things to do. He's not swimming today," Snickers says.

"Things to do? We already ate Muchos. We played fetch, took a nap, and went for a run this morning. What else could he possibly have to do?"

Apple Jack shrugs.

Safari Chip unlocks the gate to the pool.

"Last one in is a rotten Gold Rush!" Lovey yells and leads the charge to the pool.

Behind him, the rest of the Gamblers make a mad dash to the pool. They jump into the water in droves, trying hard not to land on one another. As usual, Harlan, cursed with being the slowest animal on the team, is the last to join the party.

Safari Chip and Flip aren't prepared for the sudden screams of terror they hear next. Before they can close the gate, they see each of the Gamblers frantically fight to get out of the pool. Apple Jack and Snickers help pull Harlan up while Beary and Sammie push him out of the water.

"What's wrong?" Safari Chip asks, running to his players. Before anyone can answer, he sees a large dark mass at the bottom of the pool.

"What is that?" Flip points to the object in the water.

The mass moves in a circle and rises to the top of the pool. A large muscular alligator pokes his head out of the top of the water and flashes a toothy grin at the Gamblers.

The Gamblers all gasp. They hear laughter, but it's not coming from the alligator. They look around and see the entire Gold Rush team sitting poolside laughing their heads off.

"Oh brother," Rodman says.

"The look on your faces." Jason Vyand, the Gold Rush's penguin captain and Rodman's arch nemesis, slaps his leg with his flipper. "Priceless!"

"Shut up Jason," Rodman shoots.

Jason stands up from his chair and walks over to Rodman. He throws his flipper around Rodman's shoulder.

Rodman instantly withdraws.

"Oooh! Testy," Jason snickers.

"What are you guys doing here?"

"We got to town a little early, and since we're staying here, we decided to partake in some of the amenities provided by the New Orleans Hotel. After all, we pay a twenty-five dollar a day resort fee for the use of the pool."

"Who's he?" Rodman points to the alligator.

"Him? He's our new goalie, James Vander Gates."

"Never heard of him," Rodman antagonizes Jason.

"Oh, but you will." Jason turns to his teammates. "Come on fellas. Let's get out of here. It's getting too crowded."

The Gold Rush follow their captain.

"Last one out is a rotten Gambler," Jason quips.

Aaron Packer, one of the Gold Rush's two house cats, stops when he passes Kane. "I'm back from that ACL tear you and your boy Undertaker caused me last year."

"You brought that on yourself punk, but I'll do it again any time you go after Liten." Kane pushes the cat.

Packer goes to push Kane back, but Mike Metz, the other Gold Rush house cat, grabs him and pulls him away.

Iggy Iguana, Rapture, and Thin Lizard, the marine iguana, vulture, and gecko who joined Haas in being the only Gold Rush players not to cheat in last season's Cup Finals, stop to say hello.

"How's it going?" Haas asks.

"Bad," Thin answers.

"Real bad," Iggy reiterates.

"Why? Aren't you guys doing well?" Haas asks.

"Our record is ok, but those guys hate us," Rapture says.

Haas frowns. "Why don't you guys ask for a trade or something? I'm sure Coil would do it considering."

"It's because of Coil that we don't," Rapture says.

"It doesn't seem fair for us to abandon him on account of what those guys did," Iggy elaborates.

Haas frowns even more.

"Not that we think you abandoned him or us," Iggy quickly clarifies.

"I just couldn't stand to play with that guy for one more season," Haas says, referring to Jason.

"He is a jerk," Thin agrees.

"We may leave when our contracts are up, but until then we're going to try to ride it out," Rapture says.

"Hey, on a lighter note, I hear you're starting tomorrow night." Iggy pats Haas on the back. "We're finally going to get a chance to see how we fare against the great Jack Haas."

Haas laughs. "Well, you can bet in the end, it's not going to be pretty for you guys."

His former teammates oooh at him playfully, talk a little bit of friendly smack, say their goodbyes, and leave.

*

Fourteen Gamblers lounge around their locker room and wait for Lovey to enter. They hide their water balloons while the fifteenth Gambler, Apple Jack, hides in his locker. For the fourth time in seven games, Lovey is the last guy to arrive.

"Where the heck were you again yesterday?" Kane demands of Undertaker.

"When?" Undertaker asks.

"What do you mean when?" Kane barks.

"I don't know what you're talking about," Undertaker says.

"Where were you while we all went swimming?" Apple Jack calls from inside his locker.

"Oh. I just had some stuff to do," Undertaker says.

"That's what you said last time," Kane says.

"Look, I just had some stuff to do. But don't worry. After tonight's game, what do you say we all go get Muchos?" Undertaker asks the other dogs.

"Sounds like a plan to me," Snickers says.

"Fine, but you better be there," Kane warns his buddy.

The locker room doors slowly crack open. Lovey pokes his head inside. He feels better about not being last when he sees his teammates out in the open. Usually, they'll hide once the second to last guy arrives.

"Is it ok to come in?" Lovey asks.

"Yeah. Hurry. Come in." Rodman motions for him.

"Am I last?" Lovey asks, being cautious before entering.

"No. Look. Apple Jack isn't there." L-Rod points to Apple Jack's locker.

Lovey looks and sees only three dogs. He looks back to Rodman, who holds up an extra water balloon and motions to him once again. Satisfied with his chances, Lovey opens the door wide and walks into the room. "This is great. I can't wait to get the creator of this little prank with his own…"

Just before Lovey reaches Rodman, Apple Jack jumps out of his locker. "FIRE IN THE HOLE!!!"

Lovey ducks and avoids Apple Jack's water bomb, but lying on the floor, he becomes an easy target for the rest of the team. He lies there, taking fifteen other balloons, including two from Rodman. He's left a soaking wet mess.

Lovey stands up, shakes off his wetness like a dog, and laughs. "I have to start getting here earlier."

The other Gamblers laugh.

"Why is it that you are always late?" Liten asks.

"I don't know." Lovey shrugs.

Safari Chip's office door opens. He and Flip come out. "Alright everyone, gather in,"

The Gamblers huddle around their two coaches.

"Listen, we signed a new player a few days ago, and he'll be joining us for tonight's game. Now, I don't want you guys scaring him off the way you scared off Bing."

"Don't worry Chip. We already fire in the holed Lovey," Apple Jack says.

Safari Chip turns his gaze to a soggy soaked Lovey. "So I see."

"Who'd you sign?" Rodman asks.

"Michael Williams," Safari Chip answers.

There's a collective gasp around the locker room.

"You signed Krazy Mike the pigeon!?" Harlan's eyebrows shoot up.

"He's not crazy," Safari Chip snaps.

"Yes he is Chip. He plays in traffic for fun," Sammie says.

"He does?" Beary asks, unable to believe such nonsense.

"Yes," Sammie answers with an exasperated sigh.

"Well... he's going to get hit by a car," Beary notes.

"He doesn't play in traffic, and he's not crazy," Safari Chip says, although he isn't one hundred percent sure Sammie's statement isn't true. "Besides, he put up decent numbers in Stockton, and we need someone on the third line."

"All I know is that if you signed Krazy Mike, you better start looking to sign someone else," Sammie says.

"Why?" Safari Chip asks.

"Because he's going to get hit by a car," Sammie reiterates Beary's earlier thought.

A cough near the locker room door draws the attention of everyone. There stands Krazy Mike with his wings folded. No one knows how long he's been there or what he may have heard. The Gamblers all put their heads down and pretend to be innocent of any badmouthing. They seem to be getting caught saying all the wrong things at all the wrong times this season.

Safari Chip walks over to Krazy Mike and welcomes him to the Gamblers locker room. "Why don't you get situated in your locker and then you can go over some of tonight's game plans with your line mates on the third line."

"Sounds like a plan," Krazy Mike says a little louder than necessary. He sets off in search of the one empty locker.

Undertaker has Kane to his right and looks at the empty locker to his left. "Oh nuts!"

Kane, Apple Jack, and Snickers laugh at Undertaker's misfortunes.

Krazy Mike pulls up a seat at the locker next to Undertaker and starts shoving his belongings inside. He looks into Undertaker's locker. "Hey Carl. Nice to meet you. I like what you've done with your locker."

Undertaker looks into his locker. There's nothing special about the way anything inside is set up. In fact, his locker is pretty messy. "Are you talking to me?"

"Well, I ain't talking to myself."

"My name is Undertaker."

"That's what I said, Carl," Krazy Mike says all too serious.

Undertaker turns to the dogs on his other side. He motions to Krazy Mike with his thumb and makes the international symbol for crazy by spinning a finger on his other paw in circles near his head. He mouths to his buddies, *he's nuts*.

*

Halfway through the third period, the score between the Gamblers and the Gold Rush remains 0-0. Both goalies, Haas and Vander Gates, play outstanding games. The new Gold Rush goalie has several tricks up his sleeves the Gamblers have never seen. One of those tricks being a nifty tail swat to stop shots.

The Gamblers finally catch a break when they get a two on one breakaway. Rodman races with the puck towards Vander Gates. He has Lovey at his side, and only Metz is near enough to try and fend off both Gamblers. Like always when Rodman and Lovey have a two on one, they crisscross and the one with the puck, this time Rodman, glides past and behind the net, taking the defender and the goalie with him. Just when it looks like it's going to be too late for a shot or a pass, Rodman taps the puck behind himself to Lovey, who one times it past the confused and stumbling body of Vander Gates to put the Gamblers up 1-0.

For the remainder of the game, the Gamblers avoid one potential momentum swinging penalty after another. Packer goads Undertaker into a fight that lands both players in the box. Twice, they escape penalty calls to Krazy Mike, once for swinging his stick menacingly at anyone who comes near him and later when he fires a puck at Pete Ivers, the Gold Rush's porcupine. Pete avoids the puck, but it's clear the shot was meant to hit him. The referees don't know what type of penalties to call on Krazy Mike's plays, so they leave him alone, plus none of them dare try lugging the crazy bird to the penalty box.

On the flipside, the Gold Rush get called on every little penalty they commit. Maulbreath gets rung up for roughing, Smooth goes to the box for cross-checking, and Jason gets called for flopping when he pretends to trip on Rodman's stick. He swears up and down he's not flopping, but he gets hauled to the penalty box anyway. It's the second time in two years that he's rung up on a call that just isn't called very often. The penalty agitates his already irritated coach even more, and it really angers Coil when Big Chick scores a power play goal.

Jason does himself no favors in the waning seconds of the game. The Gold Rush have their goalie pulled, and Jason has the puck. He tries to drive past Rodman, Lovey, Kane, and Undertaker all at once instead of passing the puck to a number of open teammates. His attempt to bust through the Gamblers defenses results in losing the puck. With the Gold Rush goalie pulled and the puck on Rodman's stick, a goal is eminent. Rodman passes it ahead to Liten. The mouse shoots a bull's eye at the empty Gold Rush net and scores.

When the final buzzer sounds, the Gamblers skate off the ice with a 3-0 victory.

Haas feels a bit vindicated at beating his former team, shutting them out nonetheless. It's his second shutout in as many games. He gets hugs and high fives from his Gamblers teammates on a job well done.

*

The Gold Rush enter their locker room lead by Jason, who throws his helmet across the room and breaks his stick over his knee. His tirade continues as he throws the broken pieces of the stick at some lockers. The pieces ricochet off the locker and almost hit Iggy.

Coil slithers into the room in time to see Jason's temper tantrum.

Jason falls into the chair outside of his locker and unties his skates. He attempts to pull the first skate off his foot, but twice it slips from his grasp and remains on his foot. His eyes roll, and he tries once again, only to have the skate slip from his flippers once more. He stands up and kicks his locker repeatedly with the blade, tearing a hole in the metal locker. As the blade goes through the locker door, Jason's skate gets stuck.

"Jason!" Coil hollers loud enough to startle Jason and the rest of the Gold Rush. "In my office now. You too Lance."

Jason yanks his foot out of his skate, but the skate remains lodged in the locker door. He follows Maulbreath into the coach's office. The two Gold Rush players take a seat across from their coach at his desk.

"I don't know what's wrong with you Jason. You're a great player, but you sure aren't a smart one, especially when we play this team. Why are you flopping out there?" Coil demands.

"I wasn't…"

"Oh you were too. Even the blind guy in the cheap seats could see that crap."

Maulbreath chuckles at Coil's joke.

"Don't laugh Lance. You're not much better. Sometimes I think between the two of you, you don't have one brain to share," Coil snaps.

"Ha," Jason says to Maulbreath.

"Sure, laugh at him. You see Jason, it's that attitude there that makes it easy for me to do what I'm about to do." Coil slithers from around his desk, reaches up with his tail, and rips the captain's C off of Jason's jersey.

Jason gasps.

The seriousness of the situation is so much that Maulbreath doesn't even chuckle.

"You need to start acting like a captain before you can wear this again. Lead your team on the ice and not in underhanded tactics, and maybe I'll give this back to you. It was your plans that cost us Haas, it was your poor decision making that cost us tonight's game, and it's going to be your tail if we lose this season. You're on thin ice buster. So shape up, and don't think for one minute that if you don't I won't ship you out, because I will."

No one has ever talked to Jason this way. He finds himself actually afraid of Coil and unable to speak.

Coil can see the fear all over Jason's face. It's an emotion he's never seen his star penguin exhibit. He hopes it's just what Jason needs to get his act together.

Maulbreath raises his paw.

"What Lance?" Coil asks.

"So, who's going to be our new captain?"

"You are," Coil says.

"Him?" Jason complains.

"But you're on thin ice yourself Lance. If you misstep even one time, I'll pull that C from you so fast it'll make your head spin, and I'll put Iggy, or Rapture, or Smooth in charge of this team," Coil warns.

Jason wants to argue, but he doesn't dare try right now. Instead, he does what he does best. He starts plotting a way to get back his spot as the team's captain. "You're right. I have to start acting like a leader. I have to focus on my opponents, make better decisions, and be less selfish."

Coil is the one who is shocked now. Jason actually sounds sincere. He wonders if he could possibly have gotten through to his all-star penguin. He eases up on his harsh tone. "Look guys, I still believe we're the best team in the league. We may not have won the last two Cups like we should have, but the bottom line is, *we should have*. We play good hockey. We just need to get back to playing smart hockey."

"We will," Jason says, keeping up his façade.

"You can count on us," Maulbreath agrees.

Coil thanks them and excuses his players. As they leave his office, Jason gets the door for Maulbreath.

"Thanks Jason."

"No sweat pal," Jason says, hiding a sneer.

Chapter 10: Undertaker's Whereabouts

Kane is eager to hang out with the other dogs after the game against the Gold Rush, but he's especially excited to finally have his best friend, Undertaker, with them. The four dogs sit at a table in the food court scarfing down a pile of Muchos.

"Did you guys see the way old Dog Shark over here popped Maulbreath out of his skates?" Apple Jack asks the other dogs.

"Man!" Undertaker says as he swallows his last bite of a Mucho. "One of these days, you're going to have to teach us how you appear out of thin air when you destroy these guys."

Kane quickly hands Undertaker another Mucho. "Eat up buddy."

"Oh brother. I've got to put my limit at three tonight." Undertaker pushes the Mucho aside.

"Limit at three!?" Kane exclaims. "You can polish of three dozen if you want to."

"I'm just not that hungry tonight," Undertaker says.

Kane shrugs. "Well, more for us I guess. You want another one Dog Shark?"

"No thanks. I have to limit myself to two," says Snickers.

"Two!?" all three of the other dogs yell.

"Hey. I'm not a young pup like you guys. I have to watch what I eat. This isn't all muscle you know." Snickers pat his belly with his paw.

"Sheesh," Kane murmurs.

"Don't worry brother. I'll help you finish them," Apple Jack assures Kane.

Kane reaches over the table for knuckles from his all white counterpart.

"Hey Undertaker. How's it going sharing a locker next to Krazy?" Apple Jack asks.

All eyes turn to Undertaker, but he doesn't answer.

Kane elbows his buddy. "Undertaker?"

"Huh?" Undertaker snaps out of his trance.

"I asked what it's like sharing a locker next to Krazy Mike," Apple Jack repeats.

Undertaker sighs. "Ugh. It's only been one game, and I'm already freaked out."

The other dogs have a laugh at his misfortune.

"Hey Dog Shark," Kane says. "You've played in the Olympics before right?"

"Yep," Snickers says.

"Are you going to play again this year?" Kane asks.

"If they ask me to I will, but the Olympic committee doesn't usually offer up spots for guys my age."

"Eh," Kane waves off Snickers comments. "They'll want you. I know I'm playing."

"Me too," Apple Jack says. "You in too Undertaker?"

Undertaker doesn't answer.

Kane elbows him again to get his attention. "What's with you dude?"

"What do you mean?" Undertaker asks.

"Your body is here, but your head sure isn't," Kane says.

"I'm here," Undertaker swears.

The other dogs look at him suspiciously.

"Hey Kane, let's see who can eat the most Muchos the fastest." Apple Jack grins ear to ear.

Kane puts his front paws on the table and lowers his head to the nearest plate. Apple Jack does the same. Snickers stands up, gets between them, and counts to three. The two dogs race to finish their Muchos. Apple Jack has a slight lead on Kane for a while, but he starts choking on a Mucho, and though it makes Kane laugh and snort as he chows down, Kane continues eating and wins the contest. He raises his paws in triumph and wipes his mouth and nose of chili sauce and slobber. "Yes!"

Snickers high fives Kane.

Kane turns to high five Undertaker, but Undertaker is once again lost with his head in the clouds. "Hey!" Kane shouts.

Undertaker jumps. "What?"

"What's with you man?" Kane demands.

"I'm just tired dude. I should probably call it a night. Hit the hay early," Undertaker says. He stands up from the table, says good night to his friends, and excuses himself.

The other dogs watch him leave.

"Something's going on with him," Kane says.

"Let's follow him," Apple Jack says.

The three dogs get up from the table and run in the direction in which Undertaker left. It takes them a while to spot their teammate, but they eventually find him in the crowded casino. They hunch down and try to blend in so as not to be seen. The black dog bypasses the elevators that lead to the Gamblers rooms and out the front doors of the hotel. Undertaker wa;ls outside and jumps into a cab.

"I knew it!" Kane says. He leads Apple Jack and Snickers into the next closest cab. "Follow that cab!" Kane tells the driver, pointing out Undertaker's cab.

The cabby turns around. "Hey. Is yous guys the Gamblers?"

"Yeah. Now follow that cab," Kane says again.

"Can I get your autographs?" the cabby asks.

"I'll get you a team autographed stick if you just follow and don't lose that cab," Kane orders the cabby.

The cabby turns around, puts on his serious face, pulls his cap down a little tighter, and grips his wheel firmly. "Buddy, for a team autographed stick, I'll follow that cab to the moon."

The cab driver slams the pedal to the floor and sends the Gamblers flying back into their seats. After the dogs get situated, Snickers and Apple Jack put their heads out the window, letting the cool night air blow in their whiskers.

Kane pulls them back inside. "Get in here. We don't want Undertaker knowing we're following him."

For a brief and wild moment, their cab weaves in and out of lanes, speeds past buildings, and even runs a red light or two. Finally, their cab catches up to the one carrying Undertaker.

"Ok driver. You can slow it down a little now," Snickers says.

The driver does as instructed.

Undertaker's cab pulls up outside of a known cat club called Kibel and Bitz.

"What the heck is he doing here?" Apple Jack's jaw drops.

"He must be going in to start some trouble." Kane grins from ear to ear.

"Why wouldn't he invite us then?" Snickers asks.

"I don't know, but it's a good thing we came. He's going to need some backup. Come on." Kane waves to the others and hops out of the cab.

After telling the cabby to wait for them, Apple Jack and Snickers follow Kane. The three dogs enter the club. Three hundred cat heads turn to them, and though together they are capable of mixing it up with any one cat, they know they don't have what it takes to take on an entire club full of cats.

Kane gulps hard.

"Just play it cool," Snickers whispers. "Let's just find Undertaker and get him out of here."

"You said it," Apple Jack says.

The dogs slowly venture into the joint in search of their buddy. They get a lot of unwelcoming stares as they walk around. Avoiding eye contact is the only thing that keeps them from an unwanted confrontation. They walk all the way to the back of the room and stand on a platform to get a better view.

"Where is he?" Snickers asks.

"I don't know," Kane says.

"Hey ugly," a voice shouts.

The three dogs turn and see a fat, shabby, rough looking alley cat.

"You fleabags are in the wrong place," the alley cat says.

"We're just looking for a friend. When we find him, we'll be leaving," Apple Jack says.

The alley cat grunts. He'd prefer they leave now, but as long as they're not there to stay, he'll let them be for a while.

"There he is." Kane points to a table in the far corner.

Undertaker sits in a booth across from someone the dogs can't see because he or she is blocked by the booth's wall.

Kane motions for the others to follow him and leads them to Undertaker's table. They're all shocked when they lay eyes upon their buddy holding paws with a black female cat. Their jaws hit the floor.

"WHAT THE HECK IS THIS!?" Kane yells.

Undertaker jumps and lets go of the cat's paw. "What are you guys doing here?"

"What are we doing here? What are you doing here?" Kane demands.

Undertaker is at a loss for words. He's caught, and he knows it. It's time to fess up. "I'm visiting my girlfriend."

"Well you better not let her catch you holding paws with this cat, or she's going to be mad," Apple Jack says as serious as can be.

Everyone, including the cat, gives Apple Jack a befuddled look.

"Guys, this is Elmira, my girlfriend," Undertaker introduces the two parties.

"Oh," Apple Jack says a bit confused. It takes him a second, but then it really hits him. "Ohhh! Oh... no."

Kane starts panting uncontrollably. This can't be happening. His best friend in the whole world can't be dating a cat. He stumbles backwards a bit and grabs at his heart.

Snickers grabs ahold of Kane and keeps him from falling down. "You ok Kane?"

Kane tries to talk but can't spit out any words.

"What's the matter buddy?" Undertaker asks.

"What's wrong? What's wrong? You're dating some nasty kitty cat, and you're asking me what's wrong? I guess Krazy Mike's crazy must be contagious, and since you share a locker next to him, you were the first one affected. Is this why you've been ditching us lately?" Kane barks.

"I wasn't ditching you guys. I was going to introduce you to her eventually," Undertaker says.

"Uh huh." Kane isn't buying what Undertake is selling.

A large grey cat that works as a bouncer for the club approaches the table with the loud dogs. "Is there a problem here gentlemen?"

"No problem," Undertaker says.

"Ma'am?" the bouncer asks Elmira.

"It's fine," she assures the bouncer. "We're all friends."

"Speak for yourself," Kane mutters under his breath.

"What was that?" the bouncer asks.

"I said speak for yourself," Kane says, brashly stepping up into the face of the bouncer, unwilling to back down.

"Just calm down Kane." Snickers pulls Kane away.

"Yeah, Kane. Just calm down. Maybe you fellas ought to be leaving," the bouncer suggests.

"Don't worry. We're leaving," Kane says. He turns back to Undertaker for one last word. "Just remember bro, between us, it is, was, and always will be canines before felines."

Kane leads the other dogs out of Kibel and Bitz.

Undertaker remains for a few minutes but calls it a night earlier than he wants. He heads back to his hotel room to try to make peace with Kane, Apple Jack, and Snickers, but all are asleep upon his arrival.

Chapter 11: Hitting The Road With Krazy Mike

Before the Gamblers hit the road for their next road trip, Big Chick interviews potential babysitters for El Pollos Locos. He knows his cousins will fight him about the idea, so he sends them to the arcade while he interviews the candidates.

At the end of his final interview, he doesn't have a frontrunner. None seem right. They're all too soft or too mean, too lax or overly attentive, and too ditzy and absentminded.

"I don't know what I'm going to do," Big Chick says aloud as he closes his front door on the last applicant.

Big Chick doesn't walk far from his door before it slams back open. In walk Chicken, Noodle, and Soup. The loud slam startles Big Chick, causing him to jump.

"Hey Big Chick. Who was that girl?" Soup asks.

"I was interviewing babysitters for you guys while I'm gone on the next road trip with the team," Big Chick admits.

"Babysitters?" Chicken asks angrily.

"We don't need no stinking babysitters," Noodle echoes Chicken's sentiments.

"Yeah. We can take care of ourselves," Soup protests.

"You might be able to take care of yourselves, but you've been doing it on my dime, and I can't afford for you to take care of yourselves," Big Chick informs them.

"But, you're a famous hockey player. You're rich," Chicken says.

"Kind of. I mean, I'm rich, but I'm not Rodman rich. I don't have five hundred dollars to give you guys each weekend to blow at the arcade," Big Chick argues. "Don't worry anyway. I haven't found anyone I like."

"Good," says Noodle.

"Don't you have to get going?" Soup asks.

"Where?" Big Chick asks.

"To the game," all three chickens reply.

Big Chick looks at the time. El Pollos Locos are right. He only has fifteen minutes before pregame warm-ups. Big

Chick runs to his bedroom, grabs his bag, and takes off for the arena.

"Are you guys coming to tonight's game?" Big Chick hollers as he runs out the door.

"Of course," Chicken hollers back, sticking his head out the front door.

"We'd never miss one of your games." Noodle joins Chicken at the door.

"We'll be in the front row next to Alston." Soup says, joining his fowl brethren.

*

Big Chick hustles down the hallway that leads to the Gamblers locker room. He burst through the doors.

"FIRE IN THE HOLE!!!" Apple Jack jumps out of his locker and fires a water balloon at Big Chick.

Big Chick stops dead in his tracks, tries to duck, but only succeeds in blocking his chest from the water balloon with the top of his head. One by one, Big Chick is hit with sixteen water balloons. The Gamblers have a laugh at their chicken, but he has no time for jokes.

Safari Chip comes out of his office and yells, "Warm up time."

Big Chick rushes to get into his gear while the other Gamblers rush to the ice.

That night, the Gamblers host the Seattle Rampage and get their butts whooped. Other than some bickering between Undertaker and Kane, the first and second lines play fine, but they never get any offense going. However, on the third line, Krazy Mike causes several distractions and commits a number of penalties that lead to two Rampage power play goals and one Rampage shorthanded goal in their 3-0 win over the Gamblers.

After the game, the Rampage find their locker room filled with Double Double Bonus Banana Split Sundaes compliments of Safari Chip and the Gamblers. They scarf down the delicious treats and make their way to the Gamblers locker room to thank them for the ice cream delights. Safari Chip apologizes to Buck Wild again for his comments about his pirate hat and Buck Wild assures him he has already forgotten about it.

The Gamblers and the Rampage decide to break curfew that night so the Gamblers can show the Rampage how to have a really good time in Las Vegas.

Throughout the course of the evening, word gets out about Undertaker's new girlfriend. The rest of the Gamblers think it's kind of weird, but none of them get down on him for it like the dogs do. In fact, Big Chick sympathizes with Undertaker and pals up with him while the other dogs alienate him. Big Chick uses the situation to his advantage. By night's end, he has himself a babysitter for El Pollos Locos.

*

The Gamblers hit the road for three games against opponents from the original IAHL, the Stockton Lightning, the Bakersfield Trains, and the Ontario Californians. They lose all three games for various reasons. Undertaker and Kane fight, argue, and bicker on and off the ice, rendering their defense on the ice and their friendship off the ice non-existent. In one game, the referee drops the puck, and Kane drops his gloves. The only problem is that his opponent in the fight is Undertaker. The two dogs fight, scrap, bark, bite, and claw at each other. They both get fighting penalties that put the Gamblers on a five on three penalty kill for five minutes.

In each of the three games, Krazy Mike fires at the Gamblers own net on more than one occasion. The purpose of these shots is to try and hit his opponents with the puck, but his aim isn't what it once was, and several times, Harlan and Hass are forced to stop shots from someone on their own team. They aren't always successful.

L-Rod struggles on the faceoff. His faceoff winning percentage falls well below the league average. Safari Chip tries

Goose and Krazy Mike in the center position a time or two, but they're even worse.

Worst of all is the fact that, other than Lovey, not one of the Gamblers can get any sort of offensive consistency going. Rodman finds himself in the worst drought of his career. He has only one goal and one assist in his last ten games.

With their 0-3-0-0 road trip, the Gamblers drop all the way down to fifth place behind Reno, Bakersfield, Stockton, and Fairbanks. Even though it's early in the season, Safari Chip knows he needs to do something drastic to turn his team around if they're going to reach their goal of a threepeat. Even with the new four team playoff setup, the Gamblers aren't currently one of the teams in the playoff picture.

The Gamblers aren't the only team not fairing as well as they should. The Alaska Gold Rush struggle as well. Without Haas in net, and Vander Gates not living up to the hype, they find themselves in the middle of the pack, floating back and forth between eighth and ninth place.

Contributing to the Gold Rush's woes is the unchanging play of Jason. The rest of the Gold Rush, under stern warning from Coil, have really cleaned up their act. However, even after losing his captain's status, Jason continues to try every underhanded tactic and work every cheating angle he can. In a last ditch effort to get through to his once promising penguin, Coil drops Jason all the way down to the third line. It's a move that is met by much opposition and resistance by Jason, but Coil gives him two choices: Get on board with the changes and do better or leave the team.

*

The Gamblers return home and hold, at the suggestion of Harlan, Haas, Undertaker, and a few others, a players only meeting without Krazy Mike. They agree to take a vote as to whether or not to keep Krazy Mike or send him packing. They further agree that the vote has to be unanimous. It's decided there and then that Krazy Mike is too much of a distraction to keep around. His presence on and off the ice is detrimental to the team and its goals. Plus, he scares half of them.

Rodman makes a phone call and gets Safari Chip and Flip to come to the locker room.

"What's going on guys?" Safari Chip asks.

"Chip, we have to talk to you about something," Rodman starts.

"We know we have not been performing up to standards and expectations," Liten adds.

Safari Chip waves them off. "Don't sweat it fellas. There's plenty of time to turn this thing around."

"We know, but we think we could turn it around a lot quicker if it weren't for one thing," Rodman says.

"What's that?" Safari Chip asks.

"You have to get rid of Krazy Mike," Sammie says.

"Yeah," Harlan agrees emphatically. "He's got to go."

Safari Chip is shocked to hear his players talking this way about a teammate. "Why are you guys so against Mike?"

"He scored two goals against me last game!" Harlan exclaims.

"He swings his stick at our opponents," Maverick says.

"He swings his stick at us," Goose adds.

"He's going to kill someone someday," Moose speculates.

"He scares me," L-Rod says.

Undertaker covers his mouth with his paw and kneels down to L-Rod's level. "He scares me too dude."

"Besides all of that, Ms. LeJuene called to question me about the potential ramifications of Krazy Mike's influence on L-Rod," Rodman says.

"What?" Safari Chip is aghast.

"I think she's trying to cook up an excuse to use Krazy Mike as a reason to take L-Rod away," Rodman says.

Safari Chip shakes his head frustrated. He doesn't like being bullied into making decisions. He waves his hands in the air. "Whoa! Whoa! Whoa! Everyone just calm down. Mike is part of this team. He isn't going anywhere, so you all better just get used to that idea real quick. This isn't Survivor. We don't just vote people off the team for personal reasons."

"They're not personal reasons," Harlan argues.

"Yes they are," Safari Chip shouts. "Pay attention more and maybe you'll block some of those shots that take peculiar bounces back to you Harlan. And stop calling him Krazy Rodman. If it wasn't for guys like you perpetuating that sort of image on him, then maybe you wouldn't have social services investigating whether or not you're taking good enough care of L-Rod. And you Liten… I expected more from you."

Liten looks to the ground feeling ashamed. Rodman, Harlan, and the rest of the guys join him.

"We don't cut guys just because they have a few issues. If we did that, half of this room or more wouldn't be here. I mean, you three along with Snickers are my captains. You shouldn't be trying to kick Mike off the team. You should be working with him to help make him a better player. Help make him a better teammate. Gosh!" Safari Chip shakes his head.

The Gamblers don't have anything left to say, so Safari Chip takes it as his cue to leave the room.

Chapter 12: Told You So

The Gamblers feel bad about angering Safari Chip the way they did. Except for the time he defended L-Rod to the media, they've never seen him that mad. In a matter of minutes, the L-Rod press conference went viral and became one of the most watched and most infamous press conferences of all time.

They decide to do as Safari Chip said and help Krazy Mike. That's what they would do for anyone else on the team after all. However, Krazy Mike doesn't make it easy. He continues swinging his stick like a weapon, shooting at the wrong net, and freaking out L-Rod and Undertaker. He's even seen by several players and El Pollos Locos playing in traffic. They confer on more than one occasion as to whether or not they should mention it to Safari Chip. Some are afraid to bring it up to their coach, and others are scared not to tell him. In the end, they don't want to make waves, so they hold their tongues.

*

Before the Gamblers next home game, Rodman waits impatiently for L-Rod to get ready.

"Come on L-Rod. We're going to be late," Rodman calls from their living room, holding his bag that has been packed and ready to go for three hours.

"I'm hurrying," L-Rod calls back from his room as he searches all over for his left glove. His right one was on the nightstand, just where he left it the night before. He can't figure out why the other one isn't also there.

After three more minutes pass, Rodman calls again. "What are you doing L-Rod?"

"I'm looking for my other glove."

"Why don't you just use a set of team gloves tonight?"

"Gross!" L-Rod objects from under his bed with a flashlight. He scans over the mess that's amassed there.

Rodman waits another minute before he walks into L-Rod's messy room. He doesn't see the little penguin anywhere. "L-Rod?"

L-Rod pokes his head out from under the bed. "Yeah?"

"We're going to be late."

"Well, go on ahead without me then."

"It's no wonder you can't find your glove. Look at this room. How do you find anything in here?"

"What are you, my dad?" L-Rod asks sarcastically.

"Actually, yeah, I am." Rodman pulls the adoption license from his wallet and waves it at L-Rod with a chuckle.

"Just go. I'll be there in a minute." L-Rod climbs out from under the bed and dives into a pile of clothes.

"Alright, but you better get there before Lovey, or you're going to get fire in the holed."

L-Rod doesn't respond.

Rodman leaves his little buddy and walks to the front door. He calls out one last thing. "And you're cleaning up that room after the game tonight."

L-Rod sticks his tongue out at Rodman from inside his room just as the front door closes.

Rodman pokes his head back in their room. "I saw that."

L-Rod's eyes go wide. How could Rodman have seen that? He brushes it off and goes back to looking for his glove. The longer it takes to find the glove the more frustrated he grows. He stops and thinks about the night before. He came in from practice, dropped his stick in the hallway, went into his room, tossed his bag across the room onto the pile of dirty clothes, set his gloves on the nightstand, and hopped into bed to watch TV. Then, it dawns on him. He saw a moth flying around his TV screen and he threw his glove at it.

L-Rod scurries to check behind the TV, and sure enough he finds his other glove there. He grabs it, packs it in his bag, and rushes to the front door. There's a chance he could catch up with Rodman. He's stopped in his tracks by a very loud knock as he reaches for the handle to his front door. He pauses, tilts his head, and wonders who would be knocking on their door this close to game time.

Without looking through the peephole, because it's too high for him to reach, he opens the door. He's alarmed to find Ms. LeJuene standing there. He's pretty sure she can't take him away, but he wishes Rodman wouldn't have left.

"Hello Canter," Mrs. LeJuene smiles wickedly.

"What do you want?"

"I'm here on business. Where is Rodman?"

"We've got a game in an hour and a half. He's down in the locker room."

"He left you alone?" Ms LeJuene seems appalled.

"I'm a big penguin. I can handle myself," L-Rod snaps.

"Well, I still have to talk to him. Why don't you lead me to your locker room?"

"Whatever," L-Rod pushes past her with his bag and leads her down the corridor to the elevators.

*

Rodman enters the locker room without any fear of getting fire in the holed. He knows he's at least got L-Rod beat. The place is pretty well filled up already. Even Lovey is there.

Apple Jack walks over to Rodman and hands him a water balloon. "Looks like your little buddy is going to get it today. We thought for a second we might be getting you both."

Rodman takes the balloon. "I told him to hurry."

*

L-Rod leads Ms. LeJuene down the hallway to the Gamblers locker room. "What sort of business do you have with Rodman?"

"It has come to our attention that he may have placed you in an environment that is unsafe for you, and I've come to investigate whether or not these claims are legit."

"Unsafe? What are you talking about?"

"It seems there is a new player on your team. Someone whose mental stability may put you at risk both physically and psychologically," Ms. LeJuene says.

"Krazy Mike," L-Rod whispers.

"Yes. Krazy Mike."

They reach the doors to the locker room and stop.

L-Rod turns to Ms. LeJuene. "Wait for just a second. I want to check something." He gets down onto his belly and peeks under the door. He doesn't see the shadows of anyone moving around. They must all be hiding. He stands back up.

To say Ms. LeJuene's is confused about L-Rod's actions would be an understatement.

L-Rod opens the locker room door and holds it open for her. "Ladies first."

"Thank you Canter." Ms LeJuene enters the room.

"It's L-Rod." He shoves her in the tail with his foot.

Ms. LeJuene stumbles into the center of the room, but manages to keep from falling. She plants her feet and turns to the locker room door as it slams shut. From behind her, she hears Apple Jack scream fire in the hole, but she doesn't have time to turn around to see what's going on before she starts getting pegged with water balloon after water balloon.

Rodman tries to hold up the release of his balloon, but it's too late. He was throwing blindly as he jumped out of his locker. His balloon nails her right in the snout.

It only after the last balloon is thrown that the Gamblers realize what they've done. A hushed silence falls over them.

"That ain't L-Rod," Lovey says.

"Uh oh." Rodman almost chokes on the two small words.

The locker room door opens again, and L-Rod pokes his head inside. He takes one look at Ms. LeJuene and starts laughing his head off. His laughter starts the other Gamblers laughing. Ms. LeJuene seethes at what has happened to her and the fact that the Gamblers find it funny. She cuts their laughter short with a loud angry growl. The room goes silent again, and Ms. LeJuene storms out without speaking to Rodman.

Safe and sound from the social services lady, L-Rod makes his way to his locker next to Rodman's.

"What was she doing here?" Rodman asks.

"She said she had to talk to you about my safety."

"Your safety?"

"Yeah. She said something about putting me in an unsafe situation with Krazy Mike on the team."

Safari Chip walks out of his office and looks around his team. He counts his players as he always does and notices he's missing one player.

"Where's Mike?" Safari Chip asks.

"Didn't you hear?" Beary asks.

"Hear what?" Safari Chip is baffled.

"He got hit by a car," Sammie answers.

Safari Chip jumps in place and grabs his safari hat tight. "Is he ok?"

"He is in the hospital with several broken bones and wings. He is doing fine, but he will not be playing hockey any time soon," Liten informs him.

Safari Chip is stunned. He doesn't know what to say.

"I told you," Sammie says.

Safari Chip looks to Flip. "We better go visit him after the game."

Flip nods in agreement.

"And you guys are coming with me." Safari Chip points to Rodman, Liten, Harlan, and Snickers.

The other dogs laugh at Snickers misfortune.

"I don't know what you're laughing at Undertaker," Safari Chip says. "You're coming too."

Undertaker's laughter stops instantaneously.

Kane and Apple Jack temper their laughter, so they don't draw Safari Chip's ire too.

"Now, let's go. Warm up time," Safari Chip says and claps his hand.

The Gamblers rush for the locker room doors. They play the Fort Collins F-14s that night and get back to the business of winning, beating them by a score of 6-1. Rodman breaks out of his slump, scoring two goals, Big Chick gets one, Sammie scores one, Beary adds another, and Lovey scores yet another goal.

After the game, Rodman pulls up a seat next to Lovey at his locker. "Hey Lovey."

"Hey Rod. What's up?"

"You've been playing some great hockey this year. You're putting up some really good numbers," Rodman says.

"I've got a secret weapon, a lucky charm if you will."

"What is it?"

Lovey pulls out the camouflage and yellow bandanas that Beary gave him on opening day. "Just like you, I've got a lucky scarf... or scarves rather. Ever since I started wearing these, my numbers have been off the charts."

"You wear them during the game?" Rodman asks.

Lovey nods.

"How come I never see them?"

"I wear one around my head, under my helmet and the other one around my arm, under my jersey."

"Interesting," Rodman says.

Safari Chip comes out of the coach's office with Flip. "Alright captains. Let's go."

"Gotta go Lovey. I'll catch up with you later." Rodman stands up to leave.

Liten, Harlan, and Snickers join him.

"You too Undertaker," Safari Chip says.

"Oh, but Chip. The guy creeps me out. He doesn't even know my name," Undertaker complains.

The look Safari Chip gives Undertaker lets the dog know there is no getting out of this hospital visit.

"What's the matter Undertaker? Can't be away from your kitty cat for a night?" Kane antagonizes.

"No. I'm not even going to see her tonight anyway."

"Uh huh," Kane says disbelieving.

Instead of furthering the argument, Undertaker joins the rest of the Gamblers on their way out of the locker room.

*

Safari Chip knocks on Krazy Mike's hospital room door and pokes his head inside. "Mike?"

"Who's there?" answers an alarmed voice.

"It's Safari Chip."

"Who?" the voice asks even more alarmed.

"Safari Chip. The coach of the Gamblers. Is this Michael Williams room?"

Krazy Mike jumps from the side of the door. He lands, with both of his wings wrapped in casts, right in the face of Safari Chip, scaring the monkey and sending him jumping back into the hallway. The other Gamblers have to catch their coach to keep him from falling on his tail.

Krazy Mike pokes his head out of the room. "Who are you? What do you want?"

"Mike, it's the Gamblers," Flip says.

"We came to see how you're doing," Rodman adds.

Krazy Mike stares them down with doubt washed all over his face.

The Gamblers don't know what to do. They do know that his crazy staring is freaking them out though. Krazy Mike obviously doesn't have a clue who they are. Even Safari Chip starts to wonder if his team was right this whole time.

Then, suddenly, Krazy Mike recognizes one of them. He locks eyes with Undertaker. "Carl!? You came to see me?"

Undertaker waves nervously. "How are you Mike?"

Krazy Mike walks out of the room to Undertaker. He whispers to the dog, "Be careful inside this place. They've been probing my brain, trying to get all my secrets. I think they're trying to clone the perfect hockey player."

Snickers leans over and whispers to Rodman, "I thought you were the perfect hockey player."

Krazy Mike hears Snickers' comment and shoots him a look of utter disdain.

Safari Chip has seen enough. "Well Mike, it was nice seeing you. I'm glad to see you're getting the care you need."

"You're not leaving me are you?" Krazy Mike demands.

"Yeah. We've got to get back to the hotel before curfew."

"You can't go yet. We haven't even discussed our plan."

"What plan?" Harlan asks.

"The plan to bust me out. Isn't that why you guys came?" Krazy Mike asks.

The Gamblers look at each other confused and concerned.

"Tell you what. I'll go lie down on my bed. You guys procure some scrubs. Then, come back and push my bed right out the front door. No one will ever suspect a thing." Krazy Mike runs into his room before the Gamblers have a chance to protest.

"We are not springing him," Undertaker says emphatically and somewhat noisily.

The other Gamblers shush him.

"Undertaker is right. We cannot help Krazy Mike escape. He is in need of some serious mental help," Liten says.

"I know," Safari Chip says. He looks around, finds a doctor, and flags him down. "Hey doc. Come here."

"Yes?" the doctor asks.

"What's the prognosis on Michael Williams?" Safari Chip asks.

"Are you family?" the doctor asks.

"No, I'm his coach."

"I'm sorry. I cannot violate a patient's right to privacy," the doctor informs the Gamblers.

"But, I'm Safari Chip of the Gamblers. Mike is one of my players. I just want to know what's being done for him."

"I don't care if you're Safari Chip from the Gamblers…" the doctor starts, but stops momentarily only to interrupt himself. "You're Safari Chip of the Gamblers."

"Uh huh."

"Mike's one of your players?" the doctor asks.

"Uh huh."

"Well, I guess it won't hurt to let you know how he's doing. He's pretty banged up, broken wings, sprained ankles, cracked ribs, and a concussion."

"Is the concussion what is causing him to act all crazy?" Rodman asks.

"He was crazy before," Snickers whispers to Rodman again.

Flip slaps Snickers. "You're supposed to be setting an example."

"Sorry," Snickers says.

"This is not his first concussion. He's has had many concussions throughout his career, and they very well may be taking a toll on his mental state. But don't worry. We're doing everything we can for him. We're observing him, getting him the rest he needs, and monitoring his brainwaves," the doctor assures them.

"Thanks doc. Take good care of him. He hasn't been with us for very long, but he's still one of my guys. You can send all his bills to me at the New Orleans Hotel," Safari Chip says and shakes hands with the doctor.

"Will do."

Safari Chip leads the Gamblers to the elevators.

Undertaker stops to talk to the doctor. "He can't get out can he?"

"I doubt it. We have very tight security here," the doctor promises.

"Good." Undertaker wipes the sweat from his brow.

Chapter 13: Kane And Jason Explode

Over the next couple of weeks, the Gamblers search for someone to take Krazy Mike's spot. Flip goes out on several scouting excursions while the Gamblers continue playing games with their forwards rotating turns on the third line. One of the good things about the players rotating turns on the third line is that when Rodman or Big Chick play with them, it gives L-Rod a break from having to take faceoffs. L-Rod plays a lot more relaxed on the wing, and his numbers come up while doing so.

L-Rod isn't the only Gambler whose points start piling up. Rodman, after tying the red and white striped scarf that Beary gave him to his arm, under his jersey the same as Lovey does, also gets back on track. He gets two assists in his first game while wearing it, a goal and an assist in his second game with the scarf, a hat trick in his third game, and he compiles a total of six goals and eight assists in his next seven games. The Gamblers win six of those games and climb into fourth place.

All around, all the Gamblers start playing better. The only blemish to their current stretch of games is that the arguing between Undertaker and Kane grows more heated with each passing game. Kane is so bothered by the fact that his best friend spends all of his free time with a cat instead of him and the other dogs that he becomes distracted on the ice. In a game in Alaska against the Gold Rush, Kane skates around the ice discombobulated, as though he has no idea where he is. Everything around him is a blur. He's bumped hard by Ranger, the Gold Rush's honey badger, and nearly falls down. The hit spins him around and when he stops, the first player he lays eyes on is Packer. The sight of the cat reminds him of seeing his buddy holding paws with Elmira. Kane grows incensed. He throws down his stick, flips off his gloves, and skates with a purpose at Packer.

The cat turns in time to see Kane coming at him, but he doesn't have time to protect himself. Packer drops his own stick and tries to get his gloves off, but before he can flick his wrists,

Kane already has the cat's jersey pulled over his head. He uppercuts the cat. Packer falls to the ice like a sack of bricks. Metz races over to protect his teammate only to suffer the same fate. His jersey is pulled over his head, and one swift punch to the face sends another cat to the ice seeing stars.

From behind Kane, Maulbreath tries to sneak up and take him by surprise. He grabs Kane's shoulder, spins him around, and goes to throw a punch, but Kane blocks it. Seeing another cat in his face only enrages the dog even more. He delivers Maulbreath a punch to the gut that doubles the tiger over. He pulls another jersey over the head of its owner, but this time he knees his opponent in the face instead of throwing a punch. Maulbreath joins his brutalized teammates on the ice.

Kane spins around in time to see Ranger and Auggie Froggie approaching him at the same time. They stop upon seeing his snapping, growling face. Saliva foams up on the sides of the rabid dog's mouth.

Undertaker, who has taken the ice on a line change, steps up beside Kane in an effort to show his friend that despite their squabbles he's still on his side. His intent is to help Kane take on their foes, but Kane whips his head around at Undertaker and punches him in the face too.

Undertaker falls to the ice. "What the heck Kane?"

The referees sneak in, grab the vicious dog, and drag him to the penalty box. They aren't quite sure what to charge Kane with, but they settle on the league's first ever twenty minute major for four fights, one with his own teammate.

Safari Chip yells at the officials for their ruling. He demands they go read the rulebook and make a proper call. A twenty minute penalty kill is unheard of and utterly ridiculous. The referees stick by their decision, and after the carnage on the ice is cleared off, the game resumes.

Inside the penalty box, Kane fumes as the Gamblers begin a period long penalty kill. He slams his helmet on the ground and throws his gloves into the corner. He sits on the bench and takes a couple of deep breaths to calm himself. The heckling of the Gold Rush crowd makes it hard for him to settle his nerves.

"Big tough guy Kane, pulling guys' jerseys over their heads. Why don't you fight like a man?" one fans yells.

"Yeah. What's your problem punk?" yells another.

"He's just angry because his buddy's in love with a cat," a third fan yells.

Kane turns his head in the direction of the newest heckler, a mistake for sure. The move lets the guy, an obese warthog, know that he's got Kane's attention.

"That's right Kane. You heard me. Your buddy, Morty, ain't nothing but a filthy cat lover," the guy taunts.

Kane jumps up onto the bench. His initial reaction is to scale the penalty box wall and jump into the crowd, but he composes himself and just stares at the guy until he meows at Kane. It's then that Kane reaches down, picks up the water bottle provided to him by the penalty box attendant, and sprays the warthog and several other nearby fans with water. The fans jump back and gasp, but Kane laughs.

The warthog goes nuts. He steps over a row of other Gold Rush fans and stands on the top of their seats. The crowd cheers him on, so he decides to give them what they want. He swan dives at the penalty box. He doesn't make it over the glass, but he crashes into it so hard that the glass gives way and he falls into the box with Kane.

Knowing he's probably already got a suspension coming, and that he can probably get out of further trouble by claiming self-defense, Kane takes the opportunity to relieve some of his frustration by pounding the woozy warthog like a side of beef.

Security and the referees rush to separate the player and fan. The fan is cuffed and removed from building, and the referees take Kane off the ice altogether, sending him to the locker room for his own protection.

On the Gamblers bench, Safari Chip turns to Apple Jack and Snickers. "You guys need to get them to make up."

Despite Kane's bonehead mistake, the Gamblers give up only one goal during their record long penalty kill. At the end of the twenty minute penalty, the Gold Rush lead by just one goal, and that lead is erased in a matter of a seconds by goals from Rodman and Lovey.

The Gamblers aren't the only ones having internal problems. The Gold Rush's season is spiraling out of control with the inability of their former captain to get back on track. The Gold Rush have lost one game after another. Jason complains constantly about his role on the team, and that only gets him less and less ice time. He never figures out that whining isn't going to work. Reflected in his play is the attitude of someone who doesn't care about helping his team. He has no fire, takes too many shots, and he refuses to play defense.

During the game against the Gamblers, in a flash, it becomes apparent to Jason what he has to do. In the third period, after a lengthy shift, he races to gather to puck behind the net while his line gets off the ice. He grabs the puck as the first line hits the ice, and he takes the puck out from behind the net. Jason appears to make a pass Maulbreath's way, but he purposely undershoots it, giving the puck to Liten.

Liten, not expecting the puck, fumbles it on his stick.

Jason and Maulbreath both head for Liten in an attempt to regain the puck. Jason rears his stick back like a baseball bat.

Liten gathers the puck and looks up in time to see Jason swinging his stick at him. He has just enough time to dive out of the way at the very last second. Jason misses the mouse not only because Liten dives, but because Liten isn't Jason's.

Maulbreath, skating in from behind Liten, gets clocked in the knee with Jason's stick. The tiger falls to the ice in a heap. He lets out a howl that echoes throughout the entire arena and silences the crowd. He grabs his knee and rolls around the ice.

Whistles blow. Play stops. The referees rush to the play and pull Jason away.

"What's going on?" Jason demands.

"That's a game misconduct," the referee says.

"For what?" Jason screams.

"What do you think?" the referee asks sarcastically.

"For a slash? I didn't even hit Liten. I hit my own teammate on accident," Jason continues pleading his case.

"That's going to be a match penalty too," the first referee informs Jason.

"FOR WHAT!?" Jason is aghast.

"Intent to injure."

The referees and Jason reach the tunnel. They toss Jason off the ice to raucous boos from the crowd.

Jason turns to the two referees. "You hear that booing? Those are my animals. They don't want me thrown out."

Rapture skates up and joins the referees. "They're not booing your ejection. They're booing you."

"No they're not," Jason says arrogantly, but he stops and looks at the crowd. Their angry faces, glares, and screams all seem to be directed at him. It makes him worry.

Rapture skates away without another word.

Jason makes his way to the locker room, and sweats out the next thirty-five minutes, waiting for his team to return. When they do, it's with another loss and Maulbreath out for the next several months with a broken knee.

Coil slithers into the room silently.

Jason had expected to hear the livid yelling of the snake from the ice all the way to the locker room.

The Gold Rush go about their business getting ready to leave. No one talks to Jason even when he talks to them.

Some of the Gold Rush make their way out of the locker room before Coil comes out of his office. The snake grabs Jason just before he can leave. The snake slithers right up to Jason's ear and whispers. "Get in my office now."

The snake sounds so serious that Jason doesn't challenge him even a bit. He waddles into Coil's office and takes a seat.

"Don't sit down. This won't take long," Coil says.

"What's the matter Coil? If this is about what happened to Maulbreath, that was an accident. I…"

Coil slides into his seat and pushes a piece of paper Jason's way.

Jason picks the paper up. "What's this?"

"Your unconditional release," says the snake.

"You're joking."

"No, I'm not. You are no longer a member of this team, and you are no longer welcome in my arena, so grab your gear and get out."

"You can't be serious."

"You've cost me a two time Cup champion goalie, you've alienated your teammates, and now you've knocked our captain out for most of the season. I couldn't be more serious."

Jason is speechless.

"Just go," Coil says.

Jason turns and walks out of the office. He stops at the door, turns to Coil, and says, "I'm the best player in this league. You think I won't catch on somewhere else? I'll have teams begging me to play for them. You'll regret letting me go."

"I regret the night I signed you. I can't believe I had my pick of you and Rodman, and I went with you."

Jason slams the door as hard as he can. Some pictures of Coil's Cup champion teams fall off the wall and the picture frames break. He wonders where he'll finish the season as he empties out his locker. He's too good to go unsigned, but he doesn't have any clue who will sign him. He takes a last look around the Gold Rush locker room. Two years ago he walked into this room and was essentially crowned king. He was meant to be the face of the franchise for at least the next decade. Now, he's being thrown out. He grabs his empty locker, pulls it away from the wall, and slams it to the ground. Nothing breaks, not even the locker itself, but it makes a thunderous crash, and scares the dickens out of Coil in his office.

The snake comes out to check what happened and sees the locker on the floor, but Jason is gone. The locker is the least of his problems though. He has to figure out how to replace Jason and Maulbreath and turn his team's season around.

Chapter 14: Apologies

Back in Las Vegas, Lovey heads to the locker room for
the Gamblers next game. He rounds the corner in the tunnel that
leads to the Gamblers locker room. His footsteps draw the
attention of Liten, who is about fifty feet ahead of him, and
Undertaker and Snickers, who are talking just outside the locker
room doors.

All four Gamblers stop in their tracks. The same thought
races through all of their heads. *If I don't get in the room first,
am I going to be last?*

Lovey books it for the room.

Liten turns and runs as fast as he can.

The dogs burst through the doors immediately, making
sure they're not last.

Lovey almost catches up to Liten, but the mouse has too
big a head start on him. They fly through the locker room one
after the other. To Lovey's surprise, he's met by Apple Jack
holding out a balloon for him and Liten. Someone else must not
be there. He looks around and takes a survey of the players there.
Moose is missing, so Lovey wipes the sweat off his brow and
heads for his locker.

Apple Jack grabs Liten before he can go to his locker
and whispers something into his big floppy pink ears.

Lovey stops in front of his locker and looks for his black
home jersey. Everything in his locker appears to be a t-shirt, a
suit, or a jacket. He grabs the hangers with his free paw and
pushes all of the clothes to one side so he can go through them
one item at a time. Instead of his jersey, Moose, hiding behind
all of Lovey's clothes, pops out at him. Lovey is so startled he
drops his water balloon and it pops on the floor.

"FIRE IN THE HOLE!" Moose yells.

Lovey turns to run from Moose, but he runs right into
the line of fire of fifteen other water balloons. He loses his breath
when the first excessively cold balloon explodes on him. He isn't

able to regain his breath before the other balloons start nailing him. Each one feels colder than the last.

As always, his teammates laugh at Lovey's misfortune.

Lovey finally catches his breath and shakes off his bath. "Why is it so cold today?"

"We put the balloons in the refrigerator overnight," Apple Jack chuckles.

Lovey removes his shirt and wrings it out. "Even when I think I might not be last, you guys still find a way to get me."

"You should have seen him running down the hallway," Liten laughs.

After a hearty laugh at Lovey's expense, the Gamblers prepare themselves for their first home game of the season against the Five Ohhh!. They know they owe the Reno team another apology, and they have everything they need to make Safari Chip's Double Double Bonus Banana Split Sundaes for their opponents after the game. The sundaes were a big hit with the Rampage and their coach, and the two teams had a great time on the Strip after their game. The Gamblers felt like they made a lot of new friends on the Rampage, and they hope for the same outcome tonight with the Five Ohhh!.

The game isn't as brutal as the teams' first meeting, but it's still a hard fought battle. Neither side talks much smack. In fact, neither team says much of anything to the other side. They let their play do the talking. In the end, the Gamblers, with goals from Goose, Liten, and Undertaker, whose girlfriend watches from just behind the bench, distracting and agitating Kane, come out on top with a 3-2 overtime victory.

The Gamblers rush off the ice to their locker room and change out of their hockey gear. They're all in a hurry to meet up with the Five Ohhh!.

Safari Chip leads his high spirited bunch down the tunnel. They knock on the locker room door of the Five Ohhh! and wait for someone to answer. They wait, knock, wait, knock, and wait some more. Finally, Safari Chip cracks the door open and pokes his head inside.

The room is empty.

Safari Chip pushes the door open fully and walks inside. His team follows close behind. They discover not only are the Five Ohhh! gone, but they left their Double Double Bonus Banana Split Sundaes behind, untouched, and melted.

"What the heck is going on here?" Safari Chip takes off his safari hat and scratches his head. "You sent them the note didn't you Flip?"

"Yeah," says Flip who holds up a piece of paper that was left on one of the tables. "Here it is."

"Nooo!" Liten, the team's ice cream aficionado, lays eyes on the wasted sundaes. He runs over to the melted desserts, sticks his finger into the mess, and licks off the warm remnants. "How could they do this?"

"You know what this is?" Safari Chip asks aloud to no one in particular with his hands on his hips.

"Murder," Liten answers while pouring the sundae out of its bowl onto the table.

"Well, it's not that bad. But it is a big slap in the face," Safari Chip says.

The Gamblers all nod in agreement. It looks as though they have a new foe in the league.

Chapter 15: El Pollos Locos Join The Team

Big Chick rolls out of bed and moseys on down his hallway to his kitchen where El Pollos Locos are sitting at the breakfast table, each with his own bowl of cereal.

"Good morning." Big Chick salutes his cousins.

"Hey," all three chickens greet him back.

Big Chick grabs some lemonade from the refrigerator.

"Hey Big Chick," Noodle calls.

"Yeah?"

"We had an idea," Soup says.

"What is it?"

"We think you should let us try out for the open spot on the team," Chicken says.

Big Chick laughs. "No."

El Pollos Locos stare an angry hole through the back of Big Chick's head. He can feel their angry gazes as he pours his lemonade into a cup.

Big Chick turns to them tentatively. "What?"

"We want to try out," Chicken says in all seriousness.

"No," Big Chick says.

"Yes," Noodle argues.

"No," Big Chick stands firm.

"Why?" Soup demands.

"You're too little."

"That's what they said about L-Rod," Soup argues.

"He's still bigger than you."

"We could be pretty good players," Chicken says.

"How are all three of you going try out? We only have one spot open?"

"We'll each play one game. Whoever does the best gets the contract," Noodle says as though there were no other answer.

"No," Big Chick says one final time.

*

"Absolutely not!" Safari Chip declares.

"But Chip, you don't know what it's like sharing a hotel suite with these chickens. Twenty-four hours a day they're bugging me about a tryout. I'm going out of my mind. You've got to help me," Big Chick begs.

"They're too little."

"I know, but you try telling them that."

"I will. Just send them in here," Safari Chip says.

Big Chick smiles. "Ok."

*

Two nights later, Chicken suits up to play on the third line for the Gamblers. He and the rest of El Pollos Locos drove Safari Chip even more nuts than they drove Big Chick, crying, whining, clucking, and holding protests outside his office door with picket signs and megaphones. They even got a petition signed by all of the Gamblers to let them try out, so Safari Chip finally gave in.

Chicken gets first cracks. He dons a jersey that bears the name Chicken and the number eight on back. He chooses eight on account of he is a tad pudgy and proud of it, and eight is the roundest of all the numbers.

For Chicken's debut game, the Gamblers are pitted against the Idaho Potatoes, who, like the Gamblers, are surging. The new standings still have Reno at the top and Bakersfield in second place, but Fairbanks has climbed from fourth to third and the Gamblers are in the playoff picture in fourth place with Idaho on their heels in fifth. A bad stretch has Stockton dropped all the way from third to sixth. The slumping Gold Rush continue dropping, all the way to eleventh place and have four of the former AKHL teams ahead of them in the standings.

Chicken sits impatiently on the bench waiting for his turn on the ice. "I can't wait to get out there."

"Just remember," L-Rod, his line mate, warns, "You've got to stay relaxed. Don't panic if you get confused. And if you do get confused, just try to find an open spot on the ice if we're on offense, or try to help block the net if we're on defense."

"Check." Chicken gives L-Rod a thumbs up.

The game gets underway. The first line goes out and does there thing for a little under two minutes before giving way to the second line. The second line gets stuck on the ice playing defense for almost three minutes, and then Apple Jack gets called for a penalty, and the Gamblers have to send out their penalty kill units, which don't include Chicken.

Chicken looks up to the scoreboard's timer. Almost eight minutes of game time has passed, and he has yet to even step on the ice. "It feels like we're never going to get out there."

"It happens some nights. You just have to be patient," L-Rod says.

Goose nudges Maverick and points to L-Rod. "Look at the little guy over here. In one season, he's gone from being the most impatient guy on the team to preaching its importance."

"Way to show some leadership skills L-Rod." Maverick leans over Goose and gives the little penguin a hoof pound.

L-Rod smiles. He appreciates that his teammates notice how much he's grown up.

"Third line! Go! Go! Go!" Safari Chip yells from his end of the bench.

L-Rod hops up and grabs Chicken. "That's us!"

Chicken stands on his own two feet and looks at the throng of Gamblers approaching the bench in a frenzy. He hops up and tries to scale the wall but misses the first time. He tries again, but he doesn't have the hops to make it. The bench door isn't far, but it's blocked by a bunch of the guys coming in. All of a sudden, Chicken feels himself being hoisted off the ground. Moose has him in his hooves and sets him down on the ice.

"Thanks," Chicken says.

"No sweat," Moose says, and the two of them rush to the play to help Harlan from the oncoming Potatoes attack.

Chicken races into the Gamblers zone and tries to find a player to defend, but each time he finds someone, another one of the Gamblers is already there defending that player. This in turn leaves the Potatoes player he's supposed to be guarding wide open. The Potatoes get several shots on goal because of this, but Harlan blocks them all.

Chicken gets really confused when he can't find anyone to block, so he tries to do like L-Rod advised him. The problem is he gets the advice backwards. On defense, he finds an open spot on the ice. He is no help in defending against the Potatoes attack, and he essentially puts the Gamblers on a penalty kill.

Luckily for the Gamblers, Maverick steals the puck from one of the Potatoes and clears it behind the Gamblers own net.

L-Rod sees the puck making its way around the boards to Chicken. He points and hollers, "There Chicken."

Chicken sees the puck coming, panics, but still drops his stick and tries to corral it. The puck bangs into his stick, jumps over it, and continues moving towards center ice. He turns and races for it. Just as he's about to touch it with his stick, one of the Potatoes gets there first and steals it away. The sudden appearance of the Potatoes player scares Chicken into crouching down and shielding his face with his stick. After a few seconds, Chicken peeks out from behind his stick. He sees the Potatoes that got to the puck before him get slammed brutally into the boards by Maverick. The puck is jarred loose.

Without thinking, Chicken jumps all over it. He grabs the puck and takes it over the blue line into the Gamblers offensive zone. Potatoes start swarming in on him, causing Chicken to panic and pass the puck behind himself without looking to see who or if anyone is behind him. Luckily, the pass lands on L-Rod's stick. L-Rod shoots but misses.

The puck goes behind the net and is collected by Moose. He is crowded quickly by Potatoes now, so he passes it to Goose, who is also behind the net, and he taps it backwards to L-Rod on the wing.

Chicken, meanwhile, tries to find a good place to stand on the ice. Everywhere he goes, he's blocked and guarded. He tries to recall L-Rod's advice once more, and he gets confused again. On offense this time, he does what L-Rod told him to do on defense. He rushes to the front of the net.

As Chicken stands in front of the net, L-Rod passes the puck to Maverick near the blue line. The horse is unguarded and has a wide open lane to the net. He rears back and blasts a mammoth shot at the net.

The puck speeds through the air and clanks off the pole to the side of Chicken's head, scaring him half to death. Chicken feels the whoosh of the speeding puck past his head. He jumps at the clank it makes as it hits off the pole. Once his wits return, Chicken frantically searches for the puck's whereabouts.

The puck bounces to L-Rod, who passes it right back to Maverick. The horse blasts another shot.

Chicken's eyes go wide as he stares down the one hundred and twelve mile an hour puck flying at his face. He ducks instinctively, but leaves his stick high above his head. Maverick's shot flies at Chicken's smaller than regulation sized stick with such force that it shatters the stick into hundreds of tiny splinters and flies into the net.

The goal lights go off, and the slot machine jackpot noise plays over the arena speakers. The official scorers credit Chicken with an IAHL goal as the puck touched his stick last. Maverick and L-Rod get assists.

The Gamblers rush to celebrate with Chicken. They hug him and pat him on the back, but Chicken is mortified.

"What's the matter dude?" Moose asks.

"I'm done," Chicken says and skates to the bench.

His line mates are confused.

Safari Chip opens the bench door and pats Chicken on the back as he enters. "Good job Chicken. How does it feel to have your first big league goal?"

"I quit," Chicken says, still trying to get his bearings.

"What's the matter?" Safari Chip asks.

"Thanks for letting me try out Chip, but I'm done. Those guys are too big and strong for me." Chicken walks down the bench and pulls up a seat between Big Chick and Rodman.

"Nice goal Chicken," Big Chick pats his little cousin on the head.

"It was an accident. I was just trying not to get hit."

Big Chick and Rodman laugh.

"Well, it all worked out in the end. But I've got to get out there." Rodman stands up and jumps over the wall.

"Thanks for letting me try out Big Chick, but you were right. I'm too little to play this game right now."

Big Chick puts his wing around Chicken and gives him a one-winged hug. "I'm glad you got to experience it, and I'm glad I got to play in a game with you."

The Gamblers go on to beat the Potatoes by a score of 3-2. Chicken's goal is the difference maker, and Safari Chip makes sure to give the little guy the actual puck that shattered his stick and scored the goal.

The only other excitement in the game is caused when Snickers pulls the same move he did in the second game of the season. He sneaks up out of nowhere and puts a hit on Bing that completely obliterates the chimp. The hit is clean and legal, but it is also one of the most vicious hits anyone has ever seen. After the hit, just like the first time Snickers did it, he and Derlargo fist fight and both players land in the penalty box.

*

A few nights later, Noodle does his best to hide his number from the team while he's in the locker room. While the other chickens run around and play with the Gamblers, he sits perfectly still in his chair with his back to his locker, the same locker that has been occupied now by Bing Hope, Krazy Mike, Chicken, him, and after tomorrow night's game, Soup too.

The second of the El Pollos Locos to get a shot in the IAHL agreed on number twenty-three after he was told all numbers could be only two digits long. However, after a secret after curfew mission with his yellow feathered brethren in which they broke into the tailor's office, stole the numbers they needed, removed the number on Noodle's jersey, and sewed on the three digits that currently rest on his back, Noodle now wears the number one hundred on his jersey along with his first name.

Liten notices Noodle sitting like a statue and mistakes his behavior for nervousness. He walks over to Big Chick and taps him on the shoulder. "Is your cousin feeling ok?"

"Which one?" Big Chick asks.

Liten points. "Noodle. He has been sitting motionless for half an hour. I think he might be nervous about playing tonight."

Big Chick takes in what Liten is seeing. The mouse may be right, so he walks over to Noodle. "Hey buddy. You ok?"

Noodle cranes his neck up to look Big Chick in the eyes. His only response is to give Big Chick a thumbs up.

Big Chick raises a questioning eyebrow.

Behind them, their coaches come out of their office.

"Game time!" Safari Chip shouts.

The Gamblers run for the door. Noodle pulls up the rear so no one can see his number.

Safari Chip, who always follows his team down the tunnel, is waiting at the door as always.

"After you," Noodle says as he reaches Safari Chip.

"It's ok. I'll follow you," Safari Chip says.

"Coach, can we walk down together? I have questions."

"Sure thing," Safari Chip says.

Noodle frantically comes up with a few questions to keep Safari Chip occupied as they walk down the tunnel. Noodle makes sure to enter the ice at the same time as Safari Chip. He goes one way, and Safari Chip goes the other way towards the bench. The only problem is Noodle starts skating in the wrong direction and heads right into the oncoming traffic of his teammates. The Gamblers have to glide, swerve, and jump over the little guy to avoid hitting him.

At one point, it looks as though Moose is going to bowl Noodle over, but Big Chick skates in at the last moment and snags Noodle out of harm's way. He turns Noodle around and starts him skating in the same direction as the rest of the team.

"Careful man," Big Chick warns.

"Thanks," Noodle says.

One by one, the Gamblers start to notice Noodle's number as they skate up behind him. Safari Chip is too busy going over game plans with Flip on the bench to notice though. The Gamblers all think it's funny. They give Noodle high fives, knuckles, and pat him on the head.

The referees indicate game time, and the second and third lines hit the bench. Unlike Chicken, Noodle waits patiently on the bench for his turn on the ice.

In the blink of an eye, The Gamblers go up 2-0 with goals from Liten and Big Chick. After Big Chick's goal, Safari Chip sends the first line back out.

Noodle continues to wait patiently.

Finally, L-Rod asks Noodle. "You ready?"

"I'm ready."

"Good, 'cause here comes the first line. We're in!" L-Rod jumps to his feet and jumps over the wall.

Noodle hops to his feet and follows L-Rod.

Noodle isn't as big as Chicken, and he's not as fast as Soup, but he's the smart one of the bunch, and sometimes he's a smart-aleck. So, when he hits the ice and Safari Chip sees the little chicken wearing the number one hundred on his back, the Gamblers coach is puzzled but not altogether surprised.

The Gamblers are on offense as the third line takes the ice. Noodle goes right after the puck. He's determined to score a goal just like Chicken. He thinks he's got a real shot at it too since tonight's game is against the team in last place for goal tending, defense, and last overall place in the standings, the Albuquerque Quake.

Goose beats Noodle to the puck and starts a succession of passes that go round and round the ice from him to Maverick to Moose to L-Rod and back to Goose over and over again. Noodle is always chasing the puck and never in position to take a pass. He almost gets his stick on it once, but he narrowly misses it as it goes from Moose to L-Rod.

L-Rod passes the puck to Moose on the blue line and skates over to Noodle. "I know you want the puck, but you have to get into the right position. Why don't you go stand in front of the net and try to block the goalie's view for right now? We'll work on a plan to get you the puck on the next shift."

"Check." Noodle gives L-Rod a thumbs up and races for the front of the net. He stands in front of the goalie and turns around. The goalie, a bobcat, is much taller than Noodle and has no problem seeing over the little chicken. Noodle understands this fact, so he starts jumping up and down on the ice, trying to obstruct the goalie's view.

"What are you doing creep?" the bobcat asks.

"I'm blocking your vision," Noodle says.

"Well knock it off." The bobcat pushes Noodle while he's in the air and causes him fall face first to the ice.

Meanwhile, Goose coughs up the puck and play moves the other way.

Noodle shakes the stars out of his eyes and stands up. He turns to the bobcat and screams, "HEY!"

The volume of the scream jolts the bobcat backwards.

Before the puck ever crosses the blue line, the Quakes player who stole the puck from Goose gets demolished by Maverick. Both players fall to the ice, though the Quakes player flies about eight feet through the air before he lands.

Moose skates in and grabs the loose puck. He turns, avoids another Quake, skates to his right a bit, rears back, and fires a shot at the net.

L-Rod sees Noodle with his back to the play and the puck heading straight for Noodle's head. "Noodle! Look out!"

Noodle turns around just in time to see the puck coming at him. He raises his stick to block it, and although the puck doesn't shatter his stick, the force of the shot sends Noodle backwards and spinning around in circles. He, his stick, and the puck fly past the goalie.

The goal lights go off.

One referee indicates a goal.

The Gamblers race to celebrate with Noodle, but he crawls out of the net, drops his stick, and declares, "I'm done."

Another referee waves the goal off and indicates no goal.

The third referee skates in and convenes with the first two referees. They decide to review the goal. While they review the tape, the Gamblers personnel show one replay after another of Noodle flying into the net with the puck from different angles. The puck appears to hit off of Noodle's stick and cross the line before Noodle's spinning body does. The goal should stand.

Noodle walks into the bench and informs Safari Chip that hockey is not for him. He thanks him for the opportunity and apologizes for not being able to finish the game.

Safari Chip assures him it's ok all the way around and then razzes him for his number.

"Oh. Yeah. Sorry about that too," Noodle says.

Safari Chip muses the feathers on Noodle's head. "It's ok you crazy chicken. I just hope you had fun on your one shift."

"I did."

Big Chick makes his way over to Noodle. "Are you done?"

"I'm done," Noodle says emphatically.

Suddenly the arena goes nuts. Big Chick and Noodle turn to see the referee indicate that the goal counts.

"It's a goal Noodle!" Big Chick hugs his little cousin.

Noodle tries to respond, but Big Chick's hug is too powerful. The big guy squeezes the air right out of his little cousin's lungs and shakes him forcefully.

The Quake mount a comeback in the final minutes of the game, scoring twice in the final six minutes, but the Gamblers hold on to win 3-2. Once again, it's a goal from one of El Pollos Locos that makes the difference.

*

One night later, El Pollos Locos sit around near Soup's locker as the littlest of them gets ready for his debut game.

"Look Soup, we're not trying to talk you out of playing," Noodle says.

"But we've both played, and we know what it's like out there," Chicken says.

"And?" Soup asks.

"It's scary," Chicken says.

"You calling me a chicken?" Soup asks.

Both Chicken and Noodle squint at Soup.

"I mean, are you calling me a coward?"

"Not a coward," Noodle says.

"Well then, what?"

"You're…" Chicken hesitates.

"Yeah?" Soup stamps his foot.

"Nice," Noodle says.

"Nice?" Soup asks. "So what?"

"So, the other teams are mean and rough," Chicken says.

"And they call you names," Noodle ads.

"They called you names?" Chicken asks.

"Yeah."

"What did they call you?"

"Creep. Didn't they talk like that to you too?"

"No!" Chicken says emphatically.

"Well, Big Chick told me that sometimes it happens. Not everyone in the IAHL is a gentleman like Soup." Noodle holds his wings out to his brother.

"Look guys, I appreciate your concern, but you both had your turn. I'm not afraid, and I won't let their name calling and taunting bother me. Besides, I don't want to be the only El Pollo Loco without an IAHL goal," Soup assures them.

Chicken and Noodle are pretty sure that Soup isn't going to like what he sees and hears on the ice, but it's his right to play.

Safari Chip comes out of his office and calls game time.

Chicken and Noodle head to their seats in the stands, and the Gamblers head to the ice with Soup in his jersey with the name Soup and the number 316 on the back. He had asked Safari Chip for the three digit number, and when Safari Chip asked him if he was going to find a way to wear it anyway, Soup didn't lie and told him yes, so Safari Chip granted Soup his number.

The Gamblers play the F-14s the night of Soup's debut. The F-14s aren't as bad as the Quake, but they're still one of the bottom three teams in the league.

During the pregame skate around, Soup can't help thinking about how his brothers have already bowed out of the competition to take the seventeenth and final spot on the roster. If he can just have a decent game, he's got a good shot of getting a full time contract. Chicken and Noodle both scored goals though, so he knows he's going to have to at least match their feats, and breaking their record with another goal or at least an assist wouldn't hurt.

As Soup skates around, thinking about what he has to do in the game, he inadvertently wanders too far down the ice and bumps into a leopard on the F-14s.

"Hey! Watch where you're going you midget canary," the leopard scolds Soup rather angrily.

Soup snaps out of his trance. "What did you call me?"

"Midget canary," the leopard says and skates off.

Soup covers his ears, but he's too late to block out the offensive name. The name angers Soup. He skates after the leopard. "First off, I'm a chicken, not a canary. Second, if I was a canary, I wouldn't be a midget. I'm way taller than any canary I know. And third, you shouldn't say midget. It's rude."

The leopard keeps skating.

"Did you hear me?" Soup shouts.

A toucan on the F-14s skates by Soup. "You better get out of here and stop chasing after Cosmo, little boy."

"Not until he apologizes for his rude remarks."

"You do know he's one of the top fighters in the league, don't you?" the toucan asks.

"So?"

"So, how do you think you're going to get him to apologize? He'll break you in half quicker than you can blink, and he won't think twice about it."

"Is that a threat?"

"It's a warning. Now get back to your own team dufus."

Soup covers his ears again. "You guys are mean!"

"You guys are mean," a salamander taunts in a snide voice as he skates by.

Big Chick skates into the mass of F-14s and grabs Soup. He steers his little cousin back to the Gamblers side. "You better stay over here dude."

"Why?"

"Because Cosmo Tenenbaum is over there."

"He's mean. And I'm going to get him to apologizes before this game is through," Soup declares.

Big Chick sighs heavily. Before the game starts, he grabs Maverick and Moose and asks them to keep an eye on Soup in case Cosmo tries to pick a fight with him.

The game starts shortly thereafter, and both the first and second lines play nonstop for over a minute. There's plenty of offense, but both teams fail to score. The nonstop action moves the game along, and whereas Chicken and Noodle had to wait a long time to get in the game, Soup finds himself being rushed out after a little more than two minutes of game time.

As Soup and the rest of the third line take the ice, the F-14s, including Cosmo, gather the puck that was dumped in by the Gamblers second line. One of the F-14s takes the puck up the ice and tries to shoot it to Cosmo near center ice.

Racing at Cosmo for his apology is Soup. The chicken skates right into the path of the puck, kicks it with his skate, and finds himself suddenly skating towards the F-14's goalie.

Players all over the ice hit their breaks and chase after Soup, who is very fast. Soup slips between two F-14s and cruises into the Gamblers offensive zone. The chicken's speed actually works against him. He approaches the net too fast to take a shot. He has to glide around the back of the net, but he avoids losing the puck when the goalie tries to swipe it away.

Everything happens so fast that Soup doesn't know quite what's going on. As he comes out from behind the net, the F-14s and the rest of the Gamblers have caught up to the play and are waiting for him. He's met first by Cosmo, who tries to levy a hit on Soup, but Soup spins out of the way at the last second.

Cosmo slams into the glass hard, but recovers quickly and jumps up to chase Soup again. A not so legal check from Moose slams Cosmo right back into the glass and goes uncalled.

Soup wraps around the front side of the net. He rears back like he's going to fire, but he hesitates. He waits. And waits. And waits. He waits so long that the fans, the Gamblers, and especially the F-14s grow impatient.

"Shoot it!" the salamander yells.

"Come on you yellow bellied chicken. Shoot!" the toucan yells.

"Yeah. Shoot rookie!" another F-14, a pig, yells.

Soup furrows his brow. He rears his stick back a little further and swings. The puck flies through a mess of bodies and sticks. It flies just under the glove of the F-14s goalie, ricochets off the post, and rattles around the back of the net.

The referee indicates a goal. The goal lights go off. The slot machine jackpot noise is played over the arena speakers.

Everyone, including Soup, is taken by surprise.

The F-14s have a Dalmatian named Brad. He smiles as he says to Soup. "Nice shot little dude."

"Are you cracking whip?" Soup demands.

"No bro! That was awesome," Brad says sincerely.

The Gamblers swarm Soup to celebrate. The usual hugs, high fives, and pats on the back go around, but when they're done, Soup still sees the F-14s mad dogging him, so he calls them out. He points from one F-14 to another. "You're a jerk. You're a jerk. You're a big jerk," he informs the salamander, toucan, and Cosmo before moving on to Brad. "You're pretty cool, and you're a jerk." Soup finishes with the pig.

Brad laughs at his teammates and gives Soup knuckles.

"But I'm done," Soup says and skates to the bench. He's greeted by Big Chick and the rest of the Gamblers with high fives.

For the third game in a row, it's an El Pollos Locos goal that is the difference maker in the outcome of the game. In this game however, the El Pollos Locos goal turns out to be the only goal in the game as the Gamblers go on to win 1-0.

*

After the Game the Gamblers celebrate the successful debuts of El Pollos Locos in the locker room. Even the coaches are happy with the way things turned out.

Safari Chip says to Flip, "I know they're too little to play fulltime, but I'm going to miss those little chickens. And it really stinks that we don't have a second winger for our third line."

"Well, the Olympics start in a week, and that will give us two weeks to figure something out," Flip says.

"That's true."

"I know you'll be coaching the American team, but I'll make it a point to find us a permanent fixture for that line while you and the guys are gone," Flip assures Safari Chip.

Chapter 16: Pink Jerseys And Beary's Big News

Shortly before the Olympics, the Gamblers again play the Five Ohhh! in Las Vegas. They don't know what to expect from because of the way things ended after the last game. They're not too concerned though. It's just another game. If the Five Ohhh! haven't gotten over themselves, they won't be the first team to feud with the Gamblers.

Most of the Gamblers wait in the locker room with water balloons in hand snickering and giggling. The only two not yet in the locker room are Beary and Lovey. Beary's never late, and Lovey's always late. So, they know who's going to be next through the door, and Apple Jack has a water balloon ready to toss to the panda when he comes in.

A loud crash from the other side of the doors draws their attention to the entrance. The crash is Lovey bursting through. He comes in with such force that he falls down.

A collective sigh goes around the room. They were all really hoping to get Lovey again. Something about his frantic efforts not to be last, yet always being last, makes pegging him more fun than anyone else.

Lovey pauses for just a second to make sure he's ok. When he's sure he's not hurt, he looks up from the ground and tries to tell the guys something, but he stammers because he is so out of breath and eager to tell them his news. Finally he's able to spit it out and he yells to them, "Beary's getting married!"

The rest of the guys let down their guard.

"What?" Harlan asks.

Lovey continues speaking from the ground. "I just passed Beary in the hallway. He was telling Chip he's getting married and was asking for the night off."

"Who's he getting married to?" Harlan asks. Beary's his best good buddy. He would know if Beary was getting married, and he's never even heard one word about a girlfriend.

"I don't know, but that's what I heard him telling Chip," Lovey assures all of his stunned teammates.

Harlan is happy for his buddy, but he's also very confused. The rest of the Gamblers feel the same.

"Did you say he's not playing tonight?" Apple Jack asks.

"Yeah. He was asking Chip for the night off," Lovey says.

"So you're the last one here?" Apple Jack asks.

"I don't know. I'm..." Lovey starts.

"FIRE IN THE HOLE!" Apple Jack fires his and Beary's water balloons at a defenseless Lovey on the floor.

The other Gamblers follow suit, and for what seems like the fiftieth time, Lovey gets the short end of the season long water balloon joke. After the last balloon is tossed and all the laughter subsides, Apple Jack reaches his paw to Lovey and helps him off the ground.

The locker room door opens just as Lovey plants his feet on the ground. Safari Chip and Beary walk in together.

"Who are you getting married to?" Harlan blurts out.

Beary runs to his teammates, excited to tell them all about his bride-to-be. "Her name is Mary. I wanted to take the night off to set up an engagement party so you could all meet her, but Chip talked me into playing, so she's setting it up now."

The Gamblers hoot, holler, squawk, squeal, bark, and nay.

"Let's get the party started early by going out there and beating the Five Ohhh!," Safari Chip says.

The Gamblers erupt in another joyous outburst.

"And remember everyone, it's Ladies Night tonight. You'll each find your special Ladies Night jerseys in your lockers," Safari Chip reminds his players.

Each Gambler reaches into his locker and pulls out a jersey that looks just like their regular jersey except pink with black and white trim. The colliding dice logo is still red with black letters. Their names and numbers are a darker shade of pink with white outlines.

"What the heck is this?" Undertaker holds up and examines the pink monstrosity with an apprehension to put it on.

"It should suit you just fine Princess Kitty," Kane snaps.

"Shut up Kane." Undertaker pushes Kane.

Kane pushes Undertaker back. "Don't touch me with your filthy cat paws Morty."

"Don't call me Morty, Keith." Undertaker pushes Kane again.

"I'll call you whatever I want punk." Kane pushes Undertaker with two paws this time and sends him stumbling backwards.

Snickers steps in between the bickering dogs and separates them. "Knock it off guys. Just put on the jerseys and stop fighting."

"I'll put on the jersey, but I'm done with that guy." Kane points a finger at Undertaker and walks away. He stops and turns back to Undertaker. "Canines before felines."

Undertaker frowns. He knew his relationship with Elmira was going to be rough on his canine comrades, but he never thought it would ruin his friendship with his best friend in the whole world.

Rodman and L-Rod pull their jerseys over their heads. They look down at them with the same anxiety felt by everyone else in the room.

L-Rod looks up to Rodman and shudders. "Ugh."

"You said it," Rodman agrees and shudders too.

They look at the locker next to theirs. They see Lovey smiling and lacing up his skates. The pink clearly isn't bothering him a bit.

Lovey can feel their eyes on him. "What?"

"What!?" Rodman asks flabbergasted.

"What?" Lovey repeats.

"How could you do this to us?" L-Rod grumbles and walks away.

"How could I do what?" Lovey asks confused.

Rodman shakes his head and follows L-Rod away.

A few lockers down from Lovey, Big Chick has his pink jersey on and is looking at himself in the mirror. He turns from side to side to check out his profile, pats his belly, and smoothes out his jersey. "Does this make me look fat?" he asks aloud.

Sammie glances over at him. "Yeah, it does."

"Nuts." Big Chick puts his wings to his hips.

One of the few players to have a good time with the pinkness of the situation is Haas. He sits at his locker and dyes his ears pink for the night's game

When it's time to play, Safari Chip and Flip come out of their office to yell game time but are stopped in their tracks at the sight of their pink team.

The Gamblers turn to their silenced coaches.

"Game time?" Rodman asks.

Safari Chip nods his head unable to spit out the words.

The Gamblers walk, in no hurry, to the locker room door. Safari Chip and Flip pull up the rear.

Lovey waits at the door and stops his coaches. "I didn't want you guys to be left out, so I got a pink safari hat and jacket for you Chip and a pink Gamblers hat and tie for you Flip."

The coaches reluctantly accept their gifts and put them on. If their team has to suffer this way, they might as well bear it with them. Plus, they don't want to hurt Lovey's feelings. He spent a lot of time designing these jerseys and getting things ready for the special jersey nights. The nights are drawing full houses, and they're also bringing in oodles of money for charity with the auctioning of the jerseys after the games.

The Gamblers hit the ice. They're all happy when the lights in the arena are mostly off for their introductions. In their custom colored spotlights, it makes it hard to see how pink their jerseys are, but when the light comes up, all seventeen Gamblers are seen perfectly from their opponents just across the ice to everyone high up in the cheap seats.

The Five Ohhh! take one look at their pink clad opponents and laugh their heads off.

The Gamblers cringe, but their cringing soon turns to anger.

"What are they laughing at?" Lovey asks.

"What do you think they are laughing at?" Kane snaps.

Lovey looks down at his pink jersey. "Oh nuts."

"Thank you for these pink jerseys and this humiliating experience," Liten sarcastically whispers to Lovey.

The Five Ohhh! don't let up. Ratone skates to the Five Ohhh! bench laughing so hard that he falls to his knees and grabs the boards to keep from falling completely to the ice. Samanya isn't as concerned with falling to the ice. He rolls around on his back, laughing like the obnoxious awkward teen he's become. Mad Man laughs so hard he has to skate off the ice to run to the Five Ohhh! locker room to keep from peeing his hockey pants.

Sammie Two grabs the Gamblers official cameraman and brings him onto the ice. He positions the cameraman in front of Sammie Lou, and slips his arm around Sammie Lou's shoulder. "Ok man. Get a photo of me and my cousin."

The cameraman snaps the photo.

Sammie Two races to check it out. "Oh, that's great. I'll meet you after the game. I'm going to need at least fifty copies. Oh boy is the family going to get a kick out of this photo. I think I'll have it posterized and display it in my living room." Sammie Two turns to Sammie Lou. "If you want, I can get it made into Christmas cards, and we can send them out to the family."

Dislike and a few of the other Five Ohhh! approach Rodman, Lovey, and the rest of the Gamblers.

"Nice jerseys," Dislike mocks.

"They're still cooler than yours," Rodman says.

"Not really," Ox laughs.

"Yeah. Not really. I saw them online a few days ago. I made sure to dislike them on Facespace," Dislike pokes.

"Did you dislike the fact that they're for charity, or did you dislike the fact that your mom already put in a bid on mine? I mean, after all, I am her favorite player," Lovey shoots back.

Dislike lunges at Lovey, but Ox holds him back.

It's the Gamblers turn to have a laugh.

The Five Ohhh! heckling continues when their dogs skate over to the Gamblers dogs. Crush grabs a pinch of Apple

Jack's jersey near the shoulder. He pretends to examine it a little closer, all the while snickering obnoxiously.

"You've got about two seconds to let go of my jersey," Apple Jack warns.

"Before what?" Crush asks.

"Before this." Apple Jack jumps on top of the pit bull and starts pummeling him.

This prompts Undertaker, Kane, and Snickers to preemptively grab the Five Ohhh! dog nearest to them and start fighting them too. Whistles blow and the referees skate to break up the mêlée. It's hard enough for the three referees to separate the eight dogs, but when the rest of the players on both teams take a cue from the dogs and start fighting before the game even starts, it's impossible to separate everyone.

Unable to get the situation under control, the referees eventually give up. They back off and let the teams fight it out.

In the midst of all the fighting, Greg can't find his Gamblers counterpart, Beary. He skates from one fight to another looking for the other panda bear. He finally finds Beary trying to pull The Colonel off of a frantic Big Chick. He grabs Beary from behind, spins him around, and rears back a fist.

"No wait! I don't want us to fight," Beary screams.

"Too bad," Greg says.

"Seriously. I want to be friends. Can't we all just get along?"

"No."

"I have to tell you something though," Beary says.

Greg doesn't want to hear anything Beary has to say, and he lays the Gamblers panda out with one punch.

Harlan sees his best friend get clocked, so he wraps up his fight with Marlon by delivering him a head-butt that lays the other turtle out. Harlan shakes off his wooziness and skates at Greg, gripping his goalie mask in his flipper. The Five Ohhh! panda turns around and is met by a swing of Harlan's mask to the side of his head. The hit is so hard and vicious that Greg hits the ice like a sack of bricks, and Harlan falls down with him.

"Don't mess with BNR chump," Harlan says to the unconscious Five Ohhh! panda and goes to check on Beary.

Maverick, Goose, and Moose make short work of Iceman, Slider, and Deuce and rush to help Big Chick, who is hysterically screaming as The Colonel sits on top of him, plucking feathers from Big Chick's head. Goose and Moose arrive first and try to pry the fox off, but he's too strong and pushes them away. Maverick kicks off his skates as he reaches the scene of the crime, drops to all fours, and mule kicks the fox in the face with his hind legs. The kick sends The Colonel flying through the air. The fox lands on his back dazed and hurt, but he still manages to stand quickly back up. Maverick rushes at him, continuing the fight for Big Chick while Goose and Moose help Big Chick to his feet and get the big guy to safety.

Lovey and Dislike trade violent thumps back and forth like two MMA fighters. Both are unconcerned with defense. They hit, rip, scratch, and claw at each other, making shreds of each other's jerseys.

Joey Ratone pulls Liten's tail and drags him around the ice. Liten squeals in pain until Rodman catches up to them and delivers an elbow to Ratone's head that frees Liten. For his good deed, Rodman receives an elbow from a sneak attack by Ox. Rodman is momentarily dazed, but before Ox can really pummel Rodman, Liten repays the favor by sneaking up behind Ox and punching him in the back of his knee. Ox falls to one knee, turns around, and gets whipped in the face by Liten's tail.

Even the normally laidback Haas trades a few punches with Rabbit X.

Safari Chip, Flip, and the Five Ohhh! coach, a Spider Monkey named Rezza, scream at the referees to get this thing under control, but the referees won't budge. They don't want to risk life and limb trying to stop thirty-four rabid hockey players from mauling each other.

When the referees refuse to put a stop to things, Rezza shouts from his bench at Safari Chip. "Hey idiot! Why don't you call off your thugs?"

Safari Chip points to himself with one of his long fingers. "You talking to me?"

"You're the only idiot I see here with a gang full of thugs, so I guess so."

"You're talking to me!?" Safari Chip repeats unable to believe his ears.

What ensues from this point is a tirade of yelling from one head coach to one another. They yell at and over each other so loud that neither can hear what the other is saying. When Rezza realizes his screaming isn't getting him anywhere, he flinches at Safari Chip. The Gamblers coach in turn stands up on the boards and invites a fight over his way. Rezza accepts right away. He and Safari Chip join their players in the brawl.

Being the only one of sound mind, Flip takes it upon himself to start breaking up the fights. He starts by separating the two littlest players on each team, players he's coached before. He separates L-Rod and Samanya by placing L-Rod in one penalty box and Samanya in another. He tells the officials inside to lock the door and not let them out until things settle down.

Flip then starts breaking up one fight after another until he has both teams on their respective benches where they continue to mad dog and yell at each other.

"Stop looking at them," Flip orders his team.

The Gamblers do as they're told.

"You too Chip," Flip orders the Gamblers head coach.

Safari Chip does as he's told and turns to face his team.

"Your lip is bleeding!" Big Chick gasps.

"He hit me!"

"Who?" Rodman asks.

Safari Chip points to Rezza. "Their coach."

The Gamblers look to the Five Ohhh! coach, who looks back at them with a snarl.

"Did you hit him back?" Liten asks.

"You're darn right I did. You can't tell, but HE'S GOT A BLACK EYE UNDER THAT BLACK FUR!" Safari Chip yells loud enough for the Five Ohhh! coach to hear.

Safari Chip looks at his team. Up and down the lineup, he sees guys with cuts, scrapes, scratches, bruises, bloody lips, puffy eyes, plucked feathers, and dark red blood stains in all shapes and sizes upon their nice pink jerseys, which are also ripped, torn, and disheveled. "Now that we've got some blood on our jerseys, and we look a little bit more like men, let's go out there and really kick some butt," Safari Chip shouts to his team.

There's a familiar Gamblers outburst on the bench.

When the game starts, Lovey scores the game's first goal and makes his way to Dislike. He tells the other bear, "Why don't you dislike that on Facespace?"

The goal, coupled with Lovey's comments, enrage Dislike so much that he picks another fight with Lovey. After they serve their penalties, the bears come out of the box and immediately start fighting again. They each get thrown out of the game in the third period when they get into a third fight. Lovey's third fight is with The Colonel on behalf of Big Chick and Dislike's is with Snickers.

The fights don't end there. The Colonel gets into his second fight of the night when he goes after Maverick for kicking him in the face before the game. Apple Jack fights Crunch. Kane fights Hoss. Undertaker fights Stunner. Snickers fights Crush. Sammie Lou and Sammie Two get into two fights, and Rodman steps in and takes a fight with Ratone when he tries to pick one with Liten. Twelve fights and one hundred and thirty-eight penalty minutes set IAHL records for most fights and most overall penalty minutes in one game.

In the end, with additional goals by Rodman and Moose, the Gamblers skate off the ice with a 3-2 victory. All the bruises, scratches, cuts, scrapes, and plucked feathers are worth it in their minds. The rips, tears, and blood stains in their jerseys pay off too. They set records for the amount of money they collect in the jersey auction as everyone wants a battle tested jersey.

The Gamblers feel good as they exit the ice, and they feel even better with the promise of a postgame party to celebrate Beary's engagement.

Chapter 17: Beary's Engagement Party

The Gamblers tend to their wounds, shower, and race to their hotel rooms to grab their finest suits. They weren't anticipating an engagement party before the game started. They meet in the elevator room and go down together to one of the New Orleans Hotel ballrooms.

Beary and his bride-to-be run paw in paw to the Gamblers as they enter.

"Hey guys. Meet Mary," Beary introduces his secret girlfriend.

There's a flurry of greetings from all the Gamblers at once.

"Mary, this is Harlan, Rodman, L-Rod, Lovey, Liten, Safari Chip, Flip, Sammie, Big Chick, Chicken, Noodle, Soup, Haas, Kane, Apple Jack, Snickers, Undertaker, Maverick, Goose, and Moose."

"Hello everyone. I'm so glad to meet all of you," Mary, a panda bear wearing the pink Beary Nelson Riley jersey she won at the auction tonight and pink bows in her fur, says.

"I see you won Beary's jersey tonight. Thank you for your charitable donation," Safari Chip tells Beary's fiancé.

"You're welcome. I was happy to do it and happier to finally have a jersey of my charming Bear Bear."

The Gamblers all oooh and ahhh.

"Bear Bear?" Harlan asks a bit disgusted.

"Oh stop." Beary blushes.

"So why did you keep Mary a secret?" Harlan demands.

"Well…" Beary starts.

"Awww, who cares. This is supposed to be a party." Lovey holds up his boombox. "So let's start celebrating."

The Gamblers run to the dance floor as Lovey sets up the boombox.

Safari Chip grabs Mary by the paws and leads her to the dance floor. He shouts to Beary as he leads his fiancé away, "Does the coach get the first dance?"

"Wait guys. We're still waiting for Mary's brother," Beary says.

"He can join in when he gets here," Sammie says.

"But we have to tell you guys something about Mary's brother," Beary says.

The ballroom door opens up and draws everyone's attention that way. A panda bear pokes his head in and steps inside. He walks closer and closer to the Gamblers. Halfway to the dance floor, he comes into the light. The Gamblers stifle gasps as they recognize Greg Claymore of the Five Ohhh!.

"Mary?" Greg asks shocked to find his sister with the Gamblers.

"What's he doing here?" Apple Jack asks.

"He's my brother," Mary says.

"Him?" L-Rod points to Greg.

"What are they doing here?" Greg demands of his sister.

"They're my fiancés teammates," Mary answers.

"Him?" Greg points to Beary.

"Yes, him," Mary says.

"How?" Harlan asks.

"We met after the first game in Reno," Mary explains.

"We kept it a secret because we thought you guys might make it hard on us if you knew too soon," Beary adds.

"We were hoping that both teams would eventually calm down, but after you didn't accept their banana split sundae apology, it looked hopeless," Mary explains to her brother.

There's a long awkward stare down between Greg and the Gamblers. The silence is broken by the ballroom doors opening again. In walks the entire Five Ohhh! team. They stop at the sight of Greg fuming. They look further into the room and they're just as surprised as Greg to lay eyes on the Gamblers.

"What's going on Greg?" Ox asks.

Greg screams at the top of his lungs and charges with his fists balled and aimed at Beary. Just as he's about to pummel the Gamblers panda, Harlan steps in and clotheslines the angry Five Ohhh! panda. Greg hits the floor like an anvil, and the Five

Ohhh! jump into attack mode. They rush the Gamblers in
defense of their fallen buddy.

"No!" scream Beary and Mary at the same time.

The Gamblers meet the Five Ohhh! halfway, and a
repeat of the pregame brawl takes place. Gamblers and Five
Ohhh! alike rumble, tumble, and fly across the room. Tables and
chairs get knocked over. Players get knocked over. Even Mary
gets knocked over by Greg when he gets up and tries to go after
Beary again. This time, upon seeing his future wife knocked
down, Beary doesn't try to reason with Greg. He knocks his
future brother-in-law down with a punch to the face.

Mary picks herself off the ground and makes a mad dash
for the door. Beary follows her, and both pandas run from the
ballroom.

Inside the ballroom, the fight continues. Ox and Ratone
hold Rodman down on the ground while Mad Man climbs on top
of a table and prepares to deliver a flying elbow drop.

Safari Chip side steps an attempt by Rezza to rush him.
He trips the Five Ohhh! coach and runs to the table where Mad
Man is preparing to jump onto Rodman. Safari Chip tips the
table over, thwarting Mad Man's attempt to injure his captain.

Liten, who had been knocked down by Ratone, picks
himself up and runs to help Safari Chip save Rodman. He tackles
Ratone, freeing Rodman's legs. Rodman swings his legs up and
kicks Ox in the snout, causing the ox to let him go.

On the other side of the room, Maverick is sure to step in
for Big Chick with The Colonel before the fox can get to Big
Chick, who hides under a table. Maverick has the upper hand for
a while, but Ice Man comes in and pulls the horse off of his
teammate. Together they rough Maverick up for a minute.

Big Chick watches Maverick get pummeled until he
can't watch the horse take a beating on his behalf anymore. He
stands up, flipping the table in the process, runs up beside Ice
Man and The Colonel, grabs them by their necks, and bunks
their heads together.

"Thanks buddy," Maverick says.

"No problem," Big Chick says.

Out of nowhere, Goose goes flying past them and slams into the wall.

Big Chick points to Slider, the culprit of the attack. "Let's get him."

"Yeah," Maverick agrees, and the two Gamblers chase Slider around the room.

Dislike tosses a chair at Lovey, but Lovey ducks out of the way. Lovey throws a chair back at the black bear. Dislike also ducks out of the way, and grabs a plate off of one of the tables. He chucks the plate like a Frisbee. It nails the white teddy bear in the forehead, making a dull thump as it hits Lovey and sends him falling to the ground momentarily blinded and dazed.

When Lovey's vision returns, he tries to stand up, but a barrage of dishes rains down on him. Lovey is forced to roll behind a turned over table to take cover. Momentarily, he finds himself out of the line of fire. He peeks out from behind his table and sees Dislike picking up another table. Lovey doesn't like the looks of things, so he grabs his own table with a growl and uses it as a shield as he runs at Dislike with the table top out in front of him. He runs the black teddy bear over like a freight train.

L-Rod hops on Samanya's back and pulls the bigger peewee penguin to the ground. He has his wind knocked out as they hit the floor, but he manages to hang on. L-Rod doesn't try to hurt the bully penguin, but he holds him down for El Pollos Locos to tickle.

"Hey! Stop! That tickles," Samanya protests, but El Pollos Locos don't stop. After a long while, Samanya can no longer handle his tickle torture. "Stop. Please. I'm going to pee my pants."

El Pollos Locos don't stop, and L-Rod feels something warm and wet. "Oh gross!" L-Rod lets go of Samanya, pushes the bigger penguin off of himself, and runs away.

"Ewww." Chicken points to the puddle.

"Gross," Noodle whispers.

"That's just not right," Soup says.

The dogs and Moose fight atop the ballroom stage with the Five Ohhh! dogs and Deuce. They knock over the podium and its microphone, causing a loud high pitched screech that momentarily stops all the fighting as everyone reaches up to cover their ears. The noise dies down and the fighting continues.

Kane grabs Stunner and throws him through a projection screen that was going to display a slide show of pictures of Beary and Mary. Stunner splits the screen right in two and falls off the backside of the stage. Kane turns around just in time to see Undertaker knock Hoss out with an uppercut. He runs to his best friend, spins Undertaker around, and socks him in the face.

Undertaker hits the floor with a thud. He looks up disbelieving and livid. "What the heck Kane?"

"Canines before felines," Kane yells just before Apple Jack gets thrown into him by Crunch.

Sammie Lou takes a bunch of shots from Sammie Two. He defends himself from Sammie Two's assault, but he refuses to hit him back.

"Fight back," Sammie Two screams as he throws each punch.

"No!" Sammie Lou yells back. "I don't hate you, and I won't fight you."

"Then you're going to get pummeled," Sammie Two warns.

Harlan and Haas hold up their flippers and paws to Marlon and Rabbit X.

"Look fellas. We're goalies. We've already done enough fighting for one day. What do you say we sit this one out?" Haas asks.

Rabbit X makes a fist and pounds it into his other paw. He goes to throw a punch at Haas, but Harlan jumps in his way with his shell out in front. Rabbit X breaks his paw on Harlan's shell. He lets out a loud shrill and waves his broken paw in the air, trying to shake it off.

With the Five Ohhh! rabbit out of the way, Harlan and Haas make a move towards Marlon.

Marlon throws up his flippers. "Ok. Ok. Ok. We'll sit this one out."

Harlan kicks a chair Marlon's way, and Haas motions for him to sit.

The ballroom doors fly open, and the room is flooded with every single security guard employed by the New Orleans Hotel. The security guards outnumber the hockey players three to one. They swarm the room and start putting everyone in handcuffs. Once the security guards have the riot under control, they turn the two teams over to Beary and Mary.

Beary paces in front of his teammates and rivals, tisk tisking the subdued animals. "Well, well, well. This sure is a fine how do you do."

"I wasn't going to let that punk hurt you again Beary," Harlan says.

"And we weren't going to sit back and let you beat up our brother," Ox shouts.

"Well, we…" Goose starts.

"STOP!" Beary screams at the top of his lungs.

The room goes silent.

"Enough is enough. Can't we all just get along?" Beary asks.

"NO!" all thirty-eight Gamblers, Five Ohhh!, and El Pollos Locos shout.

"Well you better start getting along with them," Mary sternly warns Greg and points to Beary and the rest of the Gamblers. "Because I'm going to marry Beary. He's going to be around a lot more, and I won't stand beside while you and your cohorts pound his brains in each time your team plays his."

"And you guys better stop flying off the handle bars each time we run into them," Beary warns his teammates. "They're going to be in the league for a long time, and we can't go on like this for the next fifteen years."

"I haven't gotten to know them yet," Mary speaks to the Five Ohhh! while pointing to the Gamblers. "But they seem like very nice young men. They welcomed me to their fold upon their arrival, and to hear Beary talk about them, you wouldn't think that there could be a nicer group of animals."

"And they're fellow hockey players. We've probably got a lot in common with them," Beary adds.

"So, if you guys are going to come to the wedding," Mary goes on.

"Then you better shape up, because we won't allow for any shenanigans like this," Beary warns.

The two teams sit in silence. Both of them are going to need some time to digest the situation.

Security escorts the Five Ohhh! out of the ballroom and uncuffs them in the foyer. From there, they make sure the Reno team leaves the hotel peacefully. The Gamblers are uncuffed inside the ballroom once word arrives that the Five Ohhh! are out of the building.

Beary asks for some privacy with his teammates, and security obliges him. Beary looks upon the Gamblers in their suits, which, just like their pink jerseys, are torn, tattered, and bloodied. Before he can speak, Beary is interrupted.

"We're all really sorry about this Beary," Rodman says.

"Yes. We did not mean to ruin your engagement party," Liten agrees.

"Yeah, sorry buddy. But, why did you invite them?" Harlan asks.

"That was my fault," Mary says. "I invited my brother. I didn't know he was going to bring his whole team."

"We thought it would be good to break the news to him first. That way maybe we could have avoided this. We didn't know he was going to bring the entire Five Ohhh! team with him."

"Either way, we're sorry things turned out the way they did," Safari Chip apologizes. "I guess we better all get going now though."

"Why?" Beary asks.

"Well, look at this place. We ruined the evening," Rodman says.

"That's ok. We won't let a little mess end the whole party. I want to get to know my Beary's buddies," Mary says.

"Really?" Sammie asks.

"Yeah," Beary says. "We'll get another ballroom and start this party from the beginning."

The Gamblers hoot, holler, bark, squawk, squeal, nay, and make a mad dash for the exit.

L-Rod grabs ahold of Rodman. "Hey."

"Yeah?" Rodman asks.

"I have to go upstairs to change."

Rodman looks down and sees pee all over L-Rod's suit. "Did you pee your pants?"

"No!" L-Rod is insulted. "Samanya peed on me."

"Boy. Those Five Ohhh! guys sure are sickos aren't they?"

"You said it."

The Gamblers hit the ballroom next door. They get to know Mary, watch the slide show of pictures from Beary and Mary's early courtship, and have the grand time they had planned to have from the onset.

"This turned out to be a nice evening after all," Harlan says to his buddy.

"Yeah it did," Beary agrees.

"Mary's a great girl man. I'm happy for you. But do me one favor?"

"What's that?"

"Don't let her talk you into another engagement party with just her side of the family. I don't want them Reno guys getting you all alone."

"Good thinking," Beary agrees and pats his reptilian friend on the shell.

Chapter 18: Flip Finds A Replacement

Before the Gamblers hit the road for their final five games before the Olympics, Flip calls for Safari Chip to come to their office.

"Hey Flip. What's the big news?" Safari Chip asks as he fights his way through the crowd in the locker room.

"I found a forward for the third line," Flip says.

"Really? That's great. Are you ready to go? You can tell me all about him on the way to the airport." Safari Chip motions for Flip to follow him out of the locker room.

"Wait. He's here. You can meet him yourself."

Safari Chip stops in his tracks. "He's here now?"

"Yeah. In your office."

Safari Chip notices that something is off about the way Flip is acting. He's not quite right. In fact, he seems nervous. The whole situation makes Safari Chip uneasy. "Who is it?"

"Take a look for yourself?" Flip says.

Safari Chip walks slowly to his office door. He keeps an eye on his assistant the entire time. Safari Chip reaches for the handle, turns it, pushes the door open, and peeks inside. Upon seeing the player, he jumps back into the locker room, slams the door shut, and turns to Flip. "What's he doing here?"

"He's who I found to play on our third line," Flip says.

"Don't you know who that is?"

"It's Jason Vyand."

Safari Chip jumps in the air, grabs his safari hat, and clenches it tightly. "He can't play on our third line.

"Why?"

"Why?" Safari Chip exclaims. "Why? Because he's Jason Vyand."

"So?"

"So he cheated Rodman out of his shot at a Gold Rush contract, which I'm not complaining about because it worked out fabulously for us. He's mean, ruthless, selfish, a cheater, and he has no respect for the game or anyone on this team." Safari Chip answers.

"He's changed," Flip says matter-of-factly.

"He took out his own teammate by whacking him in the knee with a stick. He's so vile and reprehensible that the Gold Rush cut him, and he's such a distraction that none of the other fourteen... nay, fifteen teams want him even though he's an all-star caliber player," Safari Chip argues. "Isn't he suspended for what he did to Maulbreath?"

"No. Just cut. But seriously, he's different," Flip says.

"It's only been a few weeks. How can he be different? No one changes that drastically in a month."

"I think being out of hockey has really traumatized him. It's the one thing he truly loves, and he realizes his actions have cost him that. All I ask is that you talk to him," Flip pleads.

Safari Chip is hesitant.

"I coached him for three years. He wasn't always bad."

"I'll talk to him. No promises, but I'll talk to him," Safari Chip finally gives in.

Flip opens the door and leads Safari Chip into the office. The monkey eyeballs Jason like a seal eyeballing circling sharks.

Jason stares at the ground.

Safari Chip takes a seat behind his desk, staring at Jason the whole time. He leans forward in his chair, rests his elbows on the desk, and interlocks his fingers.

Flip motions for Jason to take a seat in the the only other chair in the office.

As soon as Jason sits down, Safari Chip shoots upright in his chair and pounds his fists on the top of his desk. "You sure have a lot of nerve coming in here asking to play with this team."

Jason shoots right out of his chair. Even Flip jumps back startled.

"I knew I shouldn't have come," Jason says to Flip.

Flip gives Safari Chip a disapproving look.

Safari Chip tones down his anger and thinks more carefully about his words. "I'm sorry. I shouldn't have lost my cool." He motions for Jason to sit down again.

Jason looks to Flip and gets the ok, so he takes a seat.

Silence fills the room.

Flip finally breaks the ice. "I guess I'll start by telling you, Chip, why I brought Jason here." Flip waits for some sort of acknowledgment, and Safari Chip motions for him to continue. "Aside from being one of the best players in the IAHL, Jason is the type of player who can elevate the play of those around him."

Safari Chip points at Jason. "From what I've seen, you're also the type of player who can elevate the anger, frustration levels, and disharmony of those around you."

"As his former coach, I know sometimes Jason can get in his own way and be his own worst enemy, and I know the things he's done have negatively impacted not only the Gamblers but his own team too. But, he can also be a valuable teammate in the right situation," Flip argues.

Safari Chip grumbles lightly in the back of his throat. He wasn't expecting to find Jason in his office, and he's in no hurry whatsoever to extend him an offer. Just sitting this close to the Gamblers chief antagonist makes him uncomfortable.

Flip can see Safari Chip's consternation. "What are your concerns Chip?"

"How the rest of the guys would feel, what this could do to our locker room, whether or not he would try to sabotage us."

"I'm not looking to sabotage you guys," Jason says.

"What about your past behavior should make me believe otherwise?" Safari Chip asks.

"Nothing," Jason answers meekly.

"I don't understand," Flip interrupts. "I know Jason and Rodman are the biggest of rivals, but outside of some cheap shots and tough play, what has he done so wrong?"

Safari Chip looks at Flip confused. Then, he realizes that most of what Jason has done to the Gamblers has stayed out of the media.

"He cheated Rodman out of the Gold Rush contract back in South Africa, going so far as to spike his passion fruit juice with Sleepytime Tea. He bribed Sammie into rejoining the team for the Cup Finals two years ago in the hopes that Sammie would secretly work against us and help the Gold Rush win the Cup in exchange for a spot on their team the following season. The only reason it didn't work was because, as angry as he was, Sammie has a conscience and decided to do the right thing after Jason injured Liten. He concussed Lovey on opening night last year and gave him a complex that turned our gentle teddy bear into the league's number one fighter. What was it you told him? You better get tough or get out?" Safari Chip stares Jason in the eye.

Jason nods.

"He has taken numerous dirty shots at Rodman, Lovey, Liten, Sammie, and Big Chick. Any time they were in his line of sight, they were targets. Then, in last year's Cup Finals, he talked his team into bugging our hotel rooms in Alaska in an effort to get our game plans and use them against us. Game three of the Finals last year was the butt whooping that is was on account of them cheating." Safari Chip turns to Flip. "In fairness to him though, we found out what they did and used the mics to send them bogus information for game four."

Flip is astonished. He can't believe what he's hearing.

"He's wouldn't shake flippers with Rodman at any point in their first season. He's mean, arrogant, dishonest, disruptive, and flat out unethical. And, I'm pretty sure he injured Maulbreath on purpose." Safari Chip turns back to Jason. "Sorry kid. I know I can't prove it, but I call it like I see it, and I saw the film. It looked deliberate to me."

Jason looks away from Safari Chip, an admission of guilt to be sure.

"Look Flip, I appreciate you trying to find us a high-caliber player, and I really admire your devotion to the players you've coached, but we have a legitimate shot at a threepeat, and I'm not sure I'd be willing to risk that with this addition to the roster," Safari Chip says bluntly.

"He's right Coach. I shouldn't have come." Jason stands to leave.

Flip stops Jason from leaving. "Wait." He turns to Safari Chip. "Won't you at least let me tell you what I think he can do for us, and let him tell you why he wants to be a Gambler?"

Safari Chip is skeptical. He's not sure he'll believe anything Jason has to say, but out of respect for Flip, he lets them both talk. "Sure, but I'm going to bring some of the guys in here. I want their opinions on this matter."

"Fair enough," Flip says.

Safari Chip walks to his office door, opens it up, and calls for his four captains, Lovey, Sammie, and Haas.

The seven Gamblers walk to Safari Chip's office wondering what it is that they could have done. Office visits are usually reserved for punishments or reprimands. Safari Chip holds the door open, and they walk in one by one. Inside, they all lock eyes on Jason sitting in the chair in front of Safari Chip's desk. Their tummies flip flop and sink.

"What's he doing here?" Haas asks.

Safari Chip shuts the door. "Well, Flip has been searching for a replacement for Mike on our third line. He comes to us today with one of his former players."

"Him!?" Lovey exclaims.

"Chip, you're not really considering him are you?" Sammie asks.

"It depends on the outcome of this meeting. I brought you guys in here because you're my four captains and the three guys most adversely affected by Jason's past actions. Flip wants a chance to tell us why he thinks Jason will be a good fit for the team, and Jason wants to tell us why he deserves a chance to play with us," Safari Chip answers.

All eyes turn to Flip.

"Chip filled me in on all of the things that Jason has done to not only you guys, but to even his own teammates over the past two and a half seasons, and it's deplorable. I think even Jason would admit that," Flip starts. "But I coached this guy since he was a little penguin chick in peewees. I know it's hard for you guys to see it, but he's not all bad. He's got a competitive drive to win so fierce that sometimes it manifests into violence and treachery, but I believe we can use his desire to win to our advantage. I've seen him play the game the right way, and when he does, he's second to almost none. He'd be a huge upgrade on our third line too." Flip addresses his next comments to Safari Chip and Roman specifically. "We could put him in at center and move L-Rod to the wing, thus fixing our faceoff problems and givr L-Rod the ability to just play. Plus, think of what an advantage it would be to have Jason Vyand on our *third* line!"

The idea appeals to the Gamblers for a second, but their fears of how volatile he can be set back in and the appeal quickly vanishes.

"Jason," Safari Chip opens the door for him to talk next.

As he speaks, Jason looks down at the floor and then up into the eyes of one Gambler at a time. He makes sure to not look any one of them for too long. He also frequently and nervously scratches his head and eyebrows with his flipper. "If there was ever someone who didn't deserve to ask for an opportunity to play with a team, it would be me asking to play for this team. I'm here though because The Coach asked me to come, and fifteen other teams have already said they don't want me. I didn't think there could be any worse feeling than losing the Cup Finals back to back years, but not being able to play hockey at all is worse. I just want back in the game. I want to help a good team get even better. I want to win. I'll do whatever I have to do. I'll play third line. I'll carry everyone's bags. I know *I'm sorry* doesn't even begin to erase all I've done to you guys, but exile from the game has really got my head straight. What I did to you guys was wrong, and I want to make amends."

"What do you guys say?" Flip asks. He's anxious to start working things out between the Gamblers and Jason so they can patch up their differences and get the once promising penguin signed to a Gamblers contract.

"No," Lovey says adamantly and without hesitation.

"Yeah," Haas agrees. "I left the Gold Rush to get away from this guy, his cheating ways, and his bad influence."

Jason's stomach sinks.

Flip turns to the others. "Is it a no for all of you guys? Rodman?"

"I don't know," Rodman says.

"Harlan?" Flip asks.

Harlan shrugs.

"I don't get it," Flip stammers.

"They might need some time to really think it over. I know I do," Safari Chip says.

"Rodman, you know Jason," Flip tries again to get someone on his side.

"That's what worries me," Rodman says.

"You guys won all sorts of championships together growing up," Flip continues.

"I know, but he's changed," Rodman says.

"And he's changed again for the better." Flip turns to Sammie. "Sammie, you got two second chances. If anyone on this team knows about forgiveness and redemption it's you."

Sammie's caught off guard. "Ummm…"

"Let's sleep on it for a while, and we'll give you and Jason an answer after the road trip," Safari Chip says.

"No!" Flip says angrily. "If you guys don't want him to play with us, then be man enough to say it to his face now."

"No," Lovey reiterates his stance.

"Whatever." Flip throws his flippers in the air. He motions for Jason to follow him. "Come on Jason. Let's get out of here. I regret to inform you guys that I will not be able to accompany the team on its upcoming road trip." Flip stops as he passes by Rodman. "I expected more out of you Rodman."

Rodman throws his flippers up now. "What the heck?"

Flip storms out of the locker room.

Rodman turns to Safari Chip.

"Don't worry. He's just upset," Safari Chip says.

"Sorry guys, but I can't play with that guy," Lovey says.

"Me either," Haas says.

"Was that Flip with Jason Vyand?" Beary pokes his head inside the office.

Safari Chip takes a deep breath and sighs. This was not the way he wanted to end the first half of the season.

The Gamblers leave the coach's office and head back into the locker room where Elmira and Mary have come to pick up El Pollos Locos. They volunteered to watch the chickens anytime the Gamblers go out of town. Accompanying Elmira and Mary is one of Mary's friends, a grizzly girl whose white fur has colored specks of dyed fur like sprinkles on a cupcake.

Lovey, the last of the Gamblers to exit the coach's office, walks out huffing and puffing. He's so mad about just seeing Jason in the same locker room that his fur almost turns red. His anger disappears like a Mucho on one of the dogs' plates when he locks eyes with the girl grizzly.

"Who is that?" Lovey asks aloud.

"That's Mary's friend Sprinkles," Beary answers.

Lovey stares at her with his jaw slightly ajar.

Beary takes one of his fingers and closes Lovey's jaw. "She came with Mary and Elmira to pick up El Pollos Locos. But she also came because she's a big Lovey Bara fan."

"A Lovey Bara fan? How could she like that guy? I mean…" Lovey says rather disgusted. "Oh wait. I'm Lovey Bara." He stops again. "She wants to meet him? I mean me."

"Oh brother. Not you too Lovey. Is everyone on this team going girl crazy?" Kane rolls his eyes and walks away.

Beary pushes Lovey over to the girls and introduces him to Sprinkles. The two teddy bears are quite shy at first, but they start talking about hockey and one thing leads to another, and before they know it, they've set up a date for the three Gamblers and the three girls to go out once the Gamblers come back home.

Safari Chip tells his team to put the incident involving Flip out of their minds, but it's easier said than done as everyone is reminded of it each time they look for Flip and he's not with them in the limo, on the plane, at the hotel, or on the bench.

Chapter 19: On The Road Woes

The Gamblers five game road trip pits them against four
of the original teams, and all of the teams they are scheduled to
play, except the Gold Rush, are just outside of the playoff
picture. The Rampage, Lightning, Potatoes, and Fishermen are
the fifth, sixth, seventh, and eighth place teams respectively.

In the visitors' locker room of the Fishermen's arena, the
Gamblers sit around preparing for the game.

"I wonder if we are ever going to get someone to fill the
open spot on the third line," Liten says as he laces up his skates.

"I know. I thought Chip and Flip would have had
someone before the Olympics started," Harlan says.

"Flip looked around, but I think when he found Jason, he
put all his baskets in one egg," Rodman says.

"All his baskets in one egg?" Liten questions.

"Huh?"

"You said all his baskets in one egg."

"Did I?"

"Yeah, You did," Lovey assures him.

"I meant eggs in one basket." Rodman scratches his head
and thinks about it for a second to make sure that sounds right.

"I wish they'd hurry up. Not having a third forward is
really cutting into our playing time," L-Rod says.

"Preach on little brother." Goose high fives L-Rod.

"Yeah," Maverick agrees. "We've been relegated to
mostly penalty kill situations."

"And with the clean game you guys on the first two lines
play, the only time we see the ice is when Kane fights
Undertaker," Moose jokes.

"Well fear no more," Safari Chip's voice calls from the
office provided to him by the Fishermen.

All heads turn to their coach. They see only Safari
Chip's safari hat clad head poking out from behind the door.

"I've found someone who can play on the third line,"
Safari Chip informs them.

"Who?' L-Rod asks.

Safari Chip opens the door all the way and walks outs of the office. He stands before his team a few inches taller and a lot bulkier in a Gamblers jersey, pads, and skates.

"You're going to play on our third line?" Rodman asks.

"Yeah." Safari Chip beams.

"Who's going coach us?" Harlan asks.

"I am. There have been a handful of player/coaches. Now, I'm joining their ranks," Safari Chip explains.

"When was the last time you played?" Kane asks.

"It's been a while," Safari Chip beats around the bush. "But it's like riding a bike. You never forget how to do it."

"How old are you?" Undertaker asks.

Safari Chip grows a bit agitated. "Forty... one."

The Gamblers don't respond, but their faces all show concern.

"Snickers is thirty-eight. He's not that much younger than me," Safari Chip says.

"But I've been playing and conditioning myself every month for the past eighteen seasons," Snickers points out.

"Do you guys not want me to play?" Safari Chip asks.

Rodman can see they've hurt their coach's feelings. "It's not that. I, personally, would be honored to play side by side with you Coach... Errr I mean Chip. We just don't want you to put yourself at risk out there."

"Yes. I think it is a very noble gesture, and it shows how deeply you care for your team that you would lace up at a moment's notice to play with us," Liten agrees.

"We just don't want you getting hurt," Beary says.

"Yeah. We need you Chip," Big Chick agrees.

"I appreciate your concern guys, but I'll be ok," Safari Chip assures them. "And who knows, you might even learn a thing or two from your old coach."

The Gamblers don't think this is the best idea ever, but they don't want to hurt his feelings again, so they force some smiles and welcome their coach into the fold of players.

"You know this puts you into the mix for fire in the hole, don't you?" Apple Jack warns his coach.

Safari Chip produces a water balloon from behind his back and pops it over Apple Jack's head. "Oh, I know."

Apple Jack shakes off his wet head while the rest of the guys have a laugh.

"So I guess there's just one thing left to say," Safari Chip says.

"What's that?" Rodman asks.

"GAME TIME!"

Safari Chip rushes for the door in his Gamblers jersey with the number ten and just the name Chip on the back. He leads his team down the tunnel with the speed of a spring chicken. His energetic leadership onto the ice to do some warm up laps around the net impresses his players.

"You ready Chip?" Rodman asks as warm ups wrap up.

"I feel like I never left the game," Safari Chip responds.

Rodman smiles. "Just make sure you stretch enough. We don't want you pulling a muscle or anything."

"Don't worry about this monkey." Safari Chip points to himself.

The referees call for the starters to head to center ice for the American and Canadian National Anthems. After the anthems, the Fishermen's coach, a chinchilla named Felix, looks over at the Gamblers bench and sees Safari Chip in a uniform and skates. He calls to the Gamblers bench. "What's this?"

At first, Safari Chip pays him no attention. He barely hears the chinchilla's words, and he doesn't think they're directed at him anyway.

"Don't tell me *you're* playing Chip," Felix calls louder.

Safari Chip and several Gamblers turn and look.

"Yeah, I'm playing," Safari Chip says.

Felix laughs and scoffs at the notion. "A little past your prime aren't you?"

"I'm still better than half of the players on your team," Safari Chip shoots.

"You should be. You have a hundred more years worth of experience," Felix pokes fun.

"Oh, why don't you just shut up you wannabe monkey?" Sammie steps up for his coach.

"No need for name calling," Safari Chip quiets Sammie.

Felix smiles smugly at Sammie being scolded.

"After all, Felix still hasn't gotten over the fact that when we were players twelve years ago, we both made it to just one Cup Finals and my team beat his team. You see, Felix has never won a ring as a player or a coach," Safari Chip pokes back.

Felix fumes.

"And now, I have three rings," Safari Chip finishes.

While the two coaches take potshots at each other, the game gets underway.

Rodman loses the first faceoff, and the Gamblers head out on defense. The Fishermen set up and get off a few shots. Nothing gets past Harlan. He even catches the puck in his glove on the Fishermen's third and final shot of the series. Play stops and the teams switch lines.

Safari Chip finds himself waiting as impatiently to get onto the ice as El Pollos Locos. When the first line comes to the bench for a line change, he almost calls the second line back to the bench to let the third line go before them so he can get out there, but he composes himself, reminds himself that he's the coach and has to do what's right for the team.

With the second line on the ice, Big Chick wins his faceoff, but an errant pass sends the puck back to the Fishermen before the play ever makes it out of the Gamblers defensive zone. Harlan is forced to make a couple more quick saves, and he again succeeds in keeping the puck out of the net.

Sammie applies tremendous pressure on the Fishermen player he defends and eventually jars the puck away. He passes it ahead to Big Chick and the Gamblers finally go on offense. Big Chick dumps the puck into the Gamblers offensive zone. Beary and Snickers chase after it behind the net. They are followed closely by two Fishermen. The other three players on each team head for the bench for a line change that sends L-Rod, Goose, and Maverick onto the ice for the Gamblers.

Safari Chip chomps at the bit to get out there.

Maverick joins Snickers and Beary in the fight for the puck behind the net. His emergence allows Snickers to race for a line change with Moose.

L-Rod rushes to the traffic jam behind the net, squeezes into the middle of it, and kicks the puck out. Everyone from both teams, except Beary, give chase.

Beary races to switch with Safari Chip. As he nears the bench, someone flicks the puck out of the new mass of players that have swarmed upon it, and the puck glides all the way past center ice and heads for the Gamblers offensive zone.

Beary hits the Gamblers wall, and Safari Chip jumps over. His eyes are as big as the moon at the sight of the puck all by itself nearing the Fishermen's net. He knows without looking that nine other players are racing up behind him. Ahead of him, he sees the Fishermen's goalie skating out to tap the puck out of the zone, so Safari Chip turns on his jets to get to if first.

The goalie sees he's going to lose the race and retreats back to defend the net.

Safari Chip has the Fishermen right where he wants them. Scoring this goal should be easy. So it surprises him when he finds himself suddenly falling face first to the ice just before he reaches the loose puck. He hits with a thud, drops his stick, and struggles to regain his breath as the ice knocks his wind out.

All of the Gamblers on the bench stand up concerned for the wellbeing of their coach.

Safari Chip regains his breath, but he feels a new pain emerge. His quadriceps feel as though someone has grabbed ahold of them in the middle, squeezed them as tight as they can, twisted them, and then pulled them in opposite directions.

A referee checks on Safari Chip, and he assures the referee that he's not hurt too bad. Safari Chip attempts to stand up. He stumbles once and falls to the ice, but on the second try he makes it up. He can barely walk, much less skate, and he heads for the bench. He holds up his hand and motions for Rodman to take his spot.

Rodman waits impatiently for Safari Chip to make it to the bench. He can see his team struggling as the Fishermen have regained the puck and are back on offense. The Gamblers, without Safari Chip, are essentially on a penalty kill. Finally, Safari Chip reaches the bench and Rodman is able to jump over the wall. As soon as he hits the ice though, the Fishermen push the puck past Harlan and go up 1-0.

The Gamblers go on to lose 3-1. Safari Chip finishes the game, despite the pleas of his players to take it easy. They admire his determination, but he struggles to makes it to the tunnel. Once inside, he falls to his knees and allows the dogs to carry him to the locker room.

Safari Chip sits out the second game of the road trip, another loss, this time to Buck Wild's Seattle Rampage. From Seattle, the Gamblers head to Stockton to play the Lightning. Safari Chip returns to the lineup, still suffering from his muscle pull, and though he doesn't reinjure the muscle, all the heavy skating takes its toll on him and his quads feel just as bad as they did the night after the game against the Fishermen. The Gamblers lose to the Lightning 3-2 in overtime.

The fourth game of the road trip pits the Gamblers against the Idaho Potatoes. Because of his quad pull, Safari Chip is forced to bench himself for the second time in three games. He's frustrated for himself and also for his team. Not only is he not able to play, but he feels like he's letting his players down. His frustrations grow when the Gamblers blow a three goal lead in the third period and lose 4-3 for their fourth straight loss.

With each loss, another team or several teams pull closer to the Gamblers in the standings. In fact, the Rampage overtake the Gamblers for fourth place, dropping the Gamblers one point out of the playoff picture.

The final game of the road trip is against the Gold Rush.

Safari Chip steps out of his office and calls upon his team. "Gather 'round everyone."

The Gamblers circle around their coach.

"I've got something to say. I got a little carried away thinking I could go out there and lace up my skates again. I'm not much help with these bum legs, and I feel I've let you down, so I'm going to alert the press before tonight's game that I am once again officially retired," Safari Chip informs his players.

To his surprise, there's a collective groan.

"Oh come one now. You guys know I haven't been any help out there."

"But, you have been hurt," Liten says.

"Yeah," Big Chick agrees.

"If anyone has let anyone down, it's us who've let you down," Rodman says.

"How do you figure that?" Safari Chip is astounded.

"We've lost four games in a row and haven't been playing our best hockey," Rodman says.

"But we are ready to start doing just that," Liten adds.

"Start doing what?" Safari Chip is confused.

"Playing our best hockey," Liten clarifies.

"And if it's cool, we'd like you to delay your retirement at least until you find a replacement for yourself," Sammie says.

"Yeah. Let us at least get you a goal." Lovey smiles.

"One of the reasons you guys haven't been playing your best is because I've been more focused on what I'm going to be doing in the games instead of instructing you guys on what you should be doing. At this point in my career, I think I'm best suited as your coach, not your teammate," Safari Chip argues.

"Come one Chip. Play at least one more game with us. We want to win at least one game with you as our teammate, and we promise we'll win tonight," Rodman argues.

"How can you promise that?" Safari Chip is skeptical.

"Because I'm Rodman T. Penguin, and these are the Gamblers. We can beat anyone, anytime, anywhere, and we just happen to be playing the team we like beating the most."

"It would take a miracle to beat us tonight," Liten agrees.

Everyone can see Safari Chip thinking about it.

"Come on Chip. One more game," Beary says.

"One more game," Harlan repeats.

"Come one Chip," Apple Jack whispers.

"One more game old man," Snickers jokes.

From here, a *one more game Chip* chant breaks out.

"Alright!" Safari Chip yells. "One more game."

The Gamblers hoot, holler, squawk, squeal, nay, and bark.

The guys talk Safari Chip into mixing up the lineups for this game. They have Safari Chip put himself on the first line so he can be out there with the best defensive line in the league in Undertaker and Apple Jack and also with the two highest scoring players in the IAHL over the past two and a half seasons in Rodman and Lovey. Meanwhile, Liten moves to the third line to add some leadership and guidance to some guys who are usually left to fend for themselves.

Early in the game, the Gold Rush, who are playing without Jason and Maulbreath for the first time in over two seasons, get a soft goal when a loose puck squibs behind Harlan, and he accidently kicks it into the net while he attempts to find it.

Safari Chip almost takes himself out of the game right then and there, but Rodman and a few others remind him that it's just one goal and that they have plenty of time to catch up.

At the end of the first period, the score is 2-0 in favor of the Gold Rush. After two periods, the score is 3-0.

Safari Chip gathers his team around him in the locker room during the second intermission. "Look here guys. I know you don't want me to come out of the game, but I am. I'll serve you a lot better as your coach and not your teammate."

His comments are met by unanimous disapproval.

"Awww come on now Chip!" Lovey argues.

"You said you'd give us one more game," Goose says.

"I know, and I hate to disappoint you guys, but my legs are killing me, we're losing again, and the bottom line is that I'm just not helping you guys out there."

"If we're going to lose this game, and mind you we won't, at least let us get you an assist or a goal," Rodman begs.

"Yeah. Let us get you a point," Big Chick agrees.

"Please?" Undertaker begs.

"Please?" Lovey repeats.

"A point for me is not nearly as important as a win right now. I want you guys focused on winning," Safari Chip argues.

Apple Jack waves an angry paw at his coach. "Whatever. We see how it is."

Safari Chip's eyes go wide with shock. He looks around the room and sees all his players staring back at him with angry or disappointed eyes. It hurts to know he's letting them down, so, with a sigh, he says, "Fine. I'll give it one more period."

The room erupts with the usual Gamblers cheering.

"But!" Safari Chip says with a stern tone.

All the cheering stops, and everyone gives him their undivided attention.

"If I play, we better win," Safari Chip demands.

The Gamblers cheer again, and then go about their business re-lacing their skates, re-taping their sticks, and tending to the normal cuts and scrapes.

Intermission ends, and they head back to the ice with as much determination as they've brought to their last two Cup Finals. They know it's not going to be easy. The Gold Rush are playing better hockey without their two biggest antagonists. It's the opinion of Safari Chip, Rodman, and many of the others that the reason for the Gold Rush's good game is because they're actually playing hockey instead of trying every underhanded tactic know to animal-kind.

The third period starts with a faceoff loss by Rodman. Both teams head towards Harlan, but everyone hits the breaks pronto when Safari Chip steals the puck from the stick of Iggy and shoots it ahead to Rodman.

Rodman and Lovey race side by side towards Vander Gates. They have Metz and Packer to contend with, and the cats apply excellent pressure, forcing Rodman and Lovey to move away from each other. Almost as though they know what the other is thinking, Rodman hits the breaks and comes to a dead stop. Meanwhile, Lovey crisscrosses around Metz towards Packer to Rodman's side of the ice. Rodman taps the puck ahead to him, and Lovey handles it on his stick.

The teddy bear continues racing at the net but knows his path is blocked by Packer. He also knows that Metz is chasing him from behind. Out of the very corner of his eye, as he's checking on Metz, Lovey sees Rodman speeding towards the net on the other side of the ice, so he grinds to a spinning halt as he passes by the back of the net and fires the puck to Rodman, who completes a modified version of their crisscross play and scores.

For all his efforts, Lovey gets run over by Metz. The hit is pretty violent and dirty with Metz's stick raised high and near the middle of Lovey's neck. Lovey sees a quick flash of red light behind his eye lids as he falls to the ice seeing only black after the burst of red. He jumps up quick though and goes to fight the house cat, but Packer holds him back.

Metz sees Lovey lunge at him even in Packer's grasp. He takes a cheap shot at the restrained teddy bear, slapping him across the snout. He laughs, but his laughter is cut short by Safari Chip, who tackles him to the ice from behind and pummels him with rights and lefts about the head.

Packer lets go of Lovey so he can go after Safari Chip, but as soon as he lets go of Lovey, the teddy bear turns around and pops him in the nose.

Referees race to break up both fights. The Lovey/Packer fight is easier to break up, but it takes both of the other referees to pry Safari Chip off of Metz. Once both fights are broken up, the referees assess penalties and send both of the Gold Rush cats, Lovey, and Safari Chip to the penalty box for five minutes.

Lovey takes a seat on the penalty box bench and looks out onto the ice to watch the game. Safari Chip sits down next him and looks at Lovey. Lovey is too into the game to notice his coach's staring, so Safari Chip makes a fist and slugs his teddy bear on the upper arm. Lovey looks over, wondering what he did to deserve the hit. Safari Chip holds out some knuckles. The teddy bear smiles, and they exchange a knuckle bash.

"Nice steal," Lovey says.

"Did I get an assist on that goal?" Safari Chip asks.

"Heck yes. We both did. But you got an extra one for assisting me in that butt whopping of Metz and Packer too."

Safari Chip chuckles. He and Lovey look over to the Gold Rush's penalty box and see Metz and Packer looking back at them. The two Gamblers spit their tongues out at the cats.

The referees also tag Metz with a late hit penalty, and his added infraction puts the Gamblers on a power play. Halfway through the power play, Big Chick hits one of his pinpoint precision shots, getting the puck through a tiny hole between Vander Gates skates and the pole. The goal gets the Gamblers to within one goal of a tie with half a period to play.

A little less than five minutes later, the Gamblers tie the game on a breakaway goal by L-Rod. His goal fills the entire arena with an overwhelming feeling of a momentum change. The play of the Gold Rush appears to change from that of a team trying to win to that of a team trying not to lose. They play back on their heels and their skittish play causes them to fumble the puck, have passes picked off, and whiff on a couple of shots.

With just seconds to go in regulation, the Gamblers second line rushes to the bench for a line change. So many players try to change spots at the same time that many of them bump into each other.

"Watch out Kane!" Undertaker says as they bump chests trying to switch spots.

"You watch out Morty," Kane barks and takes his spot on the bench.

Ahead of him, the Gold Rush have a three on two against Apple Jack and Lovey, so instead of arguing Kane any more, Undertaker races to get into the play.

Iggy passes the puck sideways to Auggie Froggie as they cross the blue line, and Auggie immediately taps it sideways in the same direction to Rapture near the boards.

Lovey charges with his stick held out in front to try and disrupt Rapture's shot, but Rapture doesn't shoot. He sends the puck back to Auggie, who fires a one timer at the net.

Harlan gets some help from Apple Jack, who whacks the puck out of the air away from the net with his stick like a baseball player swinging his bat. The puck flies past all three Gold Rush players on offense and the oncoming Rodman, Undertaker, Packer, and Metz. Everyone on the ice grinds to a halt and turns to chase the puck.

The winner of the race is the last Gambler to get on the ice for their line change, Safari Chip. He grabs the puck with his stick and pulls it in close as Metz flies by and tries to take it from him. Safari Chip makes a move with his still very sore and painful legs towards Vander Gates.

Packer reaches Safari Chip next. The cat bumps him and hits him with the end of his stick, but Safari Chip shrugs it off. He keeps pushing, forcing his legs to move him forward despite the excruciating pain his muscles cause him with each stride.

Metz spins around after passing Safari Chip, turns his focus back to the monkey, and charges back at him. He dives onto his belly in the hopes that he can cause Safari Chip to stumble and fall, even if it means getting a tripping penalty.

Safari Chip knows that his legs won't hold him up much longer. For him, it's now or never. So he musters up all his strength, flips the puck over Metz's sliding body, manages to jump over the cat, and lands wobbly-kneed on the ice. He gathers the puck and fires it just before his legs totally give out.

Everyone holds their breath as the puck glides across the ice. It looks like a shot that will be blocked easily as it heads directly at Vander Gates' body. The alligator drops to his knees., but as he does, the puck seems to pick up speed. It rushes right through the five hole and rattles around the back of the net.

The goal lights go off, the crowd groans, and Safari Chip falls down.

"Chip! You did it!" Rodman yells as he dives on top of his coach.

"That was awesome!" Lovey joins the celebration.

"So much for not being any help," Apple Jack dives onto the pile.

Undertaker jumps on top of pile of Gamblers. "CHIP!!!"

At the bottom of the pile Safari Chip's face keeps going back and forth from a smile to a wince. He thanks his players for their commendations and then says, "Guys, do me one favor?"

"What's that?" Rodman asks.

"Get off me! You're breaking my legs!" Safari Chip squeals.

The Gamblers hop off of their injured coach as fast as they can. They all offer him a flipper or a paw to help him up.

"Are you ok?" Rodman asks.

"No. I can't stand up."

"Someone, go get Chip," Lovey says.

The other three Gamblers look at Lovey perplexed.

"What?" Lovey asks.

Apple Jack points to Safari Chip.

"Oh yeah." Lovey slaps his own forehead. "I was just thinking that it's usually Chip who helps us off the ice when we get hurt."

"Too bad Flip's not here," Undertaker says.

"Yeah," Rodman agrees. "I'll go get Big Chick. He'll be able to scoop Chip up and get him to the locker room no problem."

"No!" Safari Chip orders.

"No?" Rodman asks.

"Well, you can go get Big Chick, but have him take me to the bench. I want to be out here for the end of this game."

Rodman skates towards the bench and hollers for Big Chick to come onto the ice.

The head referee skates over to the Gamblers standing around Safari Chip. "Is he ok?"

"I'll be fine," Safari Chip says.

Rodman arrives back to the scene with Big Chick. The chicken scoops his coach off the ice like a little girl picking up a doll and brings him to the bench.

Once the other two Gamblers are off the ice, their first line, with Liten in Safari Chip's spot, go and take the final faceoff of the game. They polish off the final twenty-four seconds by scoring two empty net goals, one by Rodman, and another by Liten.

The Gamblers win 6-3. This time they're the team that steals a win after their opponents drop a three goal lead in the final period. High fives, hugs, and congratulations go round from all the Gamblers to Safari Chip after the game and all the way home. Their only win of the road trip, in the fashion that they won it, is worth all the struggles they went through to get it. Safari Chip reminds them that they have dropped back into fifth place with all their losses and that they have a lot of work to do once the Olympics conclude in order to ensure themselves of a threepeat.

Chapter 20: The Olympics

The Gamblers fly into Calgary, Albert, Canada for the Olympics. They ride a bus to their hotel together, comparing who will play who when and if they advance. The way the Olympics are set up, each of thirty-two teams plays another of the thirty-two teams in a single elimination tournament. The brackets are set based on how well each country fared in the previous Olympics. As it turns out, no Gambler is set to square off against another Gambler in the first round.

Upon their arrival to the hotel in which all the Olympic hockey players are staying, the different sets of players say an awkward and anxious goodbye to one another as they set off to meet their countrymen and new teammates.

For the most part, the American and Canadian players know the guys they'll be playing with from the IAHL, and the Americans even get the bonus of having Safari Chip as their coach.

Rodman and L-Rod are pretty familiar with many of the players on the South African team, whether they played with or watched them in the South African Hockey League. Playing with his old Chill teammates is going to be a blast for Rodman.

Other Gamblers, with fewer IAHL players and no Las Vegas teammates on their team, find it harder to adjust. Liten is surrounded by cats on the German team. Sammie Lou is ostracized by many of the Australian players as Sammie Two has already arrived and spewed a bunch of rumors that his cousin is a hotshot Gambler who is only interested in padding his own stats. Beary finds out from his coach that China has no goaltender and that he is to be in net for the entire Olympics. This is a fact that does not sit well with him. He hasn't played in net for over eight months, and he was not anticipating going back in for the Olympics. He doesn't even have his own pads. Under a lot of duress, and the threat of being kicked off the team if he does not cooperate, Beary gives in and agrees to play goalie. As for Harlan, well, the Galapagos Island team is a complete mess.

Once the initial team meetings disband, much to the delight of many of the Gamblers, they're eager to get back to hanging out with the guys they know. They all meet up in the hotel lobby to go to dinner together. Their numbers grow as some of their Olympic teammates, who are good friends when they visit Las Vegas with their IAHL teams, join them. Baylor Adams, a raccoon from the Californians, Gavin Christopher, a flamingo from the Lightning, Ross Ambrose and Brad Fryar, a hedgehog and a peacock from the Cacti, Ed Norton, the aardvark from the Rampage, El Pollos Locos, Dolvy, Spoedige, Pikkewyn, and even Iggy and Rapture all join the Gamblers.

Dinner is fun. The players have lots of laughs and talk some friendly smack to one another about who's going to beat who and who's going to win gold.

"I hear you're playing goalie," Harlan says to Beary.

"Yeah." Beary sounds bummed.

"That's cool," says Haas, who has one ear dyed with red, white, and blue stripes and his other ear dyed with the Olympic rings for the games.

"I guess," Beary mumbles.

"What's the matter?" Haas asks.

"I just feel I would be more help on offense. Offense isn't something my country is known for in hockey, and I could change that." Beary fiddles with the food on his plate.

"So, why don't you just tell your coach you'd rather play on the wing?" Harlan asks.

"On my team, you don't tell the coach what you'd rather do," Beary explains.

There's a brief silence. The other goalies don't know what to tell Beary.

"No matter. I'll play for them this year, because I want to play for my country, and I want to play in the Olympics, but next year I'll become an official U.S. citizen, and I'll play for America in four years," Beary says.

Haas' eyebrows shoot up. "That's harsh."

Beary just shrugs.

"Who do you guys have with you from the IAHL?" Goose asks Maverick and Moose.

"Man, we're so deep in Five Ohhh! and Gold Rush players on our team," Maverick says.

"Yeah. It totally sucks playing with the enemy," Moose grumbles.

Goose laughs his beak off.

"How many of those guys are Canadian?" Rodman asks.

"Geez, let me think. There's Ox, Dislike, Hoss, Stunner, Maulbreath, Smooth, Jimmy Peanuts, Metz, and Packer." Moose counts out all the players from the Gamblers two biggest rivals.

"And we've got Bing and Derlargo on our team," Maverick adds from their list of foes.

Goose continues laughing until Maverick pushes his friend and the two squabble a bit before Moose separates them.

"Anyone else got pros on their team?" Rodman asks.

"I've got my cousin and all four Sherman brothers," Sammie says.

"That's not a bad lineup," Safari Chip notes.

"Yeah, but our goalie is some young kid from Sydney that no one has ever heard of. He's only even played one full season in college." Sammie sounds less than enthused.

"You never know what you're going to get though. Remember that. No one thought we'd do anything a few years ago, and look at us now," Safari Chip reminds Sammie.

"True," Sammie agrees.

"I have a few guys from the league, but mostly I am surrounded by cats. House cats, alley cats, Siamese cats, black cats, tigers, mountain lions, panthers, cheetahs, the list goes on and on. It is absolutely ridiculous," Liten gripes.

The Gamblers and their friends laugh at this one.

"I have not one IAHL player," Harlan informs his buddies.

"Adios Galapagos!" Apple Jack jokes.

Harlan frowns, but the rest of the Gamblers and their friends laugh hard at their white dog's joke.

"Ummm, I'm on your team." Iggy raises his hand.

"They asked if there were any professional players," Rapture jokes with his Gold Rush cohort.

Iggy punches Rapture in the wing.

"Oops. Sorry about that Iggy," Harlan says.

Liten turns to Beary. "What about you?"

"I've just got me and Greg," Beary says.

Apple Jack goes to make the same joke, but Beary beats him to it.

"I know. Adios China," Beary says.

"I was going to say sayonara," Apple Jack says.

"That's Japanese," Beary informs him.

"Huh. Who knew?"

"I did." Snickers raises his paw.

"I did too," Kane says.

"Well, we've got the Chill," L-Rod boasts.

"Are they letting Jason play?" Safari Chip asks Rodman.

"Nope. He didn't make the roster," Rodman answers.

"Hmmm," is Safari Chip's only response.

"Chill, Shmill. We've got fifty percent of the best team ever." Lovey puts his arms around Big Chick and Snickers. "The Las Vegas Gamblers."

The arguing about who will bring home gold continues throughout the night. After dinner, the guys do some sightseeing and make sure not to miss the lighting of the Olympic torch. Watching the flames grow around the circle of the massive fire pit gives many of the players and the other Olympians goosebumps. Its lighting signifies to all of the competitors that the games have begun.

With the light lit, the night getting late, and his team playing in one of the early games, Safari Chip shouts to his players, "Ok my players, my Olympic players, curfew is now in effect. Let's hit the hay." He turns to his non-American Gamblers. "You guys can stay out all night if you want."

"Ohhh! Look at this guy with the jokes," Rodman laughs.

Everyone heads back to the hotel to get a good night's rest. None of them want to be lumped into the one and done category.

*

The first day of the Olympics sees all of the Gamblers playing against a team without other Gamblers. Better yet for the Gamblers, all of their countries win in the first round and advance to the second round, including Harlan and the Galapagos Islands and Beary and China. Both goalies turn in stellar performances, shutting out their opponents and winning by a score of 1-0. Most animals watching the games consider their wins to be upsets as they are seeded as the twentieth and twenty-first teams in the field of thirty-two, and they take out the higher seeded Greenland and Spain. There are two other upsets in the first round as the lower seeded Portugal and Curacao eliminate the higher seeded Japan and Italy. All of the upsets are grouped close together in terms of the rankings and are all near the middle of the pack where teams are more evenly matched.

The Gamblers celebrate all of their first round successes with a party in one of the hotel ballrooms. Not all of their Olympic teammates join them, but the majority of them do, as well as do many of their Olympic opponents, Olympians from other sports, and some other random animals they've never met.

On the fourth day of the Olympics, the second round begins. This round makes it so that at least one Gambler will be eliminated from their quest for an Olympic medal as the Galapagos Islands are pitted against number two, Canada. The rest of the Gamblers still find themselves facing teams with none of their Las Vegas teammates.

Harlan plays his heart out in the game against Canada. His players are no match for the standouts of the Canadian team, which is riddled with IAHL players. If it weren't for Harlan's stellar goal tending, the score would be 20-0 in favor of Canada. Anyone watching can tell immediately that the fairness of the game is about as fair as the Las Vegas Gamblers playing against St. Mary's School for Orphaned Girls.

However, at the end of regulation, the score is 0-0. The Galapagos team, which is mostly made up of birds and Harlan and Iggy, heads to its bench for some last minute instructions before overtime. The team's coach devises a plan, goes over it with everyone and sends out his best six players, Harlan, Iggy, a Galapagos Penguin named Alfredo, a Flightless Cormorant called Jose, a Waved Albatross named Jarvin, and a Great Frigatebird named Pablo Ortiz.On the flipside, the Canadians send out their best six guys as well, Max Derlargo, Dislike, Lance Maulbreath, Smooth Jackson, and Maverick with Marc Magz in net. Even with their best players on the ice, the Galapagos team is totally mismatched against the Canadians.

The puck drops and Derlargo wins easily. The Canadians get what seems to be a hundred shots off at Harlan before he's finally able to clear the puck out of the zone. He has to do it himself though as his teammates are virtually no help. They mostly look confused and discombobulated.

The Canadians regain control of the puck and come back into their offensive zone with little effort. Unfortunately for the Galapagos team, they're unable to make a line change. The Canadians get off several more shots, and they make some changes on the ice while doing so. One by one Maverick, Smooth, Dislike, Maulbreath, and Derlargo make way for Ox, Metz, Packer, Bing, and Shaun Cary of the Cacti.

The Canadians continue bombarding Harlan with shots. They know they're in control, but their frustrations mount as they can't get anything past him. Still, despite Harlan's sixty-seven blocked shots, the Canadians play arrogantly, like they have nothing to lose.

The Galapagos team, except for Iggy, having played for almost six minutes without a line change, all race for the bench at one time, leaving Harlan and Iggy to fend of five top IAHLers.

Miraculously, somehow, Harlan is able to spin and dive, and block the puck from getting past him into the net throughout the onslaught. At one point, he dives for the puck and a bunch of players, mostly Canadians, dive in on top of him.

It appears Harlan gets there first, and everyone is sure the whistles will be blown to stop the play when the puck disappears. But, out of the bottom of the pile, where no one but the referees can see, the puck pops out.

"Where is it?" Harlan shouts to Iggy.

"I don't know." Iggy pops his head up to look. He spots it before anyone else, and he tries to pry himself out of the mess of players without drawing any attention.

Magz sees the puck from the other end of the ice as well. He screams for his players to get it before Iggy can, but they can't hear the owl over the noise of the crowd.

"Get off me," Metz threatens one of his own teammates.

"Wait shhh," Ox says to his Canadian brethren.

"What? I don't hear anything," Packer says.

"Shhh" Ox shushes the other house cat.

The faint sound of Magz's stick banging on the ice to get their attention can be heard.

Ox peeks out of the pile and back towards their goalie. He sees Iggy racing towards the puck with every last ounce of energy he has left. He stands up and points his stick at Iggy. "GET HIM!"

The Canadians all jump to their skates and race to get the Marine Iguana.

Iggy skates as fast as he can to ensure he wins the breakaway, but he's dead on his feet. He knows the Canadians will catch him. He can feel them on his tail as he crosses the blue line. Each stride is slower than the last, and he feels as though he's making no progress. It's a miracle no one interrupts him when he rears back his stick. For him, it's now or never. If he doesn't score, he's pretty sure the game will be over in a matter of seconds, and it won't be team Galapagos moving on.

Ox is the first one to approach Iggy. He reaches out his stick, hooks it around Iggy, and pulls him with an illegal hook just as the iguana fires. Ironically, Magz had Iggy's shot blocked, but because of the motion of the hook, Iggy's shot goes in the complete opposite direction. It takes Magz by surprise and goes past him into the back of the net.

The second biggest possible upset in the Olympics has just happened. The Canadians, who win almost every four years, are ousted by a little known team from the Galapagos Islands with just two IAHL players. The Galapagos team goes nuts, charging the ice as though they've already won gold.

The crowd goes bonkers, and the world goes crazy. The Galapagos Island team becomes the talk of the world. They become the Cinderella team that everyone is rooting for.

Maverick and Moose give Harlan the most props after the game for his outstanding stay in the net. Losing is no fun, but they're glad if they have to that they lose to Harlan.

Another Cinderella team turns out to be team China, who pulls off a similar upset in the final game of the day when they knock out number three Russia. Beary pulls off another shutout as well, winning his game 1-0 in overtime just like his best buddy Harlan. The media starts talking about how great it would be if these two goalies, teammates in the IAHL, could lead their countries to the finals against one another.

Sandwiched in between the two mind blowing shutouts are the other Gamblers games. Lovey leads the number one seeded USA over Curacao with a hat trick in their 8-1 win. Liten factors into number six, Germany's 3-2 win over Greece with an assist on the team's first goal. Germany was down 2-0 early, but they scored a goal in each of the three periods, trying the game in the second and going ahead for good halfway through the third. Rodman and L-Rod become the first father/son duo in Olympic history to score a goal and an assist on the same play. L-Rod scores on an assist from Rodman in the second, and then in the third, Rodman scores on an assist from L-Rod. Even though they're ranked seventh and they take on an opponent who is supposed to be relatively equal to them, the South African team crushes the tenth seeded Czechoslovakian team 7-3. Sammie Lou, doesn't factor into his team's 4-0 win, but his ninth seeded

Australian team completes a minor upset over eighth seeded France. Also advancing in major upsets are Iceland and Portugal, who eliminate Switzerland and Sweden.

The Gamblers and their friends celebrate with music, dancing, and food in the ballroom yet again. Even Maverick and Moose, despite being eliminated, party it up. They're just happy to have been a part of such an awesome game.

Two days later, the Olympics continue on with most of the Gamblers loaded up on the favorite's side of the bracket, and the two underdog Gamblers having to go up against the best two remaining teams.

In the first game of the day, Beary and China are pitted against Liten and Germany. The intensity of the match is like that of an IAHL Cup finals game. Both teams hit each other hard and fight nonstop for control of the puck and the game. The Germans play like the better team, but as he's done throughout the first two rounds, Beary plays like a brick wall. He stops everything the Germans throw at him, including three very close shots by his buddy Liten. In the end, it's an early goal in the second period scored by Greg that is the difference in the game. Beary completes his third shutout in three games, beating another team he was supposed to lose to by a score of 1-0. The best part about this win though, is that Beary has lead his team into the final four, and three of those four teams win medals.

A photographer captures a great photo of Liten enthusiastically congratulating his Gamblers teammate after the game. The photo will go on to be an Olympic icon, symbolizing the true meaning of the Olympics.

The second game of the day sees Sammie Lou and the Australians destroy Iceland 9-4. Sammie Lou finally has a breakout game, scoring a hat trick and overtaking his cousin for first place on the team in goals scored and overall points as he adds two assists for five total points. It's a fact that doesn't sit well with Sammie Two.

The third game of the day pits Rodman, L-Rod, and the rest of the South Africans against upstart Portugal. The penguins are determined to not be the third in a line of teams upset by the eighteenth seeded team. From the get go, the South African team treats the game as though they are the underdogs. Dolvy gives up some early goals, putting his team in an 0-2 hole in the first five minutes, but he calms down, and eventually his team gives him a reason to relax. They tie the game on goals by Spoedige and Rugby. The game remains tied after two, but in the third, the South African team erupts for three goals in four minutes. The final score is 5-2, and South Africa advances to the medal round.

After their game, Rodman, L-Rod, and many of the players from both teams that just played rush to get showered and dressed. No one wants to miss seeing if Harlan, Iggy and team Galapagos can stand up to another test when they take on Lovey, the rest of the Gamblers, and team USA.

Patients for the day's final game to begin are at an all-time premium. No one can sit still as they wait for the game to begin. Rodman and the other non-American Gamblers feel torn. They want both teams to win since they have good buddies on each side, but they kind of want to see Harlan win a little more since he's such an underdog and may never get a chance to go this deep into the tournament again. For most, disappointment quickly overrides their excitement as team USA takes a three goal lead, scoring early and often. After the 3-0 start for team USA, Harlan finds his goalie game again. The turtle blocks their next thirty shots, but his players can't get anything past his Gamblers counterpart on the other end of the ice, Jack Haas. Harlan leaves the net towards the end of the third period for an extra attacker, and the Americans score an empty net goal. Team U.S.A. wins 4-0. The crowd and the Americans give team Galapagos a standing ovation. The American Gamblers even lift Harlan onto their shoulders and do a lap with him around the ice.

There's no party in the ballroom after round three. Four of the seven teams with Gamblers on them remain, and three of them will receive a medal of some sort. There's only one day between round three and four, and many of the Gamblers have to practice the next day. Parties can wait.

The day between the rounds drags on and on for the Olympians. All they want to do is get back onto the ice and play.

Finally, the day arrives. The first game of the day is between number one USA and the tournament's second Cinderella team, number twenty, China. The question on everyone's mind is, can Beary complete another shutout and advance his team to the gold medal round.

As it seems to have gone in every round previous, Beary does indeed shutdown his opponents, only to have his team score no goals for him. In the final seconds of the game, just when it looks like overtime is eminent, Goose grabs a loose puck, passes it out to Snickers, and he gets it to Baylor Adams, who has managed to break free from everyone on the weak side of the net. The raccoon one times the puck at the net. Beary looks at the puck as it passes his head. He throws his glove up and gets a piece of it with the tip of the glove, but it gets passed him and goes into the net. Seconds later, another Cinderella dream is squashed as the USA beats China 1-0.

Just as they did for Harlan, the Americans skate their panda around on their shoulders for a lap around the ice. The poor guy, playing a position he wasn't prepared to play, took a team with practically no talent and upset three teams on their way to the final four while giving up one goal in four games. For Beary to go out that way, it seems almost unfair.

Harlan greets Beary in the tunnel as the teams come off the ice. "You're gold man. I don't care what medal you win, or if you win a medal at all. You're a dang good hockey player."

"You are too man. You did just as well," Beary says.

Harlan grabs Beary around the neck and puts him in a playful headlock. He gives the panda noogies. "But you better promise me you'll win bronze!"

"Alright!" Beary pushes Harlan away to free himself from the turtle's grasp. "I promise!"

Beary and the American Gamblers rush to get ready to watch the game between Rodman, L-Rod and South Africa against Sammie Lou and Australia. It's picked by all the experts to be one of the best games of the Olympics. With all of the Cinderella teams out of action now, most everyone is rooting for South Africa to play the USA in the Finals. South Africa, with Rodman, probably should have been seeded number one or two. They would make for the best game against team USA.

The South African/Australian game begins with a lot of defense. No one scores in the first period. Rodman scores the game's first goal in the sixth minute of the second period, but it's answered immediately by Sammie Lou. He shoots Rodman an index finger and waves it at his buddy, telling him you won't be eliminating us just yet. Rodman laughs and points back at his friend and temporary foe.

In the third period the Australians go up late on a goal from Sammie Two, who is determined to get back to within a point of Sammie Lou on the team's top point list. Although it worked out well for his team, the bad part is that is Sammie Two, not Sammie Lou, who is the one playing for his own personal record rather than for the team's record.

Rodman scores again in the third and waves his flipper at Sammie Lou the same way he waved at Rodman earlier. This time, it's Sammie's turn to laugh and point back.

The game ends 2-2 and heads to overtime. The Australians have a great scoring opportunity with Sammie Lou a few minutes in, but Sammie Two, still playing for himself, checks his teammate and disrupts his shot.

"What the heck Two?" Sammie Lou shouts.

Sammie Two's response is to punch Sammie Lou in the eye. He falls to the ice seeing bright flashes. Then, something lightly hits his fur. He won't know it until later when he's told by a teammate, but what hit him is spit from Sammie Two's mouth.

Whistles don't blow, because there's no Olympic rule about hitting your own teammate the way there is in the IAHL. Instead, the two distracted koalas leave their team on a five on three disadvantage at the other end of the ice.

Rodman wraps around the net and tries to score, but his shot is blocked. The puck is whacked by the goalie out to the boards where it's collected by Spoedige. He taps it to the blue line for Mosienko. He sends it across the blue line for Rugby, who blasts a shot at the net.

The shot is blocked again, but it rebounds to L-Rod. He shoots and the shot is blocked, but it rebounds again. This time, Rodman collects the rebound and fires it through the five hole of the Australian goalie, completing his hat trick and sending his team to a 3-2 victory and, more importantly, to the gold medal round.

There are two days off between the gold medal round, so the Gamblers throw another get together in the hotel ballroom. This one gets crashed by everyone and gets so out of control that hotel security gets called and has to come in and put a stop to it at three in the morning.

After one day off, the bronze medal game is held between China and Australia. Most people pick Australia to win based on their ranking in the world, but the Australians suspend Sammie Two from the team and the rest of the guys look like the way their game against South Africa ended is still weighing on their minds. Most of their players play sluggish and disinterested. They make it easy for Beary to earn his fourth shutout in the Olympics, and he leads team China to yet another 1-0 win and the bronze medal.

A day later is the big one. The world sits in anticipation of who is going to win the gold medal. Team USA has half of the Gamblers, but South Africa has Rodman, L-Rod, and several top IAHL players. Two of the subplots in the game are how Rodman will fair against Big Chick during faceoffs and who will emerge victorious between Rodman, who is world renowned as the best player in the world, and Lovey, who is for the most part considered the second best player in the world.

The first question is answered immediately. Rodman and Big Chick know about the stories being broadcast about who will win the faceoff battles, and they both want to be the one who comes out on top. In the case of their first faceoff ever against one another, Big Chick gets the drop on Rodman. It's an arduous battle on the initial drop. They struggle to keep each other's stick away from the puck, but in the end Big Chick wins with a huge smile. It means a lot to him to beat the best player in the world, and Rodman can't help but chuckle and hand it to the big guy.

After the faceoff, Lovey and Big Chick switch spots so the world can get its first glimpse of what it's been waiting for, Rodman vs. Lovey. On both ends of the ice, the two buddies give each other all they have. They check each other, poke at each other, push each other, deflect one another's shots, and do their best to make sure the other doesn't score. All the while, they show the rest of the hockey world that it's completely possible to play your best hockey while playing a clean game.

It takes a while for either team to get any consistent offense. The first two goals of the game, the first by Pikkewyn of South Africa and one from Baylor Adams of the USA, are ugly shots that just happen to find a path to the net and a hole in the goaltenders. The teams head into intermission tied 1-1.

The second period sees more relaxed teams that play better. The real fun begins when Rodman scores two goals in a row. Both of his goals come on assists by L-Rod. Rodman talks some friendly smack to Lovey in the hopes that his jokes will energize the white bear into rallying his team.

And, that's just what happens. After Rodman's second goal, Big Chick wins his sixth faceoff in eight tries against Rodman, and team USA goes on the attack.

During team USA's offense, Rodman takes a look around his first line opponents. He sees Lovey, Big Chick, Goose, Undertaker, and Apple Jack surrounding him. They really are an intimidating bunch. He wonders if everyone who plays the Gamblers is this nervous, knowing any one of them can score at any moment.

Goose makes a move around Rodman from behind and gets nailed with a pass from Big Chick, who then races to the front of the net. Rodman was anticipating ta pass to Lovey on the other side of the ice, and he stumbles a bit as he tries to adjust and chase after Goose, who is already being guarded by L-Rod.

The two South African penguins bump into each other and fall down, allowing Goose to take a shot.

The puck is sure to be stopped by Dolvy, but Big Chick is there to redirect the shot into the net, pulling team USA to within one goal of a tie.

Rodman claps for Big Chick, and the giant chicken bows to him.

Not long after that, Lovey ties the game with a goal of his own. It's a beautiful shot in which he has to deke and spin around Rodman. No one has ever made Rodman look as bad as Lovey does on that shot. Rodman can only applaud his opponent's good play.

The second period ends with both teams still tied.

The third period begins with an early goal from the third line of the Americans. A one timer from Gavin Christopher to Brad Fryar gives team USA its first lead in the game. After this goal, the game dies down a lot. The Americans play very conservative, trying to eat up a lot of clock to preserve their one goal lead. The South Africans on the other hand, have a hard time breaking through the stout defense and goaltending of Undertaker, Kane, Apple Jack, Snickers, Brad Fryar, and Haas. At one point, Rodman and L-Rod try to tie the game by attempting Rodman and Lovey's patented crisscross move. They cut through Undertaker and Apple Jack like a hot knife through butter, but Lovey barges in and disrupts the play. He manages to deflect L-Rod's shot into the crowd at the last second.

With play stopped, Lovey stands with his paws on his hips, shaking his head with a slightly annoyed smile as he stares Rodman down.

Rodman can only laugh and shrug.

Turnabout is fair play though, and Lovey tries to seal the win for team USA by pulling the same stunt with Goose. This time, it's Rodman who has to disrupt the play. He thought Lovey might try that so, as he sees the play developing, he gets himself in perfect position to block Lovey's shot. He gives Lovey the same shake of the head with his flippers on his hips.

Lovey laughs this time and shrugs.

The tides turn a bit when Undertaker draws a penalty and gives the South African team a five on four power play for two of the final three minutes. Rodman's coach takes a huge gamble once the South Africans gain control of the puck. He waves for Dolvy to come to the bench so they can add a sixth attacker and go six on four. With this many minutes left in the game and only a one goal deficit, this approach is quite unusual.

Spoedige, one of the IAHL's fastest players, breaks free from all the defenders, gets lost on the ice, and reappears on the weak side of the net. He watches Mosienko blast a shot at the net, waits for the rebound, and takes Haas by surprise. Before Haas even knows Spoedige is there, the lights are flashing and the South African team is celebrating.

Safari Chip calls his team to the bench. Before he puts his second line out, he goes over some intense game plans.

"It's only going to work if Undertaker can stay out of the box," Kane gripes.

Snickers slaps Kane upside the head. "Just shut up and listen."

The second line goes out. Safari Chip tells his first line to rest quick. His plan is to put them in for the final two minutes of the game.

The second line doesn't score, and at the same time, both teams make a line change, putting their best guys on the ice.

South Africa has possession of the puck. Pikkewyn gets the puck to Rodman. They know whose flippers they want the puck in at crunch time. Rodman waits for a shot to develop, but it never does. He moves the puck around ice to Pikkewyn, Spoedige, and L-Rod, and they keep sending it back to him. He knows if South Africa is going to win gold, it's going to have to be on a Rodman T. Penguin goal. He finally takes the puck and tries to knife his way through the USA defense.

The Americans know he's going to be coming eventually, and they're ready for him when he does. Big Chick jumps in his path first. Rodman spins around him. Goose skates in his way next. Rodman passes the puck through Goose's legs and regains control of it on the other side. Lovey gets in front of him next, and Rodman dekes him out of his skates, returning the favor of making his buddy look bad. From here, Rodman has the dogs to worry about. He looks to take a shot, but Undertaker is in his way and stays in his way all the way to the net. Rodman is forced to go behind the net and try a wrap around. Undertaker follows behind him, tapping at him with his stick. Rodman shrugs off the dog's tapping and moves to complete his wraparound. He's met by Haas, who is there to block Rodman's path to Olympic immortality, and for added coverage, Apple Jack drops his stick in front of Haas' leg pads, doubling the blockage in front of the net. Apple Jack also levies a clean hit on Rodman that sends both players to the ice.

Undertaker winds up with the puck on his stick much to his own surprise. He fumbles it at first, but he finally gets it mostly under control and passes it to Big Chick.

Team USA and team South Africa head for the other end of the ice. At four on four, there is no breakaway and no odd man advantage. Rodman and Apple Jack jump to their feet as quick as they can and race after their respective teams.

Big Chick passes the puck to Lovey just before the blue line. All seems pretty evenly matched as the teams cross the blue line until Lovey turns on the jets and blows past L-Rod.

Pikkewyn and Rugby swarm the bear to block his shot.

Lovey fires.

Dolvy whacks the puck aside at the last second, but it goes right to Goose, who fires another shot at the net. Dolvy knocks this shot down and tries to clear it out of the zone, but at the last moment, he sees Rodman coming into the zone, and he tries to pass it to him instead. The change in the movement of his stick from a blast to a pass makes for a bad pass right to the oncoming stick of Undertaker.

The dog chomps at the bit to blast the puck, and when he puts his stick on it, there's no chance for Dolvy to react. The puck nearly rips through the netting as it hits the back of the net.

USA goes up 5-4 with just seconds to go in the game.

"Nuts," L-Rod says from where he stands on the ice.

"You said it," Rodman says as they watch their Gamblers teammates celebrate without them.

It's a bitter pill to swallow knowing they're probably not going to win the gold medals. It's a feeling Rodman and L-Rod had hoped to never have. Both of them wanted the gold... bad.

Now is no time to wallow though. There are still twenty-five seconds left in the game, and they know as long as they have the puck, a stick, and a prayer that they still have a shot.

Unfortunately for Rodman and the South African team, Big Chick wins another faceoff, and Dolvy never gets a chance to leave the net for a sixth South African attacker because the USA team keeps the puck in their offensive zone.

The clock runs out of time with the score 5-4. The Americans rush the ice. Rodman watches them from afar with a heavy feeling in his gut. If this is what losing the championship feels like, he makes a vow to himself to never lose a Cup Finals.

Rodman and L-Rod join their South African teammates on the bench. They wait for the American's celebration to die down, and once it does, the two teams engage in the customary end of game handshakes. The smile on the faces of his Gamblers teammates does give Rodman a little bit of solace, especially the smile on the faces of Safari Chip and Lovey.

After the handshakes, the medals are awarded. The South African team receives their silver medals first. They're humbled at the applause they receive from the fans and the Americans too. To show there are no hard feelings, they in turn give the Americans just as big an ovation when they receive their gold medals.

On the plane ride back to Las Vegas, Rodman tells his teammates, "Boy, am I glad to not be playing against you guys anymore. And I don't mean just the Americans. You guys are all the toughest guys in hockey. I would hate to be our opponents."

It's a sentiment held by every player on the plane. They're all glad to be back on the same team.

Chapter 21: The Unthinkable

The day after the Gamblers arrive home from the Olympics, Safari Chip walks into his office with the Gamblers jersey he wore on their last road trip. He folds the jersey up, puts it in a protective case, and hangs it on the wall above his desk next to the first jersey he had made after he bought the team. He admires it for a minute, thinking to himself how fun it was to be back on the ice again, especially with this group of guys, even if his legs were, and still are, killing him. He would have loved to have won more than one game, but the thrill of getting a game winning goal and going out a winner makes up for all the losing.

Retired once more, and with his team teetering back and forth between a playoff spot, Safari Chip knows it's time to get serious. It's time to get a new forward to solidify his third line and start winning again. Before he can set out to find a forward, Safari Chip dials Flip, but there's no answer.

Safari Chip sighs and leans back in his chair. There's a red light blinking on the answering machine in his office. He crosses his fingers that it's a message from Flip and presses play.

"Hey Chip. This is Lou Brown in Anchorage. I know you guys are in need of a winger, and I have one, his name is Andy Hitt. He's not a player the caliber of say Maverick, but I propose a trade, Andy and one of my defenseman, Cutter Morgan, for Maverick. I think the trade will be mutually beneficial. Give me a call. We can discuss the deal in more detail." The machine clicks off.

A trade?

Safari Chip had never thought of that, and he's not sure he likes the idea. Maverick isn't the best player on his team, but he knows his team is exceptionally talented. On most other teams, Maverick would be on the first line. It's no wonder Lou wants him. The horse would make any team he goes to better and any team that loses him would become immediately worse.

On the flip side, Safari Chip also knows that Andy Hitt isn't the type of player who would flake out on his team. He would definitely stabilize the offense on his third line, and as long as Cutter, is even serviceable, then the Gamblers could once again find themselves steady.

Safari Chip tries to imagine a team without Maverick. He tries to imagine a locker room where the horse and his best friend, Goose, aren't squabbling over the most trivial of things, a room where Maverick isn't combing his long mane and checking his big toothy grin for food between his teeth, and one where the joyous uproars in their locker room don't include a ridiculously loud nay.

Try as he might, Safari Chip can't see this locker room. But, he has to at least consider the offer since he has no other ideas. He sighs, picks up the phone, and begins to dial Lou. His dialing is interrupted by a knock on his door. "Come in."

Flip pokes his head inside the office. "May I come in?"

"Sure." Safari Chip sets the receiver back on the phone.

Flip sits down in the chair on the other side of Safari Chip's desk. "I uhhh…"

"Don't even say it," Safari Chip interrupts. "No need for apologies."

"All the same, I feel I owe you one. I should have been there on this latest road trip. You guys could have used me."

"Yeah we could have," Safari Chip says emphatically.

"Have you decided what you're going to do about the final roster spot?"

"Not yet, but I got a message from Lou Brown. He's offering Andy Hitt and Cutter Morgan for Maverick."

"What!?" Flip jumps up from his chair and slams two fists on Safari Chip's desk. "Trade Maverick? Are you nuts?"

"I don't want to!" Safari Chip leans back in his chair and puts his hands to his face to protect himself from the irate penguin across from him.

"You can't trade Maverick, especially not for those guys. I mean, Andy Hitt's ok, but Cutter Morgan's the opposite of what we need. He's a nonaggressive, score first kind of defenseman. We have plenty of scorers. We need someone like

Maverick, who isn't afraid to levy a hit on someone and who won't abandon his post unless he's got an absolute sure fire shot on goal. Besides, I think Maverick's power from near the blue line is unmatched, and he's more accurate than Cutter Morgan."

Safari Chip tries to speak, but he gets interrupted.

"Oh," says Flip. "And if you trade him, Goose will kill you."

Safari Chip sighs heavily. "Do you have a better idea?"

"I've got one." Flip walks over to the office door, opens it up, and in walks Rodman.

*

The Gamblers gather in their locker room to meet up before they head out on another five game road trip. They return to action with eight gold medal winners, two silver medalists, and one recipient of a bronze medal. With only five of them not having won a medal at all, those with one don't flaunt theirs.

"Lovey, where is your gold medal?" Liten asks.

"We decided not to wear them," Lovey answers.

"Why?" Liten is incredulous.

"We didn't want anyone to feel like we were bragging."

"Do not be ridiculous. You guys worked hard and earned those medals. You deserve to wear them. No one here would think of you guys as braggers and boasters."

"Really?" Lovey asks.

"Really. Besides, I would have liked to have seen it."

Lovey smiles, pulls his gold medal out of his pocket, and hands it to Liten. "Here. Take a look."

"I thought you said you guys did not bring them."

"I said we weren't going to wear them," Lovey corrects.

One by one, Gamblers with medals pull them out and put them on.

"Check out mine," L-Rod says to Sammie. "It's not gold, but I got to play with Rodman on the first line. I even hit him with the assist on the goal that led us into the final game."

Sammie kneels down and checks out L-Rod's medal. "I know. I was on the ice with the other team when you did."

"It's too bad about the way things ended for the Australian team." Rodman joins their conversation.

"Yeah. That put a damper on the Olympics for a lot of guys," Sammie sighs and rubs his eyebrow over his swollen eye.

Rodman takes a look at Sammie's eye. "That eye's still pretty swollen. What's up with that guy?"

"Sammie Two?"

"Yeah."

"Eh, he's just one of the many jerks up there in Reno." Sammie doesn't sound as though he wants to talk about it.

"Yeah, but why does he seem to hate you so much?"

Sammie breathes in deep, and lets out a heavy sigh. It's time to let the Gamblers in on his family secret. "He's hated me ever since we were kids."

"You knew him when you guys were kids?" Rodman is shocked.

"Of course. We're cousins."

"Cousins!?" Rodman exclaims.

"Yeah. Our moms both named us Sammie. Because I was born first, I was always called Sammie, and he got dubbed Two. I know he didn't like it at first. He always felt like he was second best, but I guess eventually he grew fond of the name, because he officially changed his last name to Two."

"He never got over his little brother complex eh?"

"I guess not," Sammie says.

"We have a word for guys like him in Germany. Backpfeifengesicht," Liten remarks.

"Back-whatta?" Sammie asks.

"Backpfeifengesicht. It means one who is badly in need of a fist to the face," Liten explains.

Lovey holds up a fist. "I'd like to be the guy to give him a fist to the face."

Sammie waves Lovey off. "Nah. Just leave him alone. It's not worth it."

Safari Chip runs around the room looking for Flip. "Flip? Flip? Has anyone seen Flip?"

No one has seen him.

Big Chick sits by his locker with El Pollos Locos. His cousins fight over the chance to wear his gold medal.

"Don't tug on it Noodle. You're going to break the strap," Chicken says and pushes him away.

"Well then share it Chicken." Noodle swipes at the medal again but misses.

"Hold on!"

"I want to try it on," Soup says.

"I've got next," Noodle shouts.

"Calm down guys. You'll all get a chance to wear it," Big Chick assures them.

"Here." Kane takes his medal from around his neck and hands it to Soup. "You can wear mine."

"What about me?" Noodle demands.

Kane looks around. He sees Undertaker holding his medal in his paw and yanks it away from him.

"Hey!" Undertaker shouts.

"Hey what?" Kane barks almost daring Undertaker to defy him. "Let the kid see your medal."

Kane hands Undertaker's medal to Noodle, and El Pollos Locos run around the room pretending to be gold medal winners.

The locker room doors crack open then. Most of the Gamblers don't pay any attention to it as Lovey has already been fire in the holed today and most of the Gamblers are immersed in conversation.

Safari Chip, though, runs to it right away to meet Flip. "Rodman," he calls across the room.

Rodman looks over to his coach and gets the high sign. His heart starts beating fast. He looks out upon his team, puts a flipper in his mouth, and whistles loudly to get everyone's attention.

Everyone stops talking and looks to Rodman.

"Hey guys listen up. Safari Chip, Flip, and I have something to tell you. We've found our seventeenth guy," Rodman says.

"Who is it?" L-Rod asks.

"He's a guy who has had a lot of success in the IAHL. He's young. He's talented," Rodman continues.

The Gamblers like what they're hearing.

"We're already the most talent laden team in the league and it sounds like we're about to get even better," Harlan whispers to and nudges Beary.

Beary nods.

"Who is he?" Liten asks.

"He's someone who can help get us out of fifth place and back into the playoff hunt," Rodman continues.

"What's his name?" Big Chick asks.

"He's right over there. I think you'll all know him." Rodman points behind everyone to the locker room doors.

The Gamblers all turn and lay eyes upon Jason Vyand. There's a collection of gasps, groans, sighs, and growls.

Lovey turns back to Rodman and says without any regard for how his comments are going to make Jason feel, "I thought we agreed not to let this guy on the team."

"We're running out of options Lovey, and if you guys can just get past the past, you'll see that with Jason, we've just elevated ourselves from a hockey powerhouse to a hockey empire," Safari Chip explains.

"All we ask is that you give Jason a chance to prove himself," Flip begs.

"He knows he's on a short leash. Just one underhanded tactic out there, and we rip up his contract," Safari Chip explains.

"In that case, he won't last long," Haas mutters.

"No doubt," Lovey agrees.

"Guys," Safari Chip says with a warning tone in his voice. "Like it or not, Jason is on the team. Work with him, treat him like you would anyone else, and you'll see this will be a good thing."

Sammie and several others roll their eyes.

Safari Chip and Flip lead Jason to Safari Chip's office. As they walk past Lovey and Rodman's lockers they hear Lovey ask Rodman how he could have let this happen. They all pretend not to hear it. They knew this was going to be tough sell to their players, but they're hoping everyone will adjust and that Jason will prove his doubters wrong.

Inside Safari Chip's office, the monkey coach instructs Jason to sit. "This isn't going to be easy Jason, but we're counting on you to be the man we know you can be. You're going to have to win these guys over, and if you can't, well, then you're at least going to have to coexist with them in some semblance of harmony."

"I can do that," Jason says.

"Good, so let's discuss a few sticking points. I've had my lines set all season long, and some of them for the better half of two seasons. The guys work well where they are, so I don't want to change my lines. What that means for you is that you'll have to adjust to playing on the third line," Safari Chip tells him.

Jason sighs.

Flip shoots Jason an irritated look.

Jason straightens up. "I mean, that's fine. Am I at least going to stay in my same position as the center?"

"Actually, you are. We need someone who can win faceoffs on that line, because L-Rod just isn't a faceoff guy, but he plays very well on the wing," Safari Chip says.

"Good. I know I can help with faceoffs." Jason smiles.

"The next matter will be what number are you going to want on your jersey?" Safari Chip asks.

"I've worn number one on every team I've ever played on," Jason responds.

"Ohhh," Safari Chip says.

"What?"

"Big Chick wears number one."

"So, tell him to give it up. I'm better than…" Jason stops in midsentence, catching himself before he makes himself look bad. "I mean, can I at least ask him if he would be willing to give it up?"

"You can ask, but don't pressure him," Flip warns.

"Are you all packed and ready to go?" Safari Chip asks.

"Yes sir."

"Good, then why don't you go ask Big Chick about the number thing. If he agrees to change, then you and he can go to the tailor's office to get new jerseys, but if he wants to keep his number, grab Rodman. He'll show you the way."

"Thank you." Jason stands and exits the office.

Back in the locker room, Jason looks around for Big Chick. At first, all he sees are a bunch of wary eyes on him. Even those who don't stare at him with complete disgust make him uncomfortable. Jason finds himself trying not to make eye contact with his new teammates. He finally spots Big Chick lacing up his skates and walks over to him under the watchful eye of Rodman and the other Gamblers. He stops and taps Big Chick on the shoulder.

Big Chick looks up. "Hi."

"Hey buddy. I'm Jason." Jason offers his flipper for Big Chick to shake.

"I know." Big Chick looks reluctantly at Jason's flipper. He instinctively goes to shake it but hesitates and holds back.

Jason retracts his flipper. "It's Martin Louie right?"

"Yeah," Big Chick answers.

"Do you go by Martin? Marty?"

"The guys call me Big Chick."

"Cool. So, I hear you wear number one."

"Yep." Big Chick nods.

"When I was on the Gold Rush, so did I."

"Uh huh." Bigh Chick nods again.

"I'd like to wear it on the Gamblers too."

"But I wear number one on the Gamblers."

"I know, but I was hoping I might be able to make a trade with you," Jason says.

"What kind of trade?" Big Chick is skeptical.

"You give me your number, and I'll give you whatever you want," Jason says and then adds quickly, "Within reason."

Big Chick thinks for a second. "I don't want anything."

"You'll give it to me for free?" Jason asks surprised.

"No. I'm going to keep it."

Jason gets frustrated. His mind starts racing, trying to think of a way to trick Big Chick into giving up his number. Then it hits him. "You know Big Chick, it would be very nice of you to welcome the new guy on the team with a gesture of camaraderie."

Big Chick puts his wing to his beak and thinks. "Well…"

Rodman walks over and yanks Jason aside. "Well nothing. He doesn't want to give up his number, and if you want to be a part of this team, you're not going to do things like that."

"Like what?" Jason asks.

"You were trying to guilt Big Chick into giving up his number and you know it." Rodman pokes Jason in the chest with his flipper.

"Alright. I'll just pick a new number."

"And stop doing stuff like that if you want to last on this team," Rodman says.

Jason nods.

"So what number do you want, so I can take you down to the tailor's office," Rodman asks.

Jason thinks about another number that suits him. "I'll be… uhhh… I'll be number eleven."

"Clever," Lovey, who can hear their conversation, says sarcastically.

"Fine. Eleven's good. We don't have an eleven," Rodman grabs Jason and leads him out of the locker room to the tailor's office.

The tailor whips together three road jerseys for Jason in a matter of minutes while he waits with Rodman. The two penguins don't say much to each other, and when they do talk it's only about the upcoming road trip.

Chapter 22: Jason's Debut

A loud knocking on the door of Rodman and L-Rod's hotel room just before curfew the first night they arrive in Portland startles the two penguins.

"I wonder who that could be," Rodman says.

L-Rod shrugs and tries to give Rodman his best *I don't know look,* but Rodman can tell L-Rod knows something. He peeks out the peephole. The entire team is standing outside his room. Rodman opens the door and peeks out. "Guys?"

"Let us in Rodman." Lovey pushes his way past Rodman and leads the charge into his room.

"We have to talk," Sammie says and follows Lovey in.

Liten nods in agreement as he enters next.

One by one, the rest of the Gamblers barge in, so Rodman steps aside and allows them in. He closes the door behind the last guy and follows his teammates to his living room.

"What's up guys?" Rodman asks as though he doesn't know what's on the minds of the fifteen angry animals in front of him.

"We don't want to play with Jason," Lovey says definitively.

"He's going to sabotage us," Sammie says.

"So we want you to join us," Haas says.

"Join you in what?" Rodman asks.

"Sitting out until he's off the team," Lovey says.

"No," Rodman says without even thinking about it.

"What?" Lovey is aghast.

"Why?" Sammie asks.

"Yeah, why? If you sit out, Chip will definitely kick him off the team," Haas says.

"Because, it's not fair to Chip, Flip, our fans, and even Jason," Rodman says.

"Not fair to Jason!?" Lovey exclaims.

"Yeah Lovey. It's not fair to Jason."

"Since when do you care about being fair to Jason?"

"Since I spoke with him for over four hours with Chip and Flip before he signed his Gamblers contract. He's actually quite upset about the way things have turned out for him since he joined the IAHL."

"How do you know he's being sincere?" Sammie asks.

"I *don't* know, but he seemed sincere."

The rest of the Gamblers stare at Rodman unmoved.

"What are your biggest fears about him being on our team?" Rodman asks his teammates.

"That he'll sabotage us," Sammie says.

"He won't sabotage us. We're the only team that will take a chance on him, and he's not going to mess that up. Plus, he wants to win."

"He gave me a concussion," Lovey says.

"And you gave him one back," Rodman counters.

"He's mean," Big Chick adds.

"He won't be mean to you. I promise. And if he is, you just let me know. I'll deal with him."

"He's the type of guy who would injure his own teammate. Just ask Maulbreath," Haas notes.

Rodman doesn't have a response to that one.

"And you know how jealous he is of you," Liten adds.

"We don't want to be scooping you off the ice like the Gold Rush had to scoop up Maulbreath is all we're saying," Harlan says.

Again, Rodman has no response, and an uncomfortable silence fills the room.

"Is there any way to convince you to boycott with us?" Lovey asks.

Rodman shakes his head no.

Lovey looks to Sammie.

Sammie shrugs and sighs.

"Alright. We'll just have to keep a close eye on him." Lovey motions for the rest of the Gamblers to follow him out of the room. The Gamblers follow, but Lovey stops in front of Rodman before passing him by. "You know, if Jason is out to sabotage us, it might not be you he goes after. He's on the third line. He might go after L-Rod, and if he does, what do you think Ms. LeJuene will do?"

The thought of Jason going after L-Rod scares Rodman. If Jason hurts L-Rod, Ms. LeJuene would surely try to revoke his parental rights. Rodman looks to L-Rod. The little penguin, having heard Lovey's words, looks nervous.

*

Before the first game of the road trip, the Gamblers sit around an unusually quiet locker room. Each has a water balloon in his hand, but when they realize the last guy in the room is going to be Jason, they don't feel like doing fire in the hole.

The locker room doors open, and Jason walks in. Overwhelming silence is the first thing he notices followed by the eyes of each and every single Gambler upon him. He doesn't move again until they all look away and go back to doing what it was they were doing before he walked in.

With Jason's back to most of the Gamblers, Lovey picks up and chucks his water balloon. It nails the newest Gambler in the back of the noggin, rocking his head forward violently. The wet explosion takes Jason by surprise. He stops in his tracks, curls his flippers into fists, grits his beak, but restrains himself from even turning around.

The single balloon attack seems more hostile than the normal sixteen balloon attack that is usually followed by tons of laughter.

Jason composes himself, uncurls his flippers, and continues on his way to his locker. He sets his bag down and starts unloading his gear.

As Jason organizes his locker, Rodman approaches him. "Hey."

Jason looks up. "Hey."

"I just want to let you know that Chip, and especially Flip, too a big risk signing you, and if you mess this up, for any reason, I'll personally see to it that you never play another hockey game in your life. Not in the IAHL, not in SAHL, not even in a rec-league."

The two penguins look each other in the eye for a tense moment.

Jason understands why he's being treated the way he is, but he still doesn't like it. The only reason he's taking it is because he wants to play hockey. He knows until he can prove himself he's going to have to just grin and bear any abuse the Gamblers dish out. "I know."

Rodman nods, turns, and heads back to his locker.

Jason looks around the locker room at a bunch of guys who hate his guts, and whose guts he has hated for a couple of seasons. Winning over the Gamblers isn't high on his list of things to do, but he hopes he can go unprovoked enough to make it through the season and prove to another team that he's worth signing in the offseason. He throws on his pads and his jersey, laces up his skates, and sits uncomfortably at his locker, trying to go unnoticed. It feels like forever for Jason, but finally, Safari Chip comes out of his office and yells game time.

*

After an early goal by Lovey in the first period, a goal that puts him two goals ahead of Rodman for the overall IAHL season lead, the Gamblers find themselves down 2-1 with a minute and a half to go in the game. The second line heads to the bench for a line change, and Safari Chip sends out his first line.

Rodman, Lovey, Liten, Undertaker, and Apple Jack fight to get the puck away from the Pirates, but they have a hard time. The Pirates get a shot off at Harlan, and the turtle makes a kick save. The puck goes to the boards on his left where it's collected by one of the Pirates.

Just as the Pirates player turns to pass the puck, Apple Jack pulls a Snickers-type move, appearing out of nowhere and obliterating his opponent. The hit causes the pass to go in the wrong direction. It lands on the stick of Lovey, who passes it ahead to Liten, and the Gamblers head out on offense.

A minute and twelve seconds remain in the game, and Safari Chip whistles loud to get the attention of Harlan. The turtle doesn't even look his coach's way. He knows what that sound means. He puts his head down and races for the bench as fast as he can. The Gamblers are going no goalie so they can have an extra attacker.

L-Rod, the team's usual sixth man, stands up and prepares to take the ice, but Safari Chip stops him.

"Don't you want me to go in?" L-Rod asks.

"Not this time," Safari Chip says.

The rest of the Gamblers look to their coach wondering which of them is going to get called. The defensemen are all pretty sure it's not going to be them, and the guys on the second line, Big Chick, Beary, and Sammie, are all tired from having just come off the ice. That leaves just Goose and Jason.

"Me?" Goose asks Safari Chip, pointing to himself.

"Nah. Him." Safari Chip points to Jason.

"Me?" Jason can't believe it.

Harlan hits the bench.

"Yeah you! Get out there" Safari Chip orders.

Jason stands up so fast he stumbles and falls down. The other Gambles laugh at him, but he stands frantically back up and jumps over the wall.

On the ice, Undertaker takes a shot that draws a lot of Pirates to one side of the net. The puck never even reaches the goalie. It deflects off of a stick of one of the Pirates and lands in front of another Pirate, who makes a nifty move around Rodman and Apple Jack and would have an all-out breakaway towards the Gamblers empty net if it weren't for Jason whizzing past him and stealing it back for the Gamblers before the Pirates can leave the Gamblers offensive zone, and heads straight for the net.

Jason takes Gamblers and Pirates alike by surprise. He approaches the net, dekes left, draws the goalie his way, brings the puck back right, spins and fires it into the back of the net.

The goal lights go off. The crowd groans. The goalie bangs his stick on the ice.

Meanwhile, Jason turns around to celebrate his game tying goal with his teammates and finds all five of them standing in the same spot they were in when he scored the goal. No one approaches him for hugs or high fives.

As happy as the Gamblers are that the game is tied, they're not sure how they feel about celebrating with Jason.

Jason's smile fades, and he heads back to the bench.

"Good job." Safari Chip high fives Jason as he enters the bench.

Flip reaches over Safari Chip to give Jason knuckles.

Rodman watches his coaches acknowledge Jason's accomplishment. He feels bad that he didn't at least point to Jason to recognize him for his goal. As the captain, he should be setting the example for the rest of the guys. So, once he arrives back at the bench, despite his animosity towards Jason, Rodman bites his pride, pats Jason on the back when he passes him, and says, "Nice shot."

"Ok first line, grab some bench," Safari Chip says.

"What?" Lovey asks. "We just took the ice. We can finish the game."

"Nah. I want you to get all the rest you can in case we need overtime. "Safari Chip turns to the other two lines. His second line still looks winded. "You guys still need a bit longer on your breather?"

They all nod.

"I guess that means you guys are in." Safari Chip points to his third liners.

L-Rod, Goose, Maverick, and Moose join Jason on the ice. They head to center ice where Jason wins his fourth faceoff in five tries, knocking the puck back to Moose.

Across the blue line, Moose passes the puck over to Maverick. The horse passes it along the boards to Goose. Goose takes it towards the net, has his path blocked, and is forced to go behind the net. There, he's pressured from either side and has to fire the puck blindly behind himself. Luckily, the puck ends up on the stick of Jason. He too gets pressured and is forced to fire the puck blindly behind himself. Maverick ends up with the puck again and fires it diagonally across the ice to L-Rod who is undefended. L-Rod one times a shot that rings off the post.

The heads of all the players on the ice spin to find the puck.

Jason spots it first because it hits off of his chest and drops to his feet. Instinctively, he rears his stick back to fire.

The Pirates goalie is the next guy to pick up the puck, and he slides in the direction of where Jason has his shot aimed.

Jason can sense the directional slide of the goalie as he's swinging his stick, and, somehow, he's able to make an adjustment mid-swing. Instead of going low on the weak side of the goalie, he fires the puck high in the opposite direction of the sinking sliding goaltender. The puck flies well above and around the goalie, bounces off the post, and ricochets into the net, setting the goal lights off once more. The shot is pretty awesome. The fact that it gives the Gamblers the lead makes it even more awesome. It's so awesome in fact that the four Gamblers on the ice mob Jason with hugs and high fives, forgetting for the moment who he is and how uncomfortable he makes them.

Safari Chip leaves his third line out for the remainder of the game, and after the Pirates pull their goalie for an extra attacker, Jason manages to pick off a pass, gain a breakaway, and score a hat trick goal on an empty netter.

The Gamblers go on to win 4-2. They win their next game against the Idaho Potatoes 5-1 and Jason scores another goal in that game. They win the third game of their road trip 3-2 over the Utah Thumpers on a goal by Goose from an assist by Jason. The fourth game of the road trip is yet another win, this time against the Fresno Fire, in which Jason has a goal and an assist. They wrap up the road trip up with a win over the Ontario Californians 6-0. Jason gets an assist in the final game as well.

Even more important than the wins and Jason's stats is the fact that it appears Jason is as promised, a changed penguin and a team player looking to resurrect his career. The Gamblers and their fans, who were just as shocked as the players, find themselves rallying around and rooting for Jason. The story of his turnaround becomes big news in the media. Before he knows it, Jason finds himself conversing, interacting, and even laughing with most, not all, but most of the Gamblers. He knows it's going to take some big time work to repair his relationship with Lovey, Sammie, and Haas. He knows he has time to do just that though, and more importantly, unlike a few weeks ago, he actually wants to make nice with them.

With their perfect 5-0-0-0 road trip, the Gamblers head home all smiles as they're once again in the playoff hunt. All their winning has catapulted them into third place behind the Five Ohhh! and the Trains. Their joy isn't hockey related alone however. Before their next home game, they have a wedding to attend.

Chapter 23: The Wedding Of Beary And Mary

Jackets are put on, ties are tied, feathers are slicked back, manes are combed, ruffled fur is straightened, and a pink carnation is slipped into a slot on Beary's coat. All the styling and preparation for the wedding takes place in the Gamblers locker room. The ceremony is going to take place on the ice.

"Hey, if we have our locker room, and the girls have the visitor's locker room, where are the Five Ohhh! getting ready?" Moose asks.

"Luckily, this is a large arena, and we had room left near the janitor's closet in the basement," Harlan jokes.

The locker room bursts into laughter.

"They're using the press room," Beary informs his teammates of the true location of the Five Ohhh!. "And fellas, I'm begging you again, please don't start anything with them today. Mary and I don't want any shenanigans at the wedding."

"Not even with Dislike?" Lovey asks.

"No!" Beary warns.

"But he already disliked the wedding of Facespace." Lovey holds up his cell phone for Beary to see.

Beary and several other Gamblers gather around to check out Lovey's Facespace page. Beary growls lightly. "What's wrong with that guy?"

"Where do I begin?" Lovey asks.

"Watch this." Rodman squeezes in and takes hold of Lovey's phone. He finds Dislike's comments about the wedding, and likes them from Lovey's page.

"Hey!" Lovey objects. "What the heck are you doing?"

"I'm liking his comments."

"Don't do that. Why would you do that?" Lovey speaks rapidly.

"It will drive him crazy that you like his comment," Rodman says.

Lovey and a few of the others chuckle.

"Guys. This is what I'm talking about," Beary warns.

"Oh, don't worry Beary. This won't cause any fights," Lovey assures him.

Harlan walks up to the crowd gathered around Lovey and his phone. "Hey Bear, was Mary able to find enough bridesmaids?"

"Oh yeah. No problem." Beary nods.

"I can't believe you made all of us groomsmen," Sammie laughs.

"I love all of you guys. I couldn't pick some of you and leave the rest of you guys out."

"Where did she find eighteen bridesmaids?" Rodman asks.

"She has lots of sisters to begin with, six of them, and she has lots of friends too. I think she was initially three ladies short, but Elmira's sisters have been helping out with the wedding details, and she invited them to join the bridal party."

"Wait. What? Elmira's sisters?" Kane joins the conversation from a few lockers down.

"Uh huh," Beary answers.

"I ain't walking down the aisle with no cat," Kane swears.

"Oh yes you are," Undertaker laughs.

"Nope." Kane crosses his arms.

"Yes," Snickers stands up to Kane. "You are."

Kane backs down.

The locker room doors burst open and in fly El Pollos Locos dressed to the nines in their own tuxedos. They rush to Big Chick.

"Hey Uncle Big Chick. How do we look?" Chicken asks.

Noodle slugs Chicken in the wing. "Why'd you call him Uncle? He's our cousin."

"Well, he's big enough to be our uncle," Chicken answers.

"His size doesn't have anything to do with whether or not he's our uncle," Soup says.

"I know…" Chicken sighs heavily. "I'm just saying. He looks like he could be our uncle."

"He doesn't look anything like Uncle Cluck," Noodle says irritated.

Soup shakes his head. "Nope. Not at all."

"He doesn't look like Uncle Cluck. He's just… I mean… Gosh! I'm sorry I ever said it," Chicken says.

"So how do we look?" Soup asks Big Chick.

"That's all I wanted to know," Chicken says.

"But you called him Uncle Cluck, and it got everything sidetracked," Noodle points out.

"I didn't call him Uncle Cluck!" Chicken throws a minor temper tantrum.

Big Chick can't help but smile at his silly cousins. "You guys look great. Are you ready to be good little ushers?"

El Pollos Locos all nod excitedly. They stand up straight and try to look professional. Being ushers is something they've been looking forward to ever since Beary asked them to do so, and they're taking the job very serious.

"You know what to do?"

They nod again.

Next to the chickens, L-Rod struggles with his tie. "Rodman, can I get some help with my tie?"

"I'd help you buddy, but I'm struggling with my own." Rodman fumbles with his.

"I can help," Jason offers.

L-Rod, one of the few Gamblers still a little wary of Jason because of what Jason has done to his favorite player, Rodman, in the past, glares at Jason a bit standoffish.

Rodman nudges L-Rod and gives him an *ease up* look. "Fine."

Jason kneels down, undoes his own tie, and proceeds to show L-Rod the process. It takes L-Rod a few tries, but eventually he gets it.

"I'll never remember that," L-Rod says.

"You will. It just takes practice," Jason assures.

They look over to Rodman to see if he's making any progress. What they find is a penguin with a wrinkled tie with the wrong kind of knot that is too tight and too low which causes the tie to hang far below his collar.

"No matter what," Jason says to L-Rod. "You can't do worse than him."

"No doubt," L-Rod agrees.

Rodman looks in his mirror at his messed up tie. "Nuts."

"Let me help." Jason grabs Rodman, spins him around, and tries to do his tie for him. The knot is so tight though that Jason can't get the ends loosened. "How hard did you pull this?"

"Hard," Rodman admits.

Jason tries for a while longer. The two penguins stumble around and make such a commotion that it gets the attention of the rest of the Gamblers. One by one, the Gamblers file over and try to help loosen the knot in Rodman's tie.

The locker room doors open again. This time, Safari Chip and Flip walk in. Everyone stops trying to untie Rodman's tie. They turn to their coaches.

With all eyes on him, Safari Chip shouts, "Wedding time!"

The Gamblers rush for the doors and head down the tunnel that leads to the ice the same way they do for a game. Rodman continues to try to loosen the knot in his tie all the way down the tunnel.

Beary and Harlan stop their teammates at the entrance to the ice.

Chairs have been set up on the ice and are filled with friends and family of both pandas including an entire section set aside for the Five Ohhh!. Red carpets stretch from both tunnels, coming together near the seats to form a V shape that leads to a single red carpet that splits the chairs down the middle. The carpet leads to a platform with a flower and hockey puck laden arch made of hockey sticks.

"So what song did you pick to walk down to?" Harlan asks Beary.

"No song," Beary answers.

"No song?"

"Nope."

"How will we know when to come out?" Harlan asks.

"You'll see. And when you do, just follow suit. All of you guys just follow suit," Beary instructs.

Suddenly, the lights in the entire arena go out. The guests gasp. The Gamblers gasp. A third gasp is heard from the ladies' tunnel.

"What's going on?" Haas asks.

Before anyone can answer, faint white lights come up and light the seating area and platform. More lights materialize, illuminating the red carpets that lead from both tunnel entrances.

The Gamblers house announcer breaks the silence by cracking to life over the arena speakers. "Attention guests of the wedding. It is now time for tonight's introductions. Coming out first, starting in groom, number seven, Las Vegas' very own, Beary Nelson Riley!"

A spot light hits the Gamblers tunnel, and Beary walks out looking as dapper as ever. He makes his way to the platform to the applause of everyone except the Five Ohhh!.

"Coming out next, the best man, number twenty, Harlan T. Turtle!"

The wedding guests love the idea of the introductions. They stand, clap, and cheer for each new intro.

"Accompanying Harlan is the maid of honor, Mary's twin sister, Carrie Claymore!"

Carrie comes out of her tunnel, joins Harlan where the carpets meet, hooks her arm around his flipper and walks with him to the platform. There, they make their ways to opposite sides of the stage. Harlan takes a spot next to Beary.

In the crowd, Dislike rolls his eyes. "I hope they aren't going to introduce every single one of his…"

"Coming out next, the first of seventeen groomsmen, number eighty-one, Sammie Lou!" the arena announcer interrupts Dislike.

Dislike rolls his eyes again. He leans over to The Colonel next to him. "Remind me to dislike this on Facespace later."

Sammie Lou accompanies another of Mary's sisters down the aisle. One by one, the Gamblers come out and lead another bridesmaid down the aisle. The first four guys after Sammie are the rest of the guys on Beary's line and his coach. Big Chick, Apple Jack, Snickers, and Safari Chip come out in order and lead the rest of Mary's sisters down the aisle.

Rodman is called next. He reaches the part where both red carpets meet and waits for the bridesmaid he'll accompany.

"Introducing bridesmaid number seven, please welcome Penny McGriff!"

As the rest of the congregation turns to lay eyes on Penny, Rodman tries some more to adjust his tie. He's too busy fighting with the troublesome accessory to notice a very beautiful penguin with her black feathers dyed pink in a purple dress with a matching purple bow atop her head. Penny reaches Rodman while he's still fiddling with his tie. She waits for him to stop fussing with it and lead her down the aisle, but he never looks up. Finally, she whispers, "What are you doing?"

"I can't get this dang tie…" Rodman says as he lifts his head. His words get caught in his beak and erased from his brain the second he lays eyes on Penny.

"You can't get your tie?" she asks.

"Huh?" Rodman asks.

Penny takes notice of his mangled tie. She reaches up, and in the blink of an eye, she has the knot loosened. She smoothes out the wrinkles the best she can, pulls the knot together delicately, and adjusts it perfectly around his collar.

"There. All better," Penny says.

"Thanks." If he could, Rodman would be blushing.

"Shall we?" Penny sticks out her flipper for Rodman to take.

Rodman takes ahold of it and leads Penny down the aisle.

Lovey comes down next with Sprinkles, followed by Undertaker and Elmira, and Kane, Liten, and L-Rod, all of whom accompany one of Elmira's sisters. Haas, Goose, Maverick, Moose, Jason, and Flip round out the introductions, each accompanying another bridesmaid of various species.

The house announcer goes silent. The crowd quiets down. The Gamblers and the groomsmen get into position. Everyone knows that the bride is the next to be introduced. They turn to the visitor's tunnel with eager anticipation.

Before Mary is announced, Lovey steps out of line, turns to the rest of the Gamblers, and calls out, "Gentlemen!"

Beary and the rest of the wedding goers turn to see what's going on.

"Attention!" Lovey shouts.

The Gamblers all stand at attention.

"Present scarves!" Lovey continues.

The Gamblers all pull out the scarves Beary had given them at the start of the season.

Beary smiles. Other than Lovey and Rodman, most of the Gamblers haven't worn their scarves much, if at all. It made Beary feel kind of embarrassed afterwards, thinking his gifts had been lame.

Even Jason, who didn't receive one from Beary, has a scaf to show his solidarity in the gesture.

"Left shoulder, arms!" Lovey commands.

All the Gamblers tie their scarves to their left arm just above their biceps.

The fact that everyone kept their scarves, and the gesture of tying them onto their suits for his wedding, warms Beary's heart. He's very thankful to be a part of the team he is on and to be friends with these guys. Plus, since everyone's scarf was given to them with a unique design to fit their individual personality, they're all different colors, tying into the color explosion theme of the wedding.

Once all the Gamblers have their scarves on, Lovey gives them one last command. "At ease, gentlemen."

In the crowd, Dislike leans back over to The Colonel. "Remind me to dislike that later too."

The Colonel gives Dislike a thumbs up.

Lovey gets back into line just as *Here Comes the Bride* begins to play over the intercom.

Before Mary comes out, the arena announcer breaks in one last time. With much less fire, and much more dignity, he announces, "Ladies and gentlemen, please rise and turn your attention to the visitor's tunnel."

The crowd obeys his commands.

"Coming down the aisle now, accompanied by her father, Fred Claymore, starting in bride, Miss Mary Claymore."

Mary comes out of the tunnel with a bouquet of different colored flowers to match the theme of their multi-colored wedding. She takes her time walking down the aisle, enjoying the moment, and giving everyone ample time to admire her in her wedding dress.

Near the platform, she turns and gives her dad a kiss on the cheek. He father smiles at her and lets her go. Mary joins Beary and the others on stage. Beary takes her paws in his, and the ceremony begins. It's a very nontraditional wedding with both pandas reading their own vows and making jokes throughout.

When it comes time for the preacher to ask if anyone has any reason to object, Greg tries to stand up and protest, but his mother grabs him and slams him back down into his chair. The commotion makes quite a loud crash and garners the attention of almost everyone. Mary shoots her brother a disapproving look.

No one objects, the preacher announces the panda bears as man and wife, and Beary is allowed to kiss his bride.

Chapter 24: The Reception

The reception starts without the newlyweds. The two families mingle amongst one another, but the hockey players choose to remain on opposite sides of the room. On the side of the room with the buffet table, the Five Ohhh! stand around hogging all the food and shooting menacing looks the Gamblers way. On the other side of the room, the Gamblers sit around one giant table, eating their meals, talking about the wedding, and paying no mind to the Five Ohhh!.

"So Rodman, that was pretty smooth the way that girl fixed your tie and walked you down the aisle," Sammie jokes.

"Hey," Rodman protests. "I walked her down the aisle."

"Uh huh," Sammie says sarcastically.

"Sure." Liten joins the ribbing.

"She sure was pretty," L-Rod notes.

"Yeah she was. Did you get her name?" Big Chick asks.

"I didn't. I was fiddling with my tie," Rodman says.

"Crash and burn." Maverick shakes his head.

"Definitely," Goose agrees.

"Her name is Penny," Sprinkles, who is sitting at the table with Lovey, informs everyone.

Lovey nudges Rodman. "You know Rod, Sprinkles and Elmira are pretty good friends with her. I bet they could set up a meeting for you."

Again, if Rodman could blush, he'd be blushing. "That's ok. I think I'm man enough to go up and talk to her myself."

Safari Chip, sitting next to Rodman on the other side, grabs the penguin's head and turns it around to get a look at the scene going on behind them. "You might be too late."

Rodman focuses in on Mad Man and Samanya talking to Penny, making her giggle.

"Nuts!" Rodman whispers.

"Awww, don't let that bother you Hott Rod. Let's just go butt in," L-Rod says.

"How?" Rodman asks.

L-Rod hops off his chair and grabs El Pollos Locos. "Just follow us."

Rodman does as L-Rod instructs, and the Gamblers entire table turns to watch.

L-Rod positions Rodman near the center of the room away from Penny and the Five Ohhh!. Then, he grabs a dinner roll off an abandoned dinner plate. He hands the roll to Soup. The littlest chicken crouches down like a football center. L-Rod steps behind Soup, playing the role of quarterback. Chicken and Noodle line up on defense across from L-Rod and Soup. Soup hikes the roll to L-Rod and runs a pattern towards Mad Man and Samanya. L-Rod drops back, watches Noodle chase after Soup, checks down Chicken, and heaves the roll across the room. L-Rod and Chicken then chase Noodle and Soup. Soup catches the roll cleanly and runs away from Noodle, who is in hot pursuit. The two chickens cut a path between Penny and the Five Ohhh! penguins, spinning their foes around and off balance.

"Hey!" Mad Man gripes after them.

Chicken rushes by next and knocks Samanya down.

"Watch it!" Mad Man yells again. He turns to help Samanya back to his feet.

While the two Five Ohhh! penguins are distracted, L-Rod stops running, gently grabs Penny's flipper, and discreetly leads her away from the Reno side of the room.

"Oh!" Penny says a bit shocked as L-Rod leads her away. "And who might you be?"

"I'm L-Rod of the Gamblers."

"Well, hello, L-Rod of the Gamblers. May I ask where you're taking me?"

Cutting through the crowd quickly, L-Rod and Penny arrive where Rodman's been stationed. "I believe you remember my friend."

"Oh yes. We met on the red carpet." Penny plays coy.

"Actually, he is my friend, but he's kind of my dad too. See, I'm an orphan, and ol' Hott Rod... I mean Rodman adopted me. And don't be fooled by my description of him as ol' Hott

Rod. He's not really old. He's actually quite young. Not as young as me, but…"

"L-Rod," Rodman calms the overzealous little guy.

"You adopted him?" Penny seems impressed.

"Yeah. It was either that or lose one of our best players to the orphanage," Rodman explains.

"I don't understand."

Rodman recounts to Penny L-Rod's entire story, how he came to Las Vegas as a stowaway from South Africa, how he wiggled his way onto the team, and how Ms. LeJuene has been threatening to take him away if anything goes wrong.

"So, it was strictly a business maneuver?" Penny asks.

"Oh! No! I mean, we definitely didn't want to lose him as a teammate, but even more than that, I didn't want to lose my buddy. L-Rod's a great kid," Rodman explains.

"I'm not that much of a kid. I've won a Cup." L-Rod pulls a necklace out from under the collar of his suit. Hanging on the chain is his championship ring. His silver medal from the Olympics flies out as well. "And an Olympic medal."

"Very impressive," Penny kneels down to L-Rod's level to admire his trophies.

L-Rod pulls her close and whispers. "If you think that's impressive, he's got two rings."

"Does he now?" Penny smiles.

L-Rod nods approvingly and looks back at the Five Ohhh! side of the room. He sees Mad Man and Samanya glaring his way. With a sly grin and a shrug, he pushes Penny and Rodman quickly towards the Gamblers table. "Well, you two will probably have lots to talk about, lots of things in common and such. Why don't you join us at our table Penny?"

"I'd love to join you guys," Penny says.

"Really?" Rodman asks.

L-Rod smiles, turns, and spits his tongue out at Mad Man and Samanya.

"You sound surprised," Penny says.

"Well…"

"Well, who wouldn't want to sit at the same table as "Thee" Rodman T. Penguin?" Penny shoots him a sly grin.

As the three penguins join the party at the Gamblers table, El Pollos Locos return from their sprint around the room and receive high fives from L-Rod on a job well done.

Once Penny is introduced to all of the Gamblers, they let her and Rodman get to know each other. Penny's fascinated by the fact that Rodman's from South Africa. She asks him a million questions about his hometown, and conversely, he's fascinated by her upbringing in Florida and asks her just as many questions. Hometowns lead to family, and from there they talk about Penny's job as a teacher, their favorite childhood memories, and a variety of other things including the fact that Penny plays hockey on a girls' recreational team.

In the middle of Rodman getting to know Penny, Beary and Mary arrive. They're swarmed by friends and family. Everyone wants to offer their congratulations. The couple meets with everyone for a brief minute, but they rush through the well wishes so they can get the party started.

The reception is like a fancy dinner, birthday party, carnival, high school Prom, comedy show, and concert all rolled into one. It starts with a fantastic Italian spread including pasta marinara, Italian style salad, bread sticks, and zeppolis.

After dinner, it's time for Harlan to give his best man speech. "So, it was a mutual decision between Beary and Mary that they wouldn't announce anything if and until they decided to get married. They didn't want to cause any bad blood between the teams." Harlan puts his flipper to his mouth and mumbles purposely into the mic. "As though things between the two teams could have gotten any worse."

The joke gets a light chuckle. Most everyone knows about the tension between the Gamblers and the Five Ohhh!, but only the players know how intense it really gets.

"It's a good thing Mary met Beary when she did. Had they met last year, there would have been no hiding him. You guys know what I'm talking about." Harlan pokes Beary in his belly and points to the Gamblers.

The Gamblers laugh uneasy. No one else reacts.

Harlan knows he's drowning. He pulls at his collar to let some of the perspiration out. He taps the mic. "Is this thing on?"

"Get off the stage," Marlon shouts from the Five Ohhh! table.

The Five Ohhh! and a few other guests laugh at that.

Harlan doesn't get off the stage however. His speech goes on for another minute or two before he finally shuts down the jokes. "But seriously, Beary, I love you man. You're the best friend a guy could ever ask for. I wish nothing but the best for you and Mary. She's a great girl, and she's part of the Gamblers family now, so don't make her mad or you're going to have sixteen angry brothers and two angry coaches to deal with."

Beary and Mary stand up. They hug Harlan, and the turtle takes his seat back at the Gamblers table.

Beary picks up the mic. "Hello everyone. We want to thank you all for coming out and sharing this special day with us. Now, without further ado…"

Mary steals the mic from him. "Let the games begin!"

El Pollos Locos get up and rush from the table. They take L-Rod with them and help the other ushers push in games such as balloon darts, whack-a-mole, bean bag pins, football toss, sink a basketball shot, and other carnival style games that are open to the guest to play.

As fast as El Pollos Locos and L-Rod rush to get the games in place, they rush even faster to play them. Noodle is a wiz at the football game. His dream is to be a professional quarterback someday. He practices morning, noon, and night.

A really intense game in which sixteen players roll a ball into one of several different colored holes in order to move a mechanical ship across a plastic ocean breaks out. There are five yellow holes, three blue holes, and one red hole in which the contestants can roll their ball. The red hole is the hardest to reach and the yellow holes are the easiest. Depending on the difficulty of the hole in which the players get their ball through, the ship moves a little or a lot.

Eight Gamblers race ships against eight Five Ohhh! players. Liten starts out on fire. He has his ship halfway across the ocean before anyone else even has theirs moved a quarter of the way to the finish. Ratone notices this and reaches around to Liten's far shoulder and gives it a tap. Liten looks to his left, and from his right, Ratone uses the distraction to steal Liten's ball. For added insult, Ratone uses both balls to move his ship faster.

"You swindler!" Liten protests when he turns back to the game and realizes what has happened.

Ratone laughs in Liten's face.

Liten pushes Ratone off his chair, grabs his ball, and rejoins the game. By the time, Liten gets back in the game, he's been overtaken by several players, including Sammie Lou and Sammie Two, who lead the pack in a neck and neck race. The dogs from both teams bark wildly and loudly from behind the action. Pushing and shoving ensues.

Sammie Lou takes the lead with only one more hole of any color to go for the win. Both he and Sammie Two roll gutter balls their next couple of tries. On their third roll, Sammie Lou gutters again, but Sammie Two hits a yellow hole and moves his boat into an even tie with Sammie Lou.

The other contestants give up their ships and come to watch the race between Sammie Lou and Sammie Two. Both koalas grit and gnash their teeth. They grab their balls at the same time and chuck them at the holes. Each gutters.

"Come on Sammie. Finish this punk," Kane barks.

"Who you calling a punk?" Hoss barks.

"Him, that's who," Kane barks back.

"Give it up cousin. You'll never beat me," Sammie Two says as he waits impatiently for his ball.

Sammie Lou doesn't respond. He stares intently at the chute, waiting for his ball. "Where the heck is my ball?"

Sammie Two looks over with a sigh of relief that Sammie Lou's ball isn't coming out, but his ball isn't either.

Sammie Lou bangs his machine, and his ball comes out. The Gamblers cheer and urge him on.

Sammie Lou knows anything other than a gutter will give him the win. He has the whole board to work with. He rolls his ball gently up the board.

"Hey!" Sammie Two protests and bangs his machine as well, causing his own ball to finally fall from the chute.

Sammie Lou's ball catches around the rim of one of the blue holes. It is going to fall for sure, but it gets hung up doing loopty-loops around the rim.

Sammie Two chucks his ball. It bangs off the back wall and comes back towards him with such force that it glides right over the red hole and heads towards the blue holes.

Sammie Lou's ball continues spinning.

Sammie Two's ball slows down a bit, but the ball still has too much force and hops over the rim of one of blue holes. It rolls slower towards the yellow holes.

Sammie Lou's ball finally starts falling into its hole.

Sammie Two's ball drops into one of the yellow holes at about the same time as Sammie Lou's. It's too close to tell who won. All heads turn to the ships.

The ships move at what seems to be the same time, but Sammie Two's boat lights the winning lamp. He jumps out of his seat and celebrates. He pumps his fists, runs in place, jumps up and down, and continually whispers yes, yes, yes.

Sammie Lou looks at him with disgust. "It's not like you just nailed the game winning goal in the Cup Finals. It's a stupid carnival game. Act like you've been there."

Sammie Two grows serious. He steps up to Sammie Lou with the Five Ohhh! behind him. "What's the problem cuz? You just can't stand to see me be better than you at anything huh?"

"It's not that. It's just that you don't know how to win with dignity," Sammie Lou says as the Gamblers rally around him.

"You're just a sore loser," Sammie Two says.

"You're a sore winner," Sammie Lou argues.

The game keeper comes over and hands Sammie Two his prize. It's a rather large stuffed alien in a tiny UFO.

"Tell you what Lou. Since you can't stand to see me win..." Sammie Two tosses the alien at Sammie Lou apathetically. "Here. Take the prize. Tell everyone you won."

Sammie Two turns his back on Sammie Lou to walk away, but Sammie Lou chucks the alien at the back of Sammie Two's head. It bounces off the Five Ohhh! panda's noggin, and though it doesn't hurt, Sammie Two turns and tries to charge Sammie Lou anyway. Greg, Ox, and The Colonel hold him back.

"Not right now Two. Not at my sister's wedding. You'll have plenty of opportunities to get him this season," Greg says.

"And just in case you guys haven't noticed, we're in first place a little more than halfway past the first half. Not bad for a couple of minor leaguers," Ox says.

"Oh get over it. How many times do we have to apologize? You guys are a good hockey team," Rodman snaps.

"Good!?" Ox snaps back. "I'd say we're pretty dang great."

Greg calls for his teammates to follow him to the next game, and they leave the Gamblers behind.

"What a bunch of sissies," Lovey notes.

"Yeah," Rodman agrees.

Soup comes up to Sammie Lou with the prize he threw at the back of Sammie Two's head. "Can I have this?"

"Sure," Sammie smiles.

"Hotdog!" Soup exclaims and runs around pretending to fly the UFO.

"I want one!" Chicken says.

"Well, let's jump into this game and each win one," L-Rod says.

By the end of the night, L-Rod and El Pollos Locos each have their own alien manned UFO.

Once everyone has used up all their game tickets, El Pollos Locos, L-Rod, and the other ushers push the games out of the room, clearing way for a dance floor.

Beary and his bride hit the floor right away for their first dance. They dance to a song called *I Love You Beary Much*. A crowd gathers around and watches their first dance as married pandas. After the first song ends, Lovey and Sprinkles and Undertaker and Elmira join them on the dance floor.

Rodman sits at the Gamblers table with Penny and a few others.

Liten nudges Rodman. "What are you doing you fool?"

"What?" Rodman asks hi co-captain.

"Ask the lady to dance."

"Oh!" Rodman turns to Penny. "Penny, would you... Ummm..."

Penny grabs Rodman's flippers. "I'd love to."

Kane sulks between Apple Jack and Snickers as he watches his best friend dancing with a cat. "This is depressing."

"What's the matter big fella?" Snickers asks as he scratches Kane behind the ear mockingly.

Kane pulls away from Snickers. "Look at him out there making a fool of himself."

"Who?" Snickers asks.

"Undertaker, out there dancing with a cat."

"Is it his moves or the fact that he's dancing with a cat that's making him look like a fool?"

"Both," Kane snarls.

"I don't think his moves are that bad," Apple Jack notes.

"You've got to get over this thing about him dating a cat," Snickers says.

"What?" Kane is shocked.

"Dude, he's in love. Let it be. Elmira's a pretty cool cat," Snickers argues on behalf of his friend.

"I can't believe what I'm hearing. Apple, do you condone this?" Kane asks.

"I don't know. I mean, I don't hate Undertaker. I'm not into cats, but Elmira's cool," Apple Jack answers.

"Even if I could get over the fact that he's dating a cat, doesn't it bother you guys that he doesn't hang out anymore?"

"Has it ever occurred to you that he's been trying to hang out, and we've been ignoring and ditching him?" Snickers shoots back.

Kane doesn't respond. Snickers is at least partly right.

"And, I don't know about you guys, but if it weren't for his game winning goal in the Olympics, we might not be wearing the gold medals we have around our necks." Snickers stands up.

"Where are you going?" Kane asks.

"Undertaker isn't going to be the only one with a cute girl on the dance floor. I'm going to ask one of Elmira's sisters to dance."

Kane can't believe his ears. He and Apple Jack turn around and watch as Snickers saunters up to Elmira's sister, Maureen, presents her his paw, and leads her to the dance floor.

Snickers and Maureen take a spot on the dance floor next to Undertaker and Elmira. Undertaker doesn't notice them at first, but when he does, he shoots Snickers a surprised but happy smile. Snickers gives him a wink and a nod.

Kane slumps even lower onto the table until he and Apple Jack feel taps on their shoulders. They turn around to find Elmira's other sisters, Nancy and Alison, standing before them.

"We were wondering," Nancy starts.

"Since our sisters are dancing with your brothers," Alison continues Nancy's thought.

"Oh they're not our brothers," Kane is quick to correct. "We don't even hardly know them."

"Well, we were still wondering if you two would like to dance?" Alison asks.

Apple Jack looks to Kane. With the furrow of his brow and a quick shake of his head, Kane let's Apple Jack know he's not interested.

Apple Jack gets up though and takes Alison by the arm.

"Wha... Hey!" Kane protests.

Apple Jack just turns his head back to Kane and shrugs.

Kane is forced to face Nancy. He stares at her unable to come up with a reason why he can't dance with her that won't make him sound like a jerk. "Oh fine." He shakes his head, stands up, and walks onto the dance floor with the cat.

Slowly, some of the other Gamblers and the Five Ohhh! start to sprinkle onto the dance floor. Some of the players dance with their own dates and others dance with the bridesmaids.

The tension between the two teams mounts as Dislike bumps Lovey and Sprinkles as they dance. Lovey shoots him an angry glance, but Dislike offers only a thumbs down.

The Colonel and his dancing partner, one of Mary's sisters, dance close to Big Chick, who dances with another of Mary's sisters. Each time The Colonel takes a stride closer to Big Chick, Big Chick glides a step away. The fox knows he has Big Chick nervous, so he continues to dance closer and closer to him, making his move faster each time. Finally, Big Chick bumps into something. He turns his head to see what is impeding his movement. The thing stopping him isn't a what but a who. Ox stands with his arms folded across his broad chest almost like he's setting a pick. He has his face really close to Big Chick's face when the chicken turns to him.

"Boo," Ox says.

Big Chick jumps in the air frightened, letting go of Mary's sister's paws. Ox takes the opportunity to sneak in and steal Big Chick's dancing partner.

The Five Ohhh! dogs pass the Gamblers dogs as they dance with Elmira and her sisters. The Five Ohhh! dogs point, laugh, and snicker. The Gamblers try to ignore them, but Crush makes a disparaging remark about Nancy that causes Kane to release her from his grasp, ball up his fists, and step up to Crush.

"What was that remark punk?" Kane demands.

Crush leans back and waves his paw across the air in front of his nose. "Dang man. Get a breath mint."

Kane pushes his adversary. Both sets of dogs step up beside their teammate in case of a fight.

Crush rears back to throw the first punch.

Crunch grabs Crush's paw and stops him. "Don't waste your energy brother. He's not worth it."

"Yeah. Besides, you don't want to have to answer to Greg for starting a fight at his sister's wedding," Stunner agrees.

Crush hesitates a moment, but eventually lowers his fist. He looks Kane in the eye. "You're lucky. But next time I see you on the ice, you're mine."

"All bark and no bite." Kane waves off Crush's threat.

On another section of the dance floor, Rodman dances with Penny. He's about to ask her if she'd like to go out with him sometime after the wedding, but before he can, he's pushed so hard from the side that he loses his grip on Penny's flippers and almost falls to the ground.

Penny gasps.

Mad Man slides into Rodman's spot. "Sorry about that, but we were rudely interrupted earlier, and I'd like to finish our conversation," Mad Man tells her.

Rodman stands up straight, making fists of his flippers.

Penny forcefully frees herself from Mad Man's grasp. "Well, I was dancing with Rodman. So, if you'd like to dance with me, you're going to have to wait, and you're going to have to ask me first."

Mad Man rolls his eyes.

"And just so you know, so you don't waste your time or mine, when you do ask, I'm going to tell you no," Penny says.

Mad Man looks insulted. He lets out a disgusted grunt. "Whatever babe. I guess you're not the kind of girl I thought you were. I mean you're turning down me to dance with that loser?"

Rodman takes a step closer to Mad Man.

"How do you call a two time Cup champion, former Rookie of the Year, and two time MVP a loser?" Penny is the one disgusted and insulted now.

"Because, there's a new top team in town." Mad Man pounds his flippers to his chest. "The Five Ohhh!." The agitator penguin walks away backwards. He bumps into Mary's parents as they dance.

"Watch where you're going son!" Mary's dad demands.

Rodman and Penny chuckle at Mad Man's scolding.

After a while, the slow dancing gets old, and someone turns on the real dance music. Those on the dance floor stop gently gliding and swaying and start jumping and moving like the wild animals they are.

The animals on the dance floor eventually clear some room to let Harlan, one of the best dancer's on the Gamblers, have some space to show off what he can do. The turtle gets down with his bad self, pulling out all of his freshest moves. He wiggles his tail and shakes his head to some Salsa music. He tiptoes across the floor really fast while clapping his flippers together. Then, while slightly hunched over, he moves slowly backwards towards the center of the floor, stops, and starts shaking his hips. The music grows faster, and he drops to his tail so he can start break dancing. He uses his flippers to prop himself up, swings his legs out in front of his body, and then rotates them in a circle around his body. Each time his legs come back around, he has to let go of the floor with one of his flippers to bypass them without knocking himself down.

"Go Harlan!" Beary cheers and claps from the edge of the crowd.

Dislike leans over to The Colonel somewhere else in the crowd. "Remind me to dislike this on Facespace too."

The Colonel nods.

Lovey, standing nearby Dislike, hears his comments. He growls at the black bear. "Well, let's see you do any better."

Dislike looks to Lovey and sneers, but he doesn't respond, and he doesn't try to outdo Harlan.

After spinning around on his flippers for a while, Harlan jumps onto his shell and spins around. He finishes with a jump that propels his whole body up with only a kick thrust. Instead of landing on his feet though, he lands a perfect split. Being able to do the splits is a perk that comes with plenty of practice and stretching on the part of a goalie.

The crowd, except the Five Ohhh!, goes nuts for Harlan.

Greg looks around at all of the guests, some of them his own family and friends, rooting Harlan on. He hates it. He feels their praise for Harlan is an act of betrayal to him and his team. His emotions overtake him, and before he knows what he's doing, he rushes onto the dance floor and pushes Harlan aside. The push is stronger than it needs to be, and Harlan stumbles to the side where he's caught by Beary and Rodman.

The crowd is uneasy at the sight of Greg pushing Harlan the way he does, but once Greg takes center stage and starts dancing, they all ease up. He has moves almost as good as Harlan. As he busts a move and hears the applause of the crowd, he realizes he's winning back the allegiance of his relations. He turns his back to his family and friends, faces the Gamblers, and sticks his tongue out at them.

Rodman turns to Safari Chip and gives him a look. Safari Chip knows the look and nods at Rodman. During Rodman's first season as a Gambler, he and the rest of the guys found out that aside from Rodman and Harlan, Safari Chip has some pretty good moves. So, Rodman and Safari Chip rush the dance floor and force Greg off with a heavy push.

Greg hits the wall of bystanders hard. He turns around to see he's been pushed by Rodman and Safari Chip. His blood boils. While the Gamblers captain and coach wow the crowd, Greg grabs Mad Man and orders him to take Rodman and Safari Chip out.

Mad Man grabs Samanya. The two penguins make their way to the center of the dance floor. They bump Rodman and Safari Chip from behind, interrupting their dancing prematurely and sending the Gamblers back to the sidelines.

Snickers points to the penguins from Reno. "What's with those guys?"

"They're just jerks," Undertaker says.

"We should get 'em," Apple Jack says.

Beary overhears the dogs' conversation. He waves a finger at the dogs and warns them, "No, no! There'll be no getting anyone."

The dogs give Beary a disapproving look, but the groom stands his ground.

Once Beary's attention is turned elsewhere, Kane whispers to the other dogs, "We should still get 'em."

"How?" Undertaker asks.

Apple Jack starts to open his mouth.

Kane cuts him off. "Don't even say it."

"I have an idea," Snickers says.

All eyes turn to him.

"Apple, I want you to go out there and push those guys off the floor as hard as you can," Snicker orders.

Apple Jack doesn't know where Snickers' plan is going, but he doesn't need to be told twice to go push someone. He makes his way through the crowd, steps onto the floor, approaches the penguins, and shoves them powerfully aside. He finds himself center stage now with all eyes on him. Snickers' plan beyond pushing the Five Ohhh! was not told to him, and he doesn't know what to do next. As he looks around at the animals staring him down, he can see a bunch of them sneering at him, looking at him like a jerk who just shoved a couple of other animals for no reason. He doesn't like being looked at like that, and he doesn't want anyone to think of him as a goon, so he breaks into his own goofy dance. He starts moving his paws up and down and shaking his tail. He plugs his nose and pretends to sink under water while shaking his head and acting as silly as he can. Immediately, his silly dancing wins over the crowd and they forget about his malicious pushing of the Reno players.

The Five Ohhh! don't forget it though. Crush saunters up to Apple Jack and pushes him back.

From the Gamblers side, Snickers orders Undertaker out to retaliate.

Undertaker rushes up on Crush and shoves him with open paws that make a loud slap.

The Five Ohhh! have had enough. Stunner, Hoss, and Crunch step out of the crowd. They help Crush up and make their way menacingly towards Apple Jack and Undertaker.

Snickers grabs Kane, and they rush out to stand beside the other dogs in their faceoff with the Five Ohhh! dogs. All eight dogs stand on the dance floor staring each other down. No one makes a move as the crowd watches uneasily for something bad to happen.

Mary grabs Beary and says to him, "You have to do something Beary. Don't let them fight."

"I'll put a stop to this nonsense." Beary leaves his bride to step onto the dance floor.

Greg sees Beary making his way to the angry dogs and mistakes Beary's attempts to make peace for an act of aggression. He rushes to stand beside his teammates.

Beary steps in between the dogs. He raises his paws as if to separate the canines. "Fellas, fellas. Let us not fight on this day of..."

Beary never finishes his sentence. Greg flies in and punches him in the face.

An all-out brawl breaks out, and once it starts, there's no stopping it. The dogs attack each other. The Gamblers and Five Ohhh! rush each other and start fighting. Even some of the wedding goers from opposite sides join in and start fighting on behalf of the team they came with.

The dogs roll around the floor, biting, clawing, and punching one another.

Kane takes his fair share of pounding from the bigger and stronger Stunner, but he holds his own.

Snickers dodges a few punches from Crush as best he can. Crush lands a few, but Snickers doesn't mind much. Crush is smaller than him, and he's really just waiting for the right moment to throw a haymaker, and when he sees his opportunity, he levels Crush, knocking him out with one shot.

Apple Jack scraps with the much larger Crunch. Crunch, for a dog his size, is very feisty and wild but not much of a fighter. He snaps, snarls, and shows his teeth as he swings erratically at Apple Jack. Apple Jack in turn laughs at the crazy dog. His laughter agitates Crunch, and the more Apple Jack laughs, the angrier the pit bull grows. Crunch gets scrappier and scrappier as Apple Jack laughs, and in turn, Apple Jack laughs more and more until his laughter becomes some much that it causes him to let down his defenses and Crunch lands a solid blow to Apple Jack's jaw. This snaps Apple Jack out of his laughter. His smile fades, and he balls up a fist. He wallops Crunch in the snout and lays him out.

Undertaker takes punch after punch from Hoss. He tries to defend himself, but the boxer is too quick for him. Undertaker refuses to fall though, and because of it, he takes more punishment than is necessary. All the while Undertaker is being hit, Elmira screams frantically for Hoss to stop. Her pleas go unanswered by Hoss, so Elmira finds a bottle of sparkling juice and cracks it over Hoss's head.

The hit surprises Hoss. He doesn't fall to the ground, but he's stunned enough to lay off his attack. He stumbles around, shakes off some broken pieces of glass, and turns to Elmira. He locks eyes with her and makes a fist.

Elmira takes a frightened step backwards unsure of what to do. She continues to back up afraid that Hoss might actually hit her. Suddenly, she bumps into something and can't get away. Her heart sinks, but what she finds she's bumped into is her sisters backing her up.

Hoss stops in his tracks. He smiles arrogantly. "You really think I'm afraid of a few cats? A few girl cats at that."

"No," says Nancy.

"But you better be afraid of that." Elmira points behind Hoss.

"That old trick eh?" Hoss laughs. "What is it? Did Undertaker suddenly come back from the grave? Here, I'll humor you." Hoss turns around and is taken by surprise. Undertaker actually is there. The Gamblers dog scoops Hoss off the ground and gives him a body slam that keeps Hoss down.

Undertaker puts his paws on his hips. "Ladies," he says to the cats.

Two cats slip their arms around him on one side and two other cats do the same on his other side, and he leads them away from the menacing Five Ohhh! dog.

Mary tends to Beary, who is still dazed on the ground. "Beary! Beary! Are you ok?"

Beary rubs his jaws. "I think so."

"Beary, they're ruining the reception," Mary cries.

Beary looks around at the riot going on in the Gamblers press room. He tries to push himself up. "I'll put a stop to it."

Beary never makes it to his feet because Greg pushes him back to the ground. "Just stay down jerk."

Mary jumps to her feet and gets in her brother's face. "Stop it Greg!"

"They started it," Greg yells back at his sister.

"I don't care who started it. I just want you to stop it."

Beary tries to get up again, but Greg pushes him to the floor once again.

Mary has seen enough. She throws a punch at her older brother, knocking him to the floor next to her husband.

Sammie Two finds his cousin in the crowd and pushes his way through the animals in front of him. He grabs Sammie Lou from behind, spins him around, and flinches at him.

Sammie Lou jumps defensively backwards. "Jerk."

Sammie Two gets serious. "What did you call me?"

Sammie Lou shakes his head and tries to walk away.

Sammie Two grabs him again, spins him around, and pushes Sammie Lou. "I said, what did you call me?"

"I called you a jerk." Sammie Lou takes a step back.

Sammie Two steps closer to Sammie Lou again and gives him another shove. "You're going to wish you hadn't called me that."

"I'm not going to fight you," Sammie Lou says.

From a few feet away, Jason sees Sammie Lou getting pushed around by his evil cousin. He starts making his way over to them to stand up for Sammie Lou.

"Well that's too bad for you, because I'm definitely going to fight you." Sammie Two makes a fist and rears back.

Sammie Lou closes his eyes and waits for his cousin to punch him. He hears a thud, but he doesn't feel anything. Upon opening his eyes, he sees Jason falling to the ground dazed and confused and Sammie Two holding his fist in pain from throwing such a hard punch. Sammie Lou deduces quickly that Jason took the punch for him. With Sammie Two still holding his paw, Sammie Lou takes the opportunity to push his cousin forcefully, sending the koala stumbling backwards and rolling over one of the table tops. He didn't want to hurt his cousin, but he needed to create some space and buy himself some time so he can drag Jason through the rioting crowd to safety.

El Pollos Locos and L-Rod run around the room looking for Big Chick, but he's nowhere to be found. They push past fighting hockey players, tussling wedding guests, and even Mary tending to Beary on the floor.

"Where can he be?" Soup asks.

"I don't know. We've looked everywhere," Noodle answers.

Chicken stands on his tip toes to try and see over the taller animals. He scans the room and still can't find Big Chick.

L-Rod jumps on top of one of the tables to get a better view of the room. He doesn't see Big Chick, but he does see The Colonel across the room flipping tables over and looking underneath each one. He does another quick scan of the room and finds Big Chick hiding behind one of the tables The Colonel is approaching. He taps Chicken on the shoulder and points out both the fox and Big Chick.

"We have to save him," Chicken says.

"How?" L-Rod asks.

"I have an idea." Noodle grabs the others, and they race to a nearby table.

"What are we going to do?" Soup asks.

"Help me take the legs off this table," Noodle instructs.

Noodle, L-Rod and the other El Pollos Locos all kick a different leg of the table at the same time. The legs fly right off and in different directions. Noodle grabs one of the wedding gifts off another nearby table. He places the gift under the center of the table top so that it rests at an angle.

Noodle places Chicken on the end of the table that rests on the floor. "Stand there Chicken."

"How is this going to help Uncle Big Chick?" Chicken asks.

"He's not our uncle Chicken!" Noodle grumbles.

"Hurry up you guys," Soup orders as he watches The Colonel get closer and closer to Big Chick.

"Stay Chicken!" Noodle demands of his brother.

Chicken does as he's told. Noodle, Soup, and L-Rod grab another table. They drag it back near the table top upon which Chicken stands. They position the second table so that it is in front of Chicken near the upward angle of his table top.

Noodle hops on top of the second table and waves for Soup and L-Rod to join him. "Come up here guys."

"What's going on?" Chicken asks.

Noodle ignores him and helps pull Soup up.

"Noodle?" Chicken asks.

Noodle whispers into L-Rod's ear and then into Soup's.

"Noodle, you're not going to do what I..."

Chicken never gets a chance to finish his sentence. Noodle yells jump, and he, Soup, and L-Rod jump onto the angled side of the table top, sending it crashing to the ground and Chicken's side of the table top flying into the air. Chicken is flung across the room like a rocket propelled missile. He flies over animals, table tops, presents, and even the wedding cake.

The Colonel approaches the table behind which Big Chick hides. He stops, smells the air, and can tell he's found what he's looking for, a giant chicken. Goosebumps appear on his flesh beneath his fur he's so excited. His heart beats fast with a tickle. He reaches for the table, grabs it firmly, and prepares to whip it into the air, but he's stopped by a sudden powerful clunk to his cranium that is Chicken as he comes crashing down like a chicken bomb. The Colonel loses his grip on the table and stumbles but doesn't fall. It takes the fox a second to collect himself. When he does, he sees Chicken laughing and sitting on the floor. The fox narrows his eyes and growls.

Chicken stops laughing.

The Colonel makes a move towards Chicken, but he's stopped once more by another blow to the head.

This time, Soup crashes into the fox and brings him to a knee. The second El Pollo Loco somersaults and rolls next to his brother in front of The Colonel. The two chickens laugh, enraging the fox even more.

Before The Colonel can make it back to his feet, a third chicken bomb in the form of Noodle flies over, crashes into, and knocks the fox to the ground.

"Take that you big stupid fox," Noodle yells.

"Yeah. Take it you bully," Soup asserts himself as well.

"That'll teach you to pick on our uncle," Chicken says.

El Pollos Locos pick themselves off the ground and rush behind the table to check on Big Chick.

"Come on big fella. We're going to get you out of here," Noodle tells his cousin.

"Where's The Colonel?" Big Chick asks.

"Don't worry about him. He won't be chasing anyone for some time," Chicken laughs.

"How do you know that?" Big Chick asks.

"Because he's been chicken bombed," Soup answers.

"He's been what?" Big Chick doesn't understand.

"Nevermind. Just follow us." Noodle helps his cousin to his feet and leads him across the room to L-Rod. The five of them make their way to where a larger group of Gamblers are so that they'll be more protected and have some backup from The Colonel and the rest of the mayhem in the room.

Elsewhere in the bedlam, Dislike sneaks up behind Lovey and pushes him. Lovey falls face first to the ground hard. He catches himself with his paws, and in a fluid motion, he spins around on the ground to see who or what pushed him. He sees Dislike laughing at him.

Dislike's laughter is abruptly interrupted by a swift smack in the snout by Sprinkles. His smile turns to a scowl, and he moves to retaliate against Lovey's girlfriend. He raises his paw and prepares to strike Sprinkles, but she makes a fist and swings at him first. She pops him square in the eye.

Sprinkles' hit on Dislike dazes the black bear long enough to allow Lovey to get back to his feet. He darts after Dislike, and the two grizzly cubs exchange rapid punches. One blow after another, they pummel each other with fists, both refusing to fall.

Near where the dogs continue their fight, Rodman bobs and weaves as he tries to avoid a fight with Mad Man. The Five Ohhh! penguin keeps moving towards Rodman, backing him up against a wall and trapping him. Mad Man takes a swing at him, but Rodman ducks out of the way. Mad Man hits the wall with his flipper. He lets out a wild squawk and keels over in pain holding his injured appendage. Rodman smiles, but doesn't even have time to laugh because he's blindsided by a hit from Ox.

As he rolls over onto his back, Rodman has only one eye open and can see Ox standing above him, getting ready to pounce. He closes the one eye he does have open and tries his best to prepare for the pummeling he's about to incur. However, with his eyes closed, Rodman never sees Penny pick up a chair and swing it at Ox. The chair explodes into a hundred pieces. Ox's eyes roll up into his head, and he falls to the ground next to Rodman. It's only because of the thud of Ox hitting the floor that Rodman dares to open his eyes. He sees the massive ox next to him and Penny standing over him with what's left of the chair.

"I owe you one," Rodman smiles at Penny.

"You can buy me dinner sometime," Penny smiles.

Just like that, without even having to ask, Rodman has the date he was hoping all night to get.

Mary eventually gets Beary back to his feet. Along with the help of some of the Gamblers, his two coaches, and some of the wedding goers, Beary is able to get the fighting stopped a little bit here and a little bit there. The only animals he can't seem to get through to are the dogs. Each time he grabs one of the Gamblers dogs, a Five Ohhh! dog sucker punches the Gamblers dog.

Kane and Undertaker whip Stunner and Hoss away from the table with the wedding cake towards Apple Jack and Snickers. Each of the Gamblers dogs catches one of the Five Ohhh! dogs. They use the momentum of the Reno players to push them towards one another and bunk their heads together. Stunner falls fast to the ground, but Hoss stays on his hind legs.

This puts the fighting to a stop.

"Oh thank heavens." Beary wipes sweat off his brow.

"Send him back this way!" Kane yells.

Undertaker motions for Apple Jack and Snickers to do as Kane has instructed.

Beary looks at the dogs by the wedding cake. Then, he looks to the dogs standing with Hoss.

Apple Jack grabs one of Hoss's arms and Snickers grabs the other.

"Noooooooo!" Beary yells.

Apple Jack and Snickers whip Hoss back towards Undertaker and Kane.

"Noooooooo!" Mary screams.

Hoss approaches Undertaker and Kane, who bend down and allow Hoss to run into their lowered shoulders. As Hoss hits them, the Gamblers dogs stand up and use their strength to lift Hoss high into the air.

The bride, groom, hockey players, and other wedding goers watch as Hoss soars through the air out of control in slow motion and does flip. Hoss comes down and crashes with a belly flop into the wedding cake.

Frosting and cake splatter all over the place. What was once a massive six tier cake is little more than a crushed pile of sweetness. Multiple ooohs are heard around the room for just a second before they're drowned out by a high pitched shriek from Mary that brings all of the animals who had just participated in the fight out of their trance. Undertaker and Kane stare at the ruined wedding cake with a Five Ohhh! dog in the middle of it.

"Nuts," the Gamblers rainbow frosting splattered dogs say in unison.

Chapter 25: Amends And New Friends

The Gamblers keep a watchful eye on the door. They wonder if Beary is going to show up for their game. No one has heard from him since he threw every one of them out of the reception. One by one, they all file in, except Beary. They even fire in the hole Harlan as he's the second to last guy to arrive.

"What the heck?" Harlan shakes off the water prank.

"What?" Apple Jack asks.

"I know I'm not the last guy here. Why'd I get fire in the holed?"

"We aren't sure if Beary is going to show up or not. And, we had to get somebody," Apple Jack explains.

"Have you heard from BNR?" Sammie asks.

"I tried knocking on his door before I came to practice to see if he wanted to walk down with me. He was with Mary in their room, and I think…"

Harlan is interrupted by the slamming open of the locker room doors that startles the Gamblers. They all jump and turn to see what caused commotion.

Even Safari Chip pokes his head out of his office long enough to see Beary looking angry, so he quickly retreats back into his office and shuts the door before Beary can see him.

Beary stands with his paws on his hips and his bride beside him with matching demeanor and stance.

"Uh oh," L-Rod whispers and stands behind Rodman.

"You can say that again buster," Beary says loudly.

"Beary, we're really sorry…" Rodman tries to apologize.

"There will be no apologies," Beary interrupts him. The panda enters the room, puts his arms behind his back, and walks slowly past each of his teammates like a drill sergeant during revelry. He stares them down with scolding eyes. "What you fellas did was despicable."

The Gamblers lower their heads. They know they did Beary wrong, and now they just have to shut their mouths and take whatever he dishes out.

"A fellow player gets one chance in this life to marry the girl of his dreams and have a party with all of his friends and family. And he requests of his teammates one thing. Just one little teeny tiny thing." Beary holds two of the fingers on his paws ever so slightly apart and pauses for dramatic effect. He lowers his head and shakes it disbelievingly.

Somehow, as angry as Beary seems, and as serious as the situation is, there's something in his tone and in the theatrics of his performance that makes the Gamblers want to laugh.

"Just don't beat up the other guests," Beary continues.

Undertaker chuckles.

Beary's head whips around to the dog. He walks briskly to him. "Oh that's funny?"

Undertaker straightens up and wipes the smirk off his face. "No."

Now it's Kane who laughs. Beary gets in his face. Kane tries to stifle his laughter, but he cannot.

"Well what is it?" Beary demands.

"I'm sorry. I just keep seeing the shocked look on Hoss's stupid face as he lay there with rainbow colored frosting all over his pretty tuxedo," Kane chuckles.

"Ruining the wedding wasn't funny, but there were funny parts in the ruination of the wedding," Apple Jack ads.

Snickers looks at the pups around him astonished. He can't believe they haven't learned by his example how to act right and keep their traps shut. "Shut up you guys."

"It's ok." Beary waves off their chuckling.

The Gamblers can't tell if the look on Beary's face is one of utter anger or depression. While they try to figure it out for a silent moment, Beary's scowl suddenly turns to a smile. He claps his paws together and points to all of his teammates. "No seriously, it's ok. It was kind of funny."

"What?" Harlan squeaks as his voice cracks.

"It was pretty cool seeing that guy go through the wedding cake, and seeing most of the Five Ohhh! get theirs," Beary says.

"You're serious?" Rodman asks, feeling a wave of relief as they're all let off the hook.

"Of course. I am. I love you guys," Beary puts his arms around Undertaker and Kane and gives them side hugs.

"What about you Mary? I am afraid we may have spoiled your special day," Liten asks.

Mary steps into the locker room with a smile. She walks right over to the mouse and playfully ruffles the fur atop his head. "Listen, I grew up in a hockey family and married into another. I know what to expect."

There's a typical joyous uproar around the Gamblers locker room. Everyone rushes to shakes paws with Beary and hug Mary and give them another congratulations.

"Now that that's over, we have a game to prepare for," Beary says.

The Gamblers beat the Fairbanks Pilots night. The Pilots happen to be one of the teams they were tied with in third place. It gives them some breathing room, but they know they're still tied with the Trains. Things don't get easier as their remaining schedule pits them mostly against teams with winning records.

After the game, Snickers grabs Kane and Apple Jack and takes them to the food court inside the New Orleans hotel. They grab trays full of Muchos and head to a table. Snickers tries to impart the importance of being good teammates and role models in the locker room on the pair. He reprimands them for their laughing at Beary's anger, as fake as it was, earlier in the day.

"Sorry, Snickers. I guess we were a little immature," Apple Jack says.

"Yeah. Sorry Dog Shark. We'll do our best to be better teammates," Kane assures him.

"Good." Snickers says. He sees Undertaker approaching the table from behind the other two dogs.

Kane and Apple Jack can see he's looking at something, so they turn to see what it is.

Kane turns immediately back around. "Oh great. What's that guy doing here?"

Undertaker hears what Kane says as he slides into the chair next to Snickers. "Hi guys."

Only Snickers greets him back. The elder dog is disappointed in the younger pups, so he lays it all out on the table for them. "To answer your question, Kane, Undertaker is here because I asked him to come. I know it came as a shock to all of us when we found him with Elmira, and I know you were hurt the most that he ditched us, but it's time to put all the bad feelings behind us," Snickers says.

Kane turns his nose up in the air.

"How you can you sit there and pretend to still be that mad after Beary and Mary's wedding?" Snickers asks.

"What do you mean?" Kane asks.

"I saw you dancing with Elmira's sister," Snickers says.

"I was trying not to be rude."

"You were having a good time." Snickers points an accusatory finger at Kane.

"I was just being polite," Kane sighs.

"No you weren't," Snickers says matter-of-factly. He points to Apple Jack. "You were having a good time too."

Apple Jack can feel Kane's gaze upon him. He turns and looks at his buddy with fear in his eyes. At first he doesn't want to admit it to Kane, but it's pretending to be angry that he really doesn't want to do anymore. He shrugs. "I did."

Kane gasps.

"Elmira said her sisters had a great time with you guys too," Undertaker informs the other dogs.

"What the heck?" Kane shouts, drawing the attention of several nearby patrons of the food court.

"What?" Snickers asks.

"I mean… I just… cats and dogs…" Kane stammers.

"What are you saying?" Apple Jack asks.

"I'm saying he betrayed us," Kane spits out.

"Last time I checked, he was still a Gambler and scoring goals for us." Snickers turns to Undertaker. "How many game winners do you have this year?"

"Three," Undertaker answers.

"One on the last road trip right?" Snickers asks.

"Yeah." Undertaker nods.

"And he's been hitting you with a record number of assists hasn't he Apple?" Snickers asks.

"Yeah. I've already got more goals this year than I did all of last season, and a lot of them have come on assists from Undertaker."

"It doesn't sound to me like he's betrayed us at all," Snickers says.

"He chose a cat over his buddies," Kane reminds them all for the millionth time.

"Get over it," Snickers orders Kane sternly.

"But…" Kane tries to argue again.

Snickers throws a threatening point of his finger Kane's way. "I've heard the stories of how you and Undertaker sat at this very table once telling Harlan that you asked him once to be nice to Beary and the second time you weren't asking, you were telling. Now, I'm telling you, Mr. Kane, be nice to Undertaker."

Kane doesn't know what to think. On one paw, he still feels hurt and doesn't want to forgive Undertaker. He wants him to feel just as bad as he did all the times Undertaker ditched them. On the other paw, he misses his buddy and wants his best friend back. He looks to Apple Jack for his thoughts.

Apple Jack shrugs. "I've really got no beef with him."

Kane looks to Undertaker but doesn't say anything.

"I miss playing on a line with you," Undertaker tells Kane.

Kane hates to admit it, but he misses playing with Undertaker too. Playing with Snickers has been great, and he's learned a lot about being aggressive both defensively and offensively and yet not to be overly aggressive. He's learned to be a scorer on top of a defender and really turned into a complete player. But, the comfortableness that comes with playing with a guy he's known his whole life like Undertaker is something that's been lacking most of this season.

Snickers kicks Kane under the table.

"Alright!" Kane barks and looks to the ceiling. "I miss playing with you too."

Snickers and Apple Jack high five from across their table.

Undertaker stands up and reaches his paw out for a shake to Kane. Kane stands up with a big smile and his paw outstretched for Undertaker, but he decides to grab Undertaker and give him a big hug instead. He crushes and shakes his friend.

"Alright, alright, alright. That's good enough," Undertaker laughs.

Kane lets him go, and the two dogs sit back down.

"Shall we eat then?" Undertaker asks and reaches for one of Kane's Muchos.

Kane slaps Undertaker's paw. "Hey! Just 'cause we're friends and line mates again, don't think for a second that you can have any of my Muchos. I don't like you that much."

The other dogs laugh until Undertaker looks at them with eyes that plead for a Mucho. They grab their trays and hold them away from the black dog and shake their heads.

"You can afford your own. You ain't no bum," Apple Jack says.

Undertaker shifts his gaze to Snickers.

"I'll share my hockey wisdom with you, not my Muchos," Snickers says.

"Nuts," Undertaker whispers and stands to go buy his own Muchos.

*

The Gamblers season continues on with Kane back on the first line with Undertaker. On the second line, Snickers, knowing he won't be around for too many more seasons, begins teaching Apple Jack all he knows about hockey. Apple Jack is the dog that most reminds him of himself, and Snickers chooses him to be his successor.

On the third line, Jason fills the seventeenth spot quite well. He even teaches L-Rod his own method for taking faceoffs. It's a method unlike anyone else in hockey, and it seems to be a method suited for L-Rod. After practicing it for a few weeks, Jason convinces Safari Chip to let L-Rod play center in a game. L-Rod wins five of the eight faceoffs he takes that night. All of the Gamblers notice the change in Jason. He seems to have done a complete one-eighty and become the perfect teammate. Even Lovey, Sammie, and Haas warm up to him.

The season seems to fly by after Beary's wedding. Despite their excellent record after the All-Star break, all the Gamblers winning isn't enough for them to catch the Five Ohhh! for first place. Before the last game of the season, the Gamblers find themselves in a four way tie for second place with Lou Brown's Anchorage Pilots, Buck Wild's Seattle Rampage, and the Bakersfield Trains. All four teams trail the Five Ohhh! by three points in the standings, making it impossible for any of them to win first place. The Gamblers hold tie breakers over all the other teams in case of a tie, but if they lose and all the other teams win, the Gamblers could find themselves on the outside of the playoffs looking in. If the Gamblers lose their game, they can still make the playoffs in variety of ways, but they'll need at least one of the teams they're tied with to lose as well. A win means a sure shot and home ice in the first round of the playoffs, so Safari Chip gives his team only one option: WIN!

Winning their final game isn't going to be easy though. They are pitted against the Gold Rush for the final game of the season. Even though statistically eliminated from the playoffs, the Gold Rush have been playing more and more like the Gold Rush of old during the final month of the season. Plus, Maulbreath is returning for the final game. He worked extra hard during his rehab in order to be able to come back for the season's finale. Initially, Coil made the decision to keep his all-star tiger out of the line up so he could have extra recovery time and be one hundred percent for the beginning of next season, but he changed his mind after Maulbreath made a strong case about being the team's leader and wanting to show his teammates what determination is all about. If nothing else, Coil decides, it would be good for the Alaska fans, who aren't used to disappointing seasons, and his players to see their captain return.

All the teams in the league have a day off before the final game. The Gamblers use the day to do a light workout and relax a bit. It's always been Safari Chip's stance that they play better when they're relaxed.

That night, Rodman and the entire team including El Pollos Locos and the coaches head out to watch Penny play in her recreational league championship game. Inevitably, the Gamblers are mobbed by fans outside the rec center, but after signing a few autographs and taking some photos, they urge everyone inside for the girls' game.

Penny's team, the Paradise Valley Haze, wear black jerseys with purple trim. The logo on her jersey is a purple hockey puck bursting through a hazy grey cloud. On her back are her first name and the number one in purple outlined in white. She wears the number one on account of her name being Penny.

The opponents of the Haze, the Green Valley Goal Scorers, wear white jerseys with blue and green trim.

"There are some big girls out there," Jason notes as he watches the girls skate.

Soup points to the ice. "Check her out. She's almost your size Big Chick."

All eyes turn to see the biggest lady on the ice. She's a chicken defense-women on Penny's team. The back of her jersey reads Chickette. Big Chick takes one look at her and falls head over heels.

Penny looks into the crowd, searching for Rodman during warm ups. She spots the Gamblers and eventually lays eyes on Rodman. He waves at her, and she blows him a kiss.

The Gamblers that catch her gesture towards him ohhh and ahhh. As always, something Penny has done would have him blushing if only it were possible for penguins to blush.

Beary leans over Safari Chip, elbows Rodman, and says, "Might you be the second Gambler to join the ranks of the wedded?"

"I don't know. I just met her." Rodman smiles.

"Just call me when you're ready to pop the question. I'll give you some tips on how to get her to say yes," Beary jokes.

Safari Chip can see Rodman's embarrassment. He laughs and slaps his captain on the back.

The game gets underway, and it quickly becomes apparent who's going to win. Most of the girls on the Goal Scorers are slow, uncoordinated, and discombobulated. Yet, many of the girls on the Haze seem to have all the tools a hockey player needs, speed, skill, puck handling, shot blocking ability, puck awareness, grace, and overall knowledge of the game.

Penny and Chickette are the Haze standouts. Penny score's the first two goals of the game and assists on the next two, putting her team up 4-0. On the defensive end of the ice, Chickette flattens anyone who comes near the net with the puck, and she usually sends the puck back down the other way. She also blocks a handful of shots from reaching her goalie. Her skills only make Big Chick fall even harder.

Several of the Gamblers comment on Penny's play. They thought for sure they'd be watching a train wreck of a hockey game with a bunch of rec league girls, but Penny and her team turn out to be quite entertaining.

The Haze win 6-2.

After the game, most of the Gamblers head back to the hotel to get a good night's rest before they play Alaska in the morning. Rodman sticks around to meet Penny after the game. Lovey, Beary, Undertaker, and Big Chick hang with him and are joined by Sprinkles, Mary, and Elmira who were also in the crowd cheering on their friend.

"Can we hang out with you Uncle Big Chick?" Chicken begs.

"Not tonight guys. You have to get back to the hotel and get some sleep. We have a big game tomorrow," Big Chick says.

"You have a big game tomorrow. We just have a big game to watch. How come you get to stay out?" Noodle asks.

"Because I'm a grown up, and you are little chicks. So please, just go back to the hotel with L-Rod and the other guys. You can hang out with him until I get back," Big Chick says.

"So..." Chicken thinks aloud. "We can hang out with L-Rod all night."

"And stay up until you get back, but we can't stay up and go out with you?" Noodle finishes Chicken's thought.

"Basically," Big Chick answers.

"Why?" Chicken asks.

"Yeah. Why?" Noodle demands.

Before Big Chick can answer, Soup speaks up. "I know why."

"Why?" the other El Pollos Locos ask.

"He wants to meet Chickette." Soup bashfully kicks the ground with his wings held behind his back.

Now it's Big Chick's turn to be ohhhed and ahhhed at.

"No!" Big Chick says defensively.

"Yeah! Yeah!" Lovey laughs.

Big Chick sighs.

"She's really nice Big Chick. You should meet her," Sprinkles urges.

"Really!? Ok!" Big Chick says overzealously then he composes himself. "I mean, yeah, sure, if you think I should."

El Pollos Locos giggle.

Noodle elbows Big Chick. "Go get her big guy."

Chicken winks and points with both wings at Big Chick. "Uncle Lady's Man."

Big Chick's teasing cousins walk away laughing.

Soup pats his embarrassed cousin on the wing. "Good luck Big Chick."

"Thanks Soup." Big Chick pats his cousin on the head and watches him run to catch up with his brothers.

The group awaiting Penny on the bleachers in the rec center doesn't have to wait long before she appears. She comes out of the locker room with Chickette. Big Chick notices her before he even sees Penny, and his heart beats fast. He stands up, sits down, looks away, sneaks a peek back Chickette's way, crosses his legs, uncrosses his legs, rests his head in his wing, straightens up, and tries to do anything to feel comfortable and look natural. All he succeeds in doing is panicking.

"What are you doing?" Lovey asks Big Chick.

"Nothing. Why?"

"You're all fidgety."

"No I'm not," Big Chick says as he continues to fidget.

Penny arrives with Chickette. "Hi everyone."

They all greet her back, and congratulate both girls on their win.

"Thanks. I mean, it's just a rec league championship. It's not like it's the Cup or anything," Penny downplays their accomplishment.

"It's still something to be proud of," Rodman says.

"Hey you guys. I hope you don't mind, but I brought my friend from the team with me. This is Chickette, and she just had to come with when she heard the Gamblers were in the crowd and that there was a chance she might be able to meet Big Chick," Penny says.

Big Chick, bashfully looking towards the ground, trying to be inconspicuous, looks up in awe. "Me?"

"She's a big fan." Penny smiles.

Big Chick straightens up with all sorts of newfound confidence. He notices that it's Chickette who looks shy. He waves to her, and she grins back at him with a bashful smile a mile wide.

Chapter 26: Lovey's Revenge

One by one, the Gamblers file into their locker room for their final regular season fire in the hole. As always, Apple Jack hands everyone their water balloons as they enter, and as always, when the locker room doors swing open and the second to last player walks in, it is Lovey who is missing and doomed to pay the watery price.

Apple Jack hands Liten his last water balloon. "Congratulations. You won't be getting ambushed today."

"Am I the last one safe?" Liten asks.

"Yep," Apple Jack chuckles.

Liten wipes his brow. "That was close."

The Gamblers rush to their lockers and other designated hiding places and wait. And wait. And wait. But, Lovey never comes through the locker room doors.

"Hey Rodman," Apple Jack calls from inside his locker.

"Yeah?"

"Lovey is coming isn't he?"

"I think so."

The Gamblers wait a few more minutes.

Snickers comes out of his locker. "Maybe someone should go check on him."

"Yeah," Rodman agrees. "I don't like this. He's never this late."

"Want me to run up to his room?" L-Rod asks Rodman.

"Sure. Be quick."

L-Rod makes his way to the locker room doors but stops when they suddenly open. He freezes in his tracks. The Gamblers that had come out of their hiding spots dive back into them and prepare to nail Lovey with their water balloons, but Lovey doesn't enter the room. In fact, no one enters the room.

L-Rod walks to the door and peeks his head into the hallway. "There's no one here."

The Gamblers come out of their lockers and other hiding spots again. They join L-Rod and examine the hallway with him. Sure enough, the little guy is right. There's no one there.

"That's weird," Big Chick says.

"You said it," Beary agrees.

A rustling from behind the players gets them all to spin around. They still see no one and nothing.

"What was that?" Haas asks.

"Something funny's going on here," Apple Jack says and makes his way towards Safari Chip's office. "Has anyone talked to Chip or Flip today?"

There's a collective shake of the Gamblers heads.

Apple Jack tries to open Safari Chip's door, but it's locked. With his and the rest of the Gamblers back's turned to the locker room door again, someone rolls a bowling ball into the center of the room.

"Where the heck did that come from?" Goose squawks.

L-Rod races back to the locker room doors. He looks into an empty hallway once more. "It came from out here, but there's still no one there."

"I'm starting to freak out man." Sammie shivers.

"Yes. It is as though there is a ghost in this locker room today," Liten says.

"There's a note on the bowling ball." Rodman grabs it while the Gamblers circle around him.

"What does it say?" Beary asks.

"It just says *revenge*," Rodman answers.

Out of nowhere, Apple Jack gets pegged in the back of the head by a water balloon. "Hey!"

The other Gamblers look to him with a little bit of shock, but then they all start laughing, but their laughter doesn't last. Undertaker and Kane each nailed with water balloons next.

"What the heck?" Undertaker shouts.

"Who did that?" Kane demands.

The Gamblers turn to the locker room doors once more and find no one there. Then, with their backs turned to Safari

Chip's office, they're all ambushed. Lovey kicks Safari Chip's door wide open and takes his teammates by surprise. He's clad in his Gamblers camo jersey from last season, black, white, and grey camo pants, the camoflague bandana Beary gave him around his head, sunglasses, and a plethora of water artillery. Included in his arsenal are two sashes full of water balloons worn around his chest in the shape of an X, two Super Soaker 5000's, both equipped with perpetual shot triggers and connected to an extra water tank worn on his back, and a squirting flower clipped to his chest.

Lovey charges the room spraying his teammates with his Super Soakers. He squirts Liten and Haas first as they're the two closest to him. They fall to the ground and drop their balloons. Lovey's attack only begins there. He runs right at the throng of Gamblers in the center of the room, taking out Harlan, Maverick, Goose, and Moose before the Gamblers can even start running.

The Gamblers do start running though. They laugh as they try to escape their crazy teddy that has obviously been fire in the holed one too many times.

Lovey jumps behind a table, detaches two water balloons, peeks over the table, spots Snickers and Apple Jack near their lockers, and tosses the balloons their way. He nails both of them in the head with dead on aim.

Rodman and L-Rod throw their balloons at Lovey, but he ducks their vain attempt at a defense. One of their balloons hits the table that shields him and the other flies far over his head. Knowing the penguins are out of ammo, Lovey stands up with his water guns and soaks them for their efforts.

Near the locker room doors, Sammie and Jason rear back with their water balloons to try and defend themselves, but they have their balloons striped from behind. They turn around and get nailed at point blank range with their own water balloons by Safari Chip and Flip. Then, the two coaches enter the room as Lovey's backup, spraying some of the Gamble who are trying to get back to their feet.

Big Chick and the dogs make their way to the table where Lovey is hiding. Their plan is to assemble a throng large enough to sustain Lovey's attack. They may not all make it, but some of them will, and then, they can take Lovey by storm, maybe even get ahold of one of his Super Soakers. As they approach the table that shields Lovey, the teddy bear pokes his head out to assess the situation.

Lovey sees the mob of oncoming Gamblers and fires a few shots, taking out Snickers and Undertaker before he hides behind the table again. He waits for a fraction of a second, unhooks two water balloons from his straps, looks out from behind the table on the other side, and chucks the two balloons. This time he knocks Kane and Apple Jack to the floor.

Big Chick, the leader of the charge, manages to make it all the way to the front of the table. He kicks it once with his giant foot and scares Lovey into standing up.

"Come on guys! Let's get him!" Big Chick shouts and motions with his wings for the dogs to help him.

But, there's nothing from the dogs.

"Guys?" Big Chick repeats.

Still, nothing from behind him.

Lovey chuckles and points behind Big Chick.

Big Chick turns to find all of his allies lying on the ground in puddles of water.

"Oh nuts," Big Chick says and turns back to face Lovey.

Lovey grabs ahold of his squirting flower, gives it two tiny pumps and squirts Big Chick in the face. Big Chick freaks out as though he's been blasted by a water cannon and runs away. All the while Big Chick runs, he gets drenched from yards away by Lovey's powerful Super Soakers.

On the other side of them room, Safari Chip and Flip hold down Liten, Maverick, Goose, and Moose by spraying them with nonstop action and not allowing them to get away.

While he was fending off Big Chick and the dogs, Lovey saw Harlan and Beary escape the locker room into the hallway that leads to the ice maker. He doesn't know what they're up to, so he heads over to the doors and pokes his head out to check things out. He sees the duo filling up a Gatorade cooler with water. Lovey pulls his head back into the locker room, hides beside the doors, and waits. While he waits, he almost gets nailed with a water balloon, but it hits the wall just above his head. He turns his focus to his new attacker and sees another water balloon coming at him. He's able to duck and fall to the floor just in time to avoid it. His new assailants are the regrouped Rodman and L-Rod, who found some stray water balloons lying on the locker room floor, no doubt those of some fallen comrade. The penguins frantically search for more water balloons that may have been dropped, but before they can find any, Lovey sprays them from the ground, knocking them to the floor with him.

With the enemy threat down, Lovey stands back up and gets into position by the locker room doors. Just as he stands up straight, Harlan and Beary burst through the door sharing the load of the Gatorade bucket that is full to the brim. They're in such a hurry to get into the room that they run right past Lovey without seeing him. Lovey aims his Super Soakers at them and fires, but nothing comes out as his water tanks have run dry. He unhooks his water guns, tosses them to the floor, grabs two more water balloons off his straps, and chucks one of them.

The first balloon hits Beary in the back of the head. The panda bear drops his side of the bucket and falls to the ground.

Harlan drops the bucket as the weight from the other side becomes too much for him to bear alone. The bucket lands upright on the ground, and though some of the water splashes out, the bucket remains mostly full.

Harlan kneels down to check on his buddy. He shakes Beary. "Beary? Beary? Are you ok? What happened?"

Before Beary can answer, Harlan gets hit in the head by Lovey's second water balloon. He falls to the ground just like his buddy, and the two of them remain there while Lovey runs up on them, grabs their Gatorade bucket, lifts it with herculean strength, and pours it all over the pair of Gamblers.

After Harlan and Beary's bath, Lovey stands up and tosses four of his remaining six water balloons at Liten, who has escaped Safari Chip's blasting, Sammie, Haas, and Jason. He saves the second to last balloon for his best friend, Rodman, but he's saving his last one for someone very special.

Lovey jumps in front of the dog known as Apple Jack. "FIRE IN THE HOLE!" He throws his final bit of ammunition.

Safari Chip and Flip run out of water in their water guns around the same time as Lovey uses his final water balloon, bringing the water attack to an end. The Gamblers stand around dripping, shaking, wringing out their jerseys, and laughing.

"I was not expecting that," Rodman says.

"How are we going to play tonight? Our jerseys are soaked," Snickers asks as he wrings out his jersey.

"We have tonight's special jerseys in my office," Safari Chip says.

"I hope these jerseys aren't pink," Undertaker says.

"No pink. These jerseys are actually pretty cool," Safari Chip laughs.

Safari Chip and Flip walk into their office and come back out with boxes. They rip the tops open and start tossing each Gambler his own red and black striped jersey. The stripes move horizontally all the way up and down the jersey. There are eight black stripes, eight red stripes, and one green stripe all of which bear a different Gamblers number in white. Goose's number zero goes in the green stripe just like it does on a real roulette wheel. The logo on the front is a roulette wheel with the words Las Vegas curved along the top of the wheel and Gamblers along the bottom of the wheel in red and black spaces. Along the back of the jersey, each Gambler has his name and number spelled out in white letters and numbers with gold trim.

"We've got some table games and slot machines in the corridor for casino night," Safari Chip explains.

Undertaker pulls his jersey over his head. "These jerseys are much better than those pink ones."

"Yeah. Good job Lovey," Kane agrees

Chapter 27: Season Finale

The Gamblers hit the ice with an abundance of fervor. Adrenaline is pumping. Hearts race. Each player feels almost as giddy and nervous as he did during the last two Cup Finals.

The New Orleans Arena is packed. Tickets aren't impossible to get, but if you got one, it wasn't easy to come by. Safari Chip makes arrangements to rope off a few standing room only sections so that the arena can accommodate an extra five hundred animals. Many of the Gamblers look into the crowd during their warm up and skating drills to find invited friends in attendance. Because of the implications of the game's outcome and also because of casino night, all of their usual and biggest fans are there. Penny, Sprinkles, Chickette, Mary, Elmira, and a few of the girls from Mary's wedding party sit together behind the Gamblers bench. Next to the girls sit El Pollos Locos. Next to El Pollos Locos are Alston Leon, Ed the elevator operator, and the entire Las Vegas Cowboys baseball team. After meeting the Cowboys when they threw out their first pitches last season, the baseball players have become huge fans of the Gamblers and vice versa. Sprinkled in elsewhere in the arena are the mayor, several of the entertainers who perform on the Las Vegas Strip, some players from the Las Vegas Aces football team, Las Vegas Jokers basketball team, and Las Vegas Tumbleweeds soccer team, celebrity chefs, casino owners, movie stars, and musicians.

Rodman skates over to Safari Chip on the bench. He has to yell over the roar of the crowd. "Chip. Do you see all the big names in the crowd tonight?"

"Yeah," Safari Chip yells back.

"If the final game of the season is this big, imagine how big the playoffs are going to be," Rodman yells back.

"You guys just focus on winning this game, or there could be no playoffs," Safari Chip warns.

Rodman flashes his coach a thumbs up.

"What's the word Rodman?" Safari Chip asks.

"Threepeat!" Rodman yells and races to rejoin his teammates. He picks up a loose puck, does a ninety degree turn, and races at the net.

Even though it's just warm ups, Harlan, who sees Rodman coming, stops eyeballing all the other pucks flying at him in order to focus on trying to stop the best player the game has ever seen. Since they're teammates, Harlan never gets to face Rodman, so during warm ups they treat each shot against one another as though it were a shot in a real game.

This time, Rodman wins.

"Nice shot Hott Rod," Harlan yells over the arena noise.

"Thanks," Rodman shouts back.

After warm ups, the teams head back to their locker rooms for the pregame intermission. It's an intermission that drags on and on. All the Gamblers want to do is get the game underway. For the fans sitting in their seats, the waiting is just as bad. The only animals that find intermission isn't long enough are the ones playing casino games in the halls.

Excitement rises when intermission finally ends, and the Gamblers are introduced. The thunderous applause they receive shakes the whole building. The cheering dies down just long enough for the national anthem to be sung by the Gamblers personal national anthem singer, a white bear named Wally dressed in the style of Liberace. Applause for Wally always erupts the second Wally finishes his last note. The Gamblers fans are very careful to never cheer too early like fans in most arenas, and no one yells anything during his performance either. That sort of behavior is disrespectful. But, when the final note is sung, they get loud like no other crowd in sports, and their hooting and hollering continues all the way through the puck drop and the first minute of the game.

Rodman loses the opening faceoff and the Gamblers go out on defense. They play a little shaky at first, and Harlan has to stop four shots before the Gamblers get control of the puck. Liten eventually does get the puck, and he sends it into their offensive zone while the other guys make a line change.

The Gold Rush regain the puck and head back towards Harlan. The Gamblers second line plays a little awkward too, and Harlan is forced to stop two more shots. He stops the second one by blasting it down the ice with his stick and forcing Vander Gates to stop the slow moving puck.

Meanwhile, the Gamblers make another change. The third line takes the ice against the Gold Rush second line of Auggie, Ranger, Pete, Smooth, and Peanuts.

Vander Gates sends the puck ahead to Auggie, and the poison dart frog heads back towards Harlan. In what initially seems like a very bad pass, Auggie sends the puck to Jason. The pass is so bad that even Jason isn't expecting to be the guy who ends up with the puck on his stick. He has his head down as he tries to steady the unexpected gift, and when he makes a move to head the other way, Ranger comes up high and hard with a cross check just under Jason's beak.

Jason feels an explosion of pain, sees stars, and falls to the ice. He hits his head hard, and though his helmet cushions the blow, it still hurts upon impact.

Whistles blow.

Maverick and Moose skate in to pick up the fight with Ranger, but the referees keep everyone separated.

L-Rod skates over to Jason and kneels down next to him. "Dude, are you ok?"

Jason's eyes are open and he can hear L-Rod's question, but it doesn't make sense to his rattled brain. His eyes spin all around as he tries to gather his wits. His beak feels broken.

L-Rod motions for the bench.

Safari Chip and Flip make their way to the ice.

"That was some shot kid. You ok?" Flip asks.

"I'm fine." Jason forces himself to talk so he can make sure his beak isn't broken. He tries to sit up but teeters a bit.

"Whoa!" Safari Chip reaches out and steadies Jason. He holds his newest player up and prevents him from hitting his head again. "Let's get you back to the bench and have you checked out."

"I'm fine," Jason assures his coaches. "I had that one coming. I expected it. It came, and now it's over."

"You still need to let us help you to the bench, and you still need to sit down for a bit," Flip orders.

"I'll rest, but let me stand up on my own," Jason pleads.

The coaches are uneasy about the idea, but they allow Jason to stand up on his own accord. They stand near him, ready to catch him at the first sign of a dizzy spell. The move gets a standing ovation from the crowd.

Safari Chip calls Maverick and Moose over. "If he comes back out, I want you guys keeping an extra close eye on him. If anyone even comes remotely close to him, I want you to bust them up. We can't afford to lose him at this point."

"You got it," Maverick says.

Moose flashes Safari Chip a thumbs up.

Jason hits the bench, Ranger hits the penalty box for two minutes, and the Gamblers send out their power play unit. The power play is anything but beneficial for the Gamblers though. They give up a short-handed goal and go down 1-0 a little more than four minutes into the game. The Gold Rush kill off their penalty and score another goal with three minutes and change left in the period. The period ends 2-0, Gold Rush.

The fact that Jason never gets back onto the ice after taking the hit from Ranger upsets Maulbreath. He was hoping to be the guy to take Jason out of the game. He crosses the fingers on his paws that Jason's absence is temporary.

The Gamblers go through their normal intermission routine, and Safari Chip rallies his before the second period starts. "Ok guys. You looked a little stiff out there."

"You want us to play relaxed," Liten interrupts.

"We play better when we're loose," Rodman adds.

"Yes!" Safari Chip shouts.

Rodman shakes animatedly. "I'm loose Chip!"

"I am loose too Chip," Liten declares.

The dogs hit each other with friendly paws. "We're loose Chip!"

Lovey ties his scarf around his forehead and tightens it like Rambo. Then, he parts his teammates, runs straight ahead, and attempts to spring board off the locker room doors for a backflip, but he hits the bar that opens the doors, and flies out into the hallway. He lands with a crash. The players can hear him call from behind the now closed doors. "I'm ok. I'm loose."

The Gamblers laugh.

Sammie smiles, winks, and points to Chip. "I'm loose too Chip."

L-Rod jumps onto Big Chick's back and holds onto his shoulders. "We're loose Chip."

Harlan moonwalks across the room. "I'm loose Chip."

Maverick, Goose, Moose, and Haas high five each other. "We're loose Chip."

Safari Chip and Flip look to Jason.

"What?" Jason asks.

"Are you loose?" Safari Chip asks.

"Well my jaw's a little loose," Jason says.

The Gamblers laugh again.

"But, are *you* loose?" Flip asks.

"I'm loose. Are you two loose?" Jason asks the coaches.

"Yeah," Safari Chip says taken aback a bit. He's never had to answer that question.

"Well, let us hear it," Rodman says.

"I'm loose," both coaches say enthusiastically.

The locker room doors open up. Lovey pokes his head in. "Are we loose?"

"We're loose! Now let's go kick some Gold Rush butt!" Safari Chip shouts.

And they are loose. They head out to the ice with the same fervor as they had in the first period but with less jitters. They battle hard from the second the puck is dropped. Rodman wins the first faceoff of the second period, and the Gamblers rack up the attack zone minutes, but no matter what they do, they can't seem to break through what has proved at times this year to be the very unstable goal tending of Vander Gates.

Try as he might, Maulbreath can't get to Jason. Every time he gets on the ice with the Gamblers third line, Jason either isn't there because he's taking every other shift off due the hit he took in the first period, or because of line changes, or because Maverick and Moose are doing their job protecting Jason.

Maulbreath skates off the ice after his sixth shift of the period and slams his stick on bench wall. It's another entire shift spent without getting his paws on Jason. He notices that the Gamblers make a change immediately after he sits, and their change includes putting Jason out there. He's running out of time in the game and the season. What he has to do can't wait until next season. He watches the play move towards the benches. Pete, the first of his teammates to skate by, is nabbed by one of Maulbreath's powerful paws. Maulbreath hoists him over the wall and take his place on the ice. He takes huge strides and whizzes across the ice to get to Jason in a hurry.

Auggie takes a shot that is blocked by Harlan and collected by Moose. Moose turns and fires a pass to L-Rod, sending the action back the other way.

Maulbreath sees the direction of the game changing and slams on the breaks. He skates the other way down the ice back towards Vander Gates and around the back of his own net.

"What are you doing?" Vander Gates asks his captain.

Maulbreath doesn't answer. Instead, he stands completely still, waiting for the play to come to him.

No one on the ice saw Maulbreath take Pete's place, because they all had their backs to the switch and when they turn to chase the puck, they are only looking at the guy with the puck. No one is expecting Maulbreath to be in front of the play. L-Rod, Goose, Jason, and several Gold Rush players all cross the blue line at the same time in a frenzy. The Gamblers take a quick look at the net and their defenders, but mostly they're focused on L-Rod and the puck.

L-Rod shoots a sideways pass to Goose just beyond the blue line. Jason's defender, Smooth, goes to help block a potential shot by Goose, thus leaving Jason wide open. Goose slows up upon seeing his shooting lane become blocked. He pushes the puck to Jason.

Jason looks down at the ice long enough to watch the puck come to his stick. He grabs it cleanly, all the while still gliding towards the front of the net. He looks up expecting to have a fraction of a second to find and then aim his shot. What he sees instead is a stick being swung at him. He has no time to avoid it. He has no time to brace for it, no time to wince, not even enough time to close his eyes. Maulbreath's stick smashes Jason in the leg, shattering the bones. Jason dives forward and ends up doing a front flip in the air. He lands like an anvil on his back but doesn't much feel the thud because the pain in his leg is so excruciating. Jason glides on his back all the way to the net where his momentum causes him to crash into Vander Gates. This slows him to a stop, but the Gold Rush goalie falls down and lands on Jason's mangled leg.

Moose bum rushes Maulbreath, tackling the tiger to the ice in defense of his teammate. He wallops Maulbreath over and over, but the rabid jungle cat is so enraged that he's able to eventually defend himself and even get the upper hand. He frees himself from Moose's grasp and knocks him to the ice. Then, he stands up and fends off an attack from Maverick. Maulbreath turns to the rest of the players on the ice, Gamblers and Gold Rush alike, with a stance daring them to try and stop him.

Finally, one of the referees steps up to the rabid tiger. He doesn't dare put his paws on Maulbreath, but he gets in his face and screams, "Get off the ice. You're out of here."

Maulbreath snorts with a smirk. The raucous boos of the angry crowd as he's skated off the ice are like music to his ears. He flinches threateningly at Goose as he passes him by and eyeballs L-Rod, who kneels protectively over Jason.

L-Rod eyes Maulbreath back with a scowl.

Maulbreath spits on the ice near Jason and L-Rod.

L-Rod fumes at the insult Maulbreath has added to the injury he's caused. The tiny penguin hops to his feet, charges at Maulbreath, jumps on his back, and tackles the tiger to one knee.

Whistles blow. Referees and players alike swarm to separate L-Rod from Maulbreath, but Maulbreath, being much bigger and stronger than L-Rod, recovers quickly, turns around, and smacks the Gamblers smallest player upside the head before anyone can stop him.

L-Rod falls hard to the ice. Maverick and Moose, having recovered from their earlier attacks, double team Maulbreath. They tackle him to the ice and try to inflict some payback, but they're restrained by referees and Gold Rush players.

Freed from anyone's grasp, Maulbreath gets to his feet and tries to attack the first animal he sees. His sights are set on Moose. Auggie races to intercept his captain. He wraps Maulbreath up but struggles to hold the tiger back.

With everyone on the ice restraining someone or trying to get their paws, wings, or hooves on someone else, it allows Goose to dive in and get Maulbreath with a shot to the jaw. Auggie pushes Goose away, but in doing so, he loses his grip on Maulbreath, and the tiger drops his own teammate with a punch and goes on the prowl, pouncing on Goose and mauling the Gamblers winger.

Players from both benches flood the ice to help stop the carnage. It takes the strength of Snickers, Apple Jack, and Big Chick to pull Maulbreath off of Goose. They finally are able to force the tiger off the ice where he's met by hotel security, who restrain him and make sure he leaves the arena and the hotel without further incident.

With the war over and the instigator removed from the ice, the referees are free to sort out the penalties. While they do that, the Gamblers medical looks over Jason, L-Rod, and Goose. L-Rod and Goose are ok to stay in the game. They have minor injuries, bumps and bruises. Jason, on the other hand, isn't so lucky. He can't walk, much less skate. He's stretchered off the ice to a standing ovation. The crowd goes especially crazy when he raises his flipper and gives them a thumbs up.

Rodman skates over to the stretcher. "You're going to be ok J-Money."

Jason nods. He tries to speak, but his words come out mumbles.

Rodman can tell it's painful just for Jason to move his beak. "It's ok man. You don't have to say anything."

Jason nods again as if saying *yes I do*.

Rodman leans in close so Jason won't have to strain.

"Don't lose this game," Jason murmurs.

"You bet," Rodman assures him. He pats Jason on the chest and lets the doctors take him off the ice.

Safari Chip motions for Rodman to come back to the bench. As Rodman rejoins his team, Safari Chip says to his players, "Put this out of your minds. There's nothing we can do for Jason right now. And there's no one on the ice who has done us wrong, so don't get into a retaliatory frame of mind. We have a game to win, and I'd like to point out that every single team that is tied with us is currently winning." Safari Chip points to the IAHL scores on the scoreboard.

The Gamblers all look. Sure enough, Safari Chip is right.

"I don't have to tell you guys what that means for us if we lose," Safari Chip continues.

"I talked to Jason as he was leaving the ice, and he told me to make sure we win game," Rodman informs his teammates.

The Gamblers all nod somber and silent.

"Let's go win this thing for Jason," Safari Chip shouts.

"And for us," Snickers adds.

"Threepeat," Liten yells.

"Threepeat on three," Safari Chip orders.

The Gamblers all throw their wings, hooves, paws, flippers, and hands into a circle.

"One. Two. Threepeat!"

"First line, take the ice." Safari Chip orders.

The first line takes the ice, but Liten comes off as the teams go four on four after the penalties assessed send two players from each team to the penalty box. Auggie serves the penalty for Maulbreath and Peanuts gets one for unsportsmanlike conduct. L-Rod and Goose both serve penalties for late hits.

The injury to Jason serves as a turning point for the Gamblers. They're able to keep their emotions in check just as Safari Chip instructed. Kane scores a goal on their first shift after Jason's injury, and Big Chick ties the game on the next shift, and as they tie their game, the Anchorage Pilots lose their lead.

The Gamblers and Gold Rush go to the second intermission tied. When the teams return to the ice, all of the other games have already started. The long delay during the Maulbreath assault has them running behind.

Lovey taps Rodman on their way to the bench. He points to the IAHL scoreboard. "The Pilots look like they're going to lose for sure."

Rodman takes a look at the 5-2 score in the Pilots/Cacti game that has seven minutes left.

"I still want to win this game," Rodman says.

"Me too buddy," Lovey says and repeats, "Me too."

"We are going to win," Liten says with a devilish grin he shoots the way of Jimmy Peanuts.

The Gold Rush's elephant shakes in his skates. He's freaked out by Liten's tiny statue, big ears, and beady little eyes. Throughout the entirety of the season, he's avoided being on the ice at the same time as Liten. The Gold Rush being eliminated from the playoffs isn't all bad for Peanuts. At least he won't have to face Liten anymore this season.

The third period gets underway. Both teams play as they should. There are no fights, no penalties, and no cheap shots. The defense on both sides of the ice is solid, and the two goalies shut down any offense that sneaks past the defenders. The game remains tied when the final buzzer rings.

"You know, these guys play pretty well when they're not cheating," Beary notes on the bench during the brief intermission before overtime starts.

"Yeah," Big Chick agrees.

"If Coil ever gets wise to the fact that one or two guys are holding his entire team back, the Gold Rush could once again become one of the best teams in the league," Haas says.

Safari Chip looks up and down the Gold Rush bench. He knows Haas is right, and eventually Coil will figure that out too. He just hopes it isn't until after the Gamblers become the first IAHL team to fourpeat.

"Look. We're in the playoffs," Maverick points to the scoreboard. Bakersfield and Seattle both won their games, but the Anchorage Pilots did indeed lose their game, 7-3.

"But if we lose this game, we're going to be the bottom seed," Rodman reminds them.

"Yeah. So let's get back out there and do what we do best," Lovey calls to his teammates.

"What do we do best?" Big Chick asks.

"Kick some Gold Rush butt."

Overtime starts with a Gold Rush faceoff win and a lot of strong offense. The Gold Rush would like nothing more than to play spoiler to the Gamblers.

Through the first sixteen minutes of period number four, the Gamblers battle hard to stay in the game. The same defensive battle that took place in the third repeats itself.

Harlan blocks a shot by Iggy and sends the puck to a tuckered out Rodman, who has been playing on the ice for over three straight minutes. Rodman takes the puck down the ice to dump it in over the blue line so his team can make a line change.

While Lovey, Liten, Undertaker and Kane skate into the bench, Big Chick, Sammie, Apple Jack, and Snickers hop over the wall and take the ice, and Beary waits for Rodman to return.

Liten, tired as he is, watches the action on the ice intently. He sees Rodman racing back to the bench and the Gold Rush doing likewise.

Rodman hits the bench, and Beary begins to hop over the wall, but he's held back by Liten.

"Whoa!" Beary shouts as he falls backwards.

Liten steadies the panda. "Sorry Beary."

"What's the deal Liten? I gotta get out there," Beary protests.

"One moment," Liten orders.

"But…"

Liten shushes Beary. The Gamblers number one alternate captain holds the panda off the ice until he sees what he's looking for. It doesn't take long before he sees what he's waiting for, Jimmy Peanuts taking the ice.

"Sorry again Beary." Liten hops over the wall.

"Hey!" Beary shouts.

"Liten! What are you doing?" Safari Chip yells.

Liten ignores them both. He sneaks into the play from behind. The conservation of the little energy he has left and the element of surprise are going to be key for Liten to accomplish what he wants to accomplish. The Gold Rush have the puck and are almost on a power play with Liten so far behind the play. They pass the puck around looking for the prime time to take a shot. Liten waits until they give the puck to Peanuts, and then, he makes his move. He speeds up to Peanuts, slams on his breaks, and sends ice flying in front of the elephant.

The elephant can sense something is afoul. He feels a tap very low around his leg, turns slowly, and sees Liten standing there grinning a toothy smile. The sight of the scary mouse causes him to freeze in horror.

"Hello." Liten waves.

"AHHHHHHHHHHHHH!" Peanuts sends out the shrillest scream anyone has ever heard. It's so loud that some of the players and the fans hold and cover their ears.

Liten takes the opportunity to steal the puck and race down the ice towards Vander Gates on a breakaway.

Players from both teams race to catch him. The nearest player to him is one of the Gamblers slowest players, Big Chick. Behind him are Smooth and Ranger. The Gold Rush duo hustles up aside Big Chick on their way towards Liten. The big fella gives them each a not so legal body check that goes uncalled.

With the Gold Rush completely knocked out of the play, Liten aims his shot, rears his stick, and fires.

Vander Gates watches the motion of Liten's stick the entire way. He stands up tall to grab the puck out of the air, but it never appears. He only has a quick second to wonder where the puck is before it's too late.

However, Liten didn't shoot it. He sent it behind himself as he swung his stick back for the fake shot. The puck lands on the stick of Big Chick, who rears back and shoots a quick shot like a bullet train over the surface of the ice. Liten jumps upon hearing the crack of the stick upon the puck. The puck sails right under him, to the net, and through the five hole of Vander Gates.

The gator drops too late. The goal lights go off. The slot machine jackpot noise that comes with each Gamblers home goal is played over the arena speakers. The Gamblers win 3-2.

Liten turns around to celebrate with his teammates. What he finds instead is Big Chick just inches from him. The biggest guy on the team plows into the second smallest guy on the team, tackling the mouse to the ice. Soon, Liten is at the bottom of a dog pile. Somehow, he manages to come out pile uncrushed.

The Gold Rush leave the ice quickly. Their offseason can't start fast enough for Coil, who, just as Safari Chip expected, has already decided to release Maulbreath and Peanuts. The announcement can't be made until the following day, but he intends to contact the players personally and hold a press conference announcing his decisions. He doesn't need a hot headed captain who is willing to purposely injure opponents. That's why he got rid of Jason. He also doesn't need peanut head elephants that are afraid of a little mouse.

The Gamblers stick long enough to take a few bows, hold up their sticks, and throw some t-shirts into the crowd. With that done, they head to their locker room where awaiting them are buckets of water balloons. They decided to hold off on the sparkling juice until they threepeat.

Lovey refills his super soaker water guns during the celebration and douses his teammates.

"That was so funny the way you scared Peanuts." Rodman pats Liten on the shoulder and smashes a water balloon over his head.

"Thank you Rodman, but it was Big Chick's goal that won the game." Liten jumps up and smashes a water balloon over Rodman's head.

"Yeah. Way to go Big Chick." Sammie fires a water balloon at the number one star of the game.

"Big game. Big stick. Big Chick," Lovey shouts and throws a water balloon at the big guy.

Soon, everyone is throwing water balloons at Big Chick for getting the game winner.

He takes the splashy bombardment with a laugh and a smile.

El Pollos Locos come into the room at one point and are not spared. They get hammered with water balloons by the bigger players, so they run into the hallway, grab a fire hose, and come back into the locker room. The first guy they take out is Big Chick. The power of their hose knocks Big Chick off his feet and sends him sliding into the lockers.

Everyone stops. They turn to see El Pollos Locos with their fire hose.

"Oh nuts!" L-Rod whispers.

"Fire in the hole!" Noodle yells.

El Pollos Locos flood the room with water. No Gambler is spared. No coach is spared. It isn't until Harlan is able to slide across the locker room floor to the locker room door through the water that has piled up about two inches deep and run into the hallway to turn the water off that their water celebration ends.

The chickens look down at their empty hose a little bewildered. Behind them, Harlan comes back into the room and pegs each of them in the back of the head with a water balloon.

"Hey!" Chicken hollers as the Gamblers laugh at Big Chick's cousins.

"Truce?" Goose asks everyone in the room.

"Awww. Does Bruce Goose want a truce?" Maverick teases.

"Hey, Bruce Moose wants a truce toose… I mean too," Moose says.

"Are there any more water balloons?" Lovey asks.

Everyone looks around the room.

"It doesn't appear so," Beary answers.

"I guess that is a truce then," Liten shrugs.

"Oh man," L-Rod says, getting very serious.

"What's the matter?" Rodman asks.

"What about Jason?"

In the excitement of their win, the Gamblers forgot they lost Jason.

"Yeah, what about Jason?" Big Chick asks.

"Are we going to be able to replace him in time for the playoffs?" Sammie asks.

Safari Chip frowns. He looks to Flip for any ideas, but Flip just shrugs at him.

"We've got to go visit him," Sammie says.

"Yeah," Haas agrees.

The Gamblers go to the hospital that night to see Jason, but he's already in surgery having his knee repaired. They're told they can come back tomorrow afternoon to see him.

"I hope he'll be ok," L-Rod says as the team leaves the hospital and piles into the team's limo.

"Me too," Rodman ruffles the feathers on the little guy's head.

Chapter 28: Jason's Replacement

Rodman has a hard time getting to sleep that night. His mind is consumed with disappointment about the way the season ended for Jason. The drastic change in Jason's attitude from the past two and a half seasons to the past few months really had Rodman looking forward to going after a championship with him. Plus, Jason made the Gamblers that much stronger. What would have been a great story was ripped from Jason, the rest of the Gamblers, and the entire hockey world in a split second.

Another thing has Rodman's mind spinning too. Who can the Gamblers get to replace Jason on such short notice? Surely not Chicken, Noodle, or Soup. They're all too little. Krazy Mike, although out of the hospital, hasn't been cleared to play, and Heaven only knows if he'd even be a help to them if he could play. He'd probably just take more shots at the Gamblers own net and needlessly put them on the penalty kill.

There's got to be someone though. Rodman gets out of bed and paces around his living room, hoping an answer will come to him. He's quiet to ensure he doesn't wake L-Rod. He walks to his giant window and looks upon the lights of the Las Vegas Strip. The water show is going on in the fountains of the Fontana. Animals are walking up and down the sidewalks. Everyone appears to be having a good time. Then, he shifts his gaze to the Pink Penguin hotel across the street. He looks upon the pink flashing neon penguin sign, and suddenly, a brilliant idea pops into his head. He's so excited about the idea that he almost calls Safari Chip right then and there, but he decides to wait until morning. The idea is so genius that Rodman now has trouble sleeping because he's so excited.

*

"Why won't you won't just tell us who it is that you found to play with us," Safari Chip begs as they make their way down the tunnel to the ice.

"I just want you to give them a chance to show you what they can do before you make up your mind," Rodman says.

"I hope it's not Krazy Mike again," Harlan says.

"It's not Krazy Mike," Rodman promises.

"Funny you mention him. I talked to him earlier today," Safari Chip says.

"You did?" Flip is surprised.

"Yeah. He's up and around. Most of his injuries are healed, and he actually seems coherent."

"Well that's good. We should send him an invite to the playoffs, let him hang out with us before one of the games in the locker room," Flip says.

"Guys," Undertaker objects. "Let's not get crazy. No pun intended."

The Gamblers reach the entrance to the ice. Rodman pulls open the door, and the Gamblers file onto the rink. Someone is already waiting on the far end of the ice. They can't tell who it is because the animal is too far away and wearing a hockey helmet with protective eyewear. It's hard to even tell what type of animal the player is, but it looks to most of them to be a bird of some sort.

Rodman directs Harlan to the net, Undertaker to center ice, and Kane to an area on the ice between the blue line and Harlan. In their positions, they look to Rodman.

"What now?" Kane shrugs.

"Try to stop the shot," Rodman says.

"Try?" Undertaker asks unbelievingly.

"There's two of us," Kane scoffs.

Rodman turns his attention to the player at the end of the ice and nods.

The player grabs the puck and heads down the ice.

Undertaker, Kane, and Harlan dig in.

Undertaker is curious to see if he can catch a glimpse of the player coming at him. As the player approaches, Undertaker takes his eyes off the puck to sneak a peek. What he finds is someone he recognizes speeding towards and swerving around him. The identity of the player alarms him even more than seeing Krazy Mike. He freezes, allowing the player get past him. All that's left to do now is whip his head around to see if Kane can stop the player.

Kane gets caught off guard by the easiness in which the player gets past Undertaker. He wasn't expecting to have to play any defense at all, because he wasn't anticipating he would even get past Undertaker. So, Kane perks up, tries to get serious, and races to disrupt the play.

The player sees the path to the net blocked by Kane. So, in an effort to get past Kane, he hides the puck behind the back side of his blade and fakes a flick at the spot between Kane's legs like he's trying to shoot the puck through and past him.

Kane stiffens up and closes his legs to try and stop the puck. Meanwhile, the player slips the puck around the feet of the dog and pulls a spin move around Kane the other way. He gathers it back up behind the second Gamblers dog and heads towards Harlan.

Harlan skates out of the net and gets into position to create a tougher shot angle. He moves backwards towards the net in step with the approaching player, keeping his eyes on the puck the entire time.

The player rears back and swings his stick. There is no attempt at trickery. The shot is a simple glove side blast.

Harlan watches the shot, watches the puck fly off of the ice, and watches the puck as it flies just above his outreached glove, over his shoulder, and into the net. Harlan turns and looks at the puck resting beyond the red line in disbelief. He saw it the whole time. How could he have missed it?

Undertaker and Kane look back in disbelief as well.

The rest of the Gamblers, including their two coaches, look upon the mystery player impressed. Rodman beams the brightest as he looks to Safari Chip for his approval.

Safari Chip half shrugs and half nods. He turns his attention to the player. "That was impressive, but before I offer you a contract, what's your name my boy?"

To the shock of everyone, the player takes off his helmet to reveal that he's not a he at all, but rather a she. Standing before them is Penny McGriff.

"A girl!?" Apple Jack exclaims.

His sentiment is echoed and whispered amongst many of the other Gamblers.

Harlan nearly chokes on a gasp.

"Oh brother," Lovey says to Sammie. "If he can't even stop a shot from a girl, we've got no chance in the playoffs."

"No doubt," Sammie agrees.

"She even got past Undertaker and Kane," L-Rod notes.

If Lovey's observations didn't dishearten every player on the team, L-Rod's does.

Harlan looks to Beary to see if his best buddy is just as surprised. His buddy is indeed surprised, but it's dismay that is all over Beary's face as he shakes his head. The gesture doesn't make Harlan feel any better.

Safari Chip pulls Rodman aside.

"Before you say anything Chip, just give her a chance," Rodman says.

Safari Chip looks to Flip.

Flip shrugs. "We don't have anything better."

"Ok. We'll give her a tryout," Safari Chip says.

The guys run back to the locker room, get suited up for an impromptu practice. Penny participates in several drills, and she proves she can hold her own, even shooting with more precision than several Gamblers during their shooting drill.

After practice, the team and Penny head to the locker room. Safari Chip holds a closed door meeting with Flip and his four captains in his office.

"I've got to tell you Rodman, I wasn't expecting that," Safari Chip starts.

"I bet. But she can play huh?" Rodman beams.

"It sure appears so," Safari Chip agrees.

Rodman can sense Safari Chip isn't sold on the idea of Penny being on the team. "But?"

"But, I don't know about having a girl on the team," Safari Chip mumbles.

"What does it matter if she's a girl?"

"It matters because she's smaller than the guys," Snickers voices his concerns.

"She's bigger than Liten and L-Rod," Rodman argues.

"Hey!" Liten objects.

"It's true." Rodman shrugs.

Liten looks to the ground a bit ashamed.

"I think what Snickers means is that because she's smaller and because she's a girl the other teams may target her," Flip says.

"Especially if we end up playing the Five Ohhh!. Those punks would love to injure her just because she's your girlfriend," Snickers adds.

Rodman hadn't thought about that. Then, he remembers something. "Well, you should see the size of some of the girls on her rec league team. They're huge, and they hit just as hard."

"I've seen some of those rec league girls, and they are big, but they're not IAHL professionals. It was a good idea Rod, but it might be best to just go with sixteen guys. We've done it in the past with as few as nine," Safari Chip says.

"Why don't we make it her choice? If you don't think she'll help the team, then you can tell her no, but if you think she can help, let her decide if she wants the risk," Rodman pleads.

Safari Chip looks to Flip for his thoughts. Flip shrugs at first, then nods. The alternate captains all nod at Safari Chip too.

"Alright. Bring her in," Safari Chip says.

Rodman goes to the door with a big smile. He opens it up and calls for Penny to come in.

"Is she going to be on the team?" L-Rod asks.

The other Gamblers eagerly look to Rodman for an answer, but Rodman gives them no indication one way or the other. He closes the door again after Penny enters.

"Have a seat Penny." Safari Chip motions for Penny to take the only seat other than his in the office.

"Thanks." Penny sits down.

"I should start by complimenting you on your hockey skills. I think we were all surprised and impressed by the way you can handle a puck."

"Thanks," Penny repeats.

"And thank you for coming down and trying to help us with what seems to be a never ending quandary of trying filling our seventeenth roster position."

"I was excited for the opportunity."

"I've discussed the idea of filling that spot with yet another guy… or uhhh… in this case a girl, and we all think you could be of great help in our quest towards a threepeat."

"But?" Penny asks.

"But we're concerned for your safety," Safari Chip says.

"Because I'm a girl?" Penny asks slightly annoyed.

"We're afraid you might be targeted for that reason," Flip joins the conversation.

"I appreciate that, but I can hold my own. You should see the size of some of the girls in my rec league," Penny says.

Rodman chuckles. "I told you."

Safari Chip takes a deep breath. It sounds like Penny wants in no matter the cost.

"There was a girl almost Big Chick's size," Harlan recalls.

"That's Big Chick's girlfriend these days," Snickers whispers to Liten.

Safari Chip ponders the idea of a girl on the team for a minute. Try as he might, he can't come up with a good enough excuse to keep her off the team. "Well, I guess there's just one thing left to ask."

"What's that?" Penny asks.

"What number do you want to wear?"

Rodman and the alternate captains pump their fists and high five. Outside the office door, a loud uproar of approval can be heard as the news travels from those who were eavesdropping to the rest of the team.

Safari Chip smiles. It appears he's made a decision that appeases the whole team. Now, he just hopes it's the right decision in terms of winning another Cup.

Penny can't control the huge grin on her face. "I wore number one on my rec team because of my name, but I know Big Chick wears number one, so how about number three since we're going to threepeat this year?"

Everyone agrees that Penny's choice of the number three is perfect.

Flip opens the office door. "Why don't you guys come in and welcome your newest teammate to the team?"

The Gamblers all rush in to congratulate Penny.

"I have to get started on the paperwork to get Penny approved by the IAHL president," Safari Chip says.

While he fills out papers, makes phone calls, and faxes forms, the party in his office continues on.

Somewhere in that party, something occurs to Harlan. "Hey."

The Gamblers and their coaches look to their turtle.

"Penny can't use the same locker room with the guys. She's a girl," Harlan says.

"Yeah," Beary agrees. "Where's Penny going to get ready?"

Safari Chip looks to Flip. He hadn't given that particular topic any thought. Flip just shrugs.

*

Rodman, Safari Chip, and Flip visit Jason at the hospital later that day.

"Tell me you guys won the game," Jason says.

"What?" Safari Chip asks. "You don't know the score?"

"No," Jason grumbles. "My TV is broke, there's no internet access in this hospital, and you'd think the staff here was from Mars the way they're not into Las Vegas Gamblers hockey or hockey in general."

"Really?" Rodman is flabbergasted.

"No fooling," Jason says.

The three Gamblers make a disheartening face.

"Awww come on. You guys didn't lose did you? Sheesh. You're always beating up on Alaska. How did you lose that game?" Jason demands, getting ahead of himself.

"Well, there's something we've got to tell you," Rodman says somberly.

"It better be that you're pulling my busted leg and that you won," Jason says with a very serious tone.

Rodman can't contain his smile any longer. "Heck yeah we won. Easy as pie."

"Good. I just hope you didn't give the guys a win one for Jason speech," Jason says not easing up on the seriousness in his tone.

"No. Of course not," Safari Chip shakes his head and lies.

Jason can tell he's lying. He shakes his own head. "Where are the rest of the guys? They don't like me enough to come visit?"

"On the contrary. They all wanted to come," Safari Chip says.

Jason looks disbelieving.

"For real. That's how this team does," Flip assures Jason.

"Then, why aren't they here?" Jason asks.

"Because we wanted to give you a reason to get out of this bed. If you want to see them, you have to get up and get your tail to the playoff games," Rodman says.

"Am I dead?" Jason asks.

"I don't think so," Safari Chip says, confused by Jason's question.

"Then, I'll be there," Jason assures his captain and coaches.

"So how bad is it?" Flip asks.

"It's shattered. The leg, the knee, the whole deal. Might as well amputate it and teach me to skate on one leg."

"It's that bad?" Safari Chip grabs his safari hat tight.

"No." Rodman wave off Jason's griping. "Someone has always had a flare for the dramatics."

"It's busted to pieces. I'll be lucky to be skating in time for opening day next season." Jason becomes more accurate in the details.

"Nuts," Safari Chip says.

"Ahhh, don't worry about me. I'll be fine eventually. What about you guys though? Did you find a replacement for me?" Jason asks.

"Yeah," Rodman draws out the word for a long second.

"Awesome. Who is he?"

"He isn't exactly a he," Rodman hesitates.

"What do you mean he's not a he?"

*

Doctors, nurses, patients, and visitors all stop in their tracks as they hear the shrill scream come from Jason's room. The scream contains only two words, and it doesn't last long, but it's loud, angry, and most of all scary.

"A GIRL!?!?"

Chapter 29: The Overtime Series

The Gamblers locker room is abnormally quiet. Everyone is on pins and needles waiting for word that Penny's paperwork has been approved by the IAHL president.

"Maybe you should go ask Chip," L-Rod suggests to Rodman.

"Nah. He said he'd let us know immediately. I don't want to bother him. Besides, Penny's not even here yet," Rodman says.

L-Rod looks around the room. All the Gamblers are dressed and ready to go for game one of the first round of the playoffs, but Penny isn't in the room. "Where is she?"

"I don't know," Rodman says.

"Did anyone change the do not disturb sign on our door?" Liten asks.

All the Gamblers shake their heads, so Rodman goes to the locker room door and opens it up. Standing on the other side, in her Gamblers uniform and with her gear, is Penny.

Rodman flips a do not disturb sign they borrowed from the hotel to the *please come in* side. "Sorry about that."

"We're going to have to come up with a better system than that," Penny tells him.

The sign was the Gamblers way of letting her know when they were dressed and it was ok for her to come in. Unfortunately, no one was put in charge of changing the sign.

Meanwhile, Penny has been given the press room as her own personal room until Safari Chip has an official room constructed for her. Her locker, however, is in the same locker room as the guys. She enters the room and unloads her bag in the locker next to Undertaker's.

*

In Safari Chip's office, he and Flip wait for the IAHL president's call, telling them that Penny has either been approved or denied to play with the Gamblers. While they wait, Safari Chip takes a look at the playoffs chart.

"It's weird how no one picked any of the former AKHL teams to even contend this year, and now two of them are in the playoffs, and one of them for sure is going to be in the Finals," Flip notes.

"Hockey is a funny game sometimes," Safari Chip agrees. He looks at the names of the other two teams in the hunt for the Cup. The Reno Five Ohhh! and the Seattle Rampage. He picks up his phone suddenly and dials a number.

"Who are you calling?" Flip asks.

"Buck Wild," Safari Chip says.

"Why?"

Buck Wild picks up on the other end of the call, and Safari Chip is unable to answer Flip's question. "Hello Buck. Hey, it's Safari Chip. I just wanted to congratulate you and your team on all that you have accomplished this season."

"Thanks Mr. Chip. Same to you and your team," Buck Wild says.

"Listen Buck, I know we got off on the wrong foot earlier in the season…"

"Ahhh, forget about it," Buck Wild interrupts. "Water under the bridge. Besides, you and your guys have always shown us a good time while we were in town. And you play a clean game. We appreciate that."

"We try."

"So are you calling just to congratulate us?"

"No," Safari Chip says with a hint of mischief. "It's no secret that my team hasn't exactly seen eye to eye with those goons from Reno, so I thought I might call you and talk a little bit of hockey before our games start, and if I happen to mention some things that worked well for us against the Five Ohhh! during the season, then maybe it might give you a leg up going into your game tonight."

"I see. Well, let's talk hockey then," Buck Wild says mischievously back.

Safari Chip gives Buck Wild every piece of advice he can about what the Gamblers did to defeat the Five Ohhh!. It's not the classiest of moves, but then again, the Five Ohhh! aren't exactly the classiest of teams.

Near the end of their conversation, Safari Chip gets a beep and has to switch over to his other call. "Hello?... Oh Mr. President... yes sir... ok then, if that's your decision."

*

Safari Chip's office door opens. Everyone turns to see the monkey. Penny stops unloading her gear and stands up at her locker when she sees a look of despair on his face.

"What did he say Chip?" Rodman asks.

"Is he going to let Penny play?" L-Rod questions.

Safari Chip doesn't say a word.

His players get anxious.

"Chip?" Big Chick asks.

Safari Chip's frown turns to a big grin. He pulls an approval letter that was faxed to him by the IAHL president from behind his back and holds it in the air. "She's all good."

The Gamblers go crazy, high fiving, hugging, and jumping around with Penny.

"So, I guess there's just one more thing to say," Safari Chip says.

"What's that?" Harlan asks.

"GAME TIME!" Safari Chip shouts.

The Gamblers grab their sticks and race for the ice.

*

Game one of the first round is a battle from start to finish. Goals from Sammie on the Gamblers and Benson Sherman on the Trains are the only goals scored in regulation. The game moves to overtime where shots on goal are thirty to twenty-nine in favor of the Trains to start the extra period.

Each team gets off ten more shots in the first overtime period, and the game heads to a second overtime. The Gamblers struggle a bit more than the Trains to keep from tiring out completely. Their previous game was a double overtime game as well. They persevere though, and they hold on for one of the strangest plays ever in the history of the league.

After a long defensive shift, Rodman pokes the puck away from Benny Sherman, and takes off on a breakaway. Lovey races with him in the hopes of pulling off their famous crisscross move, but they're both so tuckered out that most of the Trains catch up to them as they cross the blue line.

Behind Rodman and Lovey, Liten and the dogs make a line change. Seeing that they no longer have a play, Rodman dumps the puck behind the net, and he and Lovey race to the bench to let Sammie and Big Chick on the ice.

Bill Sherman secures the puck, stands next to the net, and calls out a play. He waits with one of his quadruplet brothers, Benson Sherman, behind him while the rest of the guys on their team get into formation.

The fresh Gamblers skate into the zone to apply some pressure and play defense.

Bill takes the puck out in front of the net and cuts across the ice from right to left. Benson comes out from behind the net and cuts across the ice in the opposite direction. Bill passes the puck behind himself to Benson, who isn't where he's supposed to be because he heard the wrong play called. Benson totally misses the pass, and the puck slides back towards the Trains own net. Their goalie, Rodman's old Chill teammate, Dolvy, notices the slow moving puck at the last second and drops to block it. The surprise of the botched play and the puck now moving at him, throws off Dolvy's judgment. He misses the puck, and it slides into the back of the net.

The Gamblers win 2-1.

Apple Jack gets credit for the game winning goal just for being the Gambler closest to it when it went in the net despite never having touched it.

In the other game, Safari Chip is pleased to see that his advice must have paid dividends for Buck Wild as his Rampage beat the Five Ohhh! 3-0 in Reno.

*

Game two between the Gamblers and the Trains doesn't take place for two days after game one. The IAHL set it up for both teams to play game one and have a day off. Then, the teams alternate days so that there is at least one game every day. A flip of the coin gives the Gamblers and Trains the extra day of rest, and lucky for both teams, but especially the Gamblers, that it does, because both teams are beat after game one.

The Gamblers use their extra off day to watch the game between the Five Ohhh! and the Rampage. The Five Ohhh! storm back from their 3-0 loss in game one to beat the Rampage 7-0 in game two.

The mood from the disappointing loss the Trains suffered in game one seems to carry over into game two. Their play is sloppy, beleaguered, and half-hearted. The oddity of it all is that despite their bad play, and the Gamblers good play, this game also goes to overtime with a score of 0-0.

The Gamblers outshoot the Trains in regulation twenty-five to eighteen, and a lot of their shots come really close. They ring half a dozen shots off the posts.

The teams line up for the first faceoff of overtime.

Rodman faces off with Baxter Sherman, the oldest by four minutes of the Sherman brothers, and the captain of the Trains. Behind Baxter, Rodman and the rest of the guys on the ice including the referees hear a commotion brewing that garners everyone's attention.

"Try not to put the puck in your own net again genius. We're going that way," Benson says to his brother and points to the net that Harlan is defending.

"Try listening to the call this time then, and be in position to take a pass," Bill orders.

"I heard the call. You said forty-six," Benson grumbles.

"I said forty-seven." Bill stands up straight and turns to face his brother.

Benson straightens up and moves in close to his brother.

"Knock it off you guys," Baxter orders.

Benson snorts in Bills face. "You're lucky Baxter's here."

"What do you mean I'm lucky? What's he going to do to stop me if I want to go toe to toe with you?" Bill challenges his younger by two minutes brother.

"Guys," Benny says.

"What's Baxter going to do if I do this?" Bill shoves Benson forcefully.

Benson stumbles backwards. He regains his footing without falling and hops at his brother. The two kangaroos fight. Actually, they box up and down the ice.

Kane nudges Undertaker. "Can you believe those two? They're teammates."

"They're brothers even," Undertaker says.

Liten shakes his head.

Kane sees the mouse's gesture. "What?"

Liten points to the fighting Sherman brothers. "That was you two earlier this season."

Undertaker and Kane look out on the fighting Trains.

"Nooo," both dogs deny.

After the fight is separated, the referees give both Sherman brothers five minute fighting penalties and a two minute unsportsmanlike conduct penalty. This puts the Trains on a three on five penalty kill for seven minutes and basically dooms them.

Rodman wins the faceoff, and the Gamblers go on the attack. With lots of room to maneuver, they set up and take their time. The Trains do their best to fend off any forth coming shots, and they're careful not to overcommit to any one Gamblers pass. They don't make a move to crowd the Gamblers, but that allows the Gamblers to close in and shrink the ice in front of the net.

Passes whizz and whirl from one Gambler to another. Eventually, Kane finds Undertaker with a perfect pass, and Undertaker finds an easy path to the back of the net. He blasts a shot and becomes the second dog in two playoff games to score a game winner.

*

The series moves to Bakersfield for game three. By this time, the Five Ohhh! have taken a two games to one lead in their series with a 4-2 win over the Rampage in Seattle and are one win away from the Finals. The Gamblers are hoping to wrap up their series tonight and advance as well.

The Trains, knowing they have to do something drastic to change the momentum of the series, bench Dolvy for game three. He had won the starting goalie job in training camp, and obviously got them into the playoffs, but their coach decides after two losses to go with ol' reliable, Marc Magz, their owl goalie of the last twelve seasons since he has more playoff experience.

Both teams find their offense in game three. Rodman, Lovey, and Beary all score for the Gamblers, and Bill and Benson Sherman, who have been placed on different lines, score for the Trains. After Bill's second goal, a goal that ties the game with just seconds left and keeps their playoff hopes alive, he's met at the bench wall by all the Sherman brothers, even Benson, giving him knuckles.

Bill's second goal sends the series into its third straight overtime.

Midway through overtime, Rodman and the Gamblers wrestle the puck away from the Trains and head down the ice. In front of Rodman, the Trains make a line change. As he skates past the Trains bench, another of his former Chill teammates, Spoedige, jumps in front of him and steals the puck off his stick.

Everyone on both teams come to an ice shaving halt. They all turn and chase the lightning fast Spoedige. The

Gamblers, unable to catch him, hope and pray Harlan can stop his shot, but Spoedige dekes the poor turtle right out of his shell. Harlan falls down, spinning on his belly, and Spoedige sinks an easy game winner to keep the Trains going in the playoffs.

The steal, the deke, and the goal are all so incredible that even Rodman has to give Spoedige knuckles. It's a move that gets manipulated and twisted by the media. They try to spin it such that the Gamblers and their fans should be down on Rodman for congratulating an opponent. Some reporters go so far as to say that Rodman has no respect for his own team, especially Harlan who gave up the goal to Spoedige.

Safari Chip holds another one of his famous press conferences to address the remarks of the media. Harlan sits in with him.

"I high fived him after the game too. It was a nice goal," Harlan tells reporters.

"What kind of an idiot thinks sportsmanship should be frowned upon?" Safari Chip follows Harlan's remarks. "And as for those of you who suggest that Rodman should be shunned by his own players, are you kidding me? Before he came to this team, we were losing sixty games a season. He's the first guy to practice and the last to leave. He helps his teammates on and off the ice. He's a two time MVP, and he's probably going to be a three time MVP after this season. He's a father and role model, and he's an all-around good guy. He's led us to two Cups and we're in the hunt for a third largely in part because of him. I don't care if he goes Benson Sherman on us and scores fifteen goals against us in the next game. He's my captain and the heart and soul of this team. That's how I feel. That's how my team feels. So stop wasting your time trying to stir up trouble, because it won't work with my team. Every single guy on this team is concerned with three…" Safari Chip continues his rant.

Harlan nudges his coach.

The monkey looks over to him, wondering what the interruption is about.

Harlan leans in and whispers something to Safari Chip.

"Every single guy… *and gal* on this team, including Rodman T. Penguin, is focused on three things." Safari Chip counts those three things on his fingers. "Being good animals. Being good teammates. And winning another Cup." Safari Chip abruptly knocks his microphone over and storms out of the interview. Reporters try to ask him questions, but he ignores them all.

Harlan wasn't expecting Safari Chip to leave when he did, so the turtle has to stand up quickly and chase his coach so as not to be left alone with the reporters.

*

The Reno Five Ohhh! finish off the Seattle Rampage in game four of their series with a 4-3 overtime win.

*

Much is made about the fact that the first three games of the Gamblers/Trains series all go to overtime. With all the extra hockey that has been played by these two teams of late, they both feel like they need to shake things up a bit.

Safari Chip shakes things up by switching up his lines. He moves L-Rod to the first line so he can eat up some minutes for Liten. L-Rod is quite a bit younger than Liten, and his body is a little more intact than the veteran's. He also rests Harlan in favor of Haas since Harlan has been wearing himself out blocking goals and playing crazy long minutes over the past four games, and also, so that Harlan is refreshed for game five of the series if they lose and game one of the Finals if they win. It's a win/win situation regardless of the outcome, because Harlan will be rested. Another contributing factor in Safari Chip's decision to start Haas is so that the hare can showcase his stuff and prove to the league that he still has what it takes to win in big games.

The Trains mix things up by spreading the Sherman brothers out over all three of their lines. Now, the Gamblers will have to contend with those guys for the entire sixty minutes of the game. The trains coach even moves Baxter Sherman to the second line, thinking that Rodman and Lovey are going to score no matter what, but if they can shut down the Gamblers second and third lines, then maybe they'll have a chance at getting an early lead and holding it throughout the game. Plus, the defense on the Gamblers second line should be weaker than the defense on their first line, making it easier for Baxter to score. The Trains also keep Magz in the net since he won them their last game.

Things don't always work out as planned though, and the Trains find Baxter struggles to break through the defense of Snickers and Apple Jack which is even tougher than the defense of Undertaker and Kane. Baxter gets hammered over and over, never getting any real scoring opportunities, so by the time the second period rolls around, he's moved back to the first line.

The Gamblers take an early lead on a goal from Liten. He gets the puck on a pass from Penny, and she in turn gets her first professional points. The Trains scramble to tie the game and finally do on a power play goal brought on by a roughing penalty against Snickers.

Late in the third period, Snickers makes amends for his penalty and the subsequent tying goal by sinking a slap shot and putting the Gamblers back on top 2-1. It looks at this point like a cinch that another one of the Gamblers dogs will have a game winning goal.

The Trains never quit though, and they tie things up again in the final minute of the game, ensuring for a fourth straight game, the Gamblers and the Trains will go to overtime. This overtime is quite unspectacular though as the Trains score the on their very first shot in overtime. Shane Dunleavy, a mongoose, scores on a wrap-around in the opening seconds.

*

Dunleavy's goal sends the series back to Las Vegas for the culmination of the Gamblers/Trains series. Winner goes on to face the Five Ohhh!. Loser goes home. Even before the series finishes, it is nicknamed *The Overtime Series*. The Las Vegas sports books even take bets on whether or not the fifth game will also go to overtime.

The stats for both teams are pretty similar. Both teams have scored ten goals in the series. The Gamblers have outshot the Trains 133 to 131. The Trains have a total of 45 penalty minutes to the Gamblers 43. Blocks are in favor of the Trains 65 to 64, and hits favor the Gamblers 82 to 81. It's been the most evenly matched and most exciting series in the IAHL in a long time, and it will end tonight.

Game five starts off slow. Most fans expect both teams to come out fast and furious, pucks-a-flyin'. However, it seems each team has the same idea, *let the other guys wear themselves out before we make our move.*

A ring off the post by Big Chick serves as a wakeup call for the Trains. They realize had the puck bounced one way instead of the other, they would be staring down a 1-0 deficit. They make a mad dash for the Gamblers net after the near miss and swarm Harlan with a barrage of shots over the next six minutes until they finally push one through.

Now, it's the Gamblers who are staring into the eyes of a 1-0 deficit and possible elimination from the playoffs. Worse yet, this could be the end of their dreams of a threepeat. In true Gamblers fashion, the guys regroup and go on the attack. Lovey nails Rodman with a pass on their crisscross move that allows Rodman to sink a game tying goal just before intermission.

The second period sees both teams playing cautious again. There are a couple of penalties, a few scoring opportunities, and even a Gamblers penalty shot, but no one scores. As the period ends, The Gamblers are in the middle of an all-out blitz upon Magz that doesn't end immediately following the buzzer. This causes tempers to flare.

Undertaker gets grabbed from behind and pulled into a fight with Bill Sherman. The kangaroo takes the black dog by surprise and knocks him swiftly to the ice. Kane sees his buddy fall down and jumps instinctively to protect him. He pounces on Bill Sherman, punching him repeatedly all the way to the ice.

Meanwhile, as Rodman tries to help clear the chaos in front of the net, he reaches a flipper to Lovey to help the teddy bear up, but he takes a cheap-shot to the side of the head by Benson Sherman and falls down. It's a mistake the kangaroo will wish he never made. Hitting Rodman is one of the unspoken rules in the current IAHL. The Gamblers simply will not gamble with Rodman's safety.

Lovey forces himself up, using the faces and heads of Trains players and even his own teammates to push off.

Benson Sherman catches a flash of Lovey's quick movements, so he decides to preemptively meet Lovey half way. He rears a fist back and prepares to pop Lovey, but Lovey throws his punch ahead of Benson's. The force of the punch has combined with Benson's own forward motion splits Benson's nose wide open and drops him to the ice like a sack of bricks.

The attack doesn't last long, but it's so vicious that it draws the attention of everyone on the ice. Even Kane and Bill Sherman stop fighting to look at the carnage.

Benson's snout is so lacerated that blood gushes out like water from a garden hose, freezing upon touching the ice. The sight freaks even Lovey out. He takes a nervous step backwards.

The Gamblers medical staff runs onto the ice to attend to Benson Sherman. They give him stitches on the spot to get the bleeding stopped. It isn't apparent at first, but the kangaroo needs reconstructive surgery on his face because of the injury. The lesson is once again reinforced. Never put your paws on Rodman T. Penguin.

Come the third period, only three kangaroos hit the ice. It's a fact that doesn't go unnoticed by the Gamblers. There's sure to be payback. All period long, the Gamblers keep an eye out for potential retaliations, and that makes scoring hard. They miss their first eleven shots.

Despite the Gamblers worries, the Trains had made a team decision not to retaliate during intermission. They agreed that the best revenge would be to win the game, so they play focused and effective hockey all period long, and it pays off in the form of a late goal by Baxter Sherman and a 2-1 lead with three and a half minutes to go.

Gamblers players, coaches, and fans alike don't panic. After all, this is *The Overtime Series*. Plus, the Gamblers have plenty of experience in making comebacks and winning big games.

Safari Chip sends out his third line after his team loses the lead.

Liten, who has taken the center's position with L-Rod on the first lien for tonight's game, takes the faceoff and wins.

The puck ends up on the stick of Penny. She passes it to Goose, and the Gamblers speedster takes the puck over the blue line. The Gamblers set up and start passing the puck around.

Maverick sees Penny breakaway from her defender and move to the front of the net. He taps the puck around his own defender, sending it her way.

Penny rears back to one time the oncoming puck, but she's met by a violent crash. Chris Boozer, a crow, checks Penny from the front, and her own defender crashes into her from behind. She sees stars as she gets sandwiched between the two Trains and falls to the ice unmoving.

Play continues on.

"Penny!" Rodman screams from the bench. He tries to climb the wall to check on her.

Safari Chip and Lovey hold him back.

"Wait for the referees," Safari Chip says.

Players on both teams stop to check on Penny. The distraction allows Liten to take the puck towards Magz and poke it past the owl, tying the game as whistles blow.

Two referees kneel down to check on Penny.

"Penny, are you ok?" one of the referees asks.

Penny cracks her eye open just a bit and sneaks a peek at her surroundings. She can see the goal light going off, so she opens her eyes wide, smiles, and jumps to her feet unharmed.

The Trains know they've been duped. Penny's injury was a ploy the whole time. Their coach screams from the bench to get the attention of the referees. He argues that the goal was scored after the whistles blew. Such a fuss is made that the referees decide to check the monitors to see if they can pinpoint when the goal was scored in relation to the whistles being blown.

The noise in the arena is deafening though, and it makes reviewing the play nearly impossible even with noise cancelling headphones. After a very long break in the game, the referees decide it's too close to tell. They let the goal stand.

The crowd goes bonkers.

The Trains coach waves his paws at the referees disgusted.

The game continues on until the buzzer in regulation rings. The game and the series, in the only way the hockey gods can see fit, will be determined in overtime.

Safari Chip rallies his players around before overtime starts. He reminds them to stay loose and to play smart. "And remember, the next goal scored sends the other team home, so if you want to keep playing this season, if you want to threepeat, if you want the Cup, you have to think attack, attack, attack on offense, and defend, defend, defend on defense."

Liten nudges Safari Chip.

"Yeah?" Safari Chip asks.

"I think I know what might ensure we score first." Liten shakes faintly at the thought that he might soon be realizing a third straight Cup Finals as well as his favorite treat.

"Double Double Bonus Banana Split Sundaes for everyone if we win!" Safari Chip shouts.

The Gamblers, minus Penny, go wild.

"What?" Penny asks.

"Just win," Moose tells her.

"Yeah. I didn't understand at first either, but once you've tried one, you'll understand too," Haas assures her.

The referees whistle for both teams to come to center ice. The puck drops, and overtime gets underway. Liten, back on the first line for overtime, takes four shots of his own on his first shift. Two of his shots ring off the posts. He grits his teeth and grips his stick tightly in frustration each time he misses.

A line change finally takes Liten and the rest of the first liners off the ice. From the bench, the mouse shouts words of encouragement and direction to his teammates. Safari Chip almost stops him at first, but the mouse is so animated, and his teammates on the bench find it so hilarious, and he actually seems to be motivating the other players, so e coach allows his former assistant coach to continue yelling.

The Trains take their first cracks on offense. Spoedige takes a shot that gets kicked aside by Harlan, but it gets kicked right to Dunleavy, who tries to punch the puck right back past Harlan. The turtle falls to his tail and tries to block the shot. The puck goes under his gloved flipper, but luckily for him and the Gamblers, the puck bangs off the post and flies back onto the ice.

The game remains tied.

Apple Jack grabs the puck and shoots it behind the net to get it away from two oncoming Trains players.

Dunleavy collects the puck before Big Chick can get to it and tries a wrap around this time. Harlan slides to Dunleavy's side and blocks the puck again. Dunleavy pushes against Harlan's leg pads, but he can't make Harlan budge. Finally, Harlan kicks the puck out towards the center of the Gamblers defensive zone.

Beary grabs it and races to the Gamblers attack zone with Sammie, Snickers, and several Trains players. He crosses the blue line, weaves past one defender, skates past another, crisscrosses the ice in front of Magz, then shots a pass blindly behind himself.

The puck takes Sammie by surprise, but the Gamblers koala corrals it and fires just in time to get it through a closing hole created by Magz and the goal post.

The puck lands in the net.

The goal lights go off.

The Gamblers rush the ice to celebrate.

The Trains fall to the ice, head for their bench, and sigh disappointedly, but they don't leave the ice.

Rodman and Lovey help Sammie and Beary stand up.

"What was that?" Rodman laughs.

"What was what?" Beary asks.

"What was what?" Lovey says. "You stole our move."

"Maybe we did. What are you going to do about it?" Sammie laughs.

"Nothing, as long as we're on the same team," Rodman grabs Sammie in a headlock and gives him noogies.

Lovey does the same to Beary until Harlan jumps on both of them and knocks them down.

After a brief celebration by the Gamblers, despite all the hard fought battles of the series and even the Benson Sherman injury, the Trains shake hands with the Gamblers and wish them luck.

Baxter shakes Rodman's flipper. "Beat those guys in Reno for us. We all want to see a real IAHL team with the Cup."

"Thanks. We'll do our best," Rodman promises.

"I know you will." Baxter smiles, pats Rodman on the back, and skates off.

Chapter 30: Prelude To The Finals

As he has for the past two seasons before the Cup Finals begin, Safari Chip teams with the New Orleans Hotel to plan a huge party in celebration of the Finals. This year, however, the Gamblers aren't hosting the first two games since the number one seed has gone to the owners of the best record in hockey, the Reno Five Ohhh!. Therefore, the party won't take place until the day before game three.

In the meantime, the Gamblers and the Five Ohhh! are busy in other ways. One of the most fun things they get to do is the filming of Cup Finals commercials. The theme for the Finals is an instate rivalry between the north siders from Reno taking on the two time defending champion boys from the south in Las Vegas.

The Gamblers film first.

Their commercial starts off with Rodman skating into view across the ice of an empty darkened arena. He grinds to a halt and sends ice flying at the camera. Lovey steps in from the side of the camera then and wipes the ice off the camera's lens.

"They say that what happens in Vegas, stays in Vegas," Rodman says.

"So let us show you what happens in Vegas," Lovey follows.

A montage of goals being scored by Gamblers players appears on the screen next.

Sammie appears after the goals to tell viewers, "Goals happen in Vegas."

The screen switches to a montage of shots being blocked by Harlan, Haas, and a few defensemen.

Harlan and Haas appears on screen next and deliver their line in unison. "Blocked shots happen in Vegas."

A montage of fights, mostly containing the dogs and Lovey appear on screen next.

The four dogs and Lovey get their speaking part after the fight montage. Together they all say, "Fights happen in Vegas."

The final montage is one of more goals being scored, more shots being blocked, and scoreboards showing the final scores of the games being in the Gamblers favor.

Then, Safari Chip comes on screen. "Winning happens in Vegas."

Safari Chip is followed by Rodman, Lovey and the four dogs, Liten, Big Chick, Sammie, Beary, Harlan, and L-Rod. All of them repeat winning happens in Vegas.

The final shot is the entire Gamblers team around the Cup.

"For the last two years," Beary says.

"The Cup has happened in Vegas," Big Chick says.

The final shot is a close up of Rodman. "And the Cup is staying in Vegas."

The Five Ohhh! commercial is a little different. Each Five Ohhh! player highlighted appears on screen by himself.

It starts with Ox. "They said we weren't ready for the IAHL." He turns then to watch a shot of himself scoring against Harlan on the wall behind him.

"We were told we didn't have what it takes," Dislike says and points to video of himself scoring a goal while taking a hard hit.

"We weren't skilled enough," Greg says.

A dekeing sequence featuring Greg that leads to a goal plays on the monitor behind him.

"We weren't fast enough," Sammie Two says.

A scene of Sammie Two winning a race for a puck plays.

"We weren't strong enough," Hoss barks.

Hoss and the other dogs getting into fights plays on the screen next.

"We weren't big enough," Samanya says.

A highlight of him knocking L-Rod to the ice with a big check appears on screen.

"We couldn't tend goal like the big boys of the IAHL," Marlon grumbles.

A series of Marlon blocking shots plays on the screen following his words.

"They," their coach starts, "were wrong."

"We are the big boys of the IAHL," Ox comes back on screen.

"And we're coming after the Cup," The Colonel states.

"What happens in Vegas," Ratone says.

"Eventually makes its way to Reno," Mad Man says.

The final shot of the commercial is a shot of the entire Five Ohhh! team standing around the Cup.

Other similar commercials are shot. A lot of individual promos are made. The Gamblers do a lot of commercials where they explain again that the Cup happens in Vegas and therefore will stay in Vegas, or simply that they themselves are what happen in Vegas followed by highlights of their personal achievements throughout the season. They also do promos in which they talk about threepeating. The individual Five Ohhh! commercials highlight similar high points in their season, and they talk about how hard they've fought to get to the Finals and what it would mean to win the Cup.

All of the commercials get played over and over on the network carrying the Cup Finals and ASPN. Polls are taken to see which team did a better job with their commercials. Whether it's because of their growing popularity or because they actually did a better job, the Gamblers win in a landslide. The only times they lose are in polls taken in Reno, Alaska, select cities with rival IAHL teams, and New York for some reason.

Most of the newspapers, sporting news shows, and the sports books predict the Gamblers to win in four games.

All the polls about the commercials and the predictions that the Gamblers will win only fuel the Five Ohhh! players desires to win and prove everyone wrong.

Dislike takes to Facespace, writing *so everyone is predicting the Gamblers to win. Smh.* Then he dislikes his own post. His teammates and their fans all leave him comments and dislike his post as well. A few of the Gamblers see the post and decide it would be funny to like his status. Their actions serve as more shots fired in the war that has been brewing between the two teams all season long.

*

The first thing the Gamblers do when they arrive in Reno is check their hotel room for bugs. They're relieved to find no hidden microphones anywhere.

"These guys are jerks, but at least they're not the Gold Rush," Safari Chip says.

"You said it," Rodman agrees.

The Gamblers unpack their bags and head to the arena for their turn to practice. Safari Chip holds a pretty grueling practice on the day they arrive and a light practice the next morning, the morning of the first game. He wants his team to stay sharp.

After practice, the Gamblers and the Five Ohhh! have to play the waiting game for the evening's hockey game to start. It's hard to tell which team is more excited, the Gamblers in anticipation of threepeating or the Five Ohhh!, who have seventeen players who are all trying to win the Cup for the first time.

Chapter 31: The Reno Games

Nighttime finally creeps in on the day of game one, and the two teams head to their locker rooms to prepare for the Cup Finals. The Five Ohhh! locker room is serious and tense. Not having ever played for a Cup, the Reno players are a bundle of nerves. On the opposite side of the arena, the Gamblers are cool, calm, and collected. Most of them anyway.

Moose fidgets in the seat by his locker.

"What's the matter buddy?" Maverick asks.

"I'm just nervous," Moose answers.

"This ain't no thing," Goose says.

"No thing? How can it be no thing? It's the Cup Finals!" Moose says.

"Been there," Maverick says.

"Done that," Goose tells him.

The horse and goose high five.

"Seriously, it'll be fine," Maverick tells his buddy.

"But you have to stay relaxed like Chip always tells us," Goose warns.

"I'll try," Moose says, but he thinks too much about the consequences of playing bad and he starts hyperventilating.

Maverick looks around the locker room. He finds a paper bag, grabs it, and hands it to Moose. "Here. Breathe into this. Try to relax."

Moose takes the bag and does as he's instructed.

L-Rod walks over to his line mates and takes a long hard look at Moose. "Is he going to throw up?"

"Nah." Goose waves off L-Rod's suggestion.

"He looks like he's going to throw up," L-Rod says.

"Check out the kid." Maverick points to L-Rod. "If he ain't nervous, you shouldn't be nervous Moose."

Nothing works, and Moose's condition worsens.

"Maybe he should throw up. It might make him feel…" L-Rod starts to say, but he's interrupted by the violent upchuck that comes from the depths of Moose's tummy, through his throat, and out of his mouth into the bag. Unfortunately, the bag is small and Moose's upset tummy is big. The bag tears to shreds, and vomit spills all over the locker room floor.

Maverick, Goose, and L-Rod jump back.

"Ewww! Sick," L-Rod says.

Moose coughs and spits out some lingering throw up. He clears his throat and takes a deep breath. "Oh man. Sorry. I feel better now."

"Dude! I can smell that over here," Kane shouts from across the room.

"That's because you have that crazy dog sense of smell," Moose claims.

"I can smell it too," Penny says.

"I'll get it cleaned up. Just give me a second," Moose says.

Safari Chip sits in the locker room with his team. He enjoys hanging out with his players and being a part of their conversations and hijinks. They went over most of their strategies during their light practice that morning, so there was only minimal game planning to do this evening. Mostly, he just checked to make sure the game plan details were remembered.

"At least he did it in the Five Ohhh! locker room and not ours," Safari Chip cracks a joke.

Rodman and some of the other guys laugh.

"I have an idea." Lovey runs to his locker, grabs his cellphone, runs to the puke, and snaps a photo.

"Hey. What are you doing?" Moose asks.

"That's gross Lovey," Beary says.

Lovey ignores all their comments. He's too busy posting the picture on Facespace. He titles it *A Little Present For the Five Ohhh! Compliments of Moose and the Gamblers.* Another shot fired.

Safari Chip looks at the clock on the wall. Two minutes to seven. He jumps from his seat. "Holy Toledo! Game time!"

The Gamblers jump to their feet, grab their sticks, and run down the tunnel.

With no time to spare, Moose decides to clean up his mess after the first period.

*

Game one introductions of the teams are always a big to do. Every player on each team, as well as each of the coaches, is introduced. The Gamblers receive their usual chorus of boos as the visitors, but the Reno fans take it a step further. They shout the word *sucks* as each Gambler starter is introduced.

The house announcer says, "Starting at center, number seventy-three, Rodman T. Penguin."

And the crowd shouts in unison, "Sucks!"

"Starting at right wing, number sixteen, Lovey Bara."

"SUCKS!"

Even Safari Chip isn't spared.

"The Gamblers are led by head coach, general manager, and owner of the team, Safari Chip."

"He sucks too!" the Reno crowd yells.

"Did they just say I suck?" Safari Chip asks Flip.

"I think they did," Flip answers.

"Huh," is all Safari Chip can offer after that.

On the other side of the ice, the Five Ohhh! laugh their heads off at their fans' show of disrespect to their opponents.

"Remind me to like that on Facespace later." Dislike elbows The Colonel.

"Fine, but don't elbow me." The Colonel elbows him back.

"Owww," Dislike whispers and rubs his bicep.

The lights come all the way up, and the referees call the starters to center ice.

Rodman lines up across from Ox.

"Ok gentlemen. Congratulations on making it this far. Good luck to both teams. Let's have a good clean series," the referee says.

Rodman taps Ox's stick with his as a sign of respect.

Ox takes the gesture the wrong way and uses his own stick to slaps Rodman's stick out of his flippers. Rodman's stick cracks in half and goes flying. Before the game even starts, the referees have to stop a fight from taking place. Rodman pushes Ox, and Lovey flies in to protect Rodman.

"Take a cue from what happened to Benson Sherman and leave Hott Rod alone," Lovey warns Ox with a second push.

Ox uses just one hoof to push Lovey to the ice. "Back off Bara. I'm not a punk kangaroo. I can take a slap to the face."

Undertaker and Kane help Lovey up and hold him back. The referees restrain the other Five Ohhh! starters.

"Remind me to like that on Facespace too," Dislike says and then realizes no one is standing near him.

Rodman shakes his head and races to the Gamblers bench for a new stick. He grabs the one he wants, skates back to center ice, and digs in.

Ox digs in across from him. "I have a feeling tonight's going to be a good night."

The referee drops the puck. Rodman whacks the puck back to Undertaker.

"I do too," Rodman says and shoves Ox backwards.

As Rodman skates off with his team, Ox regains his footing and races after the Gamblers captain. He meets Rodman just beyond the blue line with a vicious cross check to the back. Rodman falls face first to the ice.

Whistles blow, and play stops.

Both teams conjure around Rodman and Ox. Liten protects Rodman from further assaults while Lovey, Undertaker, and Kane push and shove Hoss, Stunner, and Dislike, trying to get their paws on Ox, who hides behind his teammates.

The referees check on Rodman. He's hurt, but he stands up on his own accord and gives them and Safari Chip a thumbs up, indicating that he's good to continue.

The referees send Ox to the penalty box for cross checking, and seven seconds into the Cup Finals, the Gamblers have their first power play. They don't let the gift go to waste either. Rodman capitalizes with a power play goal halfway through the man advantage.

Ox is freed of his temporary jail and sent back to his own bench. Rezza tears into his captain as he sits down. "You knuckle head! What do you think you're doing out there? This isn't some meaningless game. This is the Cup Finals. We can't be giving these guys free goals. I don't care what you think of them personally, professionally they're dang good. They haven't won two straight Cups on accident. So, get your head in the game if you want to keep your body in it."

Ox doesn't look at his coach while he's being scolded. He knows better than to argue. He made a bonehead mistake, and it's his team who is paying the price with their 1-0 deficit. Making the wrong face could get him yelled at even more. He just sits and takes it as he's learned to do over his many seasons of playing hockey.

The game goes on and on with physical play and very few shots. By the time the third period rolls around, the teams have combined for more penalty minutes than shots. Tripping, cross checking, slashing, boarding, and fighting penalties are called over and over. Neither team plays dirty, just very aggressive.

A quarter of the way through the third period, the Gamblers still lead 1-0 on Rodman's opening minute goal, but Ox makes amends for his opening minute mistake by catching a pass from Dislike and sinking a shot past Harlan, who loses sight of the puck in all the traffic he has in front of him.

Play continues on after Reno ties the game. The Five Ohhh! don't ease up on the Gamblers, and the Gamblers seem to avoid one catastrophe after another. It becomes pretty clear near the end of the period that the Gamblers are the team on the defensive. They feel lucky to have kept the game tied, but they also feel as though they're being punished. It will be their seventh overtime game in a row. All the extra hockey really has their bodies tuckered out. But, this is the Cup Finals. There will be no quit from the Las Vegas Gamblers.

Overtime starts with a Rodman faceoff win and a quick offensive attack by the Gamblers first line. Rodman's line does its best to end the game quickly, but all they really do is manage to put a little bit of pressure on a more rested team and tire themselves out.

The Five Ohhh! wind up with the puck after an errant pass from Liten lands in no man's land, and Dislike snatches it. Play moves the other way, and the Gamblers first line is forced to stay on the ice for a defensive shift. They fight and scrap and battle to get the puck away from the assertive Five Ohhh! team. Harlan repeatedly kicks and whacks pucks away from the net, but the Gamblers can never corral the loose puck. Finally, in an effort to just get a breather, Kane gets his stick on the puck and whips around quickly, sending the puck all the way to the other end of the ice for icing. Although play stops for a moment, the Gamblers aren't allowed to change lines on an icing call.

Eventually, they do get a line change, but this sort of play goes on and on for an entire overtime. The players on the ice, the TV announcers, the fans in attendance and watching at home all get the sense that is going to be just a matter of time before the Five Ohhh! push one across. The first overtime ends, and the teams head to the locker rooms for an extra intermission

"No more overtime games," Liten pants as he lies on one of the team's benches.

Harlan tosses his helmet aside, wipes his brow, and frantically pulls at his jersey. It gets caught on his gear and over his head. He panic as he's already sweating bullets, and his hot breath caught inside the hockey jersey makes his temperature rise even more, and it rises quickly. Harlan struggles but can't get his jersey over his head. A few of his teammates try to help the poor guy. Things go from bad to worse when Harlan starts to feel lightheaded. His flippers fall from above his head to his side, his vision fades to white, and he blacks out.

Beary and Sammie catch him before he hits the ground and gets a concussion. They set him down on his shell and remove his jersey.

"Get us some cold water," Beary orders.

"Help me get his gear off," Sammie tells Beary.

The Gamblers wingers untie Harlan's pads and remove them from the turtle. Without a jersey and pads, Harlan's body temperature begins decreasing. Undertaker and Kane come over with the team's water bucket and pour it over Harlan's body.

"Fire in the hole!" Apple Jack shouts as they pour.

That does the trick. Harlan wakes up, but he's groggy and doesn't remember what happened. "Why did you do that?"

"You passed out buddy." Kane pats the turtle's chest.

"You got too hot and we had to cool you down," Undertaker explains.

Safari Chip kneels next to his goalie. "How are you feeling?"

"Not great," Harlan says honestly.

"You just rest. We'll take care of the rest of this game."

"No. I can play," Harlan protests.

"You need to rest. It's going to be a tough series. We need you healthy and sharp." Safari Chip turns around to face Flip. "Grab the fan out of my office. We have to get it on Harlan and keep him cool."

"But Chip…"

"No but Chip. Don't worry. We've got another Cup champion on this team who is more than capable of getting us a win." Safari Chip lifts Harlan's head up to look upon Haas.

"I've got his," Haas assures Harlan and the rest of his team, but deep down, he questions whether or not he really has got it. He's lost four his last five playoff games.

Haas' false confidence is enough to allow Harlan to relax and give up his fight to stay in the game. He really does feel like poo. He's hot, out of breath, and his legs are wobbly.

Harlan isn't the only Gambler feeling like he's about to pass out. While he rests, many others suck on oxygen tubes, replenish their fluids with water and Gatorade, and even jump into the team whirlpools filled with ice cold water. Eighteen minutes of rest isn't enough for the fatigued Gamblers. When

Safari Chip tells them it's time to head back out for the second overtime period, the Gamblers feel no better than they did when they entered their locker room.

The second overtime starts with a faceoff win in which Rodman expends a lot more energy than he normally would or should just to win a faceoff. The Gamblers cross the blue line and put up as good an attack as they can. None of their shots even come close to the net though, and after they lose the puck, most of them rush to the bench for a line change.

Their plan for the rest of the game is short quick shifts, none more than forty-five seconds. Safari Chip hopes it will keep their energy levels up.

The Five Ohhh! cross their blue line, set up on offense with lots of their players figure-eighting in front of and around the net. The Gamblers find it hard to defend any one Five Ohhh! player as the puck gets passed randomly around the Five Ohhh! players.

Apple Jack watches his opponents for a good long while, and he thinks he has their passing pattern figured out. He waits for another second until he's sure he knows where the puck is going to go next. When the time is right, he makes his move to cut off the pass going from Dislike to Ox. The second he moves to intercept the puck though, he gets a cramp so bad from all the water he drank during intermission that he keels over and falls to the ice.

Ox gets the puck as it was intended, and he wastes no time ambushing a defenseless Haas.

Haas is just barely able to slide and get to the puck in time to block it, but he does and knocks it out of the air. The puck drops in front of him, and he dives to reach for it. Ox beats him to the rebound, and the Five Ohhh! captain drags the puck backwards, drawing Haas further out of the net on his belly. From there, it's an easy flip of the puck over Haas' outstretched body and a deflection off Dislike's stick to redirect the puck into the net that gives the Five Ohhh! a one game to none lead in the Cup Finals.

The Reno crowd goes ape.

The Reno players celebrate.

Snickers skates by Apple Jack, reaches out his paw, and helps the younger dog to his feet. "You ok?"

"Yeah, I just got hit with a cramp so bad it dropped me. It came out of nowhere," Apple Jack frowns. He looks around at the celebrating Five Ohhh! on the ice and the Gamblers already heading to their tunnel. "Man. I cost us the game."

"No you didn't. This is a team effort. One guy doesn't win or lose the game," Snickers puts his arm around Apple Jack and leads him to the tunnel to join their teammates.

The rest of the guys can see that Apple Jack is upset with himself. They all pat him on his leg guards with their sticks to let him know not to let it get him down.

*

After the game, the two teams take turns in the press room. Safari Chip fields all the normal questions. What does your team have to do to bounce back in game two? How have the seven straight overtimes affected his team? Why didn't Harlan finish the game? Will Harlan start in game two? He answers all the questions as honestly as he can and with dignity. The questions wind down, and he's left to rejoin his team.

The Five Ohhh! come in next. The first question for them comes from a reporter from ASPN. "Coach how big was it getting that first win?"

"The first win is always huge, especially in a five game series. It means we only have to play .500 hockey from this point on, and it means if the Gamblers are to win they'd have to beat us three out of the next four games. And, in case you guys didn't notice throughout the regular season, we don't tend to lose three out of four very often."

"Are you not even worried about losing three out of four to the Gamblers? I mean, if any team can pull that off, it's them," the ASPN reporter follows up.

"I'm not worried. I know what those guys are capable of, but my guys are just as capable. More so even."

*

Both teams have an off day between games one and two. Safari Chip doesn't hold practice. He wants his team to rest all day long, but he also wants them to spend the day together as a team. They don't leave their hotel. The day is spent hanging out by the indoor pool, playing video games in their rooms, and just talking and spending time with their friends. Mary shows up to spend some time with her husband and she brings Sprinkles, Elmira, and Chickette to visit Penny and the boys.

That night, the Gamblers, El Pollos Locos, and the girls eat dinner together. The whole day, they don't think about, talk about, or practice hockey.

The respite from hockey is just what the doctor ordered. By the next morning, the Gamblers head for their locker room together as a team. They enter feeling like the game one loss is no big deal. They're refreshed and refocused on the task at hand.

One of them gets a little too relaxed, and he falls asleep in his chair outside his locker. The rest of the team starts to notice Lovey sleeping as his snoring grows louder and louder. They punish the sleeping teddy by drawing a uni-brow on his forehead with whipped cream and tickling his nose with a feather so he slaps himself in the face trying to stop the annoying tickle. They think the slapping will eventually lead to Lovey waking himself up, but it doesn't. He continues sleeping, and other than snapping a few silly photos of him and posting them on his Facespace, the Gamblers leave him alone.

Almost immediately, Dislike dislikes the photos.

While on Facespace, the Gamblers can't help but check some of the things the Five Ohhh! are saying about the series.

Ox's Facespace has a quote from him that reads, *You heard Coach. We don't lose three out of four. So much for a Gamblers threepeat.*

The Colonel's reads, *Two more games until we dine on BIG CHICKen soup straight out of the Cup.*

Greg's page has just a picture of Beary crossed out.

Dislike's page arrogantly boasts, *Series Over!*

These comments would usually serve as bulletin board material for the Gamblers to play overaggressive and overemotional, but tonight, they just shrug it off.

"These guys obviously don't know who they're dealing with," Sammie laughs.

"Yeah. They must think…" Undertaker starts to say, but he's cut off midsentence.

The Gamblers locker room is pierced by the shrill screaming of one of their own players. The scream is so high pitched that it sounds like a little girl, and it's so loud that it can be heard all the way down the hall in the Five Ohhh! locker room.

*

"What the heck was that?" Dislike stands up and looks to the locker room door in horror.

*

Every single Gambler clutches their heart, covers their ears, or ducks instinctively for cover. Their heads whip around where they lay eyes upon Lovey gripping the arms of his chair. He pants and gasps, trying to catch his breath.

Once they know everything's ok, the Gamblers rush to check on him.

"What happened Lovey?" Rodman asks.

"Are you ok?" L-Rod asks.

Lovey struggles to catch his breath.

"Lovey?" Big Chick asks.

"Oh man. Sorry guys. I just had a really bad nightmare," Lovey spits out.

"A nightmare?" Kane waves off his teammate and returns to his locker. He's glad everything is ok, but like most of his teammates, he thought there was a real threat in the locker room. Several other players return to their lockers as well.

"What happened in your dream?" Rodman asks.

"I dreamed I was a centipede with hundreds of feet, and I couldn't play hockey anymore because I couldn't afford skates," Lovey pants.

The few remaining Gamblers around him break into hysterics.

"It's not funny. It really scared me," Lovey, who is usually quick to laugh at himself, argues.

The other Gamblers continue laughing.

Lovey furrows his mangled whipped cream uni-brow at his teammates, but eventually his heartbeat returns to normal, and he joins them in their laughter.

Snickers pats him on the back. "I used to have a similar dream. In mine, I was a snake and kept getting stuck to the ice because I couldn't wear skates."

*

Game two gets underway.

Neither team looks particularly sharp in their opening shifts, but eventually, the second line of the Five Ohhh! gets a decent attack of timely passes and well calculated shots on Harlan. Still, the turtle keeps the puck from getting past him.

The Five Ohhh! continue trying though. The Colonel makes a move to get away from his defender. He skates fast to the open side of the net and clacks his stick on the ice, indicating to Crush that he's open.

Big Chick races to close the passing lane. He positions his big body in front of the fox and turns his back to him so he can watch the play developing behind him.

The Colonel gives Big Chick a shove, but Big Chick, without even turning his head, pushes The Colonel back. The

Five Ohhh! fox stumbles and falls to his tail. He sits on the ice stunned for a minute. His keen ears pick up the laughter of some of the Gamblers fans in the crowd. This enrages him. He stands up, positions himself to Big Chick's left, and uses his tail to tickle the chicken on the right side of his face.

Big Chick slaps the nuisance away, but it comes back. He slaps it away a second time, and then turns to see what's causing the annoyance.

The Colonel pulls his tail back quickly.

To Big Chick's surprise, he doesn't see anyone or anything there. He feels a sting on the left side of his face like his feathers are being plucked. He whips his head around too late to see The Colonel duck down and speed to his right.

The Colonel stealthily kicks Big Chick's right skate sideways, causing it to slide over and take out his left foot. The giant chicken falls to the ice with a thud. Before the Gamblers on the bench can even stand to protest, The Colonel gets hit with a pass from Sammie Two and sinks a goal past Harlan.

Snickers, having watched the whole thing, turns to the nearest referee for a whistle. "You're not going to call that?"

"Call what?" the referee asks.

Snickers is too astonished to answer him back. He rolls his eyes and skates to the bench for a line change. He waits at the bench door for Big Chick while the third line takes the ice. The elder dog puts his paw around Big Chick's shoulders and leads him to a seat on the bench.

"That guy is backpfeifengesicht as well," Liten, the guy on Big Chick's other side, says angrily.

"Yeah, he is backen..fee fee, backfeef, back... He needs his lights knocked out." Snickers reaches over and high fives the mouse. "In fact Chickie, that's what I wanted to talk to you about. You've got to stand up to that guy."

"How?" Big Chick asks.

"What do you mean how? You're twice his size. Just wallop him," Snickers says.

"I don't know how to fight," Big Chick says.

"Well we're going to teach you," Snickers pats him on the back and looks to the other dogs. "Ain't that right boys?"

"I told him last year he'd be unstoppable if we could teach him," Kane smiles.

Big Chick cracks a halfhearted smile. He doesn't like the idea of hitting someone. On the other wing, he doesn't like the idea or the feeling of being hit himself, or tripped, or having his feathers ripped out.

"In the meantime, watch this." Snickers stands up and waits by the bench wall.

Snickers puts his paw out and stops Moose as he skates by the bench.

"Hey," Moose protests.

"Let me on," Snickers tells him.

Moose steps into the bench and Snickers takes an out of turn shift.

"Hey!" Safari Chip shouts when he sees Snickers skate out with the third line. "Where's he going?"

No one answers, but the other dogs smile.

Safari Chip looks to his bench really fast to make sure they're not about to get a too many men on the ice penalty. He starts counting his players, but Moose raises his arm to let his coach know it is him who is missing on the ice. The monkey breathes a sigh of relief and turns his head back to the ice just in time to see Snickers light The Colonel up with a nasty check.

The result of the hit is a double minor interference and cross checking penalty since Snickers came up high with his stick and set a pick on a player who didn't have the puck. Snickers goes to the penalty box for four minutes, but the Gamblers kill off the penalty and the message has been sent.

The rest of the period is pretty uneventful. The teams head to the first intermission with the Five Ohhh! leading 1-0.

In the Gamblers locker room, Sammie approaches Beary. "Hey Bear."

"Hey Sam," the panda greets him back.

"You see Big Chick over there?" Sammie points.

Beary turns his head and takes a gander at his center. The big guy looks downtrodden even with El Pollos Locos gathered around telling him how good he's doing.

"He looks sad," Beary notes.

"Yeah, and I think the best way to cheer him up is to help him score a goal. I was sitting near him after The Colonel scored. I think he blames himself," Sammie says.

"That's going to be tough with the way we have our hands full out there with your cousin and my brother-in-law all up in our business."

"Yeah." Sammie stops to think. "I have a plan for that too. He leans in and whispers his plan to Beary.

Across the room, Rodman approaches Penny. "Hi."

"Hi." Penny waves to him.

Rodman sits down next to her. "How's it going?"

"Good. I mean, I'm having a great time out there. I don't know that I'm helping all that much. I…"

"You're helping," Rodman cuts her off.

"I haven't scored any points yet."

"Lots of guys haven't scored points yet. It's only been four periods of hockey. At least your line hasn't given up any points. Mine has, and so has the second line. More importantly, you're keeping the third line from missing a beat," Rodman tells her.

Rodman's words make her feel a whole lot better. No wonder he's the team's captain. She jumps up and gives him a big hug. "Thanks Rodman."

Rodman hugs her back. "You're welcome."

She lets him go after a slightly longer than normal hug, composes herself, and takes a step back. "I guess I'm just used to being the leader on the team. Normally, I'm the one scoring goals."

Later, intermission ends, and both teams return to the ice. The second period gets underway. Each team creates a plethora of scoring opportunities, but Harlan and Marlon stop everything in their way. Sammie and Beary try several times to get their plan to work. The basis of their plan is really just to instigate Sammie Two and Greg. The Gamblers bears poke, prod, and crowd the Five Ohhh! bears all period long.

Finally, Greg throws down his gloves to fight Beary.

Beary whistles loudly. It's the signal to Sammie Lou that his half of the plan is working.

Sammie Lou turns his head and sees Greg in a fighting stance. So, he drops his gloves, backs up to stand back to back with Beary, and calls out Sammie Two.

Sammie Two relishes the chance to take a few more swings at his cousin. He drops his stick and gloves and moves in.

Greg moves in on Beary too.

Both Five Ohhh! bears rear back to go in for the punch. They swing at the same time, and end up punching each other in the face as Sammie Lou and Beary duck out of the way. The Five Ohhh! panda and koala fall to the ice seeing stars.

Sammie Lou picks up his stick and jumps back into the play.

The referees look at each other for the other's thoughts. There was no real fight, so they let the play continue on. While Sammie Two and Greg Claymore lie on the ice, Big Chick battles The Colonel in front of the net. The fox pushes, shoves, and hits Big Chick.

"Get out of the way you big chicken," The Colonel shouts and jabs Big Chick in the back with his stick.

"No," Big Chick stands his ground.

The Colonel taps Big Chick on the shoulder with his stick. The hit is high and almost hits him in the face. "I said…"

The Colonel never finishes his sentence. Apple Jack whizzes by and drops a shoulder into the fox's shoulder from behind. The Colonel winces in pain and turns immediately to see who hit him. Whoever it is, there's certain to be payback.

He never sees who hit him though, because his next attacker, Snickers, in typical Snickers fashion, slams into him with explosive force. The fox flies fifteen feet across the ice, leaving Big Chick completely unguarded.

Meanwhile, Sammie Lou grabs the puck and passes it to Beary. He, in turn, skates around the back of the net, drawing the attention of Marlon.

Crush and Crunch chase Beary behind the net, but Beary is able to pass the puck out to Apple Jack on the wing.

"Get it to Big Chick!" Sammie Lou yells to Apple Jack.

Apple Jack does as he's told.

Big Chick isn't expecting the pass. Everything around him is happening so fast. He's barely able to control the pass, and when he does, he sends it right back to Sammie Lou.

"You take it," Sammie Lou passes it back to Big Chick.

Big Chick shakes his head and passes it back to Sammie Lou.

"You shoot it." Sammie Lou passes it back to Big Chick.

"You shoot it." Big Chick passes it back to Sammie Lou.

"Big game. Big stick. Big Chick!" Sammie Lou says and fires it back forcefully.

Marlon's head whips back and forth at all their passing.

Beary sees Crush and Crunch scrambling to get back into the play. "Someone take the shot!"

Big Chick turns his head to Beary. He passes it to him. "You take it."

Beary doesn't hesitate. As much as he wants to get Big Chick's confidence going again, he wants to tie the game for his team even more. He one times the puck with a quickness, and blasts it past Marlon.

The Gamblers celebrate Beary's goal with him. Behind them, Sammie Two, Greg, and The Colonel seethe with anger. They look on disgusted, each plotting his next move.

The teams change lines, and the game continues.

Mad Man pesters Penny on their next shift. He points to Rodman on the bench. "I can't believe you ditched me for that guy. He's dumpy."

"He is not!" Penny argues.

"Yeah. He's fat."

Penny skates away from Mad Man.

Mad Man follows her. "Look at him." Mad Man points to Rodman again.

"Shut up."

"You're in love with a fat boy."

Penny turns around and punches Mad Man in the beak. The blast sends the Five Ohhh! penguin to the ice. She looks down upon him and sees that her punch has caused a tear to escape his eye.

Whistles blow and two referees swarm over to Penny. They detain her like they would any other player and begin to skate her off to the penalty box. Before she goes, she stops and says to Mad Man, "He's not fat, and even if he is a little pudgy, he's still the best in the world."

Mad Man sighs disgustedly.

The referees take Penny away after her final words, but she has one last message for Mad Man as she's skated to the penalty box for roughing. "And at least he's not a cry baby," she shouts loud enough for half his teammates to hear.

Mad Man wipes the tear away from his eye and tries not to make eye contact with anyone as he stands up.

The Five Ohhh! go on the power play.

Safari Chip sends out his best penalty killers, Rodman, Lovey, Apple Jack, and Snickers. The odd line ends up playing all but the final fifteen seconds of a grueling and intense penalty kill, but they do kill off the penalty and the game remains tied.

At least it remains tied until Undertaker gets a pass from Lovey and takes a garbage shot from just beyond the blue line in hopes of putting some pressure on the Five Ohhh! defense, and miraculously, the puck gets through and past about three players from each team and Marlon. The puck hits the back of the net and sets off the goal light. The Gamblers take their first lead since halfway through the first period of game one.

After Undertaker's goal, the Five Ohhh! become more aggressive in their play. They smash and crash anyone holding onto the puck. Even the littlest players, Liten, L-Rod, and Penny are not spared. The Colonel continues tormenting Big Chick to the point that the big guy becomes a nonfactor in the game. This fact worries the Gamblers. They know eventually they're going to need Big Chick's sharpshooting skills to come into play if they're going to win another Cup.

Even when they don't mean to, the Five Ohhh! punish the Gamblers. Dislike, in an attempt to disrupt a potential breakaway by Lovey, accidently hits his counterpart with a high stick to the face. Lovey's snout splits open, and he has to rush to the bench for stitches. Dislike is put in the penalty box, and the Gamblers go on the power play.

Lovey's spot on the power play is taken by Beary while he gets stiches right there on the bench. The other Gamblers sit and watch mortified as the flesh around Lovey's snout is cleaned off, and sewn up. The Gamblers grizzly cub doesn't even flinch as the needle goes in and out. Eight stitches in total.

Back on the ice, it appears that the Five Ohhh! are going to clear the puck as Stunner grabs it and fires it towards the other end of the ice. His teammates race for the bench for a line change, as well as do most of the Gamblers. However, Stunner's stick breaks as it hits the ice, and the puck goes nowhere.

Beary is the only Gambler to notice the puck resting motionless on the ice at Stunner's feet. He slams on the breaks, and takes off towards it. While Stunner looks around the ice in front of him, behind himself, and down towards Harlan, Beary sneaks in and fires the puck towards Marlon. Marlon blocks the quick shot but gives up a rebound. Beary fires again and is blocked again, but on his third try, Beary finally sinks a goal, his second of the game. It puts the Gamblers up 3-1 and sends Safari Chip's bunch into the second intermission all laughs and smiles.

The Five Ohhh! locker room is a different story. Greg pushes Sammie Two from as they enter. Sammie Two stumbles on his skates and falls to the ground. He doesn't stay there long. He jumps back to his feet and charges at Greg. Ox, Dislike, and a few others jump in to separate their fighting teammates.

"Whoa! Whoa! Whoa!" Ox shouts, holding both players at bay.

"That's for hitting me in the face," Greg shouts as he frees one of his arms from The Colonel and Dislike's grasp far enough to reach out and point at Sammie Two.

"You hit me too dummy." Sammie Two, whose arms are free as he's restrained from around the waist by Mad Man, swipes at Greg's outstretched paw.

The swipe antagonizes Greg. He jumps at Sammie Two, trying to free himself from his captors, but they hold him tight. Other Five Ohhh! players step between them to help Ox in case either fighting member of their team gets free.

"Knock it off," Ox orders. "Can't you see they planned that? It was all to make you look bad, and it worked. You looked bad, they scored, move on."

Neither likes the situation, but they do as their captain orders. They nod at each other and at Ox.

Ox allows the others to free Greg and Sammie Two. "Now shake paws."

Greg sighs. Sammie Two does as well, but he at least reaches out his paw. Greg hesitates until he sees Ox glare at him. He reaches out and gives Sammie Two's paw a few slaps that constitute enough of a paw shake to appease Ox.

"Now, how are we going to get back into this game?" Ox asks his teammates.

"They score too much," Big Deuce says.

"They don't score too much," Rezza shouts. "These guys are capable of being shut down. They only have four goals against us this series. It's our inability to score that is hurting us. We only have three goals in the series, and only two of those goals have been scored against Harlan."

"He's tough," Ratone says.

"Even when we stand in front of him to block his vision, it's like he sees right through us," Hoss explains.

"I wish they'd start Haas in one game. I hear his nerves are shaky. We could really pick on a guy like that," Mad Man says.

"Well wish in one flipper and…" Greg starts.

"Forget about it. They ain't starting Haas. Harlan's too hot right now," Ox cuts Greg off.

"It's going to take teamwork. We can't tie this thing on one shot, and we definitely can't take the lead on one shot, so play smart out there. Play good defense, and we'll make our comeback one goal at a time. Gather 'round." Rezza motions for everyone to huddle around their chalkboard. His players take mental notes of the game plans he diagrams for the third period.

Come the start of the third period, the Five Ohhh! put their plans into action. They play smart, strategic, physical, and most importantly, clean hockey. Because of their good play, dividends are paid immediately. Stunner scores with plenty of time in the period to tie it up.

Play continues on. Fight as they might, the Five Ohhh! come close a few times, but they fail to tie the game late in the period. They fight off a brief attack from the Gamblers with just a handful of seconds to go in the game. Once they secure the puck, Rezza calls a timeout.

Both teams head to their bench.

"These guys are going to pull their goalie the second they cross our blue line. You guys have to be thinking defense, defense, defense once they do. But let's try and win the faceoff and keep the puck away from them for as long as we can to kill off as much time as we can," Safari Chip tells his players.

They all nod.

He's not sure they all understand his instructions, so he quizzes them. "Big Chick?"

"Yeah Coach… I mean Chip?" Big Chick answers.

"You're taking the faceoff. What's your job after that?" Safari Chip asks.

"Play keep away," Big Chick answers correctly.

"Right. And if we don't win, Beary?" Safari Chip asks.

"Get back on defense quickly," Beary answers.

"Harlan what are you doing?" Safari Chip asks.

"Preparing for a six on five attack, checking down all six of their players, and making sure they don't score." Harlan nods.

"Right!" Safari Chip pumps his fist. Apparently, they were listening.

The referee calls for both teams to return to the ice for the faceoff which takes place near the Five Ohhh! net since that's where play stopped when time was called. Big Chick lines up across from The Colonel. His faceoff winning percentage is astronomical when facing most other teams, but Big Chick is below fifty percent when facing The Colonel. The growling that comes from The Colonel's mouth always puts Big Chick on edge and distracts him. The referee drops the puck. The Colonel snaps at Big Chick and scares the big guy into dropping his stick. This makes for an easy Five Ohhh! faceoff win.

Big Chick bends down and picks up his stick. He can hear The Colonel laughing as he skates away.

The second the Five Ohhh! gain their zone, Marlon breaks for the bench so Ox can jump on as their sixth man. Unfortunately for the Five Ohhh!, Apple Jack reaches his stick out as far as he can as Sammie Two tries to glide past him, and he pokes the puck free. Apple Jack stutter steps, unable to get good traction on the ice because he's so excited to reach the loose puck. He has to dive to reach it, and when he does, he's able to tap it to Beary.

Beary and everyone else start skating towards the empty net of the Five Ohhh!. Beary weaves past Crush and seemingly has an open and easy lane to the net. He doesn't see the oncoming Ox charging at him. He rears back to fire.

Ox lowers his shoulder to make a hard check on the Gamblers tiny panda. Behind Ox, Greg smiles at the thought of his brother-in-law being obliterated. But Ox never touches Beary. Lagging behind the play because he dropped his stick, Big Chick is in perfect position to skate in between Beary and Ox, take the blow for his winger, and stop Ox.

Beary only sees a flash of colors colliding violently and some yellow feathers flying in the air in his peripheral. He feels the vibrations of their collision. He's not sure who or what it was, but he's pretty sure without looking behind him that he has little time left to shoot, so he sends the puck gliding over the ice from about the halfway point. His shot is dead on, and he scores an empty-netter to put the Gamblers up 4-2 with under a minute to go in the game. The goal is his third of the night. If his feat had been completed in Las Vegas, the game would need to be stopped for about twenty minutes while fans throw their hats on the ice in honor of his hat trick, but in Reno, only a few hats make their way over the glass.

Once all the hats are removed, the game resumes with each team's third line on the ice. The Five Ohhh! stick to their game plan. They win the faceoff and pull their goalie. Ox jumps on as their sixth attacker, and even though it takes more than half the remaining time, the Five Ohhh! score on a shot from Slider.

"These guys just won't go away," Safari Chip says on the bench. He checks the time on the game clock. Eighteen seconds. He turns to his bench. "Ok first line. Your turn. Go finish this thing."

The Five Ohhh! send out their first line as well. Ox, though having played four straight shifts now, shows no signs of fatigue as he takes the next faceoff against Rodman. He even beats Rodman on the draw and sends his team back on offense and his goalie back to the bench for the third straight shift.

Sammie Two is the guy scheduled to take the ice as the sixth man for the Five Ohhh!, but Greg stops him and jumps over the wall in his place.

"Hey!" Sammie Two yells.

A pass goes from Hoss to Stunner. The Five Ohhh! dog shoots a shot that goes over the net. Harlan loses sight of the puck because it goes so high. He whips his head around, looking all over for it. He hears the crack it makes off the glass and breathes a sigh of relief.

The puck gets picked up by Dislike. He tries to skate around the back of the net to complete a wrap around. Harlan, who continues to search for the puck, never sees Dislike coming.

Lovey sneaks in, drops his stick in front of the goal line, and pushes the puck away from the net just as Dislike tries to sneak one past Harlan's skate. Dislike looks up stunned. He thought for sure he had the game tied. Lovey greets his counterpart with a thumbs down and his tongue sticking out. Dislike tries to punch Lovey, but Lovey dodges it and skates back out into the play.

Undertaker and Kane battle Hoss, Greg, and Ratone along the boards for the puck. Ratone frees the puck and turns to fire it to Ox, but Liten speeds in and picks off the pass. He starts skating to the other end of the ice, looking to score the Gamblers second empty-netter of the night.

Ratone and Ox are right on his heels though, so Liten passes the puck aside to Rodman, who is crowded by Stunner, and he in turn, pushes it further to the side for his best buddy. Lovey, with only Dislike on his heels, breaks ahead, aims and takes a nice easy shot. He admires his goal with his hands raised high in the air as he continues gliding towards the net.

Next to him, Rodman has his flippers raised high in the air as well.

Dislike, aware that the game is over now that the Gamblers are back to being up by two goals with only five seconds remaining in the game, crashes hard into Lovey from behind. He doesn't like being shown up, and Lovey showed him up on three separate occasions during that play.

Lovey crashes to the ice hard, but stands up quickly. He and Dislike scrap the same way they have all season long. They know they don't have long before the other guys and the referees come and stop them, so they make it count. Lovey socks Dislike in the gut, taking the black grizzly bear's wind from him, but then he gets an uppercut under his chin that bangs his teeth together. The hit stuns Lovey a bit and allows Dislike to elbow Lovey in the snout. Dislikes latest hit tears all of Lovey's stiches out and knocks him down. The Five Ohhh! crowd goes crazy, but that's where the fight ends. Swarms of players and referees engulf the scene and restrain everyone. Both bears get sent to the locker room early. Lovey spits blood on the Reno ice as he leaves, and the bears continue to jaw at each other as they skate off the ice in opposite directions.

The crowd cheers both Dislike's efforts and Lovey's ejection. They heckle Lovey really bad for about a fifteen foot stretch that leads off the ice to the tunnel. One guy even pours his drink on Lovey and yells, "How'd that butt whoopin' feel?"

Lovey looks up with his bloodied, hockey player face, smiles, and responds, "It feels a whole lot better knowing we're going to win and that you wasted your money to come watch your team lose."

His remarks get even more drinks and trash thrown on him, but Lovey just laughs it off and continues on his trek to the tunnel. Later that night, ASPN will coin a new hockey term. They name Lovey's feat in the game of scoring a goal, getting an assist, and getting into a fight the *Lovey Bara Hat Trick*. It's the sixth time it's happened this season.

The Gamblers go on a power play for the final five seconds because of the late hit call on Dislike, but it hardly matters. Rodman wins the faceoff, and neither team really tries to do anything. It's best in both their eyes to save it for the next game. Some words are exchanged between the teams' dogs after time runs out and there's a light scuffle, but nothing really happens.

Safari Chip makes a mental note that after seeing how intense the two games in Reno were, the rest of this series is going to be just as extreme and brutal.

Chapter 32: Down Time

The Gamblers catch the first flight out of Reno after game two. They're eager to get home and get some extra rest going into an off day. As they exit their limos at the New Orleans Hotel, they're met by hundreds of crazy screaming fans at two in the morning. They stop to take a few pictures and autograph threepeat signs the wild animals are waving.

Eventually, the crowd thins and the Gamblers make it through the front doors of the hotel. They walk to the elevators together and board the elevator with Ed. The goat elevator operator is excited to see him.

"Good evening sirs," Ed greets his team.

"Hey Ed," they all greet him back.

"You all looked mighty good in that game tonight," Ed compliments.

"Thanks Ed," they all say in unison again.

The rest of the ride is pretty silent. The Gamblers are tired, and Ed can see it. He doesn't bother them with chit chat tonight. He wants them to get to bed quick, get rested, and complete their threepeat. The elevator dings.

"Penthouse," Ed says with a hushed tone much different than his usual loud declaration of their destination.

"Thanks Ed," each Gambler says as they exit.

"Are we going to see you at game three?" Rodman asks.

Ed gives Rodman an annoyed look. "Now, you know better than that. Have I ever missed a game?"

"Never," Rodman chuckles and exits the elevator.

"Good night Rodman."

"See you tomorrow Ed."

The elevator doors close, but Safari Chip stops his team from going to their rooms. "Hey guys, I want to talk to you."

"What is up Chip?" Liten asks.

"I was watching the Five Ohhh! close tonight. They're going to be tough the rest of this series. They're not like the last two Gold Rush teams we've played. They don't cheat, they play tough, they play rough, the play smart, and they play together. So, if we're going to beat them, we're going to have to play just as rough and tough, we have to play even smarter, and most importantly, we have to play as a team. You guys did that tonight. Just don't let up," Safari Chip says.

The Gamblers give him a sleepy and sluggish acknowledgment and head for their rooms.

*

Most of the Gamblers spend the next day hanging out with their families. Some of them have never had their parents come to the championship game for one reason or another. With things being tense between Beary and Greg, Mary devices a plan for her and Beary to spend the first half of her day with her parents and the second half of the day with Beary's family and Harlan, who Beary decrees to be his official brother from another mother.

Neither Apple Jack, nor Snickers families can make it, so they spend the majority of the day with Kane and his little sister Twix.

"That's little Twixie?" Apple Jack says when he lays eyes upon the now grown up sister of Kane. He hasn't seen her since they were all in high school together.

"Wow," Snickers says, unable to conceal his first impressions with Kane's sister.

"Wow what?" Kane says, playing the part of the overprotective big brother.

For Big Chick, a big surprise is in store. There's an unexpected knock at his door. "I wonder who that could be," Big Chick stands up to go answer it.

El Pollos Locos rush to the door to be there when he opens it. They already know who is behind it.

Big Chick opens the door. "Grandma!" Big Chick picks her up and gives her a big hug. "I'm so glad you're here. Does this mean you're feeling better."

Grandma Louie laughs in the grip of her giant grandson. "It does. It does. But put me down!"

Big Chick does as he's told.

"And even if I was sick, I wouldn't miss my little Marty in his big championship games," she adds.

"Grandma," Big Chick mumbles. "I go by Big Chick these days."

"You go by Marty with me," she tells him sternly.

"Yes ma'am." Big Chick gives in.

Also with his grandma, are Big Chick's mom and dad, his grandpa, his aunt, and El Pollos Locos' bigger sister, Daisy.

Sammie Lou ends up spending a tense afternoon with his entire family and extended family including Sammie Two. Sammie Lou tries to speak to his cousin, but Sammie Two doesn't want any part of the conversations, giving one word answers or nods of his head whenever possible. Their family, sensing Sammie Two is being a jerk, treats him with the same lack of respect he shows Sammie Lou. The night ends with Sammie Two having had enough and walking out on his family. Sammie Lou chases after him and tries to make peace with his cousin once more. He doesn't hate the guy, and he would love to have a good relationship with him, but Sammie Two turns around and shoves Sammie Lou to the ground.

A massive pool party breaks out at the hotel pool where the families of Haas, Maverick, Goose, and Moose all hang in the warm May weather. Before the party ends, they're joined by Liten, whose family opted not to make the long trip from Germany. Prior to coming to the pool, Liten spent the majority of his day with Safari Chip, his wife, and their four sons, Mickey, Mike, Peter, and Davey at Safari Chip's house.

A knock on Rodman's hotel room door causes him to pause his video game and set his controller down. He's playing the most recent IAHL hockey game with L-Rod. Rodman is playing as the Gamblers in their home jerseys, and L-Rod plays as the Gamblers in their away jerseys since neither wants to play as any other team.

"Don't cheat this time," he warns L-Rod.

L-Rod laughs and unpauses the game the second Rodman is out of sight. He scores at will with his adoptive dad out of the room.

Rodman answers the door and finds Lovey standing there. "Hey Lovey."

"Hi Hott Rod. Got any plans for tonight?" Lovey asks.

"I'm just going to stay in and order room service with L-Rod. Penny and Flip are going to join us too."

"Ohhh. Penny eh? Nice," Lovey teases.

Rodman shrugs sheepishly.

Lovey goes to say something, but he stops.

Rodman catches Lovey's look. "What?"

"Nothing."

"No. What were you going to say?"

Lovey grimaces. "Well… I don't want to bring up a sore subject, but the guys and I have been curious…"

"About?" Rodman asks.

"How come your folks never come to watch you play?"

"That's what you were scared to ask?"

"Well, we didn't know if you guys got along. You've never really talked about them."

"My dad can rarely get time off. He's a secret service agent for the president of South Africa."

"He is!?" Lovey exclaims.

"Yeah, and my mom doesn't like to leave without him."

"That's cool I guess. I mean, it's not cool, but at least you get along with them."

"What are you doing tonight?" Rodman asks.

"My mom and dad are here. We're going to dinner."

"That's cool. Tell them hi for me."

"Will do. Have fun with your penguin party tonight." Lovey salutes Rodman, and they say their goodbyes.

Rodman returns to his video game where he finds he's down by an insurmountable number of goals. "Hey!"

L-Rod laughs his head off.

*

Each Gambler has a great night the day before game three, but come the next night, they forget about their fun and focus on the task at hand. They meet up outside their hotel rooms and ride the elevator downstairs together. They arrive at the locker room as a team. The idea of waiting for everyone and arriving all at once is founded on Safari Chip's insistence that in order to win, they're going to need to play together as a team.

They open the locker room doors and receive a surprise. Waiting for them, on crutches and wearing a suit with his Gamblers jersey over it, is Jason. He finds himself instantly surrounded by his teammates.

"Hey buddy. How's it going?" Harlan asks.

"How's the leg?" L-Rod inquires.

"Glad you're here." Sammie pats Jason on the back.

Jason is overwhelmed by their outpouring over his presence. "I'm ok. Leg still hurts. It's going to be a while before I can walk without these things. And I'm glad I'm here too."

"He's sitting on the bench tonight," Safari Chip informs his team.

Knowing Jason will be with them on the bench pumps the Gamblers up.

"Five Ohhh! better watch out tonight." Kane says.

"They're going to need some help from the real five-0 'cause we're going to steal this series tonight," Undertaker jokes.

"What is a Five Ohhh!? It has had me puzzled all season long," Liten asks.

"The five-0 are the police," Beary explains.

"They are?" Liten can't believe it.

"Yeah, why do you think they wear those stupid cop-looking jerseys?" Lovey asks.

"I did not have a clue. I thought it was just meant to make them look tough," Liten admits.

The Gamblers have a laugh at Liten's misunderstanding of American slang.

"Where does the term five-0 come from?" Liten asks.

"The TV show, Hawaii Five-0." L-Rod shakes his head.

"Ohhh." Liten finally gets it. "I thought five-0 had something to do with going five hole."

The Gamblers laugh at their teammate again.

The more Liten learns about the origins of how the Five Ohhh! got their name, the more confused he gets. "Well, how come they spell the 0, O-H-H-H with an exclamation point?"

All the Gamblers shrug. None of them have that answer.

"You guys don't know?" Penny asks.

"No. Do you?" Rodman asks.

"Well, yeah, but it's not that cool. I was reading an article from before the seasons started. It chronicled all the AKHL teams that were moving to the IAHL. It said the Five Ohhh! spell their name the way they do because it was a way to call themselves the police, and it allowed them a creative way to emphasize that their brand of hockey is exciting."

"Oh," says Rodman. "Or should I say, ohhh!?"

There's a long silence in the room as the Gamblers all wrap their heads around the idea.

"I still do not get it," Liten finally breaks the silence.

"I don't either. What's so exciting about them?" Big Chick asks.

Snickers puts his arm around Big Chick. "I'll tell you what's *going* to be exciting about them tonight."

"What?"

"When we watch you knock that Colonel on his tail the first time he picks on you." Snickers holds up a fist.

Big Chick looks terrified.

Apple Jack motions for Big Chick to follow him. "Come here big guy. We're going to show you a few moves."

Big Chick tries to resist, but the combative dogs, Maverick, Moose, and Lovey drag away. The six defensemen and the team's designated tough guy cram all their years of knowledge on fighting into the mind of Big Chick with the final minutes they have left before the game starts.

While the defense lessons with Big Chick take place in one corner of the room, most of the other Gamblers hang out with and talk to Jason until Safari Chip shouts game time. When the call comes, they all jump to their feet and head for the door. They let Jason lead the charge out of the room.

Rodman and L-Rod open the locker room doors to let him out. They're met by a blockade of sorts though. There, standing on the opposite side of the doors is Ms. LeJuene. She hasn't been seen or heard from since they fire in the holed her. The entire team gasps.

"Hello L-Rod, Mr. Penguin," Ms. LeJuene greets them.

"What do you want?" L-Rod asks with a twinge of hostility.

"I just wanted to let you know that you can't play tonight…"

"What!?" Rodman shouts and many other Gamblers.

Safari Chip fights his way to the front of his team to deal with the vindictive social services agent.

"You can't stop me from playing tonight," L-Rod defies.

The rest of the Gamblers continue to grumble and shout, causing a ruckus too loud for Ms. LeJuene to respond.

Safari Chip waves for his team to quiet down. Once they do, he's able to speak. "What is this all about Ms. LeJuene? Rodman has been taking fine care of L-Rod. You'd know that if you had bothered to check up on him at all."

"I know he has," Ms. LeJuene says.

"Then what's this about? The water balloons?" Rodman demands.

"No, this isn't about the water balloons."

"Then what?" Jason says as he steps up to Ms. LeJuene a little threateningly on his crutches.

Rodman holds Jason back, putting a flipper on his chest.

"If you would all let me explain, I will."

"Give it a try," Sammie jokes.

"I was going to say that L-Rod can't play tonight… *until* I wish him good luck," Ms. LeJuene says.

"What?" L-Rod furrows his brow.

"I'm sorry for the way things worked out earlier in the year. Sometimes in my job it's all rules and regulations, and it's easy to forget that you're dealing with real animals with real feelings. So, I wanted to come by and show my support for you," she pats L-Rod on the head, "and Rodman, and the whole team."

Everyone is shocked at the change in Ms. LeJuene's demeanor.

"Wow. Thanks," L-Rod says.

"Yeah. Thanks," Rodman repeats.

With things between Ms. LeJuene and L-Rod all sorted out, Jason calls for another charge and leads the team down the tunnel as fast as he can on his crutches.

L-Rod lags behind. He asks Safari Chip if they can leave enough tickets for all of the kids at the orphanage to come to game four.

"I think that would be manageable," Safari Chip says.

"You would do that?" she asks.

"Sure thing. I'd have done it for both games if I had known earlier that you'd be here," Safari Chip says.

"No, game four is fine. The kids will be excited," she says.

"Yeah, and we're going to win the Cup in two night's anyway, so they'll get to see the celebration," L-Rod says confidently.

"Let's not get ahead of ourselves. We have to win tonight's game first. So why don't you hurry along with the rest of the guys. I'll make arrangements with Ms. LeJuene to get her kids down here for game four," Safari Chip calms his overzealous little penguin down.

L-Rod gives his coach a thumbs up and runs to join his teammates.

Chapter 33: The First Las Vegas Game

In a five game series where the series score is 1-1, game three is always the most pivotal. The winning team will be one win away from the Cup and the other, one loss away from elimination. For the Gamblers, if they want to win their third straight Cup on their home ice, they'll have to win games three and four. If they lose either game, they'll be tasked with winning their first Cup on the road.

The first faceoff of the game is won by Rodman. The Gamblers go on the attack, and Lovey gets a shot off right away. Marlon blocks the shot, controls the puck, and sends it to Ox. Play moves the other way where the Five Ohhh! set up on offense. They make several moves to the net, take shots that get blocked by Kane, Undertaker, and Harlan, and maintain control of the puck for a very long time. They play so long on offense that they even manage to change out their entire first line while the Gamblers and their line play for over two minutes. Try as they might though, the Five Ohhh! can't push across a goal.

Tired legs and heavy breathing by the Gamblers first line, can't stop them from trying their hardest to get the puck away from their net. A scrum for the puck takes place behind the net between Kane, Undertaker, and the three Five Ohhh! forwards. Some confusion in front of the net leads to all three Gamblers forwards being on one side of the net, leaving Crush all alone for a pass that could spell danger.

Sammie Two sees this and fights hard to get the puck out of the traffic jam to Crush. He loses the battle though, and the puck gets poked out around the boards on the side of the ice with the three Gamblers and Crunch.

Rodman wins the race to the puck when Crunch eases up, seeing that it could potentially be a three man to none Gamblers breakaway if he loses the race. Instead, Crunch skates backwards on defense. Rodman, Lovey, and Liten speed as fast as their legs will carry them. They should dump the puck in and make a line change, but this three on one opportunity is something they don't get too often, and their hockey instincts take over. They all cross the blue line and head for the net.

Despite their second burst of energy, Crush is able to reach the play to make if three against two. Their easy goal isn't going to be as easy, but they still have an odd man advantage, so Rodman passes the puck to Lovey on his right, and Lovey fakes a shot at the net, drawing Crush and the goalie to his side. He then passes the puck back to Rodman in the center, and Rodman taps it to Liten.

Liten fires.

Crunch dives to stop Liten's shot. He gets an ever so slight piece of the puck, and it's just enough to send the puck a high. It goes just over the net and hits the glass.

Liten glides around the front of the net and heads for the bench as fast as he can. Lovey follows him. They desperately need a line change. Rodman goes behind the net though and fights Crush and Crunch for the puck. On their way to the bench, Liten and Lovey pass the oncoming Five Ohhh! and Snickers and Apple Jack, who have just hopped over the wall to replace Undertaker and Kane.

Crush and Crunch push, shove, hit, and elbow Rodman for the puck.

"Give it up Penguin," Crush shouts.

Their crowding and hitting gets Rodman's adrenaline pumping. He pushes, shoves, and hits them back with all his might. All the while, he makes sure not to lose the puck. The dog talk smack to him, but Rodman doesn't engage them. He knows in most cases it's better not to say anything. Saying something lets his aggressors know they've gotten into his head, and it usually incites more of the same, but not saying anything makes his foes grow frustrated. Thus, Rodman has gotten into their heads by doing nothing at all.

Rodman battles and battles with every last ounce of energy he has. He almost loses the puck as Greg becomes the third Five Ohhh! fighting through the scrum in an effort to obtain the puck, but at the last split second, Rodman is able to grab it with his skate and jam it against the boards. He holds it there until he gets reinforcements.

Those reinforcements first come in the form of Beary. He races in and squeezes between Crush and Greg, essentially pushing Greg out of the play.

"Hey!" Greg says.

"Hey what?" Beary shouts back.

"I was standing there." Greg checks Beary with his stick.

Beary turns his head over his shoulder. "Oh I'm sorry. I thought this was hockey where men fight to get the puck not ballet class."

Rodman can't help but laugh. Beary's funny words to Greg almost costs him the puck again. Luckily, Beary turns around in time to see the puck get dislodged and he grabs it before the Five Ohhh! dogs do.

"Get back to the bench Rodman. I've got this. Big Chick's waiting for you," Beary says.

"You don't have anything," Crunch barks.

"Oh hush up," Beary says.

"You sure?" Rodman asks.

At that moment, Sammie Lou comes into the scrum. "Yeah Rod, go."

Rodman has been on the ice for over three and a half straight minutes. He nods to his teammates and steps out of the scrum. Sammie Lou jumps in and takes his spot.

"You're not getting this puck," Crush barks.

"Would you stop whining Susan?" Beary antagonizes the defense.

Crush drops his stick, stands up straight, and steps up to Beary. "Who you calling Susan?"

Greg jabs Beary in the back again and causes his panda counterpart to fall forward, knocking Crush to the ice. This also causes the puck to fly off Beary's stick.

It hits Rodman in the back of his skate as he's trying to get back to the net. Rodman turns to see what hit him. His eyes light up like a Christmas tree when he sees he alone has the puck. He reaches his leg backwards to grab the loose puck and attempts a quick wrap around.

Marlon is there with a sliding stop, but Rodman maintains control of the puck. He continues trying to push it past Marlon while he wraps around the entire front side of the net. Marlon blocks the puck the whole way, and eventually, Rodman ends up back behind the net in another scrum for the puck.

"Didn't we just tell you goodbye?" Sammie Lou asks.

"I'm leaving," Rodman says when he sees Sammie Lou and Beary have the upper hand in the battle for the puck. He skates away and makes it beyond the net this time where he passes Snickers and gets a tap on the tail with Snickers' stick.

"Nice shift Hott Rod," Snickers says.

"Thanks," Rodman pants as his adrenaline winds down and the exhaustion catches up. He continues skating towards the bench where Big Chick is holding out his wing like a wrestler waiting for a tag. His legs are like cinder blocks though, and it's hard just to skate and breathe at the same time.

All of a sudden, before Rodman reaches the blue line, he hears his name being called. He turns around and sees everyone on the ice looking at him. The puck is drifting slowly towards him again. He doesn't know how it is that the puck made its way in his direction, but everyone on the ice seems frozen, waiting to see what he does with it.

What he does with the puck is rear back and fire it at the net. He means for the shot to be a hard blast just to keep it in the Gamblers zone. His fatigue and the energy he expels hitting the puck so hard causes him to fall sideways to the ice.

The next thing he knows, he's being mobbed by unfamiliar line mates. Apple Jack, Snickers, Beary, and Sammie Lou swarm him, help him up, and pull him in for a group hug.

"What's going on?" the discombobulated penguin asks.

"What do you think's going on? You scored dude," Sammie Lou says and points to the flashing lights above the net.

"That went in?" Rodman asks.

"Yeah," Snickers laughs as he shakes his captain.

Rodman smiles too tired to do anything else. His teammates help him to the bench where he's greeted with high fives, hugs, and plenty of compliments for his efforts.

The Five Ohhh! put their first line back on the ice to take on the Gamblers second line. This gives Big Chick a chance to play without the fear of facing The Colonel. He does much better during this shift than any other he's played all series long.

As the game goes on, each team plays flawlessly. Scoring becomes harder and harder. Each team is learning the moves, tendencies, and techniques of the other team, and they use this knowledge to counter their opponents. Everyone has to reach deep into their bag of tricks to pull off a move that allows them to slip past their defenders.

The final shift of the period has both teams' second line pitted against each other. Big Chick stands to the side of Harlan in front of the net to help the turtle block any potential shots.

The Colonel stands in front of Big Chick, free to take a pass or misdirect a shot towards the net.

Harlan shouts over the roar of the stadium to Big Chick. "Go get that guy Big Chick."

Big Chick hesitates.

"Go get him before he gets a pass," Harlan repeats.

The Colonel bangs his stick on the ice, trying to draw attention to himself.

Big Chick still hesitates, so Harlan skates out and pushes Big Chick towards The Colonel. Big Chick tries to sneak up on the fox. He's very quiet in his skating, his breathing, and everything else. Still, just as he's about to give The Colonel a very weak tap, The Colonel spins around growling and snorting. Big Chick screams, drops his stick, and covers his face.

Laughing, The Colonel turns his attention back to his teammates. Good thing for him he does, because a pass from Greg is coming at him fast. He gets his stick up just in time to save himself from being hit in the chest and deflects the pass.

Harlan drops to his knees to block the downward deflection too late. Goal lights go off at the same time as the buzzer sounds, ending the period. Harlan and a few of the Gamblers urge the referees to check the goal to see if it passed the line before the buzzer sounded. The Five Ohhh! skate fast for the tunnel, but they stop as their coach holds the other players on the bench. He wants his team out there for the review.

The arena roar subsides to a dull hum. Everyone waits impatiently for the call. The call takes forever, but when it comes, the referees skate away from the scorer's table indicating no goal. The call sends the arena into all out exuberant hysterics.

The Five Ohhh! coach allows his players to storm off the ice. They let the referees have it as they make their exit. They wanted that goal. In this game, they needed that goal. One goal tonight might be the difference.

*

Harlan walks up to Liten in the locker room during the first intermission. "We've got a problem."

"What problem?" Liten asks.

"Big Chick. He's a mess out there. The Colonel keeps picking on him, even when Snickers and Apple Jack stick up for him."

"Yes. I have noticed."

"We have to do something," Harlan says.

"What can we do?" Liten asks.

"Do you have your phone?" Harlan asks.

"Yes. Why?" Liten thinks for a second. "Ohhh! Good thinking Harlan."

The duo scurries off to Liten's locker to make a call.

*

To many in the crowd, period two seems like a repeat of period one. Rodman fights for his team extra hard, The Colonel continues to terrorize Big Chick, Lovey and Dislike get into a second fight, the dogs brutalize each other, Sammie Lou and

Beary battle Sammie Two and Greg during every shift, the third lines neutralize each other, and the goalies stop shot after shot. Not only does it seem like a repeat of the first period, it seems like a repeat of their entire season.

Throughout the period, Liten and Harlan explain their plan to help Big Chick to their teammates. Everyone laughs. They're sure it's going to work.

In the meantime, Big Chick is left to fend for himself. However, he's unable to do so. At one point in the period, when he has his back to the play near the glass, he reaches for the puck with his stick, swats it away, but before he can turn around, he gets boarded extra hard from behind by The Colonel.

Whistles blow. Snickers, Apple Jack, and even Sammie Lou swarm The Colonel. They pull Big Chick's abuser off of him, taking a few shots at him before referees and Five Ohhh! players can separate everyone.

On the bench, the Gamblers stand and shout in protest.

"Hey ref! What is that garbage?" Safari Chip shouts.

Even Jason stands with the rest of his teammates. He has to hop on his good leg so that he can bang his crutch on the side of the wall. "Bring that garbage my way."

Things get sorted out. The Colonel goes smiling to the penalty box. Big Chick stands up to thunderous applause and skates to the bench on his own accord. The Gambles apply intense pressure on the power play, but they fail to score.

The period ends shortly thereafter, and both teams head off the ice with the score remaining 1-0 in favor of the Gamblers.

Harlan and Liten walk on either side of Big Chick through the tunnel.

"Hey Big Chick," Harlan says.

"IIi Harlan."

"We have a surprise for you," Liten says.

"A surprise? For me?" Big Chick asks.

"Yep," Harlan smiles devilishly.

The Gamblers duo leads Big Chick to the front of the pack. They reach the locker room door, and Liten opens it.

"That's weird. Why are the lights off?" Big Chick asks.

Harlan pushes the big chicken into the room. "That's all part of your surprise."

Big Chick stumbles inside. He turns around to find the door to the locker room already half closed. In no time, he's alone in a dark room with jumpy nerves. Somehow, he's able to find the door handle in the dark, but it's locked.

Then, he hears something. The first time he hears the noise, he tries to convince himself that it's nothing, but the second time he hears it, it's the sound of a full on growl.

From outside the door, Safari Chip presses a button that turns on the lights in the locker room.

Big Chick finds himself face to face with a snarling lion that stands even a few inches taller than him. He opens his mouth to scream but promptly passes out instead.

The lion, Alston Leon, who helped Harlan and Liten get over some of their hockey fears, including Liten's fear of cats, coughs up a hair ball and flicks it aside. "Oh, dear me. I'm always doing that."

Alston bends down to pick Big Chick up, but he's only able to get him half way up. He drags the chicken to the nearest locker and props him up against it. After a few seconds, Big Chick opens his eyes.

"Hello." Alston waves.

"Hi." Big Chick waves back.

"Let's talk."

"Ok."

Big Chick and Alston talk for a few minutes. They get so into their conversation that they hardly notice the Gamblers make their way into the room one by one. Harlan, Liten, and the dogs join Big Chick and Alston in their conversation.

"Listen to him Big Chick. He knows what he's talking about," Kane says.

"He worked wonders for Liten," Undertaker adds.

"Just remember Big Chick, you're a five tool player. You can shoot, skate, pass, block, and you have size. You need to use all of those things to your advantage. In the case of standing up to The Colonel, you especially have to use your size. He's nothing but a bully, and nine times out of ten, when you stand up to a bully, they back down," Alston explains.

"What about that tenth time when they don't?" Big Chick asks.

"That's where these guys come in." Alston points to Snickers and Apple Jack.

The two dogs nod.

"I guess I could try. Hopefully, he just won't pick on me anymore though," Big Chick says. By the looks on the faces of the dogs and Alston, Big Chick knows his last words are nothing more than wishful thinking. "Ok, so tell me again how to go about standing up to this guy. What do I do?"

"Follow us," Snickers says. He leads Big Chick and the others to the corner of the locker room where the dogs have a punching bag set up.

*

It doesn't take long for The Colonel to start picking on Big Chick in the third period. He goes right after him on their first shift. The dogs wait and watch to see what Big Chick will do, but he doesn't do anything except allow The Colonel to trip him behind the back of the referees. Later in the period, The Colonel cross checks Big Chick in the back, and Big Chick does nothing again. A third incident sees The Colonel push Big Chick into the net as he races towards Marlon on a breakaway. The chicken crashes into the poles, dislodging the net.

Whistles blow, and Big Chick gets a penalty shot. Normally an excellent penalty shot shooter, Big Chick is too dismayed at his performance and the fact that he hasn't stood up to The Colonel, to concentrate. He misses by a mile and goes to the bench and to take a seat between Snickers and Apple Jack.

Big Chick doesn't say anything, and he avoids eye contact with the dogs. The dogs don't say anything either. This unnerves Big Chick, so he looks to the dog on his left and then to the dog on his right. "What?"

"What what?" Apple Jack asks.

"Why are you guys looking at me that way?"

"How are we looking at you?" Snickers asks.

"Like that," Big Chick says of their disappointed countenances.

"We're just tired of that guy picking on you," Apple Jack says.

"We thought after talking to Alston that you would take a stand," Snickers says.

Big Chick sighs. He hates violence, especially when the violence may be inflicted on him, but he knows they're right. He has to stand up to his bully. "I will."

While Big Chick and the dogs talk, Ice Man ties the game.

The next shift Big Chick plays, The Colonel leaves him alone. The shift after that though, The Colonel pressures Big Chick the entire time, poking, tapping, and checking the big guy. Near the boards, after Big Chick swats a loose puck back into the action, The Colonel glides in to check Big Chick. The big guy sidesteps him though, and the fox runs himself into the glass. This gives Big Chick enough time to skate freely away from his tormentor, to the front of the net, take a pass from Beary, and sink the go ahead goal with just a few minutes left in the game.

The Colonel, having recovered from his crash, stalks Big Chick. He sneaks up on him from behind.

Just before the fox pounces on Big Chick, Snickers yells, "Big Chick!"

Too late. The Colonel rams the chicken from behind, sending Big Chick face first to the ice. Big Chick hits hard with a thud and glides a few feet across the ice. The Colonel admires his handy work for a moment, sauntering up to take a closer look at the damage he's inflicted on the still, unmoving chicken.

Apple Jack, not wanting to see anymore, makes a move to protect Big Chick. Snickers holds him back. "Let him do it."

"Well, well, well. The Big Chicken eh? An appropriate name," The Colonel taunts as he skates closer and closer to Big Chick. He bends down to whisper in Big Chick's ears another of the many threats he's levied against his opponent all season long. "If you ever…"

If you ever. That's all The Colonel gets out of his snout before Big Chick rolls over. The chicken's eyebrows are slanted in an angry V. The feathers on his face are wrinkled like no one has ever seen from the furrowing of his brow. His beak curls back, and some of the animals will say later that they saw Big Chick bear his teeth even though chickens don't have teeth. The Colonel tries to stand back up to get away, but he gets caught by Big Chick's wing shooting up and grabbing him around the collar of his jersey. The Colonel tries to pry Big Chick's wing off so he can escape, but Big Chick sits straight up like a zombie, grabs ahold of The Colonel's jersey with his other wing, and stands to his feet.

Apple Jack and Snickers smile at the sight of The Colonel so afraid he looks like he might pee his pants. The fox cranes his neck up high so he can stare into the cold angry eyes of Big Chick. Apple Jack and Snickers stop Crush and Crunch from trying to interfere in the fight, and Sammie Lou and Beary do likewise with Sammie Two and Greg.

"What do you want?" The Colonel bellows.

"I want you to leave me alone," Big Chick snorts through a semi-clenched beak.

"Sure. Fine. Whatever," The Colonel strains himself as he fights back a terrified cry.

"I mean it," Big Chick demands.

"I know. I promise."

"And I want you to remember what's going to happen to you if you don't."

"I promise. I won't forget this."

"Not this," Big Chick says. He lifts The Colonel off his feet into the air and spins in circles. "This!"

Big Chick builds up the momentum he needs to toss The Colonel over the top of the glass into the crowd. Fans scatter to avoid the flying fox. The Colonel crashes into a row of seats in the sixth row.

"Holy Toledo," Lovey whispers on the bench.

"You said it," Rodman agrees.

The crowd, after a startled gasp and a stunned silence, laughs its head off. With the noise of the arena sure to drown out their own laughter, even a few of the Five Ohhh! join the crowd.

"What are you laughing at Ox?" Dislike demands of his captain.

"I can't help it," Ox says. "He had it coming."

Dislike is flabbergasted. "Dude, dislike."

"Well keep laughing Ox. They're winning," Rezza grumbles.

Ox shuts up. His coach is right. They need to get their heads back in the game immediately.

The Colonel and Big Chick both get tossed from the game for unsportsmanlike conduct. Big Chick leaves to high fives from his teammates and the cheers of the crowd while The Colonel leaves through the crowd with the help of the arena medical staff.

The final minutes of the game are fairly uneventful. Try as they might, the Five Ohhh! can't get the puck past Harlan, but a few seconds before the final minute of game time, they get a three on two breakaway with their third line. Ice Man, Mad Man, and Big Deuce race against Maverick and Moose towards Harlan. The Gamblers defensemen do a good job closing off all shooting lanes. Their defense makes it so that the Five Ohhh! never get a shot off, but it also causes all five players, five of the biggest players in the game, to crash into Harlan.

Harlan gets pinned between the back of Maverick and the goal post. The hit is pretty painful at first, but he can take it, until a split second later when Ice Man and Big Deuce crash into Maverick. The net doesn't dislodge like it's supposed to. Harlan feels a massive burst of pain he's never experienced before.

Somehow, he's able to avoid screaming despite the worst pain he's ever felt in his life. And, because he takes his injury like a man, the other players don't know anything is wrong.

Everyone else comes out of the dog pile without so much as a scratch, and while they're all standing up and brushing the ice off of their jerseys, Harlan manages to flip himself over onto his belly. He knows after a while what the pain is that he's feeling, and he knows it's bad.

Maverick reaches for Harlan's flipper. "Hey buddy. Grab my hoof."

"I can't," Harlan says.

"What's the matter?" Maverick asks.

"My shell is cracked."

"Oh snap! Are you serious?" Goose exclaims.

"Yeah I'm serious. Go get Chip!" Harlan shouts through the pain.

L-Rod races for the bench screaming for Safari Chip.

It takes a long while to get Harlan up and off the ice. No one can see how bad the crack in his shell is, but underneath, it's cracked like a car windshield hit by a bouncing rock. He gets a standing ovation from the crowd as he's stretchered off the ice with his flipper raised in the air for a thumbs up.

Safari Chip returns to the bench.

"Chip, shoot us straight, how bad is he?" Beary asks.

"It's bad."

"How bad?" Beary demands to know about his best friend's condition.

"His shell is cracked."

"Will he be back for game four?" Rodman asks.

"I don't know for sure, but if I had to guess, I'd say we're going to be without him for the rest of the series," Safari Chip informs his players.

There's a disappointed grumble amongst the Gamblers.

"No worries," Jason says. "We have the best backup in the game."

Haas' ears perk up. "Me?"

"You've been here before, done this," Jason pats him on the back.

"He's right," Safari Chip says. "You're in Jack."

Haas gulps. He looks at the time on the scoreboard. A minute and ten to go in this game. At least the Gamblers are winning already. He's fairly confident that he can finish the final seventy seconds of the game without blowing the lead, but the following sixty may be another story.

The Gamblers take the ice, and sure enough, Haas secures the win for his team, although it isn't as easy as he would have hoped. The Gamblers end up playing mostly defense, six on five, as the Five Ohhh! pull Marlon off the ice immediately after they win the faceoff. Twice, Haas almost gives up goals, but he's bailed out once by the poll and another time by Undertaker's stick when it whacks a sure goal away from the empty side of the net.

The Gamblers leave the ice with a win and a two games to one series lead, but they also leave without Harlan and with a goalie whose abilities at best are unsound because of his low confidence levels set to start in game four.

Chapter 34: Cracked Shell, Cracked Confidence

The hospital is where the Gamblers spend the majority of their day off between games three and four. Harlan is indeed going to miss the rest of the series, but the doctors are sure he'll be able to watch the next game from the bench. If the series goes to a game five though, they don't want him traveling to Reno.

"So you guys better win this thing tomorrow night, because I want to be there," Harlan orders his teammates.

"We'll make sure we do," Beary assures him.

"It didn't look like you got injured that bad from where we were sitting in the crowd," Mary says.

"Yeah. You took that like a man. I really thought the way everyone jumped up, and because no one screamed, that everyone was ok," Moose says.

"I'm really sorry Harlan. I feel like it's my fault," Maverick says.

"Why?" Harlan asks.

"Because I'm the one who crashed into you."

"That's not what did it. It wasn't even those two oafs from Reno crashing into us that did it. It was the fact that the net didn't dislodge like it should have," Harlan explains.

"I still feel bad," Maverick says.

"Eh." Harlan waves off the horse's silly notions.

"Can we see it?" L-Rod asks.

"No!" Rodman says.

"He can look if he wants," Harlan laughs.

L-Rod, El Pollos Locos, and a handful of curious Gamblers rush the bed to take a look. Harlan turns over onto his side and allows L-Rod to pull apart the back sides of his hospital gown. His shell looks like cracked pavement with light green tar filling in the many lines.

"Whoa!" L-Rod says.

"That's messed up," Sammie Lou says.

"You didn't scream?" Noodle asks.

"Did you hear him scream?" Chicken asks annoyed.

"The arena was noisy. He could have screamed," Noodle shoots back.

"I didn't scream," Harlan says.

"That's cool," Soup says impressed.

Harlan rolls back over and turns his attention to Haas. "So you're in buddy."

Haas gives Harlan a half smile. "Yeah"

"Awww come on now. Don't give me that nervous smile. You're Two Time Cup champion Jack Haas. You'll do just fine," Harlan says.

"I know," Haas lies.

Safari Chip stands up from the chair he's sitting in. He walks to Harlan's bed. "We better get going Harlan. We have practice in a bit."

"Thanks for visiting. I'll see you guys tomorrow night," Harlan says.

"For sure," Rodman says and gives Harlan a sideways high five so the turtle can raise his flipper enough.

Each member of the Gamblers and El Pollos Locos walks by and side fives or taps Harlan's leg. Their girlfriends and Beary's wife all give Harlan a kiss on the forehead.

*

After practice, after all the other Gamblers have left the locker room, Haas knocks on Safari Chip's door.

"Come in," Safari Chip says.

Haas enters.

"What's up Jack?" Safari Chip asks. "Sit down."

"I wanted to talk to you about game four. I don't know if I should start in goal," Haas says.

"What!?" Safari Chip can't believe what he's hearing. "Why not? Who else would we get to play goalie?"

"I don't know. Maybe Beary could start. He was phenomenal in the Olympics," Haas offers.

"You were too. You took home the gold." Safari Chip looks to Flip confused.

Flip just shrugs back at him.

"What's this all about Jack?" Safari Chip demands.

"I just think someone else might give us a better chance."

"Why you would think that," Safari Chip asks.

"What's going on Jack?" Flip asks.

Haas hesitates.

"You've been listening to the media huh?" Flip asks.

"It's not their fault. It's true. I haven't won anything in four years. I've barely even won a playoff game, much less a series. I choke in big games," Haas says.

"Don't drink the Kool-Aid kid," Safari Chip says. "You're a great player in big games, little games, practice games, pickup games, rec league games, video games. It doesn't matter what kind of game, you're good. Besides, you've played with these guys all season long. Any goalie on his best day can be bested by this group, and you've got them backing you up. But, they need you to play. I need you to play."

Haas lets Safari Chip's words sink in.

"This is why we signed you. You gave us the very best chance of winning if Harlan went down, and was it or was it not the plan to showcase to the other teams in this league that you still have what it takes to win the big one?" Safari Chip asks.

"It was."

"So, are you going to let us down, or are you going to play?" Safari Chip asks.

Haas bites down on his lip and nods his head. "Yeah. I'm going to play, and I'm going to win."

Safari Chip slams his fist on his desk and stands up.

Haas jumps out of his seat startled.

"Heck yeah! That's what I'm talking about!" Safari Chip reaches over the desk and gives Haas knuckles.

Chapter 35: The Second Las Vegas Game

Behind the Gamblers bench, in their friends and family
section, awaiting their arrival, sit El Pollos Locos, Big Chick's
mom, aunt, and grandma, Ed, Alston, some of the guys from the
last Chill team Rodman and Jason played on, Mary, Elmira,
Chickette, Lovey's family, Safari Chip's wife and sons, Ms.
LeJuene and the kids from the orphanage, and many other family
members of various Gamblers. The entire section is basically
reserved. It's the loudest section in the arena when the lights go
out. Whether booing the Five Ohhh! when they're announced or
cheering the Gamblers upon their entrance to the ice, section 105
is the craziest.

The lights come back on after the Gamblers second and
third lines come out. Safari Chip wheels Harlan in a wheelchair
from the tunnel exit to the bench. Harlan can walk, but the wheel
chair keeps him from moving around and re-cracking his shell.
Behind them, Flip steadies Jason as he makes his way across the
ice to the bench on his crutches. The injured Gamblers, both in
their hockey jerseys but no gear, get a standing ovation.

The teams finish their practice laps around their net, the
second and third lines head to the bench, and the national anthem
is sung once more by Wally the white bear. The crowd roars at
the end of Wally's final performance of the season, letting him
know just how much they appreciate him. The referees call for
both teams to head to center ice for the first faceoff of the game.

Rodman skates to center ice and does a few spins while
he waits for the Five Ohhh! center. He's extremely calm at the
moment. Two seasons ago, he would have been a bundle of
nerves. Even last year, he would have been a little anxious.
Today though, he feels inexplicably cool.

Ox joins Rodman in the faceoff circle. He snorts when
they make eye contact. "I hope you guys know this series is
going back to Reno."

"And I hope you know…" Rodman starts just as gruff as
Ox, but then calms down and changes his tone. "That no matter

what happens tonight, that this has been a good series. You guys have been worthy opponents."

Ox is taken aback. He wants to be angry, but Rodman didn't say anything rude. Not being able to be angry at Rodman makes Ox even angrier at him.

Both players dig in, and the referee drops the puck. Ox knocks Rodman to the ground and whacks the puck to Dislike. The knock down is all Rodman needs to get into a more aggressive mood. He said his peace to Ox, but now it's time to play hockey.

Dislike crosses the blue line with lots of pressure from Lovey. He shoots the puck around the back of the net where it gets picked up by Ratone. Undertaker chases the rat behind the net. He makes it impossible for Ratone to wrap cleanly around. Ratone skates to the far side of the boards behind the net, finds Ox, and fires the puck across to him.

Ox sees a small opening between Haas' skate and the pole. He one times the puck at just the right moment.

Haas looks down at the oncoming puck as it sails low through the air. He's pretty sure he won't be able to stop it, but he moves in the direction of it tries his best anyway. Luckily for him and the Gamblers, Rodman dives head first with his stick out in front of himself. He tips the puck, changing its direction. The puck goes high, hits off the cross bar, and flies into the glass behind the net.

A battle for the puck between Lovey, Kane, Dislike, and Ratone ensues. Out of view of the referees because of all the bodies in their way, Dislike elbows Lovey in the snout. The Gamblers bear feels something rip. He reaches for the stiches on his snout and gets blood on his glove. His stiches have opened slightly. The distraction of reaching up to check is enough to allow Dislike to get the puck, skate away, and fire a pass to Ox.

Liten cuts off the pass and fires one of his own to Rodman. Ox isn't sure which Gambler to go after and his feet get tangled. He falls down, and play moves towards Marlon. Rodman and Liten skate side by side for a moment with Hoss and Stunner well in front of them to prevent a breakaway. As they cross the blue line, Rodman has to decide whether to set up and wait for his team or to go for a shot. In the end, he thinks if he can push an early goal past Marlon, it might set the tone for the rest of the game. He makes a move to squeeze past both Five Ohhh! dogs, leaving Liten behind. He makes it through them before they close off his path, but their pressure makes it so that he can't aim his shot where he wants. He fires the puck anyway and nails Marlon right in the chest protector.

Marlon scoops the rebounding puck out of the air. The play is seemingly over. Everyone expects to hear the whistles stopping play as the puck is in Marlon's glove, but as Rodman and the dogs bypass the net after the shot, Marlon drops the puck. Panic sets into the turtle, and he drops to his knees and reaches for it frantically. His desperation leads him to push the puck further away, and he has to dive on his belly to grab it. Unfortunately for him, Liten swoops in, snags the puck, spins around the fallen goalie, and sinks an easy goal.

The slot machine jackpot noise played over the arena speakers is what everyone hears instead of the whistles they had expected. The Gamblers surround Liten with a group hug and playful slaps to his helmet. They high five him and go back to the bench for a line change. They're met with more high fives from their teammates and a smile from Safari Chip. The threepeat they have worked for all season long is within reach.

To remind his team that it's far from over, Safari Chip stops the second line before they head onto the ice. He calls the attention of his entire team. "Ok guys, as good as it is to have that first goal, and that first lead, remember, it's not over. These guys aren't going to give up that easy."

"Right," most of the players agree in unison.

Safari Chip is absolutely right. The Five Ohhh! don't go away that easy. For the next few shifts, they battle and battle to get the upper hand. They bombard Haas with shot after shot, but the hare stops all of them. He has three or four blocks that would qualify for ASPN's play of the day just in the first period. Each time he makes one of his eye popping stops, Harlan throws a flipper in the air and tries to stand up, only to succumb to the pain and remain in his seat. He makes sure to hoot and holler the loudest though in support of his goalie buddy.

Just when it looks like the period is going to end 1-0 in favor of the Gamblers, Sammie Two dekes Sammie Lou and Snickers and rips a nasty slap shot at the net. Haas never even sees the puck, just the goal lights going off behind him. The Five Ohhh! celebrate his goal and breathe a sigh of relief.

Haas whacks the puck out of the net. Despite all of his great stops throughout the period, the goal allows doubts to creep back in. He tries to shake the feeling, but he finds the feeling shaking him, literally. He can't control the wobble in his knees.

"Come on Haas. Get it together. You can do this. You have to do this," he tells himself.

Both coaches send out their first line to finish the period. Safari Chip was going to let his first line rest, but when he sees the Five Ohhh! have theirs out, he puts his out as well.

Ox wins the faceoff. The Five Ohhh! set up against the Gamblers and their shaky goalie. They mostly just pass the puck around while the clock ticks away. They have a play they practice for situations like this. At the four second mark, they send three guys to Haas' glove side.

Haas and a couple of Gamblers defenders all move in the same direction. The guy with the puck, Ratone, passes the puck to Ox, on the other side of the net, and he one times a shot easily past Haas with one point seven seconds left. Everything happens so fast it seems unreal.

The crowd groans, the Gamblers check and double check to make sure the puck is in the net, and the Five Ohhh! celebrate.

"Nuts," Liten says.

"Yeah, nuts," Rodman repeats.

One point seven seconds later, the Five Ohhh! head into their locker room up 2-1, and the Gamblers enter their locker room with a goalie that isn't sure he'll be able to stop one shot in the second period.

Harlan wheels himself over to Haas' locker. "Hey man."

"Hey Harlan," Haas says.

"You're doing great out there."

"I don't know if I'd say I'm doing great."

"I would," Harlan says.

"If I was doing great, we wouldn't be down 2-1," Haas argues.

"You have to stop all that negative talk. You made some dynamite saves out there. If it weren't for your goal tending, we might be down 6-1 right now."

"He's right," Beary chimes in from the locker next to Haas.

Haas sighs.

"What has you so shaken?" Harlan asks.

"I'm just not as good as you is all. I wish you could finish this game," Haas answers.

"First off, I wish I could finish this game too, but I can't. So, I need you to do it for me, for us. Second, no one is as good as me," Harlan jokes.

"Oh brother." Beary slaps his own forehead with a paw.

"And thirdly, you don't have to be as good as me. You just have to be better than Marlon. And you are."

"I just feel like he's the tortoise and I'm the hare," Haas says.

Harlan and Beary stare at the hare bewildered.

"You are a hare and he is a tortoise," Harlan says.

"I mean from that story where the hare loses the race."

Harlan angrily waves off Haas' statement. "Man, don't make me get up out of this chair and shake some sense into you. Forget that story. The tortoise cheated."

"He did?" Beary asks.

"Well, he didn't cheat, but he took advantage of a messed up situation. Run that race a million times more and I guarantee the hare wins every time. Just like he's going to win tonight," Harlan says.

Haas opens his mouth to say something again, but he gets cut off.

"I need… nay, we need you to stop stressing and start acting like the Jack Haas that won two Cups. We need a leader out there, and since we're down one, give me your jersey," Harlan demands.

"My jersey?" Haas asks.

"Don't argue me."

Haas does as he's told. He gives Harlan his jersey.

"Stay put," Harlan orders the hare and turns to Beary. "Come on Bear, we've got work to do."

Beary wheels Harlan out of the locker room. Haas doesn't know where they're going, but he grabs his backup jersey in case they don't come back in time.

In another part of the locker room, Rodman, L-Rod, Penny, and the dogs stand around Lovey. The look at his blood covered jersey from the opening minute of the game when Dislike ripped his stiches open.

"Are you going to grab a clean jersey?" Penny asks.

"Noooooooo," all the Gamblers shout together.

"Whoa!" Penny backs up with her flippers raised defensively. "What, did I say something wrong?"

"Why would I change my jersey?" Lovey asks.

"That one's all bloody." Penny points to several blobs of dried blood.

"Blood's lucky. I can't change jerseys."

"Testify," Apple Jack high fives the teddy bear.

"Boys." Penny shakes her head and walks away.

"I wish I had stiches that got ripped out," L-Rod says.

"Hey! Someone get me my phone. I have an idea," Lovey exclaims, changing the topic abruptly.

L-Rod grabs his phone for him and hands it to Lovey. "What are you going to do?"

"I need to post something to our fans on Facespace." Lovey fiddles with his phone, pulls up his Facespace page, and posts an update to get the fans involved in the game.

"Ohhh!" Rodman laughs when he reads Lovey's post. Surely it's going to get a reaction from the crowd and the Five Ohhh!, especially Dislike.

"That's good," Undertaker says.

"Mind games. I like it." Snickers points to his brain first then to Lovey.

"Looks like Lovey's getting into another fight before the night is through," Kane laughs.

The other Gamblers around him, including Lovey, all laugh.

Minutes later, just before intermission ends, Harlan and Beary come back into the locker room with Haas' jersey.

"Here." Beary tosses the jersey to Haas.

Haas looks the jersey over before putting it back on. He doesn't see immediately what difference there is in the jersey, but eventually, he lays eyes on an A on the left shoulder near his heart. It's crooked and shabbily sewn on, but Harlan and Beary didn't have oodles of time to do a good job.

"Now you're a leader. So, you have to act like it," Harlan says.

Haas smiles. He throws the jersey on, straightens it out, and gives Harlan and Beary a thumbs up. He looks up in time to see Safari Chip come out of his office. Instead of waiting for his coach's call, Haas stands up and makes it for him. "Game time! Let's go kick some butt."

"Yeah!" Harlan yells.

The others follow suit, and they head out of the locker room in a frenzy.

At the start of the period, right off the bat, Haas is tested. The Five Ohhh! win the faceoff and get down to business. Haas faces four shots in the first minute of the period. He stops every one, including the fourth shot that comes less than a second after the third. Haas twists and dives sideways to bat the puck away with his stick.

The puck moves towards the boards to his left. Lovey and Dislike are the closest players to it, but they know it's going to be a tight race to gain control of it. Dislike is in such a hurry to get to it that he trips on his own feet and falls down. This gives Lovey enough time to get to the puck and bat it to Undertaker. After winning the race to the puck, Lovey points to Dislike on his tail on the ice with one paw and gives the crowd a thumbs up with his other paw.

The crowd answers back with a thumbs up back to Lovey. The post he made during intermission read as follows: *Whenever Dislike misses a cue or missteps out there tonight, I want you GAMBLERS! (That's Gamblers with an exclamation point) fans in the crowd to give him a thumbs up.*

Dislike doesn't see Lovey's thumbs up to the crowd, but the sudden flurry of 75,000 fans raising their arms at once catches his eye. He doesn't initially see what they're doing and goes right back into the game, but they definitely have his attention.

The Gamblers play a little bit of offense but have no luck. Both teams change lines and Big Chick takes the ice with The Colonel for the first time in the period. The Colonel avoided Big Chick as much as he could in the first, and he plans to do the same in the second. At one point, while trying to block Big Chick from the net, The Colonel bumps into the big guy. Big Chick swats his wing behind himself at The Colonel. The Colonel backs up a bit to give Big Chick more space.

"What are you doing? Get back there and guard him." Marlon pushes The Colonel closer to Big Chick.

This time, The Colonel bumps Big Chick even harder.

Big Chick turns around with narrowed brow and a clenched beak. He stands up tall and puffs out his chest.

"He pushed me." The Colonel points to Marlon.

Big Chick's gaze shifts to Marlon.

Marlon shakes his head vehemently and points to The Colonel. He doesn't want to incur Big Chick's wrath either.

Big Chick points a threatening wing at both Five Ohhh! players. Meanwhile, behind him, the Gamblers can't get any offense going, because Big Chick is blocking the front of the net.

"Big Chick!" Sammie Lou yells.

Big Chick whips his head around and finds Sammie Lou, pressured by two Five Ohhh! players, firing a pass his way. Big Chick has little time to react. He tries to bat the puck out of the air towards the net, but he ends up hitting it up over the glass into the crowd.

Whistles blow. The referees indicate a delay of game penalty.

"What!? That was a shot on goal." Big Chick argues.

"It went twenty-five rows into the crowd Big Chick," the referee says as he skates the chicken to the penalty box.

The Colonel skates fast to the penalty box behind Big Chick and the referee. Just as Big Chick takes his first step inside, The Colonel swoops in and pushes him in. Big Chick stumbles and falls, banging his knees on the bench. He recovers quickly though and turns to engage his attack. The penalty box attendant and the referee hold the chicken back. It's not an easy task, and they need the assistance of a second referee.

Laughing like a hyena, The Colonel points at and taunts the angry but restrained giant until the third referee sneaks up on the fox, grabs him by the arm, and starts skating himaway.

"What? Where are we going?" The Colonel breaks free from his grasp.

"Penalty. You. Two minutes for unsportsmanlike conduct," the referee explains.

The Colonel rolls his eyes.

"Don't roll your eyes. You're lucky it's not a double minor with two more minutes for roughing," the referee says.

On the Five Ohhh! bench, Rezza goes nuts. It's a stupid move on The Colonel's part. The Five Ohhh! could have been on a power play, but instead, the teams will play four on four for two minutes.

As soon as The Colonel takes a seat on his bench, Big Chick walks to the glass that separates the two penalty boxes. He faces The Colonel and stares him down. The Colonel doesn't see Big Chick at first, but eventually he catches a glimpse of him out of the corner of his eye. He turns his head to Big Chick. "Not much you can do in there."

Big Chick points to the penalty times for himself and The Colonel. "Two minutes."

The Colonel gulps.

Play resumes with the Gamblers third line, minus Penny, who sits out because of the penalty to Big Chick, winning the ensuing faceoff. Maverick skates the puck over the blue line and passes it ahead to L-Rod. The little penguin gets pressured by his peewee nemesis, Samanya, and has to pass the puck back near the blue line to Moose. Moose passes it across to Maverick, and the horse makes a move towards the net. The move is a little aggressive, and he soon finds he's not going to have a shot, so he wraps around the back side of the net and battles Ice Man for a while, trying to maintain possession of the puck. Eventually, he makes it out from behind the net with the puck and finds Goose near the open side of the net. The horse shoots Goose the puck.

Goose drops his stick to take the pass, but he has his stick lifted up by the stick of Slider. In a last ditch effort to move the puck into the net, Goose reaches his skate out into the puck's path, hoping to stop it so he can take a quick shot once he regains control of his stick. The puck bounces off of Goose's skate and goes into the net.

The goal light's go off. The slot machine jackpot noise plays over the speakers.

The Five Ohhh! immediately swarm the referees in protest. Rezza screams for a replay from the bench. All the Five Ohhh! players make kicking motions, indicating that Goose kicked the puck into the net illegally.

"Ok! Ok! Ok!" the head referee pats the air, indicating to the Five Ohhh! the need to calm down. "We're reviewing it."

The Five Ohhh! do indeed calm down, but the crowd gets riled up. They boo loudly.

"Did you kick it?" Moose asks.

"It definitely went off my skate, but it all happened so fast. I'm not sure. I thought my skate came to a complete stop."

"Then it should be a goal," Maverick says.

"No. You kicked it plain as day," Ice Man says annoyed.

"Yeah. That crap doesn't count," Slider says.

The referees come back from the scorer's table. The review didn't take long. They wave off the goal. They make the same kicking motion that the Five Ohhh! made.

"See," Ice Man gloats.

"Whatever. It was a nice pass and try," L-Rod tells his line mates.

The third lines go to the bench and trade places with the first lines. Liten and Ratone sit out in place of Big Chick and The Colonel in their respective penalty boxes. There are still fifty seconds left on their penalties, and Big Chick continues to stare The Colonel down. He taps the glass to get The Colonel's attention again. The fox looks over at the psychotic chicken smiling wickedly. Big Chick mouths the words *fifty seconds*, and then makes the motion of pulling the thumb of his wing across his throat in a threatening manner. The Colonel gulps again.

Rodman loses the next faceoff to Ox. The Five Ohhh! head towards their attack zone and set up. Dislike, guarded by Lovey, ends up with the puck. The white bear puts some wicked defense on the black bear, but just when Lovey thinks he's got a chance to steal the puck right off of Dislike's stick, Dislike dekes him. This allows Dislike to get around him and head undefended towards Haas for a free shot. He rears back, aims, and fires.

Haas drops to his knees and closes his legs. He stops the puck with his legs pads just before it can bypass through the five hole. The puck squeaks out from his leg pads, and Haas has to dive on top of it. The Five Ohhh! players try to dig the puck out from under Haas even after the whistles blow and play stops.

Undertaker, Kane, and Rodman race in to stop the Five Ohhh! from taking cheap shots on their goalie. While the referees separate the pushing and shoving going on in front of the net, Lovey points to Dislike, mimics his swing, and acts upset that the pretend shot gets blocked. Then, he shoots the crowd another thumbs up. The 75,000 plus fans in the crowd shoot back a thumbs up Lovey's way.

Again, the reaction of the crowd catches Dislike's attention. He takes a closer look at them. He's still not sure, but he thinks that they might actually be holding their thumbs up. He turns to Lovey just as the Gamblers bear is lowering his thumb.

The same lines stay out for the next faceoff. On the wing, awaiting the puck drop, Dislike turns to Stunner behind him. "Are they holding their thumbs up?"

"Who?" Stunner asks.

"The crowd," Dislike says.

Stunner sneaks a peek. "No."

"Not now moron. Earlier."

"I don't know. You need to get your head into the game though. Don't worry about the crowd," Stunner barks.

The puck drops and Rodman wins this time. He slaps the puck Lovey's way, and Lovey takes it down the ice. He runs into Dislike, who is still distracted from his conversation with Stunner, and the two bears fall to the ice.

Whistles blow. Both bears look up in anticipation of who is going to be called for the penalty. The referee indicates Dislike for interference.

"Ohhh, come on," Dislike gripes.

The referees help Dislike up and skate him to the box. This time, he distinctly sees Lovey, sitting on his tail on the ice, give the crowd a thumbs up. He quickly shifts his gaze to the crowd and sees everyone return the gesture to Lovey.

"Are you giving me a thumbs up?" Dislike demands of the crowd with a scream.

The noise in the arena drowns out his shouting, and no one in the crowd can hear him. Their inability to answer his question drives him even more bonkers. He goes into the penalty box and throws his helmet high against the glass. It bangs off the glass so hard that it flies back and hits him in his own head.

Lovey, quick to see this and take advantage, gives the crowd another thumbs up.

Dislike sees Lovey's gesture again and turns his head to confirm what he already knows. The crowd is giving him another thumbs up. Only this time, some of the patrons behind the penalty box glass are really animated, rubbing the thumbs up in his face.

"I don't get it," Dislike shouts. "What are you doing?"

One fan points to the big screen above the arena scoreboard. Dislike turns and sees a split screen shot on the monitor. On one half of the screen is a live shot of him in the penalty box. On the other side of the screen, a fake Facespace page with Dislike's name and the same live shot of him in the penalty box for his picture appears. Instantly, the number of likes the picture receives grows bigger and bigger, faster and faster.

"Oh very funny," Dislike grumbles and breaks his stick on the penalty box bench.

Even some of the Five Ohhh! players can't help but chuckle, though they do their best to hide it from their coach and their angry grizzly.

The Gamblers play well on the power play, but find no success in scoring the tying goal. Rodman, Lovey, and the rest of the first line play for the first half of the power play before making way for the second line.

The entire time Dislike sits in the penalty box, he stews over what has taken place. The fact that the Facespace page stays on the screen the entire time he sits in the box irritates him more. The number of likes never stops growing either. As soon as the penalty is over, he jumps out of the box without his helmet and stick. He races fast to the benches.

Initially, everyone thinks he's just racing to his own bench to allow Sammie Two to get on the ice, but he doesn't go to his own bench. He drops his gloves about six feet from the Gamblers bench, drawing their attention. They look bewildered at the wild bear with malicious intent in his eyes.

About three feet from the Gamblers bench, Dislike jumps into the air. The Gamblers expressions change from confused to startled. With the exception of Lovey, who seems to be the main target, the Gamblers all scatter to avoid being crushed by the psycho projectile bear.

Lovey stands up, but he doesn't run. He catches Dislike instead and pushes him back to keep him from harming himself or any of the other Gamblers. Dislike hits his back on the inside wall of the bench. He and Lovey exchange fists of fury until the Gamblers, the referees, and eventually even the Five Ohhh! pull the two bears apart.

"Get him out of here," the head referee orders the other referees of Dislike.

"For how long?" Dislike demands.

"For the entire game," the referee informs him.

"Nooo!" Dislike shouts.

Lovey gives another thumbs up, and the crowd does the same.

Dislike tries to get at Lovey.

"You'll be lucky to play in game five," Safari Chip shouts.

"There ain't going to be a game five," Lovey remarks.

Dislike tries to break free of the referees' grasp and get at Lovey again, but he's unable.

The crowd goes absolutely bananas at Dislike's ejection. They give him thumbs ups all the way off the ice and all the way to the tunnel entrance. He makes sure not to look at them for fear he'll get so angry he does something else he regrets.

When play finally resumes, the period finishes without further incident. The teams head to the respective locker rooms with the Five Ohhh! still ahead 2-1.

Lovey rushes ahead of the team down the tunnel, eager to get back on Facespace. As some of the others file in, they make their way to Lovey's locker.

"What are you doing?" Beary asks.

"I'm liking Dislike's ejection," Lovey jokes.

Many of the Gamblers laugh.

"Hey!" Safari Chip shouts.

The Gamblers turn to their coach. He sounds angry.

"Laugh it up guys. They're winning," Safari Chip says.

"Sorry Chip," Lovey apologizes.

"Don't be sorry. I want you guys to play loose, and to be upbeat, and to have a good time. I just to make sure your heads are in the game and that you're not playing like knuckleheads. We've got twenty minutes left to win this thing on our home ice. I don't feel like going back to Reno," Safari Chip continues.

"Neither do we," Liten chimes in.

"Good. So, that means we're going to have to go out there and play our tails off. If we give up another goal…" Safari Chip stops and turns to Haas. He points to his goalie. "And by the looks of it, we won't. Haas is a dang wall out there."

"Heck yeah he is," Harlan claps his flippers together and gets the rest of the Gamblers to join in.

"But if we do, I don't care if we give up one, two, three, or ten goals this next period. I don't want to see one of my guys quit playing until that final buzzer sounds. You never know what's going to happen out there. A one goal game can turn around in a matter of seconds," Safari Chip warns his team.

"But, let's not let them score anymore, and let's get Haas another goal so he has some breathing room," Flip ads.

"Yeah!" the entire team shouts in unison.

*

The puck drops to start the third period. Rodman and Ox jostle for it. Rodman swipes it behind himself to Kane.

The Five Ohhh! start with The Colonel on the first line in place of the Dislike. During intermission, the Five Ohhh! coach read Dislike the riot act, telling him his ejection from the game was a bonehead move. No argument came from Dislike, who hopes his team can hang on for the win so he can play in game five. He also hopes he doesn't get a suspension from the league for his actions.

The Colonel is just filling in temporarily on the first line. A revolving carousel of players will replace Dislike at different times. The Colonel wants the first shift so he won't have to face Big Chick right away.

The first lines for each team continue to neutralize each other. No one scores as smart hockey is played on both sides of the ice. Outside of Lovey and Dislike, the first line players on each side, though they'd never admit it, have come to respect the first line players on the other side. For the Gamblers, it isn't like going up against Maulbreath, Ranger, Smooth, Metz, and Packer, who cheat and play dirty for sixty minutes a game. Ox, Ratone, Hoss, and Stunner take the game serious. They may play rough, but they rarely take the low road or cheap shots.

The same can't be said of the second line for the Five Ohhh!. Their forwards, The Colonel, Sammie Two, and Greg are constantly harassing their counterparts, hoping to gain some sort of underhanded advantage. With Big Chick standing up to The Colonel, it's mostly the other two that play like the Gold Rush, and that doesn't change in the third period.

Greg slams Beary into the boards as hard as he can, as often as he can. He even twice attempts to slam Beary into the glass in front of section 105 where Mary is sitting front row. The first time he does it, Greg sneaks up on Beary as the Gamblers panda tries to pry the puck away from a log jam near the boards. Greg glides in, watches his sister's face twist with terror, and he slams Beary face first into the glass.

Beary's snout mushes up against the glass and he feels a tooth crack. Beary drops his stick and loses the fight for the puck, but to his credit, he doesn't fall down. His mouth fills up with blood. He turns around, spits the blood and his tooth out, picks up his stick, and rejoins the play.

The second time Greg tries to smash Beary into the glass in front of Mary, the same scenario is playing out. Beary helps Sammie Lou try to maintain possession of the puck though Sammie Two is trying to steal it back. Greg comes from across the ice at a fast pace. Mary sees her brother racing at her husband again. She bangs on the glass frantically, screaming for Beary to turn around. She doesn't want him to get hurt again, and she certainly doesn't want him losing any more teeth. He looks silly enough with one of his front teeth missing.

Beary seems not to notice her frantic banging, pointing, and screaming. It appears he's about to be thoroughly demolished when suddenly, he spins, grabs Greg's head, and guides him into the glass face first instead. It's Greg whose snout smashes the glass and whose tooth gets knocked out this time.

Sammie Lou wins the fight for the puck and sends it out to Snickers. He takes the puck back into the Gamblers defensive zone, allowing for the second line to regroup and set up for a trip down the ice. Snickers passes it ahead to Big Chick once everyone is in position, and the Gamblers head back on offense.

The Colonel is back on the ice with the second line for this shift. He waits for Big Chick to cross the blue line before making an all or nothing move to steal the puck off the chicken's stick. He knows if he gets it, he's going to have a breakaway. On the other hand, he knows if he misses it, he'll create an open path to the net for the sharpshooting of Big Chick. The Colonel whips his stick out like he's attempting to block Big Chick from coming over the blue line, but he allows Big Chick to skate over the line with all the other Gamblers. Then, at just the right moment, he pokes at the puck, sending it backwards through Big Chick's legs.

Big Chick turns around to see if he can get the puck back, but the blazing speed of The Colonel already has him skating away towards Haas. Big Chick watches helplessly as the fox races in on net. He remembers Safari Chip's words about not quitting no matter how many goals get scored, and though he knows his speed is no match for The Colonel's, he races as fast as his legs will carry him.

Haas comes out of the net to make shooting around him harder. As the fox gets closer and closer, Haas moves further and further back, trying to keep the shooting lanes to a minimum.

The fox grows impatient. He's not sure where Big Chick is behind him, so he fires and misses. The puck goes high over the net.

Haas breathes a sigh of relief and frantically looks for the puck. By the time he finds it, it is already being scooped up by Sammie Two, who has also joined the play.

The Colonel sees Sammie Two with the puck and decides to pull a punk move in an effort to create an easy scoring opportunity for his team. He stealthily kicks Haas' skate out from underneath him.

"Whoaaaaa!" Haas shouts as he falls sideways to the ice.

The referees don't see the move, but Safari Chip, Flip, and the entire Gamblers bench do, not to mention every animal in the arena. They all stands up, boo, and shout for the referees to call a penalty.

Sammie Two never gets to finish his wrap around on the empty side of the net though, because Sammie Lou comes in and lights his cousin up Snickers style. Sammie Two literally flies two feet into the air and comes down hard on his tail. Sammie Lou even stumbles around from the force of the hit.

The puck, meanwhile, is spit out into the open by the boards. The Colonel is the closest one to it. He skates to the puck, hoping he can turn and fire it to a nearby teammate, so he can head to the bench for a line change. He turns around to make a quick pass, but instead of any Five Ohhh! teammates, the first thing he sees is Big Chick rearing down on him like a freight train. He doesn't even have time to drop his stick and raise his paws to protect himself from the hit Big Chick is about to levy.

Everything happens so fast that most of the players miss it, and those who do see the collision don't get to fully appreciate how hard a hit it really is until they see it again in a slow motion replay. When Big Chick runs into The Colonel, the fox's head whips back like a baseball being hit off a tee. The rest of his body eventually catches up, but so does Big Chick's. The Colonel gets sandwiched between the guy he's tormented all season long and the glass. At least, he's sandwiched until the glass gives out, shattering into a million pieces. The Colonel falls backwards into the first row, and Big Chick glides over the fox's body and slides into the fourth row.

The referees blow their whistles and play stops. Fans, referees, and teammates help the two players stand up and get back onto the ice. Neither is hurt, but The Colonel is shaken up.

Both teams go back to their bench for a breather while arena personnel clean the shards off the ice and replace the glass.

"Boy oh boy," Safari Chip greets his second line upon their arrival back at the bench. "You guys are one tough line. Look at you guys, putting hits on family members, breaking glass, losing teeth, and knocking opponents out."

"We're going to have to call them the black and blue line," Flip jokes.

"I want to be on the black and blue line," Lovey says in all seriousness.

"You're a black and blue line all by yourself," Rodman jokes.

All the Gamblers laugh.

Safari Chip stops laughing when he looks up at the scoreboard and sees only five minutes left in the game and his team still down by a goal. "Hey guys."

His players look to him.

"Five minutes left. It's time to score if we're going to score. Third line. You're up next. Who's going to tie this thing up?" Safari Chip asks, trying to pump his players up.

"I am!" L-Rod jumps off the bench and over the wall.

"Alright!" Safari Chip pumps his first and turns his attention to the Five Ohhh! bench and yells, "You hear that you Reno guys? L-Rod's about to tie this thing up!"

The Five Ohhh! wave off Safari Chip's warning.

"Go get 'em son," Rodman says.

"Ok dad," L-Rod jokes.

It takes the crew twenty-two minutes to replace the glass. It's a tedious task, and they have to make sure to do it right so the fans and the players are protected. They also have to make sure all of the broken pieces of glass are off the ice. If they miss even one piece, it could cause a player to trip fall, hyperextend a knee, get cut, slam into the boards, or any number of things that could cause serious harm. Once the referees are satisfied that everything has been completed properly, the game resumes.

The third lines for each team take the ice. Penny beats Mad Man on the faceoff. The Gamblers get a few scoring opportunities, and L-Rod tries his best to score, but he just isn't able to break through.

Just before the third line comes back to the bench, Safari Chip turns to his players on the bench. "Ok first line, you're next. Who's going to score?"

"I am!" all five players on the first line assert.

"Good. All five of you score. We'll be up 6-2 then," Safari Chip Jokes. "But hey guys, everyone, short shifts from here on out until the final two minutes."

Everyone gives him a thumbs up.

Play continues on, but none of the five Gamblers who said they'd score a goal actually score. The second line doesn't score either, and neither does the third line on their next shift.

At the end of the third line's shift, Samanya dekes L-Rod. He gets just enough room to fire a shot at the net. It's not the best shot, but Haas bobbles the puck in and out of his glove a few times. Players from both teams converge on the hare, trying to poke the puck past him or keep it away from the net. In the end, Haas covers it up with his glove and play stops.

Safari Chip looks to the scoreboard. It shows two minutes and two seconds left in the game. He calls a timeout.

The third line comes to the bench and everyone sits down to take a one minute breather.

"Third line, you guys look pretty tired. Does anyone want to be the sixth man after we pull Haas? Or do you want me to send Sammie out with the first line and two of you can join the second line if we have to play six on five?" Safari Chip asks.

"I want to play with the first line," L-Rod quickly volunteers.

"Alright!" Rodman high fives his little buddy.

"Who's going out with the second line then? Me or Penny?" Goose asks.

"No offense Goose, but I think if it comes down to that, I'm going to send Penny. I think as a woman, if she's our sixth man, the Five Ohhh! won't pay her much attention. They don't think she's a formidable opponent, and that might be just what we need to take them by surprise," Safari Chip explains.

"Sounds good to me," Goose, ever the team player, says.

"Let's hope it doesn't come to that though. Let's hope Rodman and company tie this thing up," Safari Chip says.

"We're going to tie this game up," Rodman assures his coach and teammates.

The referees blow their whistles and call for the teams to come back to the ice for a faceoff. Since Haas caught the puck and held onto it to end the last series, the faceoff takes place right next to the Gamblers net, so Haas has to go back in net until the Gamblers get possession of the puck.

"Looks like there's still about sixty-two minutes of left in the season," Ox says to Rodman as he lines up for the faceoff.

"You're pretty cocky for a guy who hasn't won anything yet," Rodman says.

"Oh, trust me. We've got this game in the bag. Two minutes ain't nothing when you've already shut down," Ox makes quote signs with his hooves, "the best team ever for fifty-eight minutes."

Rodman doesn't engage Ox any further. He just shakes his head and wins another faceoff. He gets the puck behind him to Kane, and Kane gets it right back to Rodman. The Gamblers captain takes the puck behind the net. He waits for each of his line mates to get into position before he skates out from behind the net. They key to scoring is not to rush anything. Two minutes and two seconds is a lifetime in hockey.

As soon as the Gamblers cross the blue line, Haas darts for the bench.

Rodman takes a quick shot. Marlon kicks the puck aside where Liten is there to get the rebound. He passes it back to Undertaker, and Undertaker shoots it to L-Rod as he races into the play like a bolt of Lightning from the bench.

L-Rod catches the Five Ohhh! and even some of the Gamblers by surprise with his burst of energy and sudden appearance on the ice. None of the Five Ohhh! checked him down as he and Haas traded places. L-Rod weaves past Ratone, squeezes past Ox, and fires at Marlon. He misses wide, but his shot is so hard and straight, it bounces off the wall and trickles back towards the net. He's able to collect his own rebound.

Marlon is the second one there. He reaches behind the net, trying to grab the puck and still block the net at the same time. He stumbles and falls to his tail as he reaches for the puck.

L-Rod reaches the puck first. He takes three quick strides to get back in front of the net for a shot and almost gets demolished by Hoss. Luckily, Kane comes in and blocks the big dog out of the play. L-Rod's able to avoid a second hit all on his own by ducking out of the way of Stunner. He slides like a baseball player with his feet out in front of himself, all the while controlling the puck on his stick near his waist. He glides past the helpless tortoise and fires the puck into the back of the net.

The goal lights go off. The game is tied. The Gamblers celebrate. The crowd celebrates.

The Five Ohhh! sigh.

It takes the Gamblers only thirteen seconds to score their goal after the puck is dropped. One minute and forty-nine seconds remain in the game.

Safari Chip contemplates pulling his first liners after their game tying goal. He did the same thing last season in the final game after the Gamblers escaped a game tying goal that was overturned upon a review. His reasoning behind the decision was that the emotional call, or in this case an emotional goal, sometimes causes the players involved to play emotionally. It worked last season as Big Chick went on to score the game winning goal in that shift. This year, however, Safari Chip decides to leave his first line out. They're mature enough and composed enough at this point in their careers that they can handle it. They've been here before, so he leaves them out.

The referees get the teams back to center ice.

Ox steps into the faceoff circle with rattled nerves. For the first time in the series, Ox feels the pressure of possibly losing. It's almost certain that the next goal will win the game with so little time left, and if the game goes to overtime, the next goal will certainly win it. He looks upon the firepower the Gamblers have. Rodman, Lovey, Liten, Big Chick, Sammie, Beary, L-Rod. All of them can score at any moment. Even the dogs, as defensemen, all have double digit goals this season. He digs in dead set on winning the faceoff.

The puck drops, but Ox loses to Rodman and the Gamblers.

Rodman whacks the puck back to Undertaker. The black dog takes the puck over the blue line against a Five Ohhh! team that looks totally deflated. Undertaker notices Hoss and Stunner moving lackadaisical towards the front of their net to help Marlon. He also has no one guarding him as Ratone and Slider get mixed up on who's covering who. Both Five Ohhh! wingers bump into each other and fumble around near Kane. So, with the lane pretty wide open, Undertaker blasts a shot towards the net.

Despite having no one helping him, Marlon stops the puck. He sees it the whole way. It flies at him high in the air, but then it knuckles and drops like a sinker ball pitch in baseball. At the last second, he has to drop to his knees to make the block. He tries to swipe at it with his glove as it bounces off his chest protector, but he misses and gives up a rebound.

Rodman, flying towards the front of the net the whole time, grabs the rebound and flicks it over Marlon into the net despite being hooked by Ox. The hook and the goal happen so fast that the referees don't have time to blow their whistles, though one of them raises an arm to indicate the penalty.

Penalty or not, it doesn't matter. Rodman scores a goal six seconds after the goal L-Rod scored to tie the game.

Ox stares at the flashing goal lights behind the net with his jaw dropped. In six seconds, his team's whole season has gone down the drain. They were winning seven seconds ago, tied six seconds ago, and now, they're losing. His stomach sinks.

Meanwhile, the Gambles jump around the ice in celebration with Rodman. They pat him on the back, Lovey slaps his helmet, and Kane picks him up for a bear hug.

Rodman laughingly struggles to get away from his canine friend. "Put me down."

Kane eventually does as he's told.

Once freed, Rodman skates fast to the bench to the earsplitting applause and hollering of the crowd. Rodman is greeted by more high fives, helmet slaps, and hollering from his teammates and coaches.

On the other side of the ice, Rezza rallies his team around. "Alright guys. We had this game, and we need to get it back. It doesn't matter how we lost control. The fact is we lost it, and we only have a few seconds to get back in it."

"Keep us out there," Ox demands of his coach.

"No. You grab some wood," the Five Ohhh! coach says.

"No. Keep us out there. We can get us back in," Ox hollers over the crowd that is still standing, clapping, jumping, and going all out crazy.

"You're too worked up. You need to take a break. Now sit down," Rezza orders.

Ox begrudgingly takes a seat. He bangs his stick on the wall and pouts, but when Rezza calls for his team to rally around him to go over their game plan, even though Ox isn't involved in the game plan, he still listens in like any good captain should. He knows the outcome of the game is more important than how the outcome is reached, so he wants to know what his teammates are going to be doing to tie the game up.

The referees call for both teams to head back to center ice. Both teams send out their second line. A faceoff between Big Chick and The Colonel takes place. The tentative fox loses his eleventh straight faceoff to Big Chick. The Gamblers go right back on the attack. They almost take an even bigger lead on a shot by Sammie Lou that sails just wide of the net.

The Five Ohhh! frantically race to get the puck. They know they can't win if they don't score. Crush and Crunch both reach the puck before any Gambler even comes close. Crush takes control of it and gives Crunch and the rest of the guys just a second to set up before he makes his move.

The Gamblers pressure Crush the second he comes out from behind the net. They know they only have to hold on for a handful of seconds in order to realize their dreams of a threepeat. Making things hard for the Five Ohhh! is the only thing the Gamblers are fixated on.

The pressure applied by the Gamblers is enough to force Crush to have to pass the puck to The Colonel. The fox can't get across the blue line onside, and he has to retreat.

With his team near their offensive zone, Rezza calls for Marlon to come to the bench so he can send out another player. Marlon hustles to the bench, and Ox jumps onto the ice before Mad Man can. He's lucky the referees don't see him, because he jumps way too early. A too many men on the ice penalty could have been the result if he had been seen.

"Ox!" Rezza shouts.

The Colonel sends the puck to Greg, and the Five Ohhh! panda is finally able to break through the zone onside. From Greg, the puck gets passed around to a few players. Sammie Two takes a shot but is denied. The Five Ohhh! maintain possession of the puck and get it back to Sammie Two, who is covered thoroughly by his cousin.

"Two!" Ox yells and motions for him to skate Ox's way.

Sammie Two doesn't know what Ox's plan is, but he trusts his captain's judgment. Maybe he sees an open shot on that side of the ice. He makes a break to get away from Sammie Lou, but his cousin follows his every stride.

Sammie Lou looks up to check on Ox. He sees Ox still standing where he was when he called Sammie Two, so Sammie Lou goes back to watching his cousin and making sure he doesn't have anywhere to go with the puck.

The second Sammie Lou's attention is off of Ox, the ox skates towards him. He collides with the Gamblers koala and knocks him to the ice. This frees Sammie Two, who takes advantage of a momentary lapse in Haas' attention as the hare checks on his fallen teammate. Sammie Two fires a shot past Haas, who doesn't see it until the last second.

The game is tied with thirty-one seconds left.

The TV announcers go bananas. "What a whacky finish to this game. Two ties, a lead change, and three goals in the final two minutes of the game."

Ox heads back to his team's bench. He's met by his coach, who appears to be livid. Ox stops in front of his coach, waiting to be reprimanded, benched, or suspended. Suddenly, Rezza's expression lightens up and he smiles. Rezza playfully punches his captain on the chest. "That's what I'm talking about. Way to be a leader out there. Way to make things happen."

All the Five Ohhh! players holler excitedly. They high five Ox and Sammie Two as he races into the bench.

"We staying out there?" Sammie Two asks.

The Five Ohhh! coach looks to Ox.

Ox nods.

"Yeah. Stay out there." The Five Ohhh! coach waves off his oncoming second line, telling them to stay where they are.

Feeling pumped, The Colonel finally breaks his winless faceoff streak against Big Chick. He knocks the puck back to Crunch, and he promptly passes it right back to Sammie Two.

Sammie Lou covers his cousin as usual. He taps him and rides him all the way into the boards. "You'll never get this puck back tonight."

Sammie Two then shoots the puck to Greg across the ice, but Beary sneaks into the puck's path and picks it off.

"So much for not getting the puck," Sammie Lou laughs.

Sammie Two shoves his cousin, but the move does little more than give Sammie a burst of speed as he makes his way down the ice towards Marlon.

Greg covers Beary as he crosses the blue line. He razzes his brother-in-law the entire time. "Where do you think you're going? You ain't going to the net. Uh uh. No way. The day you score is the day I stop griping about you marrying to my sister."

Beary ignores Greg's smack talk, but he knows Greg has him blocked, so he passes the puck back to Snickers.

"That's right. Pass it punk," Greg laughs.

Snickers passes the puck across the blue line to Apple Jack. Apple Jack holds it for a second, watching the clock. He eyeballs the ice in front of him. He has no shot. He passes it back to Snickers, and Snickers finds Sammie Lou racing into the zone all alone and sends the koala a pass.

Sammie Lou bobbles the puck a bit and has to stop to control it.

Out of nowhere a voice is heard screaming, "You're going down cousin!"

Sammie Lou looks up and sees his cousin charging into him with his elbow up. Sammie Lou takes a Sammie Two elbow to the jaw. He hears a pop and feels a crunch. His feet come out from under him, and his vision goes black as he falls to the ice.

Whistles blow, but the penalty is delayed because the Gamblers maintain possession of the puck. Sammie Lou kicks the puck inadvertently as he falls over to Apple Jack, who gets pressured by The Colonel. Apple Jack fires a risky pass into the middle of the play, hoping one of his players will come up with the puck.

Beary does indeed snag the puck, but he's still defended by Greg. Beary almost passes the puck back to Snickers, but he spins away from Greg and gets a bit of breathing room for a second. He hopes to buy enough time for his teammates to create something.

Eighteen seconds remain in regulation.

Meanwhile, Rodman skates onto the ice as the extra attacker for the delayed penalty call. He steals a page out of Ox's book, but he does it silently and sneakily. He skates into the play well behind Greg, catches Beary's eye, and calls for the panda to come his way with only a motioning flipper.

Beary nods and makes his move.

Rodman skates in behind Greg as soon as he sees Beary nod.

Sammie Two, since he doesn't have to worry about Sammie Lou, who is gingerly trying to stand up but having a hard time, skates in to defend Rodman. Sammie Two raises his elbow to take Rodman out next.

"Rodman! Look out!" Beary screams, giving up the element of surprise on Rodman's sneak attempt at a pick.

Rodman turns his attention to Sammie Two.

Greg turns his attention to Rodman.

Rodman slams on the breaks and dives out of the way to save himself. He belly flops hard onto the ice right in the path of Beary. He closes his eyes and hopes not to feel the panda bear run him over, cut him up, and/or trip and fall over him.

Sammie Two drops his elbow and puts up his paws to protect himself and Greg from the collision they're inevitably going to have.

Beary flips the puck up into the air and holds it on his stick. He hops over Rodman, lands perfectly, and makes a move for the net.

Sammie Two and Greg sound like a pair of locomotives colliding when they hit. They crumple to the ice in a heap.

Rezza slaps his hand to his own forehead. "Come on now you guys."

Beary looks at the clock. Ten seconds to go turns to nine seconds to go on the clock. He dekes Crush and shoots somewhat blindly around Crunch. He goes to the far side of the net with his shot, taking Marlon a bit by surprise.

The tortoise fully expected the puck to go to his close side, but he's still able to swing his leg out and block the puck from reaching the back of the net.

Beary never gives up on the play. He dives head first towards the net with his stick out in front of him.

Marlon swings his legs around and flips his body to make it possible to reach the puck with his glove. His eyes go wide as he stretches his glove out to cover it up. With his eyes open as wide as they are, Marlon clearly sees the blade of Beary's stick reach in first and knock the puck underneath his reach. His gaze follows the puck all the way into the back of the net.

The Gamblers go back on top, 4-3, with four seconds to go in the game. A rather intense celebration takes place on the ice as well as on the bench, but the Gamblers keep it brief, as they know in four seconds, barring a miracle, they'll be celebrating even more intensely their third Cup in as many years.

The celebration is even shorter-lived when the referee calls for Rodman to help Sammie Lou. In the excitement, everyone forgot how bad a shot Sammie Lou took. The Gamblers koala is still dazed and barely able to stand. He holds onto the wall for support. Rodman and Snickers reach him and give him added support.

"Are you ok Sammie?" Rodman asks.

Sammie Lou, bleeding from the mouth, shakes his head. His jaw is in extreme pain, but he knows without trying that moving his jaw to speak is going to hurt worse.

Rodman turns to his attention to Snickers. "We have to get him off the ice."

"Can you skate?" Snickers asks Sammie Lou.

Sammie Lou, holding his mouth shut and wincing at the pain, tries letting go of the wall. He finds for a second he can stand, and he indicates with a shake of his paw that he can kind of stand, but then, he starts dropping lazily to the ice. Rodman and Snickers each grab him before he falls all the way down.

"He can't skate," Rodman says.

Big Chick skates up. "Is he hurt?"

"Yeah, and he can't skate. We have to get him to the bench," Snickers says.

"Allow me." Big Chick hoists Sammie Lou up over his shoulder like a rag doll and skates him to the bench. He sets the koala down on the bench wall where they're met by Safari Chip, Flip, and the arena doctors.

"Let me see that jaw son. Can you talk?" the first doctor asks Sammie Lou.

Sammie Lou shakes his head.

The second doctor feels around Sammie Lou's jaw lightly. Even the light touching causes bolts of pain to shoot all throughout Sammie's head. He growls through his clenched jaw.

"Oh yeah. That jaw is broken good," the second doctor says.

"We have to get him off the ice, and to…" the first doctor starts to say.

Sammie Lou interrupts him with another groan and waving arms, indicating he has no intention of leaving he ice.

"No?" the first doctor asks.

Sammie shakes his head, points to himself, then points to the arena exit.

"You won't go?"

Sammie Lou shakes his head and points to the bench.

"But you need surgery on your jaw," the doctor argues.

Sammie Lou shakes his head again. He points to the time on the scoreboard and holds up four fingers.

"Four?" the first doctor asks.

"He means there are four seconds left in the game," the second doctor says.

"Ok. Four seconds. Then we go," the first doctor says.

Sammie Lou shakes his head again.

"No!? What now?" the first doctor asks.

Sammie Lou points to himself. He mimics the action of hoisting the Cup.

"Huh?" both doctors ask.

"I think he wants to hold the Cup first," Rodman says.

"Doesn't it hurt though?" the second doctor asks.

Sammie makes the same shaking motion with his paw, indicating that it hurts a little, even though it hurts a lot. There's no way he's going to miss the final seconds and all the celebrating.

"Ok, so you hold the Cup and then we'll go?" the first doctor asks.

Sammie shakes his head again.

"What now?" the second doctor asks.

Sammie mimics shaking the sparkling juice bottles and spraying his teammates.

The doctors look utterly confused.

"That means he wants to wait until after party time," Lovey tells them.

The doctors roll their eyes and sigh.

"Tell you what. When you're ready to be fixed up, then you come down and we'll fix you up," the first doctor says.

Sammie gives the doctors a thumbs up. He gets major tough guy credit from his teammates for sticking around.

Safari Chip puts his best guys on the ice for the final four seconds. Big Chick, since he's got the league's best faceoff winning percentage, plays center and takes a faceoff against Ox. On the wing, Lovey is joined by Rodman, who moves to the wing in place of Liten who rides the bench so Big Chick can play. Safari Chip is set to send Undertaker and Kane out to play defense, but all the dogs agree that Snickers should be on the ice for the closing seconds.

"That's fine, but I need at least one of you out there with him," Safari Chip says.

"You go," Undertaker says to Kane.

"Nah, you go. I've been a jerk to you all season long. Let me make it up to you this way," Kane says.

"Really?" Undertaker asks.

Kane nods.

Undertaker hugs his best friend.

Kane let's Undertaker hug him for a second, but then he pushes him away. "Get out there."

Both teams line up for the faceoff. Big Chick stands across from Ox. He doesn't smile, brag, boast, or taunt the ox. To Big Chick, this faceoff is as important as the opening faceoff.

The referee drops the puck, and Big Chick whacks it aside to Rodman. Rodman is chased for only a second by Five Ohhh! players as he heads to secure the puck behind his own net where Haas has already dropped his stick and is throwing his gloves into the air.

Chapter 36: Game Five

The clock hits zero. There will be no game five. The Gamblers storm the ice. Rodman tackles Haas from behind with a bear hug. Soon, they're joined by the rest of the oncoming Gamblers. The high fives and hugs go on long after the dog pile of players on the ice disbands.

The younger dogs especially, but all of the Gamblers at different intervals, continuously pat Snickers on the back, congratulating him on winning his first Cup ever at the end of his eighteenth season. The elder dog fights back tears of joy. As happy as he is, he doesn't want the other dogs seeing him cry. They see it though, and it's ok with them. After all, that's what winning this Cup is all about.

L-Rod also sees Snickers try to hide his tears. "It's ok Snickers. I cried when we won last year."

Snickers chuckles and ruffles the feathers on L-rod's head with a smile.

L-Rod rushes off after a minute to find Rodman. He runs into Big Chick first. Big Chick grabs L-Rod by his flippers and jumps up and down on the ice with the little penguin, pulling him high into the air with each bounce.

"We did it! We did it! We did it!" Big Chick repeats over and over again.

"Wooooo!" L-Rod screams as he and Big Chick bounce around.

Big Chick finally lets the little guy go, and L-Rod has to stand still on the ice for a minute. He feels like his eyes are still bouncing up and down and his head is dizzy.

Elsewhere in the crowd of Gamblers, Penny looks for Rodman too. She passes by Goose and asks him if he's seen Rodman.

Before he answers her, Goose hugs her first. "We won the Cup again!"

Penny smiles and hugs the crazy goose back. "I know!"

Goose lets her go.

"Have you seen Rodman?" Penny asks him again,

Before he can answer, Maverick glides over to them and starts naying as loud and excitedly as he can. He throws his arms out far apart from each other. Goose responds by mimicking Maverick's actions. He throws his wings apart and squawks as loud as he can. The best friends then start pushing each other in a sort of a tough guy celebration.

"Have either of you guys seen Rodman?" Penny asks.

"Rodman?" Maverick asks.

"Yes."

"Nope," Maverick answers.

"I did," Goose says.

"Where?" Penny asks.

Before Goose can answer, Moose skates in and starts screaming at the top of his lungs with his arms wide open. Maverick and Goose join him, and Penny skates away shaking her head.

On the Gamblers bench, Safari Chip walks from one end of the bench to the other, shaking hands and congratulating Flip, Sammie Lou, Harlan, and Jason. As much as Safari Chip's handshake means to them, the injured Gamblers hate being stuck on the bench. They're way too excited to be restricted to such a small celebration. It becomes too much for Sammie Lou, and he skates out there, broken jaw and all, and joins the festivities.

Not long after Sammie Lou leaves the bench, Haas and Beary come over and grab Harlan's wheelchair. They push it out onto the ice and skate the turtle around the ice for a victory lap. On their lap around the ice, they have to avoid Lovey, who is skating erratically and doing backflips for the crowd. They also bypass Liten, who is frozen solid as he stares into the crowd at a girl mouse holding a sign that says *Liten Mus is #1 in the league and #1 in my heart*.

While L-Rod and Penny search for Rodman, he is looking for them too. He makes his way from one teammate to another, hugging, high fiving, and celebrating with all of them as he goes. He makes his way to the Gamblers bench where he finds just the two coaches and Jason.

"Have you guys seen L-Rod and Penny?" Rodman asks.

"Not lately," Safari Chip says as he scans the ice.

"What are you doing on the bench?" Rodman asks Jason.

"I can't walk alone on the ice with my crutches," Jason answers.

Rodman hops over the wall, grabs Jason's crutches and throws them onto the ice. He slips his flipper under Jason's and steadies him. "You can do it with a little bit of help though."

Jason nods.

The two penguins exit the bench and Rodman helps Jason make his way across the ice. Once they get into the middle of the festivities, the other Gamblers swarm them to shake Jason's flipper.

Finally, L-Rod spots Rodman. He points him out to Penny. "There he is."

L-Rod leads Penny into the crowd gathered around Rodman and Jason. He pushes his way through the middle of the crowd and Penny follows.

"Hey Rodman," L-Rod shouts as they make it to him.

"Hey." Rodman turns his head to L-Rod.

"I've been looking for you."

"What's up?" Rodman asks.

Before L-Rod can answer, Penny pushes her way to Rodman and plants a big kiss on him in front of the whole team, including the coaches, who have made their way to the party.

The entire team ooohs and ahhhs.

Rodman is taken by surprise. He looks shocked and embarrassed, but mostly happy when the kiss is done

Penny winks at Rodman then turns to L-Rod. "What did you need to tell him?"

"I was just going to say congrats, but I wasn't going to kiss him," L-Rod says and makes the entire team burst into laughter.

Safari Chip, with all his players in one spot, puts a halt to their celebrating long enough to do the customary handshake with the other team. The Gamblers line up. Even the injured Gamblers get in line. Beary pushes Harlan's wheelchair down the line. Flip helps Jason hop along over the ice so he can shake with the Five Ohhh!.

Rodman, normally the guy at the front of the line, makes sure to be the guy at the end of the line so he can express to each player on the Five Ohhh! how impressed he was by their performance in the series and throughout the season. Most of the Five Ohhh! hear what he has to say, but they don't really listen. They're too busy moping and wallowing in the fact that they've lost the Cup.

Upon meeting Ox, Rodman shakes his hoof. The ox seems gruff and annoyed like most of the rest of his team at first. Rodman starts telling him how much he respects the game Ox played, but Ox isn't able to hear him.

"What?" Ox shouts over the crowd.

Rodman motions for Ox to bend a little lower so Rodman can talk into his ear.

Ox does as Rodman requests out of a natural reaction to Rodman's motions. If he had more time to think about it, he probably would have just brushed Rodman off.

Rodman has to shout just so Ox can hear him. "I know we got off on the wrong foot this season, and I know we were to blame for the whole thing. But I want you to know, and I want your whole team to know that after that first game, we knew what a mistake we made underestimating you guys and the rest of the AKHL teams that joined the league this year. You guys are professionals through and through. And I know for a fact that it's just a matter of time before you guys are the ones hoisting the Cup."

Ox stands back up quite amazed. Rodman's words were nothing short of sincere. He feels like a jerk for the way he allowed his team to treat the Gamblers all season long. "Thanks Rodman."

Rodman pulls Ox back down with more to say. "Just don't think you'll be hoisting the Cup next season. We've got one more to go."

Ox laughs. "We'll see about that. I don't like waiting."

The two captains shake again, and Ox skates off the ice with the rest of the Five Ohhh! so the MVP and Cup trophy ceremonies can begin.

Safari Chip is handed a microphone to make the Cup Finals MVP announcement. "It's time to award one of my players with the MVP award."

The crowd roars.

"This is always a lot of fun but a hard decision to make. It's always a team effort to get the win, but this year we had a guy who scored more goals than anyone else during the Finals, and he scored the game winner in two of the three games… Oh yeah, and he got married a few months ago," Safari Chip continues on.

The crowd knows who it is. The Gamblers do as well, and they push Beary towards their coach and the trophy he so deserves.

"Beary Nelson Riley, it is with great honor that I bestow upon you this year's Cup Finals' MVP award." Safari Chip hands his panda the trophy.

Beary holds it up in the air to the applause of the crowd, his teammates, and his coaches. A few pictures are snapped, and then Beary rushes to the glass to show the trophy to Mary. She stands on the other side, clapping so proud of her husband.

"Now what do you say we get this Cup passed around one more time?" Safari Chip says into the microphone.

The crowd roars again.

The IAHL president hands Safari Chip the Cup. The Gamblers don't move from their spot on the ice. Customarily, the Cup is handed to the team's captain first, but this year, the Gamblers have been planning something different.

When Safari Chip holds the Cup out for the first player to take it, no one moves.

"Go get it," Snickers says to Rodman.

"Nope." Rodman smiles.

Before Snickers can ask Rodman why he won't take the Cup, Undertaker, Kane, and Apple Jack push the older dog towards the Cup.

"You first old man," Kane jokes.

"What?" Snickers asks.

"Yeah, we all figure you've waited long enough to do this, so the team decided a long time ago to let you hold it first," Undertaker explains.

Snickers is overjoyed at the gesture. He's pushed all the way to the Cup and has it thrust at him. With the Cup in his paws, he's not able to wipe his tears away to hide them like he did earlier.

"Don't cry dude. Your tears are going to freeze to your face," Apple Jack jokes.

Snickers laughs, raises the Cup, and barks loudly to the crowd. He holds onto it a bit longer than normal, but that's just because it means so much to him. After all, not only has it taken him so long to win it, but the Cup is named after his grandpa and his dad won it three times. When he does finally give it up, he gives it to Rodman, who passes it to the Cup Finals' MVP, Beary, after he's done.

From Beary, the Cup makes its way around to all the Gamblers, though Harlan and Jason can't hold it at all. Even Sammie manages to hold it above his head despite his injuries. The team is called to center ice for their team photo with the Cup after everyone has had a chance to hold it and skate with it.

As soon as the photo is taken, Lovey gets an idea. He grabs the nearest Gamblers to him, Rodman and Liten, and they hop up and start doing a lap around the ice. Lovey instructs Liten to hold up three fingers. The mouse does so, and Lovey turns to Rodman.

"Hold up three fingers," Lovey says.

Rodman holds up both of his flippers instead. "I don't have fingers."

     "Oh," Lovey says a bit taken aback at the fact that he's played with Rodman for three years and never noticed his best friend didn't have fingers. "Well, skate with us anyway."

     Lovey and Liten hold up three fingers, symbolizing their threepeat. All of the Gamblers watch the three guys skating with their fingers up, and Rodman pounding his chest three times and pointing to the crowd after the third pound.

     Sammie is the first Gambler to race out and join them. He squeezes in between Lovey and Liten and shakes his head.

     "No?" Lovey asks.

     Sammie shakes his head again. Unable to speak, he simply holds up four fingers. Lovey and Liten take his cue and they hold up four fingers. The four Gamblers are then joined by the rest of their teammates. They do a few laps, those with fingers, holding four of them up at a time, and those with flippers, wings, and hooves pounding their chest four times and pointing to the crowd and yelling one word.

     All of the Gamblers, their coaches, and the crowd repeat that word over and over.

     "Fourpeat!"

Look for Hockey Penguin 4Peat coming in early 2015!

Friend Rodman on Facebook at:

www.facebook.com/rodmanthepenguin

There, you can find the rest of the Gamblers and their friends including:

Safari Chip
Lovey Bara
Big Chick
Beary Nelson Riley
Harlan
Undertaker
Kane
Apple Jack
Snickers

Liten
Sammie Lou
L-Rod
Maverick
Bruce Goose
Bruce Moose
Jason Vyand
Lance Maulbreath
Jack Haas

And don't forget to "like" Hockey Penguin on Facebook!

You can also contact the author at:
www.facebook.com/thee5hole or
hockeypenguinlv@gmail.com

Be sure to check out the official
Hockey Penguin website for what's going on with the series,
where the author might be for special events, and all other
Hockey Penguin news and happenings.
www.hockeypenguin.net

Made in the USA
San Bernardino, CA
23 February 2014